SEVEN STONES

THE COMPLETE SERIES

SEVEN STONES

THE COMPLETE SERIES

Dave Higgins

ISBN (Print): 978-1-912674-00-8
ISBN (EPUB): 978-1-912674-01-5

Set in IM Fell English SC and URWGarmondT.

Cover design: *©2018 Dave Higgins*.

Published by Dave Higgins, Bristol.

Contents

Part One	1
Part Two	9
Part Three	15
Part Four	21
Part Five	25
Part Six	31
Part Seven	37
Part Eight	43
Part Nine	47
Part Ten	53
Part Eleven	59
Part Twelve	65
Part Thirteen	71
Part Fourteen	75
Part Fifteen	81
Part Sixteen	87
Part Seventeen	93
Part Eighteen	99
Part Nineteen	103
Part Twenty	107
Part Twenty-One	111
Part Twenty-Two	117

Part Twenty-Three   121

Part Twenty-Four   127

Part Twenty-Five   131

Part Twenty-Six   137

Part Twenty-Seven   141

Part Twenty-Eight   147

Part Twenty-Nine   153

Part Thirty   157

Part Thirty-One   163

Part Thirty-Two   167

Part Thirty-Three   173

Part Thirty-Four   179

Part Thirty-Five   185

Part Thirty-Six   189

Part Thirty-Seven   195

Part Thirty-Eight   201

Part Thirty-Nine   207

Part Forty   211

Part Forty-One   217

Part Forty-Two   221

Part Forty-Three   225

Part Forty-Four   231

Part Forty-Five   237

Part Forty-Six   241

Part Forty-Seven   245

Part Forty-Eight   251

Part Forty-Nine   257

Part Fifty   261

Part Fifty-One   267

Part Fifty-Two   271

Part Fifty-Three   275

Part Fifty-Four   281

Part Fifty-Five   285

Part Fifty-Six 289
Part Fifty-Seven 295
Part Fifty-Eight 301
Part Fifty-Nine 307
Part Sixty 313
Part Sixty-One 317
Part Sixty-Two 323
Part Sixty-Three 329
Part Sixty-Four 333
Part Sixty-Five 337
Part Sixty-Six 343
Part Sixty-Seven 347
Part Sixty-Eight 353
Part Sixty-Nine 359
Part Seventy 365
Part Seventy-One 369
Part Seventy-Two 375
Part Seventy-Three 381
Part Seventy-Four 385
Part Seventy-Five 391
Part Seventy-Six 395
Part Seventy-Seven 399
Part Seventy-Eight 403
Part Seventy-Nine 407
Part Eighty 411
Part Eighty-One 417
Part Eighty-Two 421
Part Eighty-Three 427
Part Eighty-Four 431
Part Eighty-Five 437
Part Eighty-Six 441
Part Eighty-Seven 445
Part Eighty-Eight 449

Part Eighty-Nine   453

Part Ninety   457

Part Ninety-One   461

Part Ninety-Two   465

Part Ninety-Three   471

Part Ninety-Four   475

Part Ninety-Five   479

Part Ninety-Six   483

Part Ninety-Seven   487

Part One

Rain streamed down, blurring the trees and shadows into a single mass of half-resolved limbs. While the storm washed away light, it strengthened the stench of rot. Reverend Kobb pinched the bridge of his nose. The further north he came, the worse the nightmares became, and the closer the land matched the images in them.

Flicking the reins, he aimed his horse, Falcon, for the middle of the track. Away from the trees, the echoes of threat weakened, but the rain had an easier time getting to him. Changing direction mid-fall, it swept under his hat, before shifting again to pass over his drawn-up collar and ooze down his back.

Glad his humour remained dry—even if nothing else did—Kobb reminded himself this was what the Book of Blessings called an opportunity to praise the Maker's skill, to marvel at how rain was good at making things wet.

Light flickered in the distance. It looked close, but Kobb was certain he'd have time to give praise before he reached it. Fifteen soggy minutes later, a palisade rose through the murk, followed by a small hut. Unmoved by thoughts of stables, rubdowns, or shedding his dripping burden, Falcon squelched on at the same unconcerned pace.

"Greetings, the village!"

Someone shifted inside the hut. "Odd weather for travelling," called a damp voice.

"Has turned heavy. I'll be glad to be indoors."

A hunched youth emerged, holding a lantern on a pole. Beady eyes and a pallid face reinforced the impression of his voice.

The pendant at Kobb's throat glinted as the watcher thrust his light forward like a pike. "Botherer, eh? Don't hold much with people going on about how we're all sinners."

Kobb let his cloak hang open, revealing the carved butt of his Courser. "My sermons can be loud. But I keep them short."

The youth's mouth twisted as he drew the lantern back. When he dragged his shapeless cap off, Kobb realised he was smiling ingratiatingly.

"Where would a traveller get supplies?" Kobb asked.

"Tanton's. Midway along. Come to where Gamm used to live, you're too far."

Kobb settled his cape back in place. If you come to the house of a man you've never met, who doesn't live there any more, then you're in the wrong place. An omen for his journey if ever there was one.

Entering the village freed him from the random drips and gushes of overhanging branches, letting him experience the full force of the rain cascading between the rough-hewn houses. A well-designed drop crept down his chest. He chastised himself for judging the youth in haste: no sane person would be cheerful today. As the far gate came into view, he reined in and dismounted. "Don't remember how to gallop while I'm gone, Falcon."

As Kobb entered the store, a slender, balding man straightened from a barrel and peered at him. "Lambart Tanton. Help you?"

"Absolution Kobb. Looking for food." Kobb paused. "And a large horse blanket."

"Food I can do. Expecting shipment of blankets tomorrow. Want to pay now; I'll have it run over to the inn in the morning."

The light was almost gone, but the day wasn't. The rain couldn't make him wet twice. "Blanket's not important. I wasn't planning on staying the night."

"What's so urgent you need to go back out in this weather?" A woman, young from the sound of it, asked from the shadow of a doorway.

Kobb bowed to her silhouette. "Not hurrying. Just hadn't thought to stop."

She emerged into the light, revealing a functional leather coat and breeches. "Anessa Tanton. Forest gets wild around here. You'd be best to take a guide. I'd be—"

"Now you're back, girl, you can get that store room sorted." Lambart fixed her with a glare.

"Maybe I will stay over," said Kobb. "Could you point me at the inn?"

Lambert seemed to ignore him for a moment, then spat out directions. Deciding he'd be best served checking the supplies before he bought them anyway, Kobb resettled his cloak and strode into the storm.

Boots already filthy, he grasped Falcon's reins and trudged to the inn. The weather continued to exalt the Maker. Kobb led Falcon to the inn's stable, then swung his saddlebag over his shoulder and squelched around the building. He pondered why no one had put a door into the main building, or even a covered walkway. Vague ideas it might be carpentry related aside, nothing came to him.

Smoke drifted across the taproom from the fireplace, gathering the odours of sweat, damp, and less clear items on its way. Kobb blinked the fug from his eyes. From the press of bodies, whatever people did around here stopped for weather.

He peeled his cape away from his riding leathers and sidled across to the bar, nodding to the flat-faced villagers. It seemed glaring at strangers was common even if you weren't in a leaky hut. But it did mean he didn't need to attract the innkeeper's attention. "Looking for room and board. My horse is in the stable; could do with a rub down and a trough."

The innkeeper wiped his face with his rag before going back to rubbing a tankard. After glancing at the rapier on Kobb's hip and the Courser angled across his chest, the innkeeper revealed a set of dull teeth. "Don't allow weapons."

Kobb looked over his shoulder, taking in the axes, crossbows, and other dangerous objects propped on tables. Meeting the innkeeper's eyes again, he raised one brow.

"Them's tools."

"Might I rent somewhere to store my weapons?"

"Room and board's three. Another for the horse. Use of the safe's a strip."

Safe? That was a surprise. Kobb pulled out two strips. Breaking off a hunk, he put the rest on the bar. "Deal."

The innkeeper replaced the metal with a crude key. "Top of the stairs. Third door. And remember, you're not to go disturbing my customers with your noise."

Kobb squeezed between tables and mounted the stairs. If anything, the smoke from the fire seemed to prefer the upper floor to the chimney. Several short, narrow doors, about five feet apart, ran down the back wall. Eyes watering, Kobb let himself into his room. The door banged against the side of the bed.

He shouldered the door. Apart from a narrow palliasse, the room was empty. Not even a curtain over the window—although, the window was dirty enough, a curtain would have made little difference.

Placing his saddlebag at the end of the thin space, he peered at the ceiling and walls. No hooks either. But not all the nails had been hammered flush. He hung his cloak and hat as best he could. Leaving them to drip, he pulled the Book of Blessings from his jacket and began to pray.

When he ran out of good experiences, he eased himself to his feet. His left boot squelched, making him wince. Intellectually, 'look to that which is with you always before all others' made sense. However, the decades of adherence had not overcome the instinct to clean his kit as soon as he stopped.

He pulled a rag from his bag and cleaned the mud from his clothes. At the point where he was only moving the filth around, he considered the window. Apparently, the inn had been built for better things: cobwebbed and grimy though it was, the window opened.

Aware of the irony in making use of the torrential rain, Kobb washed out his rag and continued.

Soul and kit tended, he should eat and try to sleep; there wasn't a hurry, but an early start would still feel better.

When he emerged, the taproom was more packed than before. Fortunately, without his cloak it was easier to shuffle to the bar. Squeezing between two bulging jerkins, he tilted his head towards the innkeeper.

Mouth pursed, the innkeeper came over. "Didn't think your sort drank."

"Nothing in the Book against wetting a dry throat. Mug of ale, and a bite."

The innkeeper pulled a rag from the stained recesses of his apron and rubbed it across the rim of a wooden tankard. After dipping it in an open barrel, he thumped it down in front of Kobb before trudging off.

Kobb sipped the ale. Watery, with an odd under-note he hoped was resin from the tankard. Not a drink to savour, but adequate for washing away travel. And for easing the path of the dark bread and cracked cheese that the innkeeper dropped in front of him. Kobb picked up the plate and mug and shuffled away from the bar.

Most of the seats were taken, and those that looked empty were all in use by people who had gone to the jakes or were but a few minutes away. He sighed and sidled up the stairs.

The meal tasted as inadequate as it looked, but after days of trail food any variety was as good as spice and the plate was soon clear. Taking the same stance on the palliasse, Kobb collapsed into sleep.

Evil whispers and looming horrors pulled him awake. Still wrapped in nightmares of hungering trees and rocks from before the world was new, it took a moment to realise the whispering was real. The door, locked behind him when he brought his supper up, cracked open.

His hand flicked to the top of his saddlebag, grasping thin air. His Courser was in the innkeeper's safe.

Two shadowy figures crept into the room. "Told you bastard'd be asleep. Won't be so sneery without his fancy weapons," gurgled a voice, sounding like the watcher.

Recalling his frequent debates with the Master of Novice on the difference between the Blessing of Action and the Sin of Impatience, Kobb reached for the edge of the empty plate. He pushed down hard with his free arm, sitting up and snapping the plate into the leading figure's chin.

Kicking his right leg into the knee of the stunned youth, Kobb cleared room to rise.

The second thug, perhaps more used to getting his blows in before his victim realised the fight had started, still looked down at his fallen companion when Kobb's right elbow struck his ear. Turning, he caught Kobb's left fist on the nose.

Kobb stepped back.

With apparent lack of true experience in dirty fighting, the youth struggled to his feet with head still bowed.

Kobb let him reach his full height before flicking an elbow at his chin.

The watcher blocked Kobb's arm with a grunt, and then rose in both tone and stance as Kobb's knee reminded him, belatedly, to shield his groin.

Kobb locked his fingers and brought both fists down on the youth's forehead, sending him back into his companion.

In a display of some sense, if little bravery, the second thug raised his palms.

Kobb nodded at him and let him drag his companion from the room.

Closing the door behind his visitors, Kobb considered the lock. After a moment's thought, he shuffled the palliasse away from the wall.

The sound of the door banging into the foot of the palliasse roused him after dawn.

"Stranger! You stand accused of assault. It will go worse if you don't come peaceful."

Kobb reached for his leathers. Bringing him to law. Perhaps the watcher had the makings of a dirty fighter after all.

Part Two

Anessa rested her right hand on the butt of her slung crossbow and drifted behind the crowd, keeping one eye on Whistler Duffin. Stubby fingers clasped over his filthy apron, the innkeeper seemed have settled in until the entertainment was over.

Tremaine Aycock and his equally creepy son dragged Kobb out of the inn. The crowd shifted forward. While they were distracted, Anessa sprinted for the side of the inn. Pressing herself against the rough wood, she tried the kitchen door. As usual, Duffin had been too lazy to set the bolt.

Treating the filthy boards like untested undergrowth, she slid across the room and peered into the taproom. Aycock's ranting echoed through the open door, but there was no one in sight. She crept along the bar to the cash chest. A padlock, spattered with rust and other substances, lay beside it.

She gripped the lid and lifted. It creaked open, releasing a draft of stale air. Freezing in place, she strained her ears. Aycock's shouting continued without pause.

After crouching lower, she peered into the chest. A bundle of cloth with a sword hilt sticking out one end lay next to handfuls of hunks and the bone chips some villagers used in their place. She raised the edge of the cloth.

The weave felt greasy on her fingers. Kobb's sword and an object of crystal, sweeping metal, and carved wood, shaped like a crossbow without the arms, lay within. Remembering how nervous the sight of Kobb had made her father, and how he refused to explain, she pulled on her gloves before lifting them out of the chest. She resisted the urge to inspect them, sliding them to the sack of food she had thrown together while her father was opening the store.

She paused and then added a few strips to the sack. Duffin might not have been part of the plan, but he had let it happen, so Kobb deserved a refund. Easing the chest closed, she crept out the kitchen door and around the back of the inn.

The smell of rotting straw hit her as she slipped into the stable. An immense black horse, looming over the shattered remains of a trough, stared at her. She studied its shoulders for warning of an attack as she backed out of the stable.

Once outside, she exchanged the sack for her crossbow and headed for the front of the inn.

"This man laid hands on my son," shouted Aycock. "If it weren't for Duffin's forethought, he would have killed us all."

Anessa dropped to a crouch as Aycock turned back from the crowd. The angle wasn't right. A few of the east-siders were behind him. She resisted the urge to shoot anyway.

Aycock pointed at Kobb and strode forward. "I say we hang—"

Anessa caressed the trigger. The bolt skimmed Aycock's belt before spending itself in the front of Goodie Weaver's house.

Aycock's advance stuttered as the impact jolted his hip and his belt gave way.

"Ain't fair to hang a man without a trial," said Anessa, cranking her crossbow. "Particularly when he ain't done nothing wrong, and you ain't law here."

Aycock clutched at his breeches. "You could have—"

"My Anessa's a good shot," Lambert Tanton called from the middle of the crowd, "but even she can't hit something that small."

The older man whirled around as the larger part of the crowd burst out laughing.

Kobb's saddlebag thumped to the ground. Osraed Corless sidled away, trying to merge into the crowd of east-siders.

"We can't let violent outsiders take over the village," said Aycock. The east-siders nodded in support.

"I reckon Reverend Kobb was leaving anyway," said Lambert. "Ain't no need to stir things up."

"Lambert's right," shouted Goodie Weaver. "And about leaving things be, too." She added a gesture to make sure no one missed the joke.

Kobb stepped away from Dereck Aycock, seeming not to notice when Dereck's grunted in pain. Sweeping his saddlebag up, Kobb strolled towards the inn door.

"Got your stuff," said Anessa, patting a sack slung over her shoulder. She headed towards the stables. "We should get a move on before they try something."

Kobb tilted his head.

She held her breath. He couldn't turn her down now.

His eyes turned less flinty. "Agreed. Although, Falcon might have his own ideas."

Finished strapping on the fragile-looking tack, Kobb leapt into the saddle and offered her a hand.

She swallowed hard. The forest was dense in places. It made sense to go on foot. But he wouldn't let her go with him if he thought she was afraid. Watching the horse for the slightest twitch, she stepped closer and let him swing her up behind him.

The beast's back rolled underneath her as it stomped out of the stable. She wrapped her arms tighter around Kobb.

Kobb nodded to the dispersing crowd as they jolted to the north gate, apparently unconcerned by the horse's attempts to throw them.

Glad to replace the air of the village with the scent of trees, she tried to match Kobb's movements. "So, where are we going?"

"Don't know, but I will when I get there." Kobb pulled Falcon to a halt. "There was mention you had my kit."

Anessa unclasped her fingers from his cloak and half-tumbled to solid ground. She handed the sack up to him. "Dad heard them planning it last night. Didn't seem right, and I didn't want you thinking we were all... like that." And it let him see how useful she could be. "Put the food you wanted in there too."

The smell of fresh bread and sharp cheese that her dad would miss come lunchtime wafted up as Kobb reached in and settled his weapons in place. "Seems a few strips slipped in here too."

"Duffin slung your stuff in his chest with the money. Didn't even lock it. Seemed right to take something for how they treated you."

"There are Blessings enough we need not take from others." Kobb dismounted and stacked the money on a rock. Pausing for a moment, he removed a strip from the pile and dropped it in a pouch. "That said, an unlocked cash box is not a safe."

He peered at the shadows clinging to the edges of the path. "I am grateful for the company. But I got the feeling your father didn't approve of—"

"Since Mum died, he gets a little worried when I'm out, but he don't mean it. And might be better to avoid Aycock for a few days anyway."

"There's sense in that. If Aycock's the type to chew over a slight, we'll head on a ways before I eat. No reason to tire Falcon, though." Taking the reins, he pointed down the track. "Lead on."

Anessa peered sideways at the horse. It ignored her for the moment. With one ear out for changes in the sounds of small animals, she led the way along the track.

A few miles later, she pointed out a clearing near the path. A thrush bounced across the leaf mould before flitting into a tree. "Seems a good place to take a break."

Kobb nodded and unslung the sack of provisions. After breaking a loaf in half, he passed her a piece before doing the same with a lump of cheese.

She propped her crossbow against a mossy rock on the far side from the horse and sat down. The damp ground made it hard to tell, but it smelt like the rain would hold off.

She was licking the last crumbs of cheese from her fingers when terrible howls rang out from several directions. The thrush continued its song.

Anessa snatched up her crossbow. "Eaters! But they never come this close to the track."

She tried to spot a target, but—although the howls became louder and more frequent—the shadows seemed too still.

And then the rain of spears began.

Part Three

Reverend Kobb rolled sideways behind a stump and rose to a crouch, Courser and rapier in his hands. A second hail of spears peppered the ground, but he couldn't make who threw them. His eyes flicked from the shadows to Anessa and back. She seemed safe crouched behind a large boulder, and her crossbow was loaded. He could reach her in a few steps, but that might be what they expected. Or he could wait. "Tell me more of these Eaters. How do they act? Do they understand us?"

She ducked further down. "Don't know. How can you be so calm?"

"Experience. If I understand, I'm better prepared."

"They're evil. Sensible people run or hide. Don't know anyone who fought and lived."

Kobb glanced at the shafts clustered in the ground. Two rains of spears, each from several directions. But not from all sides at once. So probably two or three groups circling the clearing, throwing twice. He burst from behind the stump, sprinted at an angle to Anessa's hiding place, and dived for another rock. More spears thudded into the earth, barely missing him. Now for the risky part. He leapt up and ran hard at the tree line to the left of where one of the last groups of spears had come from.

He heard Anessa shout something but didn't stop. After flattening himself against a tree, he counted to five in his head and slashed sideways with his rapier, rolling around the tree after it.

Leaf litter scuffed as something jumped back. Kobb glimpsed a dark limb slipping into the shadows beneath a bush. Taking a step backwards, he let his Courser rise up. Short figures, barely distinguishable from shadow even from feet away, leapt from the bushes on all sides, clubs raised. Crude wooden masks concealed their faces but didn't muffle their howling.

Letting everything other than his targets fade away, Kobb turned at the waist. A heavy silence drowned their war cries as the Courser's crystal glowed. Kobb straightened, the Eater's twisted bodies already still.

Anessa's crossbow twanged behind him, followed by a whinny.

Kobb put his back to another tree. Four more Eaters ran towards Falcon from the far side of the track. Another lay on the ground, a quarrel jutting from its head. Falcon reared as the first creature approached, smashing it backwards with his hooves, but the others held back, spreading wider to flank the horse.

With no clear line of sight, Kobb sprinted towards Falcon, rapier raised. Whistling low then high, Kobb dropped and rolled left. Falcon charged right, exposing the end Eater. Kobb's Courser flickered again.

Anessa shouted incoherently.

Glancing back, Kobb saw her pressed against a tree, knife in one hand and quarrel in the other, stabbing out at a group of five Eaters. She would soon be overwhelmed. But if he went back, the Eaters would all but cripple Falcon. Neither option clearly better, he chose to trust Anessa's belief she was good enough.

He surged across the clearing and scythed down another Eater.

With one less threat to avoid, Falcon focused his efforts, hooves felling another of the creatures.

Anessa's shouting cut off mid-insult.

Kobb forced himself not to react. The last Eater, cautious of Kobb's presence, missed his chance to close on Falcon's flank, instead diving for a nearby spear. Kobb's Courser took the Eater as his fingers wrapped around the shaft.

Hoping there weren't more of the creatures lurking nearby, Kobb turned his back on the forest. Anessa, left arm cradling her gut, slumped against the tree. Wide swipes of her knife held the Eaters back but posed no threat.

Thankful he had guessed right, Kobb aimed the Courser up from the ground, taking three Eaters in the head in quick succession.

The last two broke into the forest.

Rolling onto his side, Kobb hawked and spat. Flecks of blood stood out against the muck. Death had started charging for his services a while ago. After scuffing leaf mould over the spit, he clambered to his feet. "Anessa?"

She pulled herself up the trunk by one arm, chest heaving but whole. Gaze flicking across the twisted bodies of the Eaters, she gaped at Kobb.

He crouched to clean his rapier on some leaves. Disbelief mixed with the immortality of youth. That must be how his face had looked when Certitude Gannon walked unharmed towards him through the tumbling bodies of the bandits. Kobb wondered if Gannon had felt as hollow inside at the sight of it as he did now.

"How...?" Anessa staggered over to her fallen crossbow. "Dad said you were dangerous. But there were so many. And then they fell faster than I could count."

"The Courser takes its strength from will, not metal or muscle. I need to aim, but not reload."

"And could I...?"

Kobb stood. Few had the talent, and of those not all came into it. But to come into it without training, to chance upon in nature the pattern the

Courser formed, might be like throwing bottles of brandy into a fire. He drew and spun his Courser, offering her the butt. "I do not have the Blessing of Knowing, but the attempt will answer. Point it at your target like your crossbow, picture the target falling in your mind, and squeeze the butt."

Anessa rested her crossbow on a rock and reached out. Her hand paused halfway, before snatching the Courser. Shoulders hard as oak, she thrust it towards a tangle of brambles.

Kobb felt stiffness leave his neck as nothing happened. Walking forwards, he rested a hand on her shoulder as she thrust the Courser out for the third time. "You are not called to bear it."

"Perhaps it takes time. I could—"

"It brings only the hardest of Blessings. And asks much." He slipped the Courser from her fingers and holstered it. "The reaction you saw this morning is not unusual."

"But you could..." The fire went out of her. "You could kill those who challenged you. And all who disagreed. And then... How do you bear it, Mr Kobb...? I mean, Reverend..."

"You are not of the faith, and we are companions. Call me Kobb or Absolution. And I bear it because those who accept the world as a Blessing find it is so." And because the alternative was worse than merely killing those who threatened him. "But the time for philosophy is beside a warm hearth with a full stomach. We should move on. It will be slow going from here on."

"I thought you had not been this way before. And anyway, the track is passable for miles yet."

"But the forest will not be. Especially for Falcon." Kobb looked down at the remains of the Eaters. "If they don't usually come this close to the track then something has changed. I must at least rule it out before I move on."

Anessa looked back the way they had come, before peering into the forest. "When they fled, they left some spoor. But tracking them and finding a way for your horse will not be easy. Let us hope it is not an ambush."

The day passed noon and faded as she scouted both the Eaters' route and an easier route that did not deviate too far. She returned grinning. "Some sort of ruined structure ahead. They camp there. I can get us close on foot, but your horse will make too much noise."

Kobb patted Falcon's nose. "Try not to get into trouble without me."

Following Anessa, he crept through the undergrowth. The forest ahead grew lighter. He stopped beside her and peered through the bushes. The jagged remains of columns and walls jutted from the ground, defeated by the encroaching trees but fighting to the last. Five Eaters, one clutching a staff, clustered around a fire next to a mostly intact low building. The staff-bearer threw something into the fire with his free hand, turning the flames solid black. The air turned sour.

Anessa bit back a gasp.

Kobb drew back a little. "I can deal with that few easily. You should keep watch in case others return."

"I can get us closer without noise. And it will be over faster with both of us."

Kobb inclined his head and signalled her to lead the way.

Crawling left, Anessa led the way to a point where a sagging wall concealed the fire.

Kobb crouched low and followed her across the leaf mould to the shadows beneath it. Pointing at each of their chests, he signalled she should go to opposite end.

He leaned around the end to confirm the Eaters were still clustered around the fire. Raising his Courser, he fired. The nearest Eater collapsed into the fire. Flames gusted up and then settled into reds and oranges.

Eaters dived away from the fire. Kobb took another and saw a third collapse with a quarrel in his chest.

With a howling war cry, an Eater charged towards Kobb. The staff bearer began to chant.

Kobb took the charging Eater in the head.

The remaining Eater continued to chant. The fire blazed higher, making the air shimmer.

Letting everything else drift away, Kobb aimed the Courser and caressed the butt.

The Eater's chant continued.

Kobb fired again, and a third time to no effect.

A quarrel glanced off a column several feet from the Eater.

Chant soaring in volume, the Eater pointed his staff towards Anessa's hiding place. Chunks of stone exploded up. With a terrible creak, the wall slumped further.

Kobb fired as fast as he could will.

The Eater spun its staff. Almost a blur, it disappeared behind a pile of stone. Leaping up again, it lashed out with its staff.

Kobb dived sideways as the wall shattered around him.

Part Four

Tucking his legs in tight, Kobb rolled into the shadow of the remaining wall. Massive blocks thudded into the ground only inches from his feet. Dust rained down, as others were knocked free of the lip of his narrow shelter. He pressed his elbows hard against his sides and aimed the Courser at the worst threats as best he could.

The stones shifted path—when he hit them—but lacking whatever it was the Courser most worked upon, did not shatter. Clouds of dirt and mortar covered the stench of the Eater's ritual, sucking the moisture from Kobb's mouth.

The thudding and rolling stopped. Feeling something twist inside as he forced a cough down, he swilled his mouth with saliva and let it dribble in brown strings from his lips. With luck, the Eater would think him buried beneath the rubble.

Kobb eased himself up onto his elbows and crawled around the pile of stones. Peering between two massive blocks, he saw the Eater standing a few feet away, spinning its staff above its head and flicking its gaze from place to place.

Heartbeats later, it sprinted past the fire and into the intact building.

Kobb racked his mind. Even if he could get close enough to use his sword without receiving a dose of whatever the Eater did, it was too fast to fight with a rapier. He needed an edge.

He considered the surrounding rubble. While some blocks were cracked, most of them were intact. The majority of the damage was to the mortar, or through falling. Maybe whatever the Eater had done had the same reduced effect on stone as his Courser.

By sliding slowly, he moved onto the top of a block and took a better look at the building. Two low doorways gaped, one either end of the front wall, but there were no windows—at least on the sides he could see. One corner of the roof sagged as if ready to fall.

After an aching glance at the jumble of stone at the far end of the wall, he crept between columns and the remains of walls until he stood next to the door furthest from the damaged area of the roof. He flattened himself against the wall and waited.

The chanting didn't restart. The Eater hadn't noticed him. Kobb took aim at the other door lintel and raised his Courser. Hoping his lungs would stand another use so soon after his frenzied firing and the clouds of muck, he took his shot. Not waiting to see the effect, he swung his rapier hard across the doorway.

The rumble of falling stones covered the sound of Kobb's rapier striking the Eater in the face as it ran through the doorway. Continuing his motion, Kobb rolled around the edge of the door while dropping his weapons and leapt onto the staggered Eater, locking his arms around its body.

The air thickened as the rent in the building spread.

The Eater's arms and legs blurred as it struck at him, but Kobb ignored the pain and squeezed harder. Leaning back, he raised the Eater from the ground.

Too close to wield its staff, and unable to dodge an attack that had already occurred, it thrashed as Kobb drew his arms tighter around its spine.

The Eater twisted its head around, snapping at him

Kobb felt a tearing sensation on the side of his head, followed by pain and warmth spreading down his neck. Strength trickling away, and rubble falling ever closer, he realised he would soon lose his grip on one or the other. He locked his fingers as tight as he could and threw himself forwards.

Agony spiked through his hands and forearms as they slammed into the rough floor. Blood-flecked mucus exploded from his mouth as something punched into his chest, sending his lungs into racking coughs.

He drew a breath of his own will. The Eater lay unmoving beneath him.

Shouts, not loud enough to be intelligible, penetrated the rumble of falling blocks. Anessa or more Eaters? After forcing down nausea, he rolled off his opponent and staggered out of the door.

No one greeted his sight. Grabbing up his weapons, he stumbled away from the collapsing building towards where he last saw Anessa. As he moved, he realised the shouts were inside. There must have been more Eaters deeper within.

A crossbow lay next to the remains of the wall, half-cranked. In the shadows beneath the sagged stonework, he saw Anessa's head. He crouched down. "Anessa. Can you move?"

Her eyes were closed, but the locks of hair lying across her face trembled. He gave praise for a Blessing. She was unconscious but still breathing.

Easing his aching body as close as possible to the gap, he slid his right arm in. It hit rock, just below her chest.

He drew his arm back and moved around the wall. The middle had stood better. Blocks still held by mortar formed an arch, the depths of which revealed Anessa's legs. Just one block held her in place.

The sound of falling stone quietened.

"—me. Anyone!" The shouting sounded human.

Kobb paused. The wall hadn't sunk while he fought the Eater, so might hold for a while longer. And even the thought of shifting it on his own made him feel queasy. He walked back towards the building. "I can... hear you."

"Thank you! Hurry, please."

Kobb took a step through the doorway. Murky light shifted through the clouds of settling dust, revealing jagged piles of stone. From the far corner, metal groaned. Twisted iron bars stopped the remaining roof from falling further.

Someone moved behind the bars. "Over here. The cage saved me, but it won't hold."

Pausing after each step, Kobb moved closer. The rubble shifted as he advanced, but held. Crouching, he saw a middle-aged man, hunched within a tangle of bars.

Kobb looked up. A team of workers with ropes and bars might move the stonework, but one ageing priest, bruised, half-choked, and without tools had no chance.

The cage creaked again as the roof shifted.

Part Five

Kobb froze. The creaking stopped.

"Haelen Lok," said the prisoner. "Did you see how that creature destroyed the building? Could you break the bars?"

Kobb peered through the murk. The side wall sagged inward. He was no architect, but the wall and roof looked to be taking some of each other's weight. If he blasted one of them away, the cage would take the full weight of the other before he could get off a second shot. "Not sure it would help. We need to... We might be able to..."

He backed away across the rubble to the doorway. The Eater's staff lay next to its body, mercifully still intact. Kobb took a step back towards the cage and stumbled sideways as the stones shifted beneath his feet.

The staff lodged between two blocks, preventing him from falling. Kobb held his breath. Nothing moved. Shifting his feet, he regained his footing and eased the staff free. He inched his way back to the cage, transferring his weight from foot to foot, and passed the end of the staff between two bars. "If you brace the roof with this it might hold long enough for me to get some bars out of the way."

"And if it doesn't, the roof crushes me." Haelen took the end of the staff. "Don't see a choice, though. I need you to promise something first. I was on my way to find my daughter when those creatures found me. Promise me if I die you'll save my Katrina."

Kobb's fingered the pendant at his throat. He couldn't leave a child in danger. "I promise."

Haelen drew the staff through the bars and twisted it around as best he could. For a moment, flecks of something caught the light, confirming Kobb's theory it was similar to a Courser. Hopefully, it would be as resilient.

Kobb drew his Courser. "Turn your head away. It'll get messy." Realising he had no idea which bars were bearing the least weight, he aimed to one side of Haelen and took his shot.

The bar shivered. With a graunch, the bottom sprang outward. The roof creaked, but the air was too full of muck to tell how far it moved.

Kobb dived into the choking cloud of powered mortar and dirt, thrusting his arm forwards. His fingers met flesh. Pulling his arm back, he yanked Haelen out as Haelen leapt forwards. The edge of a block bruised Kobb's aching back as the two men landed in a tangled heap. A sharp crack, like snapping kindling, rang out.

Despite wanting nothing so much as a single night's rest, Kobb struggled to his feet and staggered for the door. His passage turned faster and more assured as Haelen wrapped an arm around him and drew him forward.

The louder crack of the staff losing its battle presaged the fatal crash of the building. Gasping for breath, the two men lay on the grass.

"A Courser?" Haelen rolled over. "I hoped for rescue, but not... Has the push started?"

Kobb sat up. "I'm not in the Legion. There's just Anessa and me. We need to get her out."

"If your companion was in there, then—"

"Over there. By the wall."

Haelen eased himself upright and then helped Kobb up. The two of them trudged across the clearing, steps gaining some hint of strength as they went.

"I used to be Legion. A healer." Haelen crouched beside Anessa and ran his fingers over her head and torso. "She might just be stunned, but I'll need time and a better inspection."

"If I pull on the block, perhaps you can slide her out."

"You shifted stone last time. It's my turn." Haelen braced his hands on the bottom of the block. "Slide. Don't yank. If she is injured, we don't want to make it worse."

Kobb gripped Anessa beneath the armpits. As Haelen heaved, Kobb pulled.

She moved slightly, but Kobb could feel resistance. Arms and legs trembling, Haelen let the block settle back.

Kobb stumbled over. "My turn." His efforts were, if anything, less effective.

Haelen pumped his fingers. "What if we slide something in so it doesn't settle back?"

Hampered by the fading light, they gathered a small pile of the flattest stones they could find. By taking turns to lift the block, they wedged the remains of the wall higher. With each wedge, the pile trembled and bowed out further.

"It'll fall if we try adding more stones," Haelen said. "We have to risk hurting her."

Gripping one side of Anessa's torso each, they yanked hard. With a sound of tearing cloth, she slid from under the wall.

Haelen ran his fingers over her again, this time easing them under her torso too. "Nothing feels out of place. She'll need remedies, though, and rest." He looked over at the jagged remains of the building. "My bag is buried in there somewhere. But they didn't spend long in my camp. There might still be what I need there. If we could move her that is."

Kobb managed half a chuckle before the coughing started. Slapping his chest, he spat muck. "Falcon, my horse, has a way of finding trouble; but I doubt anyone dropped a building on him." He held out his rapier. "Wait here."

The return to Falcon was easy enough; and, freed of the need for stealth, leading him back to the clearing manageable. Falcon even consented to stand still while they settled Anessa across his saddle.

Not wishing to jolt her, the journey from the ruins took even longer than the stealthy approach. By the time they reached Haelen's camp, night had full hold.

Shards of bottles, contents now only stains, lay among tatters of tent and clothing. Kobb helped Haelen lay Anessa down on the remains of a cloak. "I'll take watch."

"I need to stay up anyway to prepare the herbs," said Haelen. "It'll be worse if neither of us gets any sleep. I've had nothing to do but sit in that cage anyway."

Kobb slumped against a tree. It made sense. "Wake me if anything seems odd."

Sleep caught him the moment his eyes closed. And then the world tumbled into a screaming abyss.

Kobb's eyes snapped open. Bitter slime coated his tongue and icy fingers crushed his temples.

Haelen crouched beside him. "You were thrashing. And muttering something."

"Nightmares. Rocks twisting like smoke. And chanting. They grow stronger as I move north."

"You barely slept. There is a potion. It might help control the nightmares. But..."

Kobb considered. Without the dreams, he might lose the way. But without one good night's sleep soon, he would soon lose the ability to fight. "But what?"

"It needs Korha venom. There are swamps to the east. There might be Korha there. But Anessa can't travel."

Korha. A creature so evil the myths claimed the Maker denied it the Blessing of Death. "Then I go alone."

Part Six

Anessa felt woozy. Everything was dark. She smelt rotting leaves and a sharper scent like crushed grass. The last thing she remembered was the wall tumbling down, and something hitting her in the stomach. Something moved nearby. Sounded like the fight was over.

The darkness wasn't uniform: there were specks of light here and there, like an old feed sack over a window. Kobb wouldn't put a bag on her head, so... So she needed to see what was going on. She twitched one arm and listened.

Something clinked, not metal, pottery maybe? Then the sound of whatever was out there moving away. Easing her right arm over her stomach, Anessa winced in anticipation; and then paused again when she wasn't racked with pain.

Something rough was wrapped around her stomach, but her arm moved freely, so she wasn't tied up. Nearby, someone whistled a tune.

She froze. Whoever it was didn't fear detection. Which was another reason it couldn't be Kobb. Two reasons, given how impossible the image of him whistling cheerfully seemed. If she was careful, the noise would cover her movements. She brought her hand up to her face.

Hessian and a mushy substance. A ragged edge hung just past her ear. Whatever it was, it was only draped over. She could lift a corner enough to see and then work out what to do next.

The whistling continued. The scent of crushed grass strengthened as she lifted the sacking. By tilting her head, she made out the back of a man clad in a filthy tunic, crouched over something. She peered around. Broken glass, potsherds, and torn cloth filled the clearing. Her crossbow lay on a pile of sacking six feet away. Which, still woozy and moving over broken glass, was five feet too far.

That rock was within reach, though. She peeled the cloth all the way off her face and eased herself into a crouch. All she had to do was—

Pain jabbed through her left leg. Biting down on a shout, she collapsed sideways.

The man sprang to his feet and walked towards her. "Anessa?"

As he crouched down next to her, she swung the rock hard.

He swayed backwards without effort. "Calm down. I'm a friend. Haelen Lok. I'm a healer."

"Kobb?"

"He's fine. Dealt with the last of those creatures. Rescued me from them." Haelen extended his hands, palms facing her. "Can I touch you?"

Anessa stared at him. The wooziness made it hard to concentrate, but he could have killed her already if he wanted; and he knew her name... She nodded.

He ran his fingers along her legs and across her stomach. "Any sickness? Blurred vision?"

"Pain in my leg. And my head's wobbly." This didn't seem so bad. The gentle brushing of his fingers was relaxing.

He grabbed her left foot and wrenched while pressing down hard on her knee.

Anessa spasmed, shooting upright. Now her stomach hurt.

"Cramp. The poultice kept you still while you slept." Haelen's fingers pressed along her leg. "Should be better now."

Blinking wetness away, she realised the pain jabbing her leg was gone now. "Thank you... I think."

"You were lucky. The blast stunned you, but the rubble only bruised you." He pressed on her shoulder. "You need rest, though. The reverend won't be back for several days anyway."

Anessa sagged back. Kobb had gone on without her. Although, she couldn't blame him: she nearly got killed by Eaters the first time, missed half her shots the second time, and then did get knocked out. "Did he say where he was going?"

"Those creatures broke most of what they didn't take. I found enough to tend you, but..." Haelen glanced away. "I needed Korha venom."

Anessa stared at him. She recalled fragments of the stories Gramma told before Dad found out and forbade it. "They're a myth."

"Some of the tales are pure fantasy, but the beasts are real enough." Haelen rested a hand on her shoulder. "And that's all they are, beasts; dangerous I'll admit, but not some dark force that can't be stopped."

Anessa stood and staggered towards her crossbow. "Maybe. But we have to help him."

"You need rest."

"You said he would be back in several days. I can get a night's sleep on the way as easily as here. But I'm not lying around while he goes into danger. You don't have to come."

"And spend all my time worrying you'd collapsed in a ditch? I shouldn't have let him go in the first place."

Scared each moment might be the last chance not to be too late, but aware that any of Haelen's surviving possessions might be the difference between saving Kobb's life and not, Anessa forced herself to help him assemble a bundle each.

Between her aching everything and not moving above a walk for fearing to attract unwanted attention, the first day's travel was less than she had hoped. But they were going in a straightish line; Kobb might be faster on horseback, but Haelen assured her the road would take Kobb miles out of his way.

Next morning she awoke cold but less stiff. After convincing Haelen to eat as they walked, they spent another day squeezing between twisted trees, before collapsing onto a patch of the least rotten vegetation they could find in the gloom.

An icy drizzle, filtering between branches too close to admit more than tatters of light, woke them. Tired and unsure of which side of dawn it was, they trudged on.

Feet numb and clothes clammy, Anessa realised it was lighter ahead and the ground sloped down. The brambles gave way to half-rotten undergrowth layered over slimy soil. The rain, taking full advantage of the wider gaps between dying trees, drove into her face. But it was lighter ahead.

They stumbled and slid through the trees, emerging on the edge of a ragged field. Clumps of grey leaves lay in rough lines through the mud. On the far side huts sagged, wrapped in tendrils of mist.

"Alcston," said Haelen. "Unless someone else was mad enough to build on the edge of a swamp. If the reverend stayed on the road, that's where it ends."

Spurred on by the thought of news, or even finding Kobb still there, Anessa forced her way across the cloying mud towards the nearest hut. "Halloo, the village."

The mist sucked away her shout, returning the village to silence. She considered the nearby huts. Shutters, too warped and swelled to be usable, covered the windows; and no smoke rose from the chimneys. But some of the doors stood partway open. When she banged on the nearest, her hand came away coated with a greenish mould.

Haelen squelched into sight. "Looks abandoned. We should move on."

Anessa peered into the murk. "I think there's someone asleep in there." She shoved on the door until the gap was wide enough to slip in. A bitter smell hung in the air. Quiet breathing came from a bed in the corner. She made out a head above a crumpled blanket. "Hallo."

Apart from a slight snuffle, they didn't react.

Anessa walked over and reached out to shake them. More of the mould coated the blanket. Her hand jerked back, catching a fold and sending the blanket sliding to the floor. A woman, curled up inside a tattered nightdress, lay on a decaying bundle of straw.

Reaching out again, Anessa tugged on the woman's shoulder. The woman rolled onto her back but didn't wake. Something wasn't right.

The woman should have woken up. Why hadn't she woken? Then Anessa realised something worse. The woman was on her back now, so why weren't her legs visible?

She bent down. The bitter odour grew stronger.

The woman's legs ended below the hips.

Murky light spilled across the bed as Haelen forced the door wide.

Anessa's legs gave way. The woman's legs ended not in the smooth stumps of deformity or an old accident, but in torn flesh and bone. Flesh and bone that—unlike her skin and bedding—bore no sign of dirt or decay.

Flushed with life, yet did not bleed.

PART SEVEN

Anessa felt hands lifting her up and helping her to the door. Staggering out of the hut, she began to hiccup, each spasm burning her throat. Not caring about the mould, she slumped against the swollen planks. Haelen might've been right about needing more rest.

Haelen stepped into view. He held out her pack and then patted her shoulder. "There's no shame in it. Seeing that and not feeling ill? That would be a bad thing."

"What... what did that?" She forced the bile down. "How is she...?"

"Korha venom is powerful. Some tales speak of them felling mighty warriors with a single blow. All I could do was stop her from suffering further."

Anessa took a deep breath and then regretted it as the scent of stagnant water flooded her nose. She'd thought coming with Kobb would be an escape from Morth, a chance to get away from the east-siders and their sneaking around. Instead, the world was the senseless, dangerous place Dad kept trying to protect her from.

Which made Haelen's actions all the more impressive. Coming with her might only be repaying a debt to Kobb, but spending his time and precious resources helping a complete stranger... "We should search the rest of the village. What if there are more villagers?"

Haelen gazed at her for a moment. Whatever he saw made him smile, but it soon faded. "I don't have the herbs to wake them up. So killing whatever did this might be the only way. I only met the reverend briefly, but I think this would have spurred him on. Which means—"

"—either he got here already and needs help, or we don't have time to wait for him." Anessa studied the churned ground. "Those might be hoof prints."

She unslung her crossbow. After a moment, Haelen drew his eating knife; it didn't make him look any more dangerous.

The mist thickened as she led the way through the village, adding to the impression the tendrils clutched at it. As she slogged on, the huts showed ever-greater signs of abandonment, swollen wood giving way to rot and collapse. The squelch of their feet broke the silence.

The ground underwent similar degradation, cloying mud melting into a foul-smelling soup. Feet later, the mist took away what little chance she had of identifying even hints of tracks. She wasn't sure if the dark shapes in the near distance were fallen huts or rotten trees. "How could anyone live here?"

"Cities don't have the same discomforts, it's true, but they aren't safer. And they have a lot more rules. Some people prefer hard freedom to a feather bed they'll never own." Haelen hawked into the mud and then swept his arm around. "But I reckon this foulness came to live here after they did."

"So, it might be—" In the distance, something cried out. She held a finger to her lips and waited.

A few moments later, it came again. "Does that sound like ahorse?"

Haelen shrugged. "It's something to head for."

Eyes drawn in every direction by half-shapes in the fog, Anessa crept forward. The ground resisted each attempt to lift her boot yet slid away each time she put it down.

Filthy water spattered her back and Haelen cried out. She turned and saw him sprawled face down in the muck. She scanned for threats, but nothing seemed out-of-place. "Haelen?"

He rolled over and sat up, spitting out mud and water. After running his hands over his legs, he picked up his knife. "Caught my foot on something. Left ankle twisted. Doesn't feel broken."

She slung her crossbow and helped him up.

His face paled under the filth as his weight shifted onto his legs. Wrapping his arm around her shoulders, he pointed at a twisted form squatting in the murk. "Help me to that tree."

Anessa wrapped her arm around his waist and took his weight. Just as she thought she had it, her right foot slid sideways. By shifting his grip on her shoulder, Haelen stopped her falling but almost went over himself. Stopping almost every other step to change their positions, they reached the tree.

Thin limbs jutted from a bulging trunk. Sap oozed from cracks in bark the colour of lead. Only the few leaves clinging to the least unhealthy twigs convinced Anessa it wasn't some armoured beast.

Haelen tugged on a branch about the thickness of his wrist. "Should take my weight."

"I'm not leaving you in the middle of a swamp."

"I'm not asking you to." Haelen drew his knife. "But I can barely walk. I can't run. I'd make it worse if we're attacked."

"Then we—"

"No." Haelen hacked at the branch. "By the time you get to the village and back it might be too late. You need to carry on. Once I can cut the branch off, I can limp back. Maybe take a look in the other huts so I'm not useless."

Anessa's thoughts refused to settle. Haelen didn't seem like he would last long at the best of times; with a twisted ankle, he was just prey. But he was right about how long it would take to help him back. The swamp seemed threatening, but all they had encountered was mud and fog. Could she let him go back on his own?

The branch tore away under Haelen's knife. He wedged a fork under his arm. Tufts of limp black leaves waved above his head. It should have been comical, but it made Anessa more nervous.

Haelen took his arm from around her shoulders. The branch sank deeper, canting him sideways, but he stayed upright. "Anessa. You need to get going. I'll be fine."

Unsure what to say, she raised a hand in salute and trudged into the mist. A few moments later, she looked back, but the fog had already hidden him from view. Heart heavy, she tried to locate the cries of the horse.

Moving first one way and then angling back as the sound shifted, she advanced. Now she was certain it was a familiar whinny. A shadow shifted in a way the mist wouldn't explain. Hoping she wasn't giving away the advantage of stealth, she sloshed as fast as she could towards it.

A loud neigh echoed ahead. The fog grudgingly revealed the silhouette of a horse.

Finding firmer footing, Anessa jogged forward. Somehow, an island of solid ground existed within the filthy soup. A squat tree jutted from the middle. Falcon, straining against the reins hitched to its branches, stood at bay on the far side.

Caked with mud and wreathed in mist, he raced towards her. Spittle exploded across her face as the reins pulled his gaping mouth up inches from her.

Kobb had been here. Gritting her teeth, she stepped closer with her palms raised. "Friend. I'm a friend."

When he didn't attack straight away, she sidled over to the reins. Between Falcon's pulling and the soggy air, the leather had swelled, but she eventually worked the hitch loose. As soon as she did, Falcon headed for the mist.

Dogs ran to their masters; maybe horses did too. Unslinging her crossbow as she ran, Anessa struggled after him. The mist shredded around his passage, adding brief maws to Anessa's imaginings of lashing tentacles. She thought she saw a flash of purple through the murk, but it was gone before she could be sure and didn't return.

Falcon surged towards a vague darker shape ahead. Then tumbled sideways as a tentacle seemed to lash out, before dissipating again.

Anessa dropped to a crouch. The murk swirled but revealed only more mist. The shadow, the size of an adult man lying on the ground, remained still. She waited.

Falcon didn't move. Eyes flicking at every shift in the fog, she crept forward.

The horse was still breathing. But he seemed smaller, lying in the swamp. She patted him on the flank. The same bitter odour as the hut filled her nostrils and a thin layer of green mould clung to her palm.

The mist shifted around her, but no attack came. Her legs felt weak. Fighting down a yawn, she peered through the murk. The creature should be ahead of her, so why couldn't she see it.

Her crossbow drooped in her hands. She needed a plan, but the cold seemed to eat away at her thoughts. She slumped next to Falcon. Now he wasn't looming over her, she realised his coat was soft like a pillow.

She couldn't hold back a yawn. The mist swirled and thickened ahead, obscuring the slumped shadow. Falcon's flank felt comfortable under her cheek. Apart from the mould, it was just like...

Part Eight

Thwang

Anessa screamed in pain as something hit her stomach. Struggling to draw breath, she noticed her crossbow next to her, no longer loaded and with one arm embedded in the mud. It must have gone off when it hit the ground, kicking the butt into her stomach. She stifled a yawn. If she'd dropped her crossbow in the mud, Haelen was right about her needing—

No. Sleep was the enemy. Grabbing the crossbow, she backed away. Torn between keeping moving to stay awake and having to rely on her knife to protect herself, she risked a brief stop to wipe away the worst of the mud from her crossbow.

Something splashed behind her.

She spun around. For a moment, she thought she saw something move, but then it was lost in the fog. After fumbling a bolt into place, she crept closer.

The mist swirled again revealing a thin shadow. Almost releasing without thought, she realised it was a withered sapling. Neck aching from trying to look in every direction at once, and new abuse reminding her stomach of old insults, she took long moments to realise the urge to sleep had faded.

She crouched and looked back. Tendrils of fog slid across Falcon. Or something that looked like fog. Ignoring the dull aches, she took aim and loosed a bolt.

The mist twisted where it had passed, but she couldn't be sure whether the remaining tendrils were a trick of vapour, or even be sure some of them had not been. The tiredness was a sign the Korha was nearby, but—unless the fog cleared—she would be firing blind. Or she could get closer. Close enough to be affected by its venom.

Falcon had fallen asleep before he hit the ground, but she had only begun to doze. She thought she'd seen a tentacle hit him. What if the venom was so strong that breathing the air it had passed through was enough to feel some effect? She slung her crossbow and unlaced her coat. Her singlet was the only vaguely clean clothing she had left. At least that would change through choice. Ripping a wide strip from the hem, she pushed it deep into the muck.

The brackish water darkened as clots of black matter rose to the surface. Anessa gagged as the damp air took on a stench that made Duffin's jakes seem fragrant. Before she lost her nerve, she dragged the strip out and tied it around her face.

Loading her crossbow, she trudged towards Falcon. Between, hopefully, less of the venom getting through and the foulness making her not want to breathe anyway, she should be safe unless a tentacle touched her. She thought she could make out several whirls of mist that were both thicker and less random than others. She crept closer.

The fog shifted, but the tentacles didn't, making her more certain they were not just a trick of her mind. Where the centre of the tentacles would be, she made out a darker patch. She wanted to loose now, but knew she might only have one chance. Lungs aching, she inched closer.

The air remained still; but the mist parted, revealing Kobb slumped in the water. A dark sphere, easily two feet across, with a horizontal line across the middle, loomed over him. She gasped as she realised it was an eye, mud and rotten leaves from the cloth filling her mouth.

Fighting down nausea, she raised her crossbow. Even battered and half-choked, her aim was true. The bolt smashed into the centre of the eye, filling the air with black ichor.

Anessa tumbled backwards as barbed tentacles lashed out of the mist. Plastered with muck—but crossbow in hand—she rolled away. Long moments later, the flailing assault slowed and then stopped.

She wiped filth from her eyes and watched the Korha for the slightest movement. Tentacles almost the colour of mist hung around a torso containing the remains of a single huge eye. The fog drifted back, obscuring the cloud of ichor. Something didn't feel right. If the mist hid the body, why were the tentacles still so easy to see?

The fog shifted again. The patch of blackness grew ever smaller.

Then blinked.

Barbed tentacles flickered out.

Not noticing the swamp claiming her right boot, she stumbled away. Something caught her foot, sending her face first into the muck.

She couldn't breathe.

She tore the rag from her face and rolled over. But the fog was even thicker at the swamp's surface and only grey met her eyes. She was still awake, so perhaps she was safe for the moment. She eased herself up.

Vague shadows came and went in the mist, but nothing struck at her. She must have tripped. The Korha had lost her.

Her crossbow was gone. She felt around but discovered only mud. Not that having a weapon would save her if the creature found her.

Why had it lost her in the fog? This was its home. If Haelen was right, it might even have brought this murk with it.

What if it was more than at home in fog? The eye had drifted back together. How could she fight fog?

Unless she wanted to leave Kobb, and the surviving villagers, to the creature, she had to try something.

Fog went faster on hot days. Dad even called it burning away. Fire might damage it.

Black gunk oozed between her fingers as she patted her pockets. Her flint hadn't been lost when she fled, but she had nothing that was dry enough to burn, let alone set a creature that large alight.

But Kobb might. She crept through the mist to Falcon. Mud caked the outside of Kobb's saddlebag, but it hadn't received a dunking. The contents might be dry. She yawned. Why had he tied it so tightly? She couldn't get a grip. If only—

Gritting her teeth, she poked herself in the stomach. She might just be tired, but she couldn't take the risk. The knot yielded, revealing folded clothes, a book, and a small iron box. Rumour had it the faithful had some strange rules, but she doubted anyone would die from the lack of a shirt. That would be terrible, or funny, rescuing him and then it turning out the book wasn't—

She slapped herself. Don't drift off. She located a shadow in the mist that seemed too solid to be a threat and slogged towards it. After longer than it should have taken, she reached the twisted remains of a tree. Her knife skipped and scraped the bark instead of cutting cleanly, but she eventually removed a branch.

The makeshift torch caught on the third attempt. A weight she hadn't realised she bore lifted. Against reason, the air seemed clearer around the smouldering cloth. She raised the torch high and advanced into the mist.

Eyes no longer heavy, she saw with horrid clarity the moment mist solidified into flesh. Her legs turned weak, as pallid muscle, studded with jagged shards of mould-covered bone, rose then smashed down.

Part Nine

Without the swirling mist to explain away the oddities, Anessa's mind rejected the sight before her, eyes clamping shut.

She retched as a bitter stench filled her nostrils. Something slammed into the swamp next to her, spattering her with more filth. She cracked open one eye as another fit of retching overcame her.

Thick grey fumes billowed around her. She staggered sideways. A withered tendril, leaden smoke trickling from fast-spreading cracks, twitched in the mud. She had hoped the torch would hurt it, but could never have imagined the fire burning it up so fast it didn't even touch her.

Eyes tearing from the smoke, she waited. Mist swirled around the remains of the tentacle, then drifted away. It was dead. With her new weapon held high, she slogged towards what she hoped was Kobb.

Two more tentacles burst from the fog.

Swinging the torch like a club, she struck at the closer threat.

As soon as the fire touched it, the tentacle folded back on itself, seeming much further away than the distance would allow. After hanging in the air for a moment, it tumbled down like a rotten branch.

Anessa lunged sideways to meet the second tentacle. With a thrust of the torch, she sent it tumbling into the swamp.

A mass of fanged limbs shredded the mist before her.

The fog gave way to smoke both fouler and more welcome as she swung the torch again and again.

Blinded and coughing, she felt something strike her across the left shoulder. Her legs gave way, and she tumbled forward. Her last sight before the murk of the swamp flooded her vision was the torch sizzling out.

A great weight pressed her into the filthy water. Lungs aching, she tried to push up, but the pressure was too great. The water bubbled in front of her as the air was squeezed from her chest.

Fighting panic, she realised the weight wasn't moving. She clawed at the mud, dragging herself forward.

The exertion burnt up her remaining breath. Unable to stop herself inhaling, she gagged as icy muck filled her mouth. Fingers scrabbling against the filth again, she forced her head up enough that the vomit didn't choke her.

Arms numb, she dragged again. The weight shifted onto her legs. Twisting sideways, she pulled one leg free then the other. After collapsing onto her back, she realised the fog had almost gone. No longer sure which pain was which, she forced herself up.

Leaden threads lay in a twisted mass across torn ground. Each seemed still and dead when she looked at it, but seen from the corner of her eye, they slipped through each other.

Her hands shook as she fell to her knees. The shaking spread until her entire body seemed palsied. She could feel the sun on her face; but, even with her coat pulled closed, the shivering wouldn't stop.

At some point, she noticed Kobb lying beneath one of the densest clusters of tendrils. The shaking slowed once she started crawling towards him. She couldn't see any wounds, but his eyes remained closed and neither shaking his shoulder nor calling his name brought any reaction.

Grabbing under his armpits, she tried to slide him free. Tendrils cracked, releasing a thick pale fluid closer to sap than blood. Unwilling to take the risk it was venom, she threw herself backwards.

Pain shot up her back as she hit the ground, followed by another down her neck as Kobb's weight folded her forward again. After drawing in several lumps of air, she confirmed his legs were free of the burnt mass. Purple light fractured as the last of the mist cleared.

Shifting from under Kobb's body, she trudged over. Kobb's Courser lay between two tussocks, filmed with dank water but unbroken. After looking from her filth-spattered clothes to his, she put it back in his holster as it was.

Kobb felt much heavier than Haelen had. She got his arm around her shoulder, only to discover his legs wouldn't hold his weight. Hoping he would wake soon, she wrapped her arms across his chest and shuffled backwards.

By craning over one shoulder, she dragged him over to Falcon. He seemed equally asleep. After lowering Kobb down, she gathered her courage and patted Falcon's side.

The green mould was gone, but he didn't react. Ready to leap backwards, she slapped his shoulder.

Falcon's head twitched, like a man settling in sleep, and then he stilled.

No help there then. Through the tatters of mist, Anessa made out more-regular shapes in the distance. Hoping it was the village, she eased Kobb up and slogged through the muck.

Uncounted pauses and deviations later, she reached the more solid ground on the edge of Alcston. Focused on the next step, she took a moment to notice the sounds of muttering.

Kobb's left arm was twitching.

She lowered him to the ground. "Kobb? Can you hear me? Absolution?"

"... Silence... waterfall."

"What?"

"Absolution is like the silence of the waterfall," said Haelen from behind her. "It's from the Book of Blessings."

Kobb snorted and rolled onto his side. He peered up at them for a moment with wide eyes, then burst out laughing. Each time it seemed he had returned to his usual serious self another spasm of chuckling curled him up again.

Anessa was wondering if the fight had turned him simple when he clambered to his feet.

"Best night's sleep in many a month." Kobb slapped Anessa on the shoulder.

Haelen stared at him with one eyebrow raised. "It might be safer to use the potion from now on."

Anessa's shoulders slumped. "It's gone. I burnt the Korha. It was all for nothing."

"Not quite." Haelen pointed at a hut behind him. "Whoever stayed there was more than just a farmer. There are bottles of venom and other things, and books of notes. The mould got in, and I'm not sure a decent person would want to touch some of it anyway, but there's plenty to make the potion and replenish my supplies."

Anessa turned as the sound of splashing echoed from behind them. Falcon galloped into the village.

Trying to remember she had just killed a horrible beast, Anessa forced herself not to run. "I'll check on the survivors. They'll have woken up too."

Kobb's smile disappeared. "We should head on before we lose the light."

"We can't just—" Anessa's mind processed Haelen's appearance. After all the slogging through filth, she had assumed the stains on his tunic were mud; but they were redder, more vibrant, than the grey brown slurry that clung to her clothes. She squelched past him.

Three bloodstained bundles, the size of sleeping people, lay along the side wall of the hut.

"The venom kept them asleep, but it also stopped blood loss." Haelen laid a hand on her elbow. "Once it wore off..."

Anessa staggered backwards. People in Morth had always claimed Botherers were just trying to trick things out of people, but they weren't. Pure evil was real.

"Kobb's right," said Haelen. "We should take what we can and go."

"My crossbow! I lost it. How will I–?"

"There were weapons in a few of the huts. I can—"

"No." Anessa swallowed hard. "You need to gather up the things for Kobb's potion." Shoulders rigid, she headed for the next hut and then the next.

She found a boot that had somehow avoided mildew. None of the crossbows were close to hers, but one of them would be usable with a little work. And the turf-hook, although dotted with rust, felt reassuring as it brushed against her leg.

Kobb and Haelen were bent over a large parchment when she returned.

Kobb glanced at the 12-inch blade on her hip and nodded sharply. "We found a map. Whoever was here was doing more than study the swamp. The writing's in code, but there are lines linking the swamp and other places to something north of here. We might finally have a destination.

Part Ten

Kobb folded the map and slipped it into his coat. Hopefully, Anessa wouldn't ask to see it. Haelen hadn't said anything—to him it probably didn't mean anything—but Anessa would notice immediately that Morth, her home, was one of the sites marked on the map.

Of course—unless he broke the code—he couldn't be certain the map led to the source of his nightmares. But, it would be an unlikely coincidence; and, even if it were, with the site of a Korha infestation marked, the other locations would probably be tainted with something equally unblessed.

Strolling over to Falcon, he formed a stirrup of his hands. "Mount up, Haelen. I'll walk a while to get the humours flowing."

Haelen shook his head. "Anessa killed a Korha. She deserves the rest more than I do."

"I can walk. I should..." Anessa shuffled in place. "...work these boots in."

Kobb straightened and pointed at Haelen's crutch. "She might need rest, but you need to be off that ankle. What would you say to a patient who tried to walk if they didn't have to?"

"I'd tell them how lucky they were to have me as their healer." Haelen moved over to Kobb. "I suppose I do need to be able to keep up with two such mighty heroes, though."

"We'll get started then," said Kobb, helping Haelen to mount. "We'll look to stop early so we can clean the muck off properly."

Motioning Anessa to lead, he glanced back at the swamp before striding out of Alcston.

The trees closed in on the path. With the rain holding off, they seemed to loom less; but the smell of rot still filled Kobb's nostrils, and he was sure not all of it came from the filth spotting his clothes. Even with the renewed energy from uninterrupted sleep, he felt as if something were pressing down on him and he was glad when Anessa identified a clearing near running water to camp in.

Haelen swung himself down from Falcon, his wince only visible because Kobb was looking for it. Reaching into his pouch, Haelen held out a bottle toward Kobb. "Anessa needs sleep. And shaking your head at me won't change that, young lady. I don't need my ankle to watch. I'll wake the Reverend later. But first thing's to fix a blanket across these trees."

Kobb took the potion absent-mindedly. "A blanket? If there's a storm the rain will gust round it."

"Anessa'll need privacy to—"

"You didn't stick up a blanket while we were heading to Alcston," said Anessa. "And I ain't bothered."

Haelen's eyes went wide. "It was just the two of us."

It was strange the way losing a child took a person. If Kobb asked Haelen, he would deny he thought of Anessa as anything other than a travelling companion, but Kobb reckoned his emotions were a whole other matter. "If one of us is staying up, we're not short of blankets. Don't know about being polite, but it would keep Falcon out of the soap."

Anessa pulled out a blanket and jogged over to the trees. "We should get on then. Won't take all of us to tie up a blanket."

Kobb unslung his saddlebag from Falcon and started brushing the horse's coat. Once he was content not a fleck of mud remained, he sought out clean clothes for himself. Looking from the stains on his current shirt to the tatters where the sleeve used to be on his spare, he reminded himself that having most of a clean shirt was a blessing.

He strolled over to Haelen, being very careful to match the healer's lack of interest in the splashing and off-tune singing coming from behind them. "So, how fast will the potion work?"

"It's gentler than the venom and you'll wake normally, but I'd not take it until you're ready to sleep."

The splashing stopped, and Anessa strolled across the clearing clutching a pile of wet clothes. "I'll get these hung out, then it's my turn to cook."

Deciding the morale boost from a fire would outweigh the risk, Kobb headed behind the blanket without commenting.

Later, curled next to Falcon with a belly full of porridge, he decided he had made the right choice. The smell of rot had faded and the tension in his muscles eased away. His eyes slipped closed.

"Reverend."

Kobb sat up. He felt awake but relaxed, and moon had passed the midpoint. The potion had worked.

Haelen nodded at him from the far side of the fire and waved a handful of papers. "Thought I might use the time."

"You can read that stuff?" Kobb strolled over and crouched beside him.

"I picked up some things since I left the Legions." Haelen's shoulders stiffened. "When my Katrina disappeared, only clue they found was a stone with symbols on. Same thing as these. It took me a while, but I managed to pick up enough of it to work out the path lead north. Most of this is about the Korha, though. I need to find—"

Kobb rested a hand on Haelen's shoulder. "Maybe it'll make more sense after some sleep."

After a moment, Haelen slumped. "You're right. I can't tell ink from stains any more."

Apart from Haelen's snoring, the rest of the night passed peacefully, as did the next three. And the days between. The scent of decay still undercut the air, but birds flitted in the trees and the weather held.

Anessa and Haelen began to unfold, breaths slightly deeper, motions more fluid, and voices more robust. But Kobb only thought more and more on what might drive the Eaters from where they lived but ignore humans travelling toward it. Could slaying the Korha have really echoed back to the source, driving the dangers before it?

The fourth morning brought Kobb a bitter release to the tension. Studying the sky as dawn broke, he watched the contrast between tree and sky flowing around the edges of the clearing; but not reaching the north. Coincidence or not, their destination was cloaked in the storm clouds he had expected to face on the journey.

"Cold breakfast, then?" said Haelen breaking Kobb's reverie. "Were the dry days the Blessing, or is it that we have breakfast?"

"A fine theological question." Kobb headed for Falcon. "Best pack now rather than later."

As they continued north, the clouds sapped the sun, reducing the forest back to a mass of half-seen limbs. But the storm didn't break.

Feeling both nauseated and very awake, Kobb stumbled to a halt.

"Something wrong?" Haelen, still not happy at to be the one who rode, made to dismount.

"I'm—" Kobb caught a flash of light from the corner of his eye, but when he turned it was gone. "I'm not feeling—"

The sky exploded with light.

"Reverend?"

Kobb shook his head. Haelen was staring at him, concern on his face. Behind him, the sky remained the same leaden tone it had been for the entire morning. "Sorry, the lightning..."

"Lightning?" said Anessa. "What lightning?"

Part Eleven

"Something's off." Kobb pinched his nose and let his breath slip out of his mouth. The churning in his stomach settled. A tingling on his skin he hadn't realised was there had gone; as if a storm had broken. But the pewter clouds still pressed down on the road.

And no natural storm had ever brought him close to vomiting; cold and wet, yes, but never like emptying his guts.

His shoulders hunched. More unnerving than a storm racking his body were the effects passing as if they had never been. It didn't make sense—and yet something felt familiar.

He closed his eyes. He almost had it. For a moment, he could feel rough palms resting on his temples; and smell the mix of sweat and leather from Gannon's armour. Remember his body seeming to turn inside out as the raw power rebounded from his mentor's will; and the way the turmoil was but memory the moment he truly saw the crystal in his hand.

Eyes snapping open, he drew his Courser. It looked inert, but the chill of the grip reached deep into his fingers.

"Which way?" asked Anessa.

Kobb realised she was pressed against a tree, jerking her crossbow to point at shadow after shadow. He holstered his Courser. "Not a threat. Least not here."

Anessa stepped back onto the track, eyes still flicking around the tree line.

"Maybe we should make camp." Haelen pulled his hood over his head. "Build a shelter before the rain comes."

"They're not rain clouds," said Kobb. "That's power. Old power. Right where the map marked it would be."

"And that's what made you...?" Anessa waved her hand in a loose circle.

"It's like... an invisible river. Those as have the Blessing, feel the currents. There are artefacts, Courser and others, that shape it, like a dam. But, if the river floods, the dam isn't enough." Kobb straightened his shoulders and strode down the track. "Best hope that was all of it; that it'll take time to build again. Sooner I get there, better the hope."

"Sooner we get there." Anessa moved past him.

As they moved on, the small rustlings and skitterings in the forest faded away. Shortly after, Anessa stopped at a bend in the track.

Kobb moved to join her. Tangled in each other, several trees hung across the path. Pacing slowly toward them, he realised the forest ended as if cut with a knife. Past the blockage the ground was churned, but scoured clean—apart from a ring of stones that Kobb was willing to bet stood at the exact middle of the devastation.

Anessa unslung her turf-hook. "We'll not be short for firewood."

Taking turns, they hacked away branches until Falcon could fit through. In contrast to clinging earth and leaf mould of the forest, dust shifted beneath their feet.

Kobb unsheathed his weapons. "One step at a time. And if I say run back, do it."

Creeping forward, he strained his senses for the slightest feeling of nausea. Much closer and there wouldn't be time to run back to the trees, but if he could send them back as soon as the power surged, he might be able to hold it long enough for them to escape the worst. A shadow flicked above him.

Drawing and aiming without thought, he barely stopped himself shooting a skein of geese. He holstered his Courser and walked on.

Anessa pointed to one side of the stones. "Are those tents?"

"Not just tents," said Haelen. "Tents that are still standing. Maybe this was days ago and whatever you felt was—"

Noted only in its loss, the sound of wings was swallowed by silence. Twisted bundles of feathers rained from the sky ahead.

"I didn't feel power." Sheathing his rapier, Kobb picked up a rock and threw it ahead of him. A puff of dust rose up where it struck the ground. He paced over to it. "Walk exactly behind me."

Pitching the stone and then moving to it, he inched his way forward. A gentle breeze stirred his hair, strong enough to ripple both the bodies of the dead geese and the tents; but nothing else moved ahead and he felt no power building.

"Wait," shouted Haelen. "Don't Coursers only affect the living?"

Kobb froze with one foot raised. They did damage stone, but the effect was much weaker. Lowering his boot to the ground, he rolled his shoulders and hurled the rock as hard as he could.

It arced through the air, struck the ground near one of the geese, and bounced past.

Anessa stared at him, face pale. "Could the curse have gone?"

"Only one way to be sure." Kobb walked a few steps closer and spat.

The wind caught the spittle, bending it away. With a sizzle it disappeared.

"Not gone." Kobb considered. Bearing crystal didn't protect against a Courser, but the Blessing of Form would let a mentor confine raw power within an apprentice, briefly. Could he shape this?

Pressing the fingers of his free hand to his pendant, he raised his Courser and stepped forward.

Despite the lowering storm, the crystal sparkled as if in sunlight. A low hum clasped the base of his skull.

And stepped forward.

Frost grew on the stock, biting at his hand. A dull ache filled his joints.

And stepped forward.

A sharp smell flooded his nostrils and he tasted copper.

Purple sparks crackled along the Courser before flickering away. Sticking to the air for a moment before fading, they painted a faint wall of light an arm's length ahead.

"Thieves!"

Kobb instinctively dropped back and into a crouch.

The glow disappeared. A man, mostly obscured by a tattered robe and waving a trowel, ran toward him from the direction of the tents.

"We ain't thieves," shouted Anessa from behind him. "You take that back."

Keeping the Courser pointed down—but not holstering it—Kobb rose to his feet. He raised his free hand, palm out. "As my friend says, we do not seek to steal from you."

The man stumbled to a halt and pushed back the hood of his robe, revealing sunken green eyes peering from between bushy grey eyebrows and a ragged beard. "You're too tall for Skithai. But you could be common bandits. Why else would you be here, eh?"

Kobb balanced the risks. This man could well be the mysterious alchemist from Alcston, but was he here to stop the threat or...? "We heard of a threat to the north. A map led us here."

"Map, eh?" The man scratched his beard. "Well, don't mean you aren't thieves just because you can read a map. But your friend didn't try a shot, which means you aren't stupid. And a person of your skills has better options than banditry. Do me a task, and I'll risk letting you in."

Kobb settled his Courser in place. "If it's honourable."

"Honour's exactly what it is. I cut a deal with a Skithai, but it turned on me. Did something to the stones and set its tribe on me. I managed to raise the power and drive them off. Could work out how to undo what it did, but it would be faster if I could get it to tell me. If I go after it then I have to let the power fade again. But you could bring the Skithai to me."

"You'll give us a moment?" Kobb turned and strolled back to his companions. He signalled them to lean close, and kept his voice low. "We aren't getting through that barrier without him."

"If he's evil, then anyone who worked with him is too," said Anessa.

Haelen frowned and then nodded.

Kobb walked neared to the barrier. "We'll do it."

The man pointed at Kobb's pendant. "Promise me."

Kobb clutched the pendant. "I promise we'll bring the Skithai back here."

"Good enough. Off with you then."

"A minor point." Kobb raised an eyebrow. "We have no idea what Skithai look like."

"Skithai. Short, ugly." The man scratched his head. "Some folk call them Eaters. You'll recognise this one by his mask: got a pair of golden antlers on it."

Part Twelve

Anessa watched the man stride back into a tent. His accusation still rankled, but she supposed anyone would be rude if they had been attacked by their allies. Not that he shouldn't have expected it: making a deal with Eaters.

She turned slowly on the spot. After facing the Korha, the prospect of Eaters didn't seem so terrifying. And, whatever raising the power meant, it had cleared the forest back hundreds of feet in every direction, so there wasn't much danger of an ambush; which was lucky, because she'd need all her attention to find a trail with the ground scrubbed clean. "Least we know what to expect from Eaters, so it'll be easier this time. Bigger problem's finding them."

Kobb frowned. "Last time, we were killing them—not trying to capture them—and we almost died. And a Courser only kills; even if I get the chance, I can't shoot the Eater."

"We worry about capturing it after we find it," said Haelen. "If it's interested in these stones, it'll probably stay close enough to watch."

Anessa swept her arm around the expanse of bare ground. "Hope so. Mid-afternoon's past, and there's hours of searching to find a trail even before we follow it."

"Maybe not," Kobb turned to face the stones. "Last time, they attacked from a place of strength with minimal flanking and fled quickly. If we find the dead, we find the trail."

"Best start further out, though." Anessa unslung her crossbow and strode away from the circle. "Don't much fancy blundering into whatever's killing everything."

The soil puffed and cracked beneath her feet, sending up a faint dusty scent. Sweeping her gaze from side to side, she scanned the tree line for anything odd. Not that she expected to see the Eaters at this distance, but no one ever got killed for paying attention. After a brief pause to be sure she was well away from the stones, she began to move sunward around the clearing.

After a moment, she stopped again. "Eaters can't throw a spear this far, Haelen, so you might as well rest your ankle."

"A kind thought, but no cause to risk it without need." Haelen raised his right foot, and then rose up on the toes of his left foot. "Wouldn't be much of a healer if I couldn't shake a sprain."

Anessa nodded. He couldn't believe sitting up there would make him a target. But she understood his desire not to spend more time on Falcon. Resettling the turf hook on her hip, she moved off.

With the sky cloaked in leaden cloud and night creeping up, she had to strain to make out differences in the dirt. Finally, in the distance, she noticed several paler patches. So far, she hadn't seen a stone much larger than a couple of fists, so was probably more than boulders. "There."

"Sharp eyes, Anessa." Kobb clapped her on the shoulder. "Maybe this won't be so hard."

She grinned. A small voice suggested Kobb was only keeping their spirits up, but it felt good to have someone recognise her skills. "We ain't found it yet. And if Haelen's right, Eaters are watching, so they'll likely be expecting us."

After taking a long look at the shadowed forest, she led the way toward the paler patches. She could make out darker patches like masks, but they looked wrong for dead bodies. It took her several more yards to realise it was the way they lay: unlike the dead geese, the Eaters' limbs jutted at odd angles and twisted like they had too many joints.

"Only six dead?" whispered Haelen. "Are we going to be facing most of the tribe?"

"There's more than six dead." Kobb pointed back toward the stones.

Anessa peered through the half-light. There were slightly paler patches if you looked for them, but they didn't have the twisted lumpiness of a body. Easy enough to get confused in this light, though. Especially if your eyes weren't sharp. Not that Kobb was old... he would just be tired. Glad the murk would hide her flushed face, she crouched beside one of the bodies. Might be something helpful.

As her fingers touched the edge of the Eater's loincloth, the entire body sank inward. A waft of foul air made her screw up her face. When she looked again, the body was only a paler smear on the ground. Not wanting to breathe in another body, she eased herself back and to her feet.

Now she knew what to look for she could make out dozens of paler patches scattered between her and the stones. Kobb had been right. Each one of those smears had been an Eater. The Stones had killed too many to count.

The thought of it pushed at her. Gritting her teeth, she forced herself to keep a slow enough pace to not miss something. "We should get into the forest. While we've still got enough light to find where they went."

"No more bodies ahead," said Haelen. "Could be that was all of them."

"Or the bodies were intact enough the survivors took them away," said Kobb.

Anessa paused. Only people cared about their dead. But, the Eaters had made a deal so they had to be more than just clever beasts. She wasn't sure if knowing how much like people they were made them seem better or worse.

Reaching the edge of the forest without finding a sign of which way the Eaters might have gone, she desperately studied the tree line. The power hadn't left the same barrier of tangled trees here, but there was no sign anyone had moved through the undergrowth either. Kobb's idea had seemed like a good plan while there was light, but with the day gone and the clouds hiding the moon there wasn't much she could do. "I've lost the trail. If it was ever here. We have to stop."

"Whatever the Reverend says about those clouds, I don't trust them not to rain on us." Haelen pulled his hood further forward. "Let's at least get under the trees before we stop."

Anessa crept into the forest. As she stepped from the blasted earth, the scent of rotten leaves and damp mud wrapped around her again like an old blanket. Even without the trees being forced against each other, they had grown close and twisted. She could make out the hint of a way clear enough for Falcon, but the gloom and the undergrowth conspired to make it seem a killing ground between blinds and dead falls.

Closing her eyes, she raised a hand. Without the sound of the others footfalls, the forest fell silent. She stilled her breath. A thrush trilled in the distance. Something felt wrong, but she couldn't point to it. She studied the shadows again. Nothing seemed out of place.

Except the thrush. There were no other animal noises, and it was past dark, so why was a thrush singing? Unless—

There was thrush song when the Eaters attacked. Sweeping her crossbow from undergrowth to shadow, she back stepped to the others. "I think they're nearby."

Kobb drew his weapons. "Which way?"

Anessa peered at the undergrowth. Shadows seemed to move in the corners of her eyes, but stilled when she looked straight on. "There's only one way we can go—unless we leave your horse. We either wait, or chance they've not set an ambush."

"And the longer we wait, the more chance they get to pick their moment," said Kobb. "We move on, but no risks."

Keeping close to the others rather than leading the way, Anessa crept through the thinner undergrowth. The thrush trilled again, nearer this time.

The realisation the song had changed hit her at the same moment an Eater spear flew over her head. From behind her, Haelen screamed incoherently.

Part Thirteen

Anessa spun around. Haelen lay on the ground, a spear quivering in the trunk behind him. Feeling felt a burst of relief, she whirled back to face the direction of the attack.

Kobb had run further down the track. Why would he—? Flanking! The first spear might be a distraction. She tried to cover both sides at once with her crossbow.

Silence slammed down and a purple light made the shadows harden. Instinctively, she glanced ahead. The undergrowth beyond Kobb had withered and fallen and several bodies lay among the dead brambles.

She turned, and tumbled backwards as a spear passed in front of her eyes.

A bitter dusty smell cut the scent of rotting leaves. Three small figures burst from the murk to her left. They moved like Eaters, but something seemed different about them.

Rolling to her feet, she loosed a bolt at the nearest, catching it between the eyes and sending it to the ground.

Angry at getting distracted, she drew her turf hook and charged to meet them. Swinging the weapon two-handed, she cleaved through a club and into the side of its owner's head. Blade firmly lodged, she felt herself jerked forward as the Eater fell.

Pain flooded her right side. The other Eater lashed out again at her hip.

Leg half-folding beneath her, she wrenched her turf hook free and flailed sideways.

Instead of leaping back as she expected, the Eater lunged forward. Its club slammed into her right elbow.

Her right hand juddered from the hilt, but her hook continued round, smashing deep into the Eater's head.

Her opponent fell to the ground, taking the turf hook with it.

Heat flooded up Anessa's neck. She'd let her weapon get trapped twice in a row. Kobb wouldn't— There hadn't been a second burst of light. Working her elbow, she looked over.

Hunched by coughing, Kobb fended off four Eaters with his rapier. His Courser hung loosely at his side.

She planted her foot on the face of the Eater at her feet and yanked at her turf hook. Acid flooded her mouth as it tore free. Trying not to think about the sound, she sprinted toward Kobb.

One of the Eaters spun to meet her, waving its club frantically.

The remaining three shifted around Kobb. Before they could press the attack, his rapier flicked up, taking the middle of the three in the throat.

Anessa tightened her grip hard enough to turn her knuckles white and jabbed at the oncoming Eater. A shock ran up both her arms as the blade glanced off the wildly swinging club.

She stumbled sideways. Gritting her teeth against the renewed complaint from her right elbow, she slashed left. But, afraid of getting her weapon caught again, she unconsciously pulled the blow. The Eater, carried forward by its charge, passed her by before the blow landed.

Spinning to follow, she saw the Eater slammed sideways as Falcon lashed out. Fluids arced from its pulped head. Its body crashed into a bush before sliding to the ground.

Anessa turned quickly in a circle. Haelen crouched, eating knife clutched in his hand, against a tree. Kobb stood over a pile of bodies, one fist pressed to his mouth.

She turned again, peering into each shadow. All the stories talked of Eaters as ravening beasts; wouldn't they with everything she had rather than holding back? But, travelling with Kobb had revealed there was a lot she was wrong about: both about Eaters and about fighting. Best to be certain.

After a third circle, she straightened. "Think that's it."

Kobb hawked loudly, before staggering over to lean against Falcon's flank.

"You're hurt." Haelen strode over to Kobb.

Kobb sheathed his weapons. "Just tired. Trying to push through must have taken more effort than I thought."

"Did anyone see antlers? Did we...?" Anessa realised why the attack had seemed odd. None of the bodies bore masks. The bitter smell of dust grew stronger as she bent over the nearest one.

Without the crude mask, the Eater's head looked narrow and angular. Pure black eyes, nearly twice the size of a person's, sat either side of a flat nose. Between the half-open lips she saw teeth like a pike. "Why don't they have masks?"

"Didn't holler and howl like before either," said Kobb.

"They've got something smeared on their faces," said Haelen. "Maybe, we—"

"Best move on." Kobb took up Falcon's reins. "Won't learn much in this gloom. This isn't a good camp anyway."

Haelen sighed and nodded. "Give me the reins. You two need to be ready if they attack again."

Anessa reloaded her crossbow and led the way further into the forest. Ears aching from the lack of noise, she forced her shoulders down and tried to stop hunching against the attack that never came.

A sudden flash of Mum, face damp, telling her to be a good girl distracted her from her obsessive scanning of the shadows. She paused. Why was she remembering Grandam's funeral? She'd wanted to put the Winter Bettanie she'd picked in the grave, but it weren't proper. Mustn't disturb a death poesy.

She could smell a death poesy ahead. The gloom was less, too. She crept forward. The scent of herbs grew stronger.

The trees thinned, leaving a small clearing. Five pale shapes lay within, radiating out from the centre.

She scanned the undergrowth, but couldn't see any sign of an ambush. Not that that proved anything. Signalling the others to move up, she crept into the clearing.

Each of the dead Eaters had been laid, feet out, with their hands crossed over their chests. Like the others, they wore no masks. A dark paste was smeared across their faces, smelling of dust and age. Scorched at one end, a bundle of herbs lay in the space between their heads.

Keeping her crossbow ready, Anessa moved to the edge of the clearing and circled.

"End of the bundle's still warm," said Kobb. "We're barely missed them."

"So," said Haelen, "choice is camp here and give them a lead or go racing off at night?"

"Ain't happy sleeping around Eaters," muttered Anessa. "Definitely ain't happy sleeping with dead ones."

Haelen chuckled. "Number of times they attacked us, they can't expect manners. Easy enough to sling them—"

Kobb knocked him flat as something, flickers of light trailing it, burst from a thicket and sped past Anessa into the distance.

Part Fourteen

Kobb's head instinctively twisted after the fleeing Eater. Butter-yellow glints shot between the harder flare of its staff. Something didn't feel right. It sprinted fast enough that they didn't have time to react; yet its path had curved, taking it within inches of all three of them.

Leaves shifted in the breeze, and the shadows tugged at the corners of his eyes, but nothing seemed out of place. He eased himself to his feet, drawing his weapons as he rose. "You all right, Anessa?"

"Startled. But ain't harmed."

"Good enough." Kobb extended a hand to Haelen. "Anyone else think that thing had horns?"

Haelen pulled himself up. "All I saw was your shoulder, then the ground. If it could run like that, why was it still here? And why didn't it attack?"

Kobb nodded at the bodies. "Looks like a funeral. Maybe it wasn't finished, and it waited, hoping we'd head straight on. Once you mentioned staying, it realised we wouldn't."

"Why didn't it sneak away?" Anessa waved her hand at the undergrowth. "They can almost climb in your trousers without being seen, so could have crept away easy at night."

"Funerals mean the dead matter." Kobb slung his weapons. "Probably hoping we'd follow once we saw it and not disturb the bodies."

Anessa peered into the bushes. "Might be right. It's left a clear enough track."

"Or it panicked and was moving too fast to be stealthy." Haelen picked leaf mould off his chest. "Either way, tracks won't help if it can run that fast."

"Probably can't, least not for long." Kobb patted his Courser. "Last few years, I've felt the weight every time I used it. Young person could fight for an hour or more, but they'd need a hearty meal after. Faster the Eater runs, sooner it needs to rest. If we start now we might catch it."

Kobb unslung his saddlebag. "It'll try to hide when it does rest, though. You've the sharpest eyes, Anessa, so best you take Falcon and we'll follow."

Anessa's hands clenched harder on her crossbow. "No... I mean, I ain't strong enough to wrestle it, and this crossbow's still pulling a bit so can't risk shooting."

"She's right, Reverend," said Haelen. "I saw that Eater fight you in the ruins. Needs a soldier."

Kobb looked from one nervous face to another. Haelen, he understood: Haelen might not acknowledge it, but letting Anessa go racing off on her own would feel like risking his daughter. But Anessa had seemed almost too confident since she brought down the Korha; why wasn't she itching to go? Regardless, they had a point. "Fair enough. Least I'll be easy enough to track, so get some rest before you follow. Don't see cause to disturb the dead, though."

"We'll leave them alone," said Haelen. "As long as they do the same."

"What!" Anessa jerked her crossbow up to point at the nearest body.

"I think he was joking," said Kobb, putting his saddlebag back and taking up Falcon's reins. "Needs practice though."

Haelen stuck his tongue out. "Wouldn't have taken you for an expert on humour, Reverend."

Kobb nodded to them both and led Falcon toward the Eater's path. As he moved deeper into the undergrowth, the crisp scent of sap fought against the fug of damp leaves and lost. Trusting that nothing else would be forcing its way so brutally through the forest, he followed the bent branches and torn leaves without pausing.

The moon had passed mid-point and the trail continued unbroken, clear enough to see even in the dark. Feet heavy and eyes gritty, he began to doubt the Eater needed sleep. He stumbled to a halt.

Warm air whiffled across the back of his neck. He patted Falcon on the nose. "You'd be happy for the rest too, eh? No use catching up if we're too tired to do anything."

Hanging his saddlebag on a nearby branch, he stripped Falcon's harness and brushed away the day. Yawns fighting against each bite, Kobb forced down half a biscuit before slumping back against a trunk.

He woke to find the rain had found him. Marshalling on leaves, drops drew together to assail his hat. He rubbed the grit from his eyes and, pulling his jacket tighter, peered into the murk.

The signs of the Eater's forced passage were clearer now, but experience suggested the rain would revive half-crushed vegetation; and the trickles and drips were already tricking his eyes and ears into detecting movement. Taking comfort that the trees would keep the wind from driving the rain directly into his face, he settled Falcon's harness into place and trudged along the crude trail.

Encouraged by the rain, the ground pulled at his boots, adding a dullness in his legs to the stiffness of a night lacking in deep sleep. The worsening storm drew the shadows closer, and washed away much of the trail, forcing Kobb to slow his pace still further and stay focused on only the closest vegetation to be sure of seeing what signs there were.

And so the track caught him by surprise. He realised the Eater's passage had met a crude path through the forest. Emerging on a sharp bend, he faced almost exactly down a gloomy tunnel between ancient trees. He glanced left, toward the south. The shadows seemed deeper and branches seemed to reach down as if grasping for what little light has slipped past them.

Ahead, the ground was rutted but appeared free of brambles and other obstructions, and the branches loomed high. That was the route he'd choose if moving at speed. Mounting Falcon, Kobb resolved to close the gap further.

Falcon, seeming as happy as his master not to be forcing through undergrowth, cantered along the path. Moving at speed drove the rain under the brim of Kobb's hat, but—although it was as wet and cold—the sense that it came from progress not the elements weakened the discomfort.

His gut suggested the Eater would have the same desire to avoid obstacles. Keeping his eyes ahead, he maintained Falcon's speed. As an unsought blessing, the rain eased as noon approached, sparing him the need to swipe the water from his eyes.

The crude track swayed left and right, but cleaved to the west for much of the day. As late afternoon took the sun beneath the trees, returning the track to murk and shadow, the path curved more sharply to the north. And continued that way.

Torn between the logical assumption the Eater would use the path and the twinge in his gut its path took it more to the west, he pulled Falcon up. Each moment he waited felt like letting the Eater get further away, but wasn't riding away from it worse? He studied the track ahead. It still looked like the route a fleeing man would choose. But it felt wrong. Hoping he wouldn't regret it, he swung Falcon round, and walked back to where the track bent away from its westerly line.

Whether it was the slower pace or the conscious seeking, he noticed a faint scent of crushed stems within the rot. Peering into the undergrowth, he made out hints of bent branch and disturbed leaf. Once he dismounted, he picked out more signs that something might have left the track. He didn't have Anessa's skill in judging size and time, but the might-be trail pointed west. It was certain enough; and faith would carry the rest.

"Sorry, old friend. It's back to trudging for a while." Resettling his weapons, Kobb lead Falcon off the path.

The twin weights of straining against the barrier and fragmented sleep against a tree conspired to press him deeper into the rotten mulch. Feet not clearing the brambles on the first attempt more and more often, he considered waiting for the others to catch up. However, stopping now would give the Eater back any lead Kobb had taken away. Ignoring the tightness across his forehead, he staggered on from crushed sprig to torn leaf. Until even stubbornness was not enough to hold back the acceptance that he was too tired to tell act from happenstance; or to respond should he find his quarry.

Washing down another biscuit with a few mouthfuls of Haelen's potion, he managed to tend to Falcon before slipping into darkness.

Purple light crackled between jutting pillars, tearing away the night but leaving nothing it its wake. Seeming to ooze from the darkness, absence bled into the ground, stealing colour from the vegetation before flowing outward. Trees, pressed close from years without the touch of axe, surged up or twisted together. Branches left jagged by storms grew sharper.

The taste of decay clinging to tongue, Kobb snapped awake, barely turning aside before vomiting. Spitting bile, he clasped his aching head. The dreams had returned.

Squinting up, he thought the sky still dark. With luck, the Eater had stopped last night and not yet moved on. Easing himself to his feet, he chuckled. Wishing his enemy the Blessing of rest when he was denied it was too sharp a lesson in the Maker's liberality not to smile.

Nodding in contrition in response to Falcon's silent stare, Kobb forced his legs to carry him forward. The dull thudding in his head, and ache in his joints remained, but after a while the effort of lifting each leg free of the muck and tangles cleared away the fog in his head.

Peering around, he realised he had lost the trail. A sensible man would stop, but he had come so far on the certainty the Eater headed due west that it seemed more effort to stop than go on. Conscious of the pale light creeping through chinks in the trees from behind, he forced himself to move faster.

Something caught his eye as he stumbled on. Focused on keeping his legs moving, it took him some moments to realise trees don't glint and sparkle. He stopped, settling against a tree as his body remembered he was too tired to move. After staring blankly into the forest for a while, he accepted whatever he had glimpsed was hidden from this direction.

Wanting to spit the cloying taste from his mouth, but unable to muster the energy to do two things at once, he aimed himself at another tree and pitched toward it. He pushed against the trunk, gaining enough momentum to convince his legs he was walking.

For an instant, the dawn fractured to his right, as if light had struck crystal. He leaned back against a tree and studied the area. The glint eluded him.

But his ears picked out a faint snore.

Part Fifteen

Kobb peered between the trees. The knee-high undergrowth had grown upward into a tangled wall of brambles and branches almost his height. It looked impenetrable, but was also the source of the snoring. There must be a way through. Gritting his teeth, he shifted his weight from the trunk next to him.

His legs bowed beneath him, but he forced his knees straight before his sway became uncontrollable. One pace at a time, he crept toward the snores. Springy tendrils hooked at his ankles and each step slipped on rotting matter, adding to the foul tang in the air. If he could—

Snap.

The snoring stopped.

Kobb froze. Hot icicles slashed his right leg as it held most of his weight. Something rustled ahead.

On the edge of falling, Kobb eased his left hand to his rapier and slid it free.

Scrabbling came from further to the left. Each blink feeling like rubbing dirt in his eyes, Kobb squinted into the brambles. The Eater had led him far from the clearing. Now it would turn like a beast at bay. Where would the attack come from?

His head snapped back as a brief scuffing came from where he had originally looked. The snoring resumed.

Biting down as hot lightning speared out from his knee, Kobb moved the rest of his weight from his left foot and slid it off the broken twig. If he could hear snores, the noise hadn't been the Eater. Or it was pretending to sleep; waiting for him to be distracted. Hoping he was Blessed, Kobb focused on the ground directly ahead, testing each footing by eye and toe.

He reached the thicket without incident. Unwilling to take the chance he was wrong about an attack, he kept his rapier up as he sank to his haunches. His legs aching still more from his stilted advance, he rested but a moment in a squat, before bracing his right arm behind him and half-collapsing into a seated position.

The snores continued. He let out a slow breath. Leaning the growing burden of his torso onto his raised legs, he peered at the brambles. Closer now to the ground, he made out scuffs and bent sprouts where small animals had slipped under; and one tangle hanging over empty space. Falling sideways as quietly as he could, he stared in.

The gap continued deeper into the wall of vegetation. A way in. Low and narrow, but a way in. Even better, a crystal glinted deeper in: an Eater staff. Keeping the rapier ahead of him, he pushed the brambles aside as best he could and dragged himself into the gap. The scent of rot faded, replaced with a subtle earthy smell. Now he was in it, he realised the tunnel was perfectly straight and the same size all the way. Tendrils that sprouted inward each curved back into the sides and roof. It was too regular to have grown.

Cursing the need to not use his Courser, and uncertain if he even could, Kobb wriggled forward. The tunnel opened out into a light-flecked bower. A single Eater, mask of polished wood with short golden antlers, gazed back at him.

The snoring continued. After a moment, Kobb decided the feeling of being watched was only the shadows in the mask; but there was no room for complacency. He reached for the end of the staff, and paused. The Eater had rested its bag on the staff. Even at his best, Kobb would have had difficulty getting the staff out without the bag falling.

Inching forward slightly, he slid his rapier into its sheath. Apologising to his shoulders for what he was about to do, he stretched his right arm toward the bag. A burning sensation twisted in his lower back, and his upper arms felt like they were tearing through his back.

But his fingertips curled over the shoulder sling. He curled them into his palm, and then drew his forearm up. The bag jerked closer.

The snoring continued.

His lower back wobbled. Arms still, he stretched first his left then his right leg back and out. As soon as his right leg was straight, he lowered his chest to the soil. His neck immediately ached from tilting his head, but he felt stable. He drew his right arm closer again.

The bag slid and bounced closer. An inch away from his face, it gaped open. A mask slid free.

Ignoring the sensation of a jagged spike driving into his shoulder, Kobb twisted and caught it with his free hand before it struck the staff. He lowered himself back to prone and swallowed the pain, before exhaling through his mouth. Could he get it back into the bag?

The snoring had stopped.

Tilting his head back, he stared across the bower into a pair of bright purple eyes. The Eater's hand already rested on the end of its staff.

Certain he couldn't reach it in time, Kobb arched his back and grabbed for his rapier.

"Don't, Anh-kru. Please." The Eater pointed at the mask in Kobb's hand.

It wasn't attacking. The Eaters took the masks from the dead. They must be important. Too important to risk damage. Keeping a firm grip on the mask, Kobb settled into a less uncomfortable slump. "Hands off the staff."

The Eater drew its hand back, and then raised both palms out. "No fight needed. No harm. Masks must be taken home, or torag-kru... evil happens."

"You're coming with me." Kobb waved the mask. "Any tricks and..."

"We deal. No harm. No tricks."

"Stay here until I call." Grabbing the end of the staff with his free hand, Kobb wrestled it past him. The Eater watched, unblinking. One-handed, each movement sent a new flicker of agony through part of his body, but Kobb dare not let go of the mask. Eventually, the staff rested alongside him. Wriggling back, and then dragging the staff alongside, he inched his way out.

As soon as he was free of the tunnel, Kobb struggled to his feet. Feeling an odd sense of guilt, he braced his weight on the staff and shuffled several feet away. "Come. Slowly."

Moments later the Eater emerged, clutching its bag. "Where do we go?"

"Back to the stone circle."

The Eater seemed to sag. Shaking its head slowly, it indicated its bag. "Long way back. With tiredness on you, will be many days. I have way to ease burden."

"You think I would trust you?"

The Eater became rigid. "Torag-kru! Only lost one would poison Blessing of wakefulness."

Blessing? It was right that offering false help was evil, but wasn't Kobb the first to follow the Way this far north. "All certitude is as the mist at dawn—"

"—cloaking stone of truth forged."

That hides the rock of the Maker's truth. The words weren't the same, but the meaning was. "You know the Way of the Maker Guiding? But how? Which Reverend showed you the path?"

The Eater made a rattling noise. After a moment, Kobb realised it was chuckling. "No. I am not convert to your faith. You are Urt-Skithai."

Part Sixteen

Anessa crept forward. The ground was mired in rotten leaves and brambles, but the trees seemed less tangled ahead. Something small and dark exploded from the undergrowth, trilling and chittering. Then the wildlife fell silent. She raised her hand.

Eyes flicking from side to side, Haelen crouched down.

Tilting her head, Anessa strained her ears. No thrushes. Wind brushed the treetops. And in the distance, the clump of hooves. Keeping her crossbow up, Anessa eased toward the nearest gap between trees. A path cut through the forest, shafts of light spearing the murk. The brief yellow glint caught her eye.

Peering, she made out Kobb leading Falcon. As Kobb moved closer, she realised another, smaller figure walked beside him. Kobb'd captured the Eater. She wasn't sure how, but he had done it. "Haelen. It's Kobb."

Several small animals fled across the track as Haelen pushed his way through the undergrowth.

After sharing a grin of victory, Anessa stepped onto the path. Crossbow lowered, she jogged to meet Kobb.

The Eater still had its staff. She dropped to a crouch and brought her crossbow to her shoulder. "Drop the staff!"

Kobb released Falcon's reins and raised his palms. "It's fine, Anessa. It isn't going to hurt us."

"Then it won't mind putting the staff down," said Haelen, appearing beside her.

Anessa glanced up. He had his eating knife clutched in his hand, and his hood pulled up. He still didn't look very threatening, but she appreciated the thought. When she looked back, the Eater had rested the staff on the ground and continued toward them.

Kobb bent and picked up the staff. As he straightened, a cloth sling bag swung round his neck, wrapping around his arm. Untangling himself, he took up the reins again and headed on.

Anessa kept her crossbow pointed at the Eater as it strolled forward. It didn't seem to be up to anything, but it could be thinking anything behind that mask. "Far enough."

The Eater inclined its head and folded into a sitting position. Despite not looking, it somehow ended up on a dry tussock.

"Doubt's understandable," said Kobb, spitting a plug of something into the bushes. "But, it's given its word. Besides, I've got something it won't risk." He patted the cloth bag.

Anessa unloaded her crossbow and slung it. As she stood, Kobb threw the staff forward.

The Eater caught it without looking.

Realising as the crossbow cleared her shoulder that the Eater had had time to do something if it wanted, Anessa let her crossbow fall back into place. "Some reason you're acting like a fool?"

Kobb moved closer. His movements were smooth and assured, but his eyes were more red than white. "My apologies. Not enough sleep. Keeping moving's not too hard, but it's not so good for remembering to explain.

The dreams are back, Haelen."

"The potion weakens over time." Haelen sounded tense. "I didn't expect it to happen so quick. I've the makings in my bag, but..." Haelen swept his arm around the forest, seeming to give equal weight to the grimy surroundings and Eater sitting nearby.

"I've lasted this long. I'll last another night." Kobb twitched his head in the direction of the stone circle. "No cause to dawdle though. You can brew a batch once I've kept my promise."

The Eater rose to its feet and ambled into the undergrowth.

Anessa hurried after it. Kobb knew what he was doing—even if he was even odder than usual—but that didn't mean she shouldn't take precautions. The Eater might work out Kobb wanted to do more than take it back to the circle. She just hoped he found a way to tell her what his plan was before they got there.

The journey back passed uneventfully. But, between her constant fear that the Eater was going to do something—a fear Haelen seemed to share—and Kobb snapping awake several times during the night, she felt both limp and twitchy by the time they reached the circle.

Passing the reins to Haelen, Kobb strode forward across the blasted soil. The Eater strolled beside him.

Anessa followed, still unsure what the plan was.

Stopping at what Anessa supposed was the edge of the barrier, Kobb drew himself up to his full height. "Greetings, the camp."

The wild-haired man emerged from a tent. Shading his eyes for a moment, he nodded sharply and disappeared between the Stones.

Anessa flicked her gaze around as the quiet, normal sounds stopped dead. The air tasted of metal and—for an instant—flickered purple.

Shoulders starting to quiver, Kobb strode forward.

Anessa resettled her crossbow for easier access and followed. Fortunately, removing the barrier was less dramatic than raising it.

Stared at head on, the Stones stood barely taller than she was, but she couldn't shake the feeling they loomed many times taller when she wasn't looking. She glanced from side to side, trying to catch them shifting. Stumbling to a halt just outside the ring, she realised—even though the Sun was clear above the trees—the stones had only the wispy shadows of a cloudy day.

"Ha! Thought you could stop me did you, Skithai?" His tattered robe streaming behind him, the man strode into sight between two stones. "Why isn't it tied, eh?"

"Came willingly, so no need coming, "said Kobb. " And, it's leaving freely, so would be a hindrance going."

The man stumbled to a halt, eyebrows almost merging with his beard in puzzlement.

Anessa frowned in agreement. Leaving...?

Unslinging the cloth bag, Kobb threw it to the Eater. Eater raised its staff, crystals flaring, hooked the bag from the air, and sped into the distance.

Anessa grabbed her crossbow on instinct, but the creature was gone before she could aim. What was Kobb's plan? Why—?

"You promised!" The man was almost puce between the thickets of hair. "You can't break a promise!"

"Promised we'd bring it back. And we did." Kobb pointed into the forest. "You want more, it went that way."

"You... why..." The man staggered sideways, falling against a Stone.

Anessa realised she couldn't hear birds. Spitting the taste of iron from her mouth, she snapped her crossbow up to point at the man. "Move away. I can loose well before you finish."

The man eased himself upright. Glaring at her, he moved away from the stone.

"Sensible man knows when to cut his losses," said Haelen.

Staring hard at Haelen for a moment, the man raised his hands in surrender. He smiled weakly and backed toward the tents. "I see how it is. I'll get my things and leave."

"Who knows what you've got hidden in there." Kobb reached into his saddlebag and pulled out a sack of oats. "It's not luxury, but it's enough to keep you going for a while."

The man's gaze flicked around, settling on Kobb's Courser. After tugging his robes straighter, the man snatched the sack and strode away south.

Anessa tracked his path for a while, before deciding he really was leaving. "What's going on, Kobb?"

Kobb rested his back on a Stone. "The Eaters worship the Maker. A sight better than most people. That, and it wanting to stop this evil as much as I do, meant we made a deal."

"You made a deal?" She wanted to trust him, but it didn't make sense.

Kobb sagged back against one of the stones. "It didn't agree to come back with me only to keep the masks safe. It needed someone to do what it couldn't. It told me what the Stones are."

Part Seventeen

Before Anessa could work out what to ask first, Haelen started chortling. The wind, slipping between the stones, undercut his mirth.

Pushing his hood back, Haelen took a deep breath. "No wonder you didn't bring the Legions with you."

Anessa glared back and forth between the two men before settling on Haelen.

"He actually believes," said Haelen, sputtering. "He truly believes."

"But, don't everyone?" Anessa slung her crossbow. "I mean most folks don't—"

"—keep bothering the Maker?" interjected Kobb, eyes sparkling.

Anessa flushed. "Weren't going to say that. Meant most folks don't expect him to pay attention to their doings. We kept the rituals and always put out the share each Maker Day."

"I'm not offended, Anessa." Kobb's mouth quirked. "Botherer isn't the worst I been called. But Haelen isn't talking about believing in the Maker. Not exactly."

"There's two types of Botherer." Haelen winked at Kobb. "The civilised ones, who do good works, maybe serve beside the Legion, and take the respect for it; and the ones who'll give up their last crust because it's better to die giving a Blessing than live."

"You trusted an Eater because it talked pleasant?" Anessa stared at Kobb. "But... that's... why would you...?"

"Why did you stop Aycock? Taking a stranger's part against your people?"

"Weren't right what they were doing" She felt heat flow up her face. "'Sides, most people don't like east-siders anyway, so weren't a risk."

Kobb pursed his lips. "And people don't like Korha either. So no danger people would disagree."

"What... no... Couldn't just leave you! Not without doing something."

"And I am most grateful." Kobb smiled.

She realised she'd done it too: risked her own life for a stranger, not once but over and over again, because it was the right thing to do. She could have turned back after the Eaters attacked the first time, or given up when the Korha nearly killed her, or... "But why's that so funny? You both— Wait! What do you mean the Eater told you what the Stones are?"

Kobb's grin died. "The Stones anchor a... a river of power between here and somewhere else. That's why they move around in my dreams. They're supposed to be connected in a certain way, but the rituals got old. Might even have been weakened deliberately. The power's leaking out into the world. Distorting it. Bringing old evils back, like the Korha."

"So you're going to perform the rituals?" asked Haelen. "Rebuild this gate before it gets worse?"

"I will." Kobb straightened. "But first we need to visit the places the power went."

Haelen drew himself up. "If a person gets a sweating disease, you try to cure it; you don't just keep mopping their brow. If we fix the gate, the evil will go away."

"It isn't that simple. Performing the rituals might make the evil part of the world again, not send it back. And even if I do work out the rituals, they might not work unless the evil is gone. I need to—"

If he worked out the rituals? Anessa looked Kobb hard in the eyes. "I thought the Eater told you what to do? And won't the evil just keep coming back?"

"The rituals aren't Skithai. That's why the shaman couldn't deal with this. It knows what's wrong, but only someone attuned to the rituals can do it. I managed to feel the barrier; I'll have to do it again with the whole circle." Kobb rubbed the pendant at his throat. "As for the evil? Evil only thrives unopposed. Stand up to it and it won't return."

"Maybe there's something in the notes we found in Alcston?" Haelen inclined his head toward the tents. "Our predecessor might have left something helpful, too. He did work out how to raise the barrier."

"We need the barrier anyway," said Anessa. "We aren't the only ones interested. If we take turns watching, we might keep a couple of people out, but that's all. And, soon as we leave, someone could just stroll in. If we can control the barrier, we don't have to worry."

Kobb shook his head. "A Courser's a terrible weapon, but it's controlled. But the barrier isn't. It scoured the ground. It's dark power."

"You said the rituals faded," said Haelen. "Maybe that's why it isn't controlled? At least review the notes. That map look like it showed—"

"You're right." Kobb sighed. "We need to find out more. We'd best start with whatever's in those tents."

Anessa chewed her lip. Dad had always been on at her to practice her letters more, but hunting didn't make her head ache; and she was plenty good enough at reading for inventory and ordering. "One of us should stay out here. Just in case."

"Another fine thought," said Kobb, relaxing. "You're the one who knows about these things, Haelen—"

Haelen went pale. "Wouldn't say I knew—"

"None of us do." Kobb sighed. "But you've studied the papers we found, so you're the closest we've got. Look at whatever notes he left before we scared him off. Anessa and I'll take a look around the circle. Make sure he doesn't come sneaking back before we have a better plan; and between her eyes and my dreams we might see something helpful."

Haelen pinched the bridge of his nose and then strolled toward the tents.

"So, what does invisible evil look like?" Anessa forced her mouth to stay level. "I was distracted last time."

Kobb snorted. "I figure you'll recognise it when you don't see it."

The wind gusted as they entered the circle, raising goose pimples on Anessa's arms. She swept her eyes around the tree line as they moved toward the centre. She didn't actually expect an attack, but focusing on the forest reduced the feeling that the Stones shifted in the corners of her vision.

But didn't help with the guilt. Whatever Kobb said about being glad she was here, he'd come most of the way before he even met her; and Haelen was more useful as a healer and for figuring all the creepy stuff. Sharp eyes were all she had, and here she was going out of her way not to look.

A distant voice whispered in her right ear.

Anessa snapped her head sideways. Nothing.

Something stroked the left side of her face and whispered nonsense.

She slapped her face. A tendril of hair tickled her fingertips. Letting the tightness in her shoulders slip away, she tucked the stray hair back in place. Just the layout of the Stones making the wind twist and murmur.

Deliberately moving her hand off the turf-hook, she glared at the nearest Stone. Same height as her father and about as narrow. No cause to be scared of something you could wrap your arms around. So what else was there?

The stone sparkled slightly in the sun. That was no use. They already knew it did crystally things, like Kobb's Courser did. The shadow was still pale. That weren't right. But it weren't giant-mist-creature not right. Nothing to be afraid of.

Ignoring the impression of words in the wind she moved closer. Now she took a proper look the Stone weren't even that scary. The patterns were pleasant. Didn't look that firm in the ground either. Might take a run up, but she could probably shove it over. Something grabbed her shoulder.

Spinning round, she fumbled for her crossbow. A dark figure loomed over her.

Part Eighteen

Searing sunlight haloed the figure. Streams of shadow bled from its edges, making it seem to flicker and twist.

The bolt twisted in Anessa's fingers, refusing to line up with the channel.

Stretching up into the sky, the figure jerked again, its arm now stretched toward her again.

She fumbled with the bolt as she leapt backwards.

"Anessa?" The edge of a cloud brushed the sun. Kobb peered at her, one arm half-raised, before glancing over his shoulder "Did you see something? You didn't answer when I called."

She slide the bolt back into its belt loop. How had she mistaken Kobb for an attacker? If she didn't calm down, he'd send her home. And that would make it partly her fault if he failed. "Thought I saw something, but it was just the sun."

She looked at the Stone again. It stood silent and immovable, light catching random flecks of crystal.

"They do go wandering, don't they."

Hoping he hadn't noticed her twitch, she faced him again. "You see it too?"

"It's good to know it's not my dreams making me see things." Kobb half-grinned. "Not that it wouldn't be better."

Why would it better if–? If they both saw it, then the Stones really were moving. Anessa leapt away from the stone. Head flicking, she checked them all. Seven rough pillars in a rough circle, the gaps between them apparently random, with a sort of long boulder in the middle.

She checked again. They still gave off the air of immobility, but she was sure they were a different distance apart now. She took a step to the left without taking her eyes off the Stones on the far side.

The sense of a pattern within the crude ring grew. And as it did, one Stone caught her eye. "Shadow's different."

Kobb took a few steps to the right and then moved back. "Stone doesn't sparkle so much either."

Looking at each other for a second, they each took a step toward it at the same moment.

When no evil powers blasted her where she stood, Anessa shook her head and walked forward more naturally. Closer to, the Stone stood out even more; in as much as it didn't stand out. A rough lump of dark rock, a little wider than her shoulders and a hand or so taller than Kobb. Sunlight pointed a dark shadow across the rough ground.

Anessa turned on the spot. Whether in the corner of her eye or the centre of her gaze, the Stone sat, dull and motionless.

The sound of running feet ended her study. Haelen sprinted toward them, waving a handful of parchment. "This is... we need to open the gate."

Anessa peered at him. "We know."

"No... I don't mean... I mean, this is where they took my daughter." Haelen pushed past them toward the centre of the circle.

Kobb grabbed Haelen's arm. "We'll find her. But we need to do this right."

"These notes refers to the gates of absence." Haelen thrust a parchment into Kobb's hand. "That's what it said on the stone they found when she got taken. Look. Same words."

Anessa wrapped her arm around Haelen's shoulder. "That's good news. You found where they came I mean."

"And I think I've worked out some of the rest." Haelen held up a dirty parchment covered in odd circular patterns and scrawled notes.

It looked random to Anessa, but Kobb seemed thoughtful.

Haelen pointed at one of the patterns. "Notes specifically say the barrier's the same thing as a Courser; only the Stones anchor it. There's no Courser in the tent. Soon as I found this, I checked. So, the lack of control... I reckon that's because he didn't know the trick of it. But you could make it..." Haelen waved his free hand in circles.

"If there is a word for how I do it they never told me," Kobb peered at the notes. "Could well work right if I do it; and the method's clear enough. Only problem is, it needs to be done inside the circle."

"But, that means you'd need to stay here." Anessa fingered the hilt of her turf-hook. "Without you, how will we find the evil?"

"And even if we could find them, it will take months to walk there and back for every stray stream of power." Haelen's shoulders sagged

Kobb's smile was large, but it didn't reach his eyes. "Falcon could—"

"How did all this gear get here?" Anessa indicated the three tents. "Ain't seen another horse, and he left on foot."

"The Skithai must have helped. Before they turned against him."

"Maybe. Don't feel right though." Anessa forced her shoulders not to curl as Kobb and Haelen both looked at her. She hoped she wasn't about to make a fool of herself. "He talked them Eaters into helping, right? So, reckon he knew them better than what we do."

Kobb's eyes widened. "If they agreed to help him, he must have lied to them about what he was doing. So he would have planned to deal with them before they found out, not keep them around to carry his tents back."

"Wait..." Haelen scanned a parchment, before thrusting it forward. "Gates of absence. Not gate. Gates. More than one. You said the power's like a river but it's trickling away. What if the connection went with it? He could raise the barrier and open a gate to somewhere else."

"We could stop anyone from entering the circle, and travel faster." Anessa grinned Haelen.

"It's not right," said Kobb. "The Book of Blessings says that power should not be embraced. Using the barrier maybe, but riding the power..."

"Not right." Haelen jutted his jaw into Kobb's face. "After all this time, I found a clue to where my daughter is, and you're worried about whether your book would approve! Well, you don't have to come. But you're not stopping me."

Kobb's hand settled on his rapier.

PART NINETEEN

Before Kobb could clear his blade, Anessa pushed herself between them. "The Eaters run fast. Real fast. And they worship the Maker don't they? So ain't travelling fast righteous?"

Kobb grabbed her shoulder and twisted. "Suddenly you are an expert on virtue? On faith? Did the Maker always speak to you, or was it only since you left your hovel?"

"Virtue?" Anessa didn't notice the pain in her hand—only the pleasing glow of its mark on Kobb's face. "Least I help people, instead of following rules honest folk laugh at."

Kobb drew his free fist back. Before the blow could fall, he doubled over.

Anessa stepped backwards as Haelen lowered his fist and grabbed for Kobb's bowed head. Grinning, she circled around the wrestling men. With Haelen distracting him, she should be able to pick her spot.

Her fingers wrapped around the turf hook. If she lined up right, she might catch both of them with a single—

The weapon slipped from her fingers. Haelen wasn't her enemy. Kobb wasn't her enemy. Why was she—? The power twisted things! She kicked the turf hook away and then unslung her crossbow. Her left hand instinctively dropped to a bolt.

Biting down on her tongue, she hurled the crossbow away, then cast her bolts in the opposite direction. Her mouth flooded with copper as she turned back to the struggling men and charged.

Her shoulder caught Kobb's chest, tearing him from Haelen's grip but sending her tumbling to the ground.

Haelen, eyes wide, brought his leg back and then paused. "Katrina?"

She was right. The Stones made people see wrong. Bloody spittle flying, she locked eyes with Kobb. "Kobb! The power got in our heads!"

He froze, knuckles white on the butt of his Courser. His jaw trembled as he forced his hand to the pendant at his throat.

As Anessa eased herself to her feet, Haelen began to sob uncontrollably.

"Get him outside the Stones." Kobb backed away. "Might not attack you."

Anessa rested her hand on Haelen's elbow and pulled gently. Body shaking, he let her lead him between the nearest Stones. As soon as she stepped through, the air felt warmer. Her shoulders sagged, a stiffness she hadn't noticed trickling away. "It worked, Kobb. I feel better."

The taste of metal coated her tongue. For a moment she dismissed it; then she realised Kobb hadn't just not answered, all the sound had gone. She spun round.

Purple fire flickered across the stones, lashing randomly over Kobb's rigid body. She needed to get him out of there.

As she took a step forward, the fire surged, tendrils bridging the gaps between the stones. Her feet stumbled to a halt.

Pimples rose on her arms. The wind, gusting in one direction then another, span up patterns of dust.

Sparks burst randomly across the scorched ground.

Sunlight bled away, making the fire seem brighter still.

Then it stopped.

Blinking away the patterns floating across her vision, Anessa looked around. What happened? Had—?

Kobb collapsed backwards, face bloodless.

Anessa rushed toward him, but Haelen outpaced her.

"Reverend!" Haelen dropped to a crouch.

Kobb's eyes cracked open. "Barrier. Directed the power. Affect us less."

"You raised the barrier." Anessa crouched at his other side. "But it nearly... You were right. Using the Stones is too dangerous."

"No.... Haelen's right. It's like a Courser." Kobb sat up. "But, that much power, and after chasing through the forest without a good night's sleep... I'll be fine."

Anessa raised an eyebrow, but the blood was returning to his face and he remained upright unaided.

Haelen rose and offered his hand. "Shouldn't have said what I did. Man's entitled to his morals."

"I've faced down enough Reverends who got a taste for telling people what to do." Kobb took Haelen's hand. "My fault for forgetting the Book of Blessings is a guide. Don't hold all the Maker's thoughts."

"Weren't none of us right." Anessa gestured around. "Stones were doing things. Barrier's up now. Best get some rest... outside the ring."

Kobb pulled himself upright on Haelen's arm. "Seems we owe you again. A Blessing that you saw through it given how strong it was. If it was only me succumbed, would make sense: these Stones have been pressing at me for months. But Haelen was taken hard too."

"Aren't the innocent supposed to be immune to true evil?" Haelen frowned. "In tales, least ways."

Anessa felt heat flood her face. She weren't innocent. Couldn't be, growing up around farm beasts.

"Would be good if life were like a tale." Kobb rubbed his eyes. "Don't mean we can't get her back. But we'll all benefit from some sleep."

"That's all it was," Anessa muttered. "Weren't as tired as the two of you."

Despite her theory, Anessa tumbled into sleep as soon as she lay down.

Only to jerk awake, eyes gritty, as Kobb shouted incoherently. Conflicted between acknowledging his pain and giving him privacy, she kept her face turned away. As her eyes crept closed, an odd pattering noise came from outside.

She untangled her legs from the blanket and peered out the tent flap. The night was black, but in place of stars, purple light flickered and sparked across the sky. An especially bright flash revealed a hooded figure slipping from the second tent.

Part Twenty

Kobb focused on the weave of the canvas above his head. A great weight pinned him to the cot and a deep hammering echoed through his head. Forcing his lungs to take and hold deeper breaths, the thudding faded. Heart no longer racing, he turned his thoughts inward. The barrier pressed against him. Incoherent syllables squeezed from his lips as he shoved back.

Easing into the feeling, he sensed the wind gusting through the stones... and something else. The power twisting and flowing from the circle to the barrier. He shouldn't be able to— He was still connected. When he collapsed, he hadn't noticed. Body arching, he forced himself out of the flow.

A sliver of light flickered across the roof of the tent. Sitting up, he pushed aside the blanket Haelen had insisted they hang between the cots. The tent flap fell closed, cutting off the image of Anessa creeping away.

Rubbing the bridge of his nose, he scooped up his Courser and rapier. A weapon clutched in each hand, he slipped out.

Freezing air bit through his shirt. Glancing up at the snow sparking on the barrier, he considered going back for his jacket. But Anessa was already some distance away. Striding after her, he noticed Haelen standing in the ring of Stones. Anessa was heading straight for him, so why hadn't Haelen spotted whatever she had? Why was Haelen in the circle anyway? If he acted as if he were just coming to see Haelen, it might distract whatever was out there; which would let Anessa sneak up on it. "Cold night for it."

Haelen spun round, a bundle of papers slipping from his hand. Caught by the wind, notes and diagrams swirled sideways.

"Haelen?" Anessa straightened. "I thought..."

Haelen lunged for the papers. Getting his feet crossed in his haste, he landed in an ungainly heap, outstretched fingers pinning his prize to the dirt. "Woke up with an idea. I wanted to—"

"I'm first to admit it's hard to step away," said Kobb. "But you'll be sharper after some rest."

Haelen fumbled the papers back into a rough pile and stood up. "One more, quick thing. I'll not sleep anyway for thinking on it."

Kobb nodded. If dreams of a threat were enough to keep him moving, then how strong must the chance to rescue a child be? Clutching his arms tight in the vain attempt to save the last of his warmth, he stumbled back to bed. The remainder of his night was blessedly free of nightmares.

Even with his jacket, the next morning was bitter. The barrier stopped the snow but not the cold it brought. Haelen was already among the Stones —assuming he'd gone to bed in the first place. Throwing oats in a pot, Kobb relit the fire. He might not be able to drag Haelen away from his research, but the smell of hot porridge might.

Anessa emerged from the other tent, almost lost inside a crude fur coat. "Seems the old man planned in being here a while. Is that porridge?"

"Grab a bowl. There's probably enough for your new friend too." Seeing Anessa's look of puzzlement, Kobb pointed at the coat.

Leaving the pot on the fire until it was a choice between burning the meal and letting it go cold, Kobb gave up on Haelen coming to him. After wrapping the handle in a rag, he grabbed another spoon and walked into the ring. "Breakfast, Haelen."

Haelen looked up. Pointing at the map clutched in his left hand with a finger more blue than pink, he grinned. "The Stones are connected to the power. Seven stones, seven threads leaking away."

Kobb nodded. "Makes sense. But—"

"This one's different." Haelen patted the nearest Stone. "Doesn't look the same. And we already dealt with one of the evils. Reckon this links to Alcston."

"If it's not evil any more, shouldn't we feel … something near it?" Anessa stomped over, and dipped her spoon in the pot. Breath fogging the air, she circled the Stone, face creased in a deep frown.

Kobb looked back and forth between the stone and Haelen's map. He couldn't sense anything odd—least not odder than the Stones in general—but what did not having your thoughts corrupted feel like? Haelen's reasoning made sense, though.

Anessa sneaked another spoonful of porridge. "Reckon you could make it travel? If it ain't corrupted, then ain't it the safest one to try?"

"I want this over, too." Kobb placed the pot next to Haelen and thrust the spoon into his free hand. "But it might be safer to take another proper look at all the papers first. Get some decent sleep and meals while we can."

Haelen sprang up, spoon pointing at Kobb like a dagger. "Only so much reading people's notes can do. Takes someone with the right gift to use the power. I'm the only one who understands half these scrawlings; but I can't do it and make the potion you need. So, either you two sit around while I do it all, or you try it. Please, Reverend. My daughter..."

"My apologies. You're right; it's not something you find in a book." Although, there were less savoury places you could gain access to the talent. "Best move well back, Haelen. Kobb sighed. If I make it work, no telling how it'll do it. Don't want to take you by accident."

Haelen grabbed him into a hug and then jogged over to the tents.

"And put a thicker coat on before you start anything." Kobb turned to face Anessa. "No need for you to take the risk, either. You've done more than most already."

Anessa pulled her coat tighter. "And if you do it, but collapse at the other end? If I'm not there to save you who knows what'd happen."

"I suppose, if you do come, Haelen might actually get some porridge."

Anessa's eyes widened before crinkling with glee.

Closing his eyes, Kobb sought inward for the odd connection he'd felt in the night. Threads of power shifted and flickered just beyond his reach. He slowed his breathing, letting the patterns flow through his mind. Following the threads, he ignored each one that touched the barrier until a simpler but more chaotic structure spasmed in front of him.

"Kobb? Are you all right?"

The structure shattered, flowing lines lashing into randomness. Pain lancing through his temples, he grabbed for them, stopping the collapse. "Fine. Need quiet."

Retracing the threads, he sifted away the ones supporting the barrier again. Fourteen overlapping lines of power remained. Headache growing, he brushed against one.

Within the chaos, lurked a rough order. A direction. Letting the merest part of his senses touch the threads, he let those that seemed to come inward drift from his perceptions.

Reduced to seven lines, the structure hung on the verge of sense. Kobb let his thoughts sink further in. There. One of the lines felt different. Holding the resonance of his Courser in his mind, he pushed aside the pain and focused on that single flow. Agony shredded his thoughts as something hurled him away.

Part Twenty-One

Kobb's blood glowed against the pristine snow. Cold biting into his knees, he tried to spit the copper taste from his mouth, but the effort set him coughing again, flooding his throat with bloody mucus.

"Kobb!" The snow crunched as Anessa dropped to his side.

Taking a gulp of chill air, he forced the pain down into his stomach. "Caught me off guard. I'll be fine."

"It worked. We're there."

Kobb straightened. Drifts of mostly white snow clung to low huts. "Haelen was right."

"Looks sort of homely with the snow." Anessa threw her arms out and spun around. "It's all worked out."

The sun hadn't moved in the sky, so the journey had been almost instant. And—even accounting for the drifts hiding some of the decay— Alcston did seem better than when they left. More normal. Maybe too normal. "Best wait until we get back before we celebrate."

Anessa's shoulders slumped. "Sorry. You probably need to rest a bit."

"Rest's always good. But that's not what's bothering me. How do we get back?"

"Same way we..." Anessa followed her footprints to the start, then jumped. The snow puffed up as she landed. Eyes wide, she flicked her gaze from side to side. "There's no Stone this end."

Kobb turned slowly on the spot. Apart from the spatters of blood and the snow churned by their feet, everything was calm. "Can't see any sign of power."

"Maybe the Stones just put you sort of near where it is. What about that finding thing you did with the barrier? I'll search around while you do..." Anessa scrunched her face up and thrust her chin forward.

"Was that really what I looked like? Constipated poultry?"

"No." Anessa's cheeks flushed to match her nose. "You looked very noble and serious, like a... Well, there might have been some resemblance... but definitely a heroic rooster."

Kobb flapped his elbows. "Then let us hope the way back is like an egg."

He closed his eyes and slowed his breathing. After waiting for the crunch of Anessa's footsteps to fade, he focused on the Blessing of Form. The structure rose up in his mind, then hung lifeless. Letting it unravel, he opened his eyes and walked a few yards east. The barrier had been obvious once he knew what to seek; hopefully, whatever gap or knot in the world marked the way back would be similarly noticeable.

With each attempt the structure came more easily; yet remained dull and static. Feet numb and thighs aching, he stumbled into a clear patch in the lee of a hut. The sun was past noon; brushing the treetops already. If he didn't freeze solid, he might finish checking the rest of the village before it was properly dark. But it would be bitter work. And that was assuming the wind stayed from the west. If it shifted round to over the swamp, the temperature—

The swamp. The Korha had been deep in the swamp. His limbs felt so heavy. Kobb slumped until he was crouched against the wall. If the end of the flow moved around then it could be anywhere. Searching a marsh in good weather, mere yards at a time, would be more than arduous. With winter settling...? He clutched at his pendant, but the darkness wouldn't lift. Without movement to fight it off, the chill crept down his collar.

Shivering, he stood. They needed a fire and food. He should spend what light remained on finding firewood to last the night, and somewhere intact to shelter. After stomping a semblance of life back into his feet, he trudged toward the centre of the village.

"Did you find it?" Anessa jogged around a corner.

Hope might sustain her when all else failed. "Haven't finished looking yet. But I don't need light to search, so a fire first. You found anything?"

"Someone's been here since the Korha died.... Not for days though: there's a bunch of Autumn's Crown on a grave, but they were dead before the snow came." She hunched deeper into her coat. "Fire'd be good. Shelter until tomorrow. If it's sunny, might melt the snow enough to make things easier."

"Better weather would be pleasant."

"Least we know the way this time." Anessa gestured at the forest.

Kobb stared. "What?"

"You don't reckon we'll find anything. You ain't one for taking rests, so if you thought you'd find it, you'd still be trudging around with me trying to make you stop. And, you got that look like Dad got when I used to tell him my ideas about going places."

Blessed are the innocent, for they see the truth without seeking. "Haelen won't be pleased."

"Well, he can get used to it. Going fast one way's better than not at all. And, the barrier'll— It's only raising needs the Stones right? You can get through it from the outside?"

"I don't know. The answer's probably in those notes Haelen's trying to decipher." Kobb squared his shoulders. "Bound to be. Once we reach the circle, he can work out how to get us inside."

"Shame he ain't here. Might notice if anything's different in that room he found."

"Different?"

"That hut full of odd stuff. Next to where we arrived. You walked straight past it, so the way back ain't there; and all the notes are gone anyway. But if this power went away maybe something else changed?" Anessa shrugged. "Without him, we'll never know."

Kobb headed for the hut. The lunatic at the Stones accessed the power, but didn't give off the feeling of one burdened with it. What if the way back was the same: waiting to be used rather than constantly pushing against sanity? He entered a small room filled with a fireplace, a broken bed, and half-a-chair. On the far side, a doorway gaped in a crude wall; whoever lived here had split the hut in two.

Sidling through the detritus, he looked into the second room. A few intact containers stood on sagging shelves. Fragments of glass, pottery, and other rubbish dotted the floor. The mould had got in, like Haelen said. He made out a darker area in the far corner, several feet square.

He moved closer. A square of dark wood, the sheen of long polishing still visible under the mould, sat in place of the functional planks that made up the rest of the floor. Grabbing a fragment of cloth from a nearby pile, he wiped away some of the muck.

"Found something?"

Kobb glanced at Anessa. "Why would someone make floorboards out of Anesh Oak?"

"Ain't even heard of it."

Kobb drew his Courser and tapped the butt. "This is Anesh Oak. You wouldn't... not unless..."

Wiping frantically, he cleared a swathe of filth away. Familiar symbols, barely visible in the gloom, marked the dark wood. He grabbed another tatter of cloth and set to work. A pattern, unknown yet also obvious, emerged. "Tapping. They were trying to tap the flow."

"And that's a good thing?"

"No. It's bad... I mean it's bad they were doing it. But, might be good for us. A Courser doesn't need to be right atop a source of power to work. So, even if it's not that close, could tap the way back; bring it here."

"So, we step on the wood and end up at the Stones?"

"Not quite." Kobb closed his eyes and let the structure rise up in his mind. With the pattern to underpin it, it required no effort to maintain it. Power flickered and shifted. Something pushed gently at him.

He straightened. A dull Stone, without even the barest of sparkle, squatted next to him. "Haelen!"

A fur-wrapped figure ran out of the sleeping tent.

"That's all it took?" Anessa frowned at Kobb.

"With the right pattern, yes."

"But what about...? You'll need that oak."

"Anesh Oak is ideal for holding patterns, but—"

"—we don't need to reuse the pattern," interjected Haelen, stumbling to a halt, "If we're only travelling once."

Kobb patted the stone. "Only six more to purify."

Part Twenty-Two

Anessa grabbed Haelen. "We did it!"

"That's good to hear." Haelen wriggled free. "But, let's get inside. I brewed up a new batch of sleeping potion. And the Reverend will want to shake the cold off after..."

Kobb rolled his shoulders. "Journey there wasn't ideal, so best if Haelen takes a poke to make sure nothing permanent happened. Wouldn't say no to something warm though; if you don't mind starting supper, Anessa."

Haelen nodded. "I'll try to be quick. Wouldn't be fair to force her to eat it all."

Kobb snorted.

Anessa stomped over to the woodpile. Weren't nothing wrong with a healthy appetite. Probably be more pleasantness and less arguing if people ate up their porridge instead of spending their time making odd writings. Only a few days wood left, maybe a bit longer if they weren't around to need a fire in the day. She peered out into the fading light. Would it be safe to lower the barrier for a while to collect wood? Or they could... She chuckled at the image of Kobb doing his mad rooster face with his jacket stuffed full of kindling. Just six Stones left anyway, so probably wouldn't be an issue.

It were a touch odd that the previous inhabitant had hauled enough barrels of water to last weeks but not built the woodpile to match. He was cracked though, so not worth creasing her head about. Adding roots to the pot and some oats for thickening, she set the soup to cook.

Waking early the next morning, she realised she'd got a full night's sleep: no keeping one eye out for threats; no Kobb shouting. Torn between the staying curled up in the warmth of the coats piled on her bed and the smell of hot oats wafting from outside, she eased her head up.

Chill air grabbed at her nose and crept along her neck. Gritting her teeth, she dived out of her nest and quickly scooped the top layer around her. After jumping up and down to shake the sleep off, she stomped out of the tent. Despite knowing it wouldn't be there, it felt odd not to have snow crunch beneath her feet.

"Morning, Anessa." Haelen looked up from the pot.

Filling a bowl to the brim, she settled next to Kobb. "What's the plan?"

"Haelen reckons we try that one."

"You worked out where each of them goes, then?"

Kobb and Haelen glanced at each other. "Not yet," said Haelen.

Anessa took another scoop of porridge. Seemed like Haelen found one of those things Kobb thought were wrong. Least they weren't arguing fit to kill this time. "That one it is then. I get to pick next though."

Haelen laughed. "The Reverend's doing the moving. If we're taking turns, seems he should have the next choice."

"Suppose that's fair." She pointed her spoon at Kobb. "But no picking a boring one."

Kobb inclined his head. "Of course not. Although, we do have to go to each of them, so..."

Anessa grinned, then went back to shovelling porridge into her mouth.

Kobb had seemed a little severe to begin with, but he was definitely more cheerful now. Must be the company, and getting closer to ending the evil.

A second bowlful resting in her stomach, she glanced around to make sure she hadn't forgotten something and joined the other two next to Haelen's pick. The Stones on either side seemed to shift in the corners of her eyes. Fixing a giant grin on her face, she winked at both of them. That'd show those Stones she weren't scared.

Kobb brushed his fingers over his pendant. "Ready?"

"Reckon so." She rested her hand on the butt of her crossbow, just in case. "So, we don't know what—?"

Something wrapped around her like damp cloth and the taste of stale milk flooded her mouth. Tearing her eyes open, she lurched sideways.

Snow crunched under her feet. Then her body cramped. Acid and half-digested oats overwhelmed the milky taste. Staggering away from the vomit-spattered snow, she turned until she found Kobb. "Thought it was supposed to be easy?"

Kobb swallowed hard. His hands trembled and sweat coated his brow. "Moving worked like I thought. Must be the corruption in the power."

Anessa looked over at Haelen. His face was a little pale, but seemed otherwise well. "How did you—?"

"Doing what I do, gives you a strong stomach. Pinching yourself helps too."

Made sense. Probably wouldn't last long as a healer if you got sick. She slipped off her gloves and pinched her left wrist hard. It brought back memories of her cousins just having a bit of fun, but the churning in her stomach did slow.

She studied their surroundings. The shattered remains of huts jutted from drifts of snow. Pines loomed up on all sides. Wide tracks, filled with jagged stumps, broke the wall of trees in several places. Pulling her gloves back on, she trudged toward the nearest hut.

Two of the corner posts remained upright. The rest of the walls and the roof lay, shattered and half-buried, in a rough line. Apart from which parts were intact, the next building was the same. "What happened here?"

"Something broke the huts apart," said Kobb. "Don't see bodies though."

"They had time to get away." Haelen walked over, waving a twisted metal object. Snow caked his gloves. "Least ways after the first time. Snow on those looks thicker. Dug this pan out. Must have been flattened when the hut was smashed. But I reckon if we dig through the ones over there, won't be anything but broken wood."

Kobb rubbed his chin. "You might be right. Something demolished those huts. Whoever lived here tried to stop it and failed, or maybe just hid. Once it was gone, they buried the dead or took them, and carried their all possessions with them. The creature came back and broke down the other huts after they were empty."

A muffled crack echoed around the clearing. Anessa spun, looking for the source. More cracks rang out. The pines to the north thrashed in a wind that wasn't there.

Part Twenty-Three

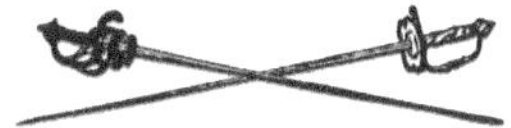

"It's coming from there." Anessa pointed at a section of tree line, her gaze flicking around the settlement. Nothing stood high enough to hide even one of them. "Maybe, we could make for the forest?"

"I don't think it'll help." Kobb indicated the pristine snow. "Even if we can't be seen, it'll see fresh tracks."

A deafening crack rang out.

"We can't do nothing!" Shivering, Anessa unslung her crossbow.

Haelen tilted his head. "What if we stand close together? It smashed these huts in a line, so if we don't get in its way..."

"Might work if it ignores us. But if it attacks fast, it would catch us all. Spread out, we make it choose between us and can flank it." As Kobb jogged for the other side of the settlement, a massive pine slammed down, hurling snow into the air.

A huge hairy shape burst through the white cloud and pounded toward Anessa. She sighted and shot. Beneath the rumble of its charge, the crossbow sounded odd.

Despite her repairs, the nut hadn't released fully; the bolt was still in the channel. Eyes locked on the oncoming mass of flesh and tusks, she abandoned the idea of firing again and ran sideways.

The boar veered to match her path.

Legs aching, she fought against the drifts; but they sucked at her feet, holding her to a fast walk. Something flared bright across the snow as a weight slammed into her back. The ground shook as the boar pounded closer.

Tumbling forward, Anessa felt a gust tug at her legs and smelt soggy fur. After the pain didn't come, she turned over and eased herself up. Haelen lay face down in the snow beside her. Inches beyond his feet, a churned track led to a slumped mass of hair and bone. Haelen must have knocked her out of the way at the last minute.

She clambered upright as Kobb stalked toward them. Steam rose from the beast, swirling around the yellowed spurs that jutted randomly out of its pelt. Fumbling a bolt into her crossbow, she peered for the slightest twitch. "A boar, but don't look like right."

"It's natural enough a Courser killed it." Kobb prodded the body with the tip of his rapier. "Wouldn't risk eating it though."

Haelen coughed and struggled up. He scrubbed his gloves across his face, dislodging clumps of snow from his beard and eyebrows.

Anessa clamped her teeth together. He'd saved her life. She shouldn't laugh.

Haelen blinked his eyes clear and glanced at a handful of snow, before staring calmly at her. "I'm alive, so my disguise worked."

Pushed over the edge, Anessa surrendered to a fit of the giggles. Ribs aching, she gulped down a draft of air, then hiccuped as the cold hit her throat.

Kobb glanced up from his study of the boar. "Maybe we should arm ourselves with snowballs?"

"Sorry." Anessa scurried over to the corpse. Closer, and with the steam dispersing, she noticed the bristles were patchy, revealing pallid flesh and odd blisters. Its head was even worse: skin torn and scarred into a single shiny mass, broken only by misaligned tusks.

"Enjoy the victory, Reverend." Haelen crouched next to them. "Cleaning the power won't all be this easy."

"Ain't over yet." Anessa pointed to the gaps in the pines and then the shattered huts. "This boar knocked down a tree, but that path's wider. Less it went back and forth, it'd need a sounder to do so much damage."

"You think there are a dozen more of them charging around?" Haelen's smile faded.

"At least," said Anessa. "Maybe they circled and came back—"

"—or maybe they kept going, and each strip is a new sounder." Haelen paled as he considered the number of gaps in the tree line.

"Whatever happened, changed their bodies," said Kobb. "Behaviour could be different too; corruption might even have made them vengeful."

"Only one way to find out." Anessa pointed south. "Remains are pointing away, so the boars left that way."

Kobb sheathed his rapier. "But they came from the north. If there are... sounders of these things rampaging around, then whatever caused it's that way."

Anessa readied her crossbow. Wanting to make up for her earlier mistake, she peered to the north. Where would be the best place to enter the forest? But—instead of starting for the tree line—Kobb remained by the boar, gaze on at Haelen.

Haelen spent a moment beating the last of the snow from his coat. "Reverend's right the problem's likely north. But don't fancy facing several of these without knowing more of what they're like. I reckon we track them south and see what we learn."

Grinning, Anessa changed direction. The snow crunched beneath her feet, as she led the way south to the nearest shatter in the tree line; and then stumbled to halt. The scent of resin choked her lungs. She'd seen a full-growth pine fall, but seeing the tangle of jagged stumps and trunks close up made the power of the boars loom huge.

She set her shoulders. Going after the sounder'd been her idea. So they smashed down trees? A normal boar'd hit hard enough to kill anyway, so these weren't more dangerous. She could do this.

After studying the gaps in the pile, she sidled through. Warm shadow wrapped around her and her footsteps fell silent. Shielded by the chaos of branches, the ground had been spared the last several snowfalls creating a needle-floored bower. She crept forward a few yards. The route was gloomy, but the boars'd forced away any obstacle. She returned to the edge. "You'll need to crouch in some places. It's clear enough where they went though."

Kobb patted the shattered end of a branch. "And we'll hear if they try to come at us from the side."

Sucking air through her teeth, Anessa slipped forward. The problem wouldn't be if the boars came from the sides, it'd be getting away if a sounder came from ahead. The more time she spent in this tunnel, the less she liked it.

But the alternatives were clambering over the top of the broken trees, which'd be exhausting if it was even possible, or following the damage from one side, which'd still leave them open to being charged. At least under here, they'd an idea where the threat'd come. The roof of trees would protect against more falls too. Reassured, she padded faster.

The stink of resin made her feel blurry. But that might be helpful: boars had bad eyesight and hearing; they used smell to find threats so, with the damage smashing through obstacles did to their snouts, they'd not notice they were being tracked. A sharp crack sounded from behind her.

She dived against the wall of fractured wood and curled as tight as she could. After a moment, she realised the ground wasn't shaking. Easing herself up, she saw Haelen holding a thick branch in one hand.

His shoulders slumped as he smiled in her direction. "Didn't mean to scare you. Wanted something better than my knife, in case... It looked as if it would come free easily."

"Stop talking," hissed Anessa, the back of her neck itching. Something was wrong.

"No cause to be—"

"Quiet." She pointed deeper along the tunnel. The subtle counter note to the breeze across the pines resolved into hooves scuffing needles. Snuffling from side-to-side as it advanced, a twisted boar staggered out of the gloom ahead.

Part Twenty-Four

Anessa readied her crossbow. The boar had the same bone spines and ragged coat as the one in the clearing, but it seemed tentative. Her guess about the resin muddling their senses must be right. She settled her weapon and took aim. No sense in killing it before it was a threat; the longer she watched it, the more she'd learn.

Shuffling sideways, the boar slammed the side of its face into a branch and then swayed back toward the centre. A beam of sunlight struck the boar's head as it staggered on, revealing its left eye socket gaped empty in an expanse of bone. Seemed like more than not smelling. Spasms running through its limbs, it charged.

Anessa's finger tightened on instinct. The bolt smacked into the boar's neck, sinking deep enough to be lost in the gloom. She began to reload.

Front legs losing order, the boar tumbled forward; but didn't stop for another six feet. A final twitch ran through its back legs, then its body collapsed.

Haelen drew his knife and stepped closer to the corpse. As he crouched down next to it, the boar slumped further. The exposed bone glinted.

Bolt settling into place, Anessa had turned her attention back to the gloom ahead when she realised the boar was in shadow. As she swung around, a jagged shape flickered up from the boar's head.

Haelen leapt to his feet as the whirr of wings filled the air.

Kobb's Courser flew to his hand.

Unfolding multiple chitinous limbs, the insect surged toward Haelen.

Anessa shook off her shock and loosed her bolt. Chips of bark exploded from a smashed trunk as it passed through the creature without stopping.

Kobb still hadn't fired. Haelen must be blocking his line of sight.

Leaping away from the oncoming mandibles, Haelen stumbled and fell, a shaft of sunlight striking his blade.

The monster lunged forward, but veered suddenly. Heavy silence swallowed Haelen's gasping as purple light wreathed the monster's form.

Eyes dull and wings tattered, the insect tumbled to the ground, from the shuff of pine needles now solid.

"How...?" Anessa wound her crossbow as fast as her arms would go. "Why didn't the other boar...?"

"I used a Courser. Maybe it killed the parasite as well."

Anessa let the crank spin back. "I didn't spot it till it were close, and I can't do anything about the real threat if I do notice it in time... I might not be a hero after all."

"Killing's not what makes a hero." Kobb helped Haelen upright. "And shooting that boar before it hit us is enough for me."

Haelen brushed needles from his trousers as best he could. "Reverend's right. If anyone's to blame for it finding us, I am. Poking the dead ain't going to tell us more than we know. I reckon we head back."

Anessa peered at the insect. Ten legs, ending in six-inch spikes, splayed beneath a body covered in triangular scales. Rubbery tendrils surrounded a cluster of seven differently sized eyes. Even dead, it gave her the creeps.

"Boar acted odd. First one blasted through those pines and came hard at me. This'n wandered till it realised we were here, like it had shaking fever... well, not the same, but I reckon something happened ahead."

"She's right. Behaviour was different." Haelen winked. "One of the basics of healing and I missed it. If you're not careful, Anessa, you'll have my place and the Reverend's."

She felt a flush rise up her neck. Suddenly glad of the gloom, she readied her crossbow and moved off. Haelen's praise running through her mind, she breathed a little easier. But only a little: tracking beasts she couldn't hurt, even if they were sick, made the Korha seem easy.

Ahead the path brightened, gaps between the tangled wood becoming larger and more frequent. At the range of her sight, something hunched in the shadows. Pointing ahead and then pressing a finger to her lips, she crept closer.

Bone spurs and matted fur emerged from the murk. But the boar's legs splayed beneath its slumped, motionless body. Alert for the slightest flicker or twitch, she moved forward. Kobb and Haelen followed, weapons ready.

Close now, she saw the fletchings of bolts between the spurs. Someone killed it, but had the insect–? Branches creaked to her left.

She rolled away, and automatically brought her crossbow up. A young man in muddy leathers dropped between two slanted trunks, crossbow hanging in one hand. She jerked her finger off the trigger. "Who are you?"

The hunter fell to his knees, sweat glistening on his forehead. "Attacked... get home..."

"The boars attacked you?" Haelen ran forward. "Let me take a look."

The young man slumped to the ground, letting the crossbow slip from his fingers, as Haelen poked and peered. Eventually, Haelen straightened. "Can't find wounds or breaks, but you do need rest. We should make camp for the night."

"Might want a safer spot. Not sure I fancy boar for supper." Kobb rested a hand on the hunter's shoulder. "You have any companions that might be out there? Or see how many boars survived."

The man mumbled something.

Kobb crouched down. "Didn't catch—"

The hunter's left hand clamped around the butt of Kobb's Courser. Heels digging into the dirt, the man's legs kicked hard. Stolen weapon clutched tight, he rolled past a wide-eyed Haelen and rose to his feet.

Part Twenty-Five

Kobb rose smoothly, rapier singing out to point at the man's heart. From the corner of his eye, he saw Anessa raise her crossbow. Shifting his weight onto his front foot, Kobb adjusted his guard to account for his target's likely choices.

"Stay calm." Haelen turned, palms raised. "We want to help."

"Killing stone..." Gripping the Courser by its middle, the man waved it in the air. "Come through. Danger wrong."

"Don't have to be bad." Anessa waggled her crossbow. "But we ain't doing nothing until you put that down."

The patterns on the Courser's hilt stayed dull and not even daylight glinted from the crystal. The hunter wasn't holding it as if he intended to use it either. Something about it had scared him. Could he have seen something similar? Settling into a neutral stance, Kobb let the point of his rapier drop to a defensive guard.

Eyes wide and head twitching, the man backed away. "Lawless... don't want to."

If he were going to attack, he would have. But that didn't mean he wouldn't get spooked. Kobb sheathed his rapier. "Anessa, put your weapon up. We're all safe here."

"What about boars? Even if we ain't threatening each other, there's more out there."

"Boars gone." The hunter nodded, his upper body rocking in time. "I go home. Safe."

Anessa frowned for a moment before slinging her crossbow.

"We can help you." Haelen smiled. "We should rest first, though."

Kobb considered the man's grip on the Courser. It was more than not intending to use it: none of his fingers touched the sigils. It could be chance, but there were two reasons a person might recognise a Courser.

Strolling forward, he started gathering fallen branches. "Better get a meal on. Hunger doesn't best feed hunger."

"You scour?" The hunter bent from the waist and fumbled up some twigs with his free hand. "Together worship. Take —"

Kobb snapped upright and hurled his armful of branches at the man's head. Anyone who saw a Courser being used might think it a stone that killed. But a simple hunter wouldn't know about scouring, much less suggest that sort of worship.

Reeling backward, the man lost his grip on the Courser. Kobb lunged forward.

Only to fall short as the man folded oddly, grappling Kobb's chest.

Courser tantalisingly out of reach, Kobb snapped his arms up, hoping to break the hold.

The hunter's arms jerked open. But before Kobb could take advantage, his opponent re-established his grip. Hands clasping each other's arms, the two men tumbled to the ground.

The hunter continued to twitch. For a moment, Kobb thought he could take advantage. But, the odd movements were matched by an unnatural strength.

Their rolling ended as the man's knees drove into Kobb's gut. Gulping air, Kobb stared up at his opponent.

And at Anessa stepping in. The flat of her turf-hook struck the hunter's head. With a sickening crunch, his head snapped forward and he tumbled to the ground. Blood oozed from his nostrils, cutting the pine scent with copper.

"I just... I wanted to distract him." Anessa spun away and retched up what remained of her breakfast.

As Kobb sat up, he noticed dark fluid leaking from the back of the hunter's head. Fragments of bloody bone glistened between already matted hair.

The misshapen mess shifted. Hurling himself flat, Kobb rolled away as an insect flickered into view.

"Reverend!" Haelen scooped the Courser up and pitched it toward Kobb.

Fingers wrapping around the butt as the creature swung to face him, Kobb fired. Bark and twigs rained down as the power passed through the insect.

Swerving sideways, it flew into the shadows. Its tendrils drew in for a moment as a bolt whisked through it. Otherwise unaffected, it came at Kobb again from the side.

Light. The other one hadn't gone straight for Haelen; it had swerved around the sunbeam. Kobb shot at the branches above the insect, creating a new spear of sunlight.

Ichor trickled from the creature's abdomen as it jerked back into the gloom.

Kobb shot repeatedly, raining wood and sunlight over his target.

Wings losing their rhythm, it spiralled to the ground.

Ignoring the deep ache in his lungs, Kobb unleashed his Courser on the fallen insect again.

Purple light flickered across its chitin. When the power faded, the insects wings were still and its eyes dull.

Kobb collapsed back on his side, hawking bloody spittle. Only to jerk upright as someone groaned behind him.

Struggling around, he saw the hunter twitch. Throat juddering, the man let out another ragged noise and then stilled.

After casting a quick glance at Kobb, Haelen crouched beside the hunter. Peering into his eyes for a moment, Haelen moved round to study the back of his head. "Apoplexy. Monster left without him dying."

"Apo— He's only sick?" Anessa helped Kobb sit up. "You can save him?"

Haelen shifted the hunter's limbs, arranging him in an odd sideways sprawl. Straightening, he answered. "If I had everything I needed, and somewhere he could rest in the warm, maybe. Even then, there's something wrong about his skull. Cracked like morning ice."

"You mean I...?" Anessa pressed a hand to her mouth.

Haelen put an arm around her shoulder and turned her away. "You did right. Tap like that would only have stunned a healthy man."

Kobb gripped his pendant and raised his Courser. The others wouldn't approve, but it wouldn't be the first secret he kept. And he needed to be certain.

A moment of silence and the hunter was released.

"Sunlight hurts them." Kobb eased himself upright. "And more reliably than a Courser."

Haelen gave Anessa's shoulder a final squeeze, before turning back. "I reckon that one was in this boar first. Came out and went into the hunter. The boars don't have cracked skulls, and this poor fellow's ain't broken enough to let that creature out. That flickering they do, maybe they can be only half there. Dodge it that way"

"So why did the first two just die?" Anessa reloaded her crossbow.

"Using a Courser takes it out of a person. Right, Reverend?" said Haelen. "Makes sense they're here less they see a need."

Anessa kicked the insect. "So, we catch them by surprise, we can kill them. But what if they took more people? I'll kill a boar, but..."

"If Reverend's right about sunlight, I reckon trepanning'll drive one out." Haelen made a twisting motion with one hand. "Old remedy. Hasn't been used for longer than I've been a healer: supposedly, if you drill a hole in someone's head it lets the evil out. Thought it was nonsense, but..."

Kobb nodded. "We have a plan. Stay in the light. If we meet a boar, aim for the head. If one of them's in a person, we try Haelen's idea."

"North, then." said Anessa.

Part Twenty-Six

Kobb holstered his Courser and stood.

"Shame to waste that." Haelen pointed at the broken branches scattered across the area. "And we'll all be better for a rest."

Shivering, Anessa glanced at the hunter. "Day's only half gone. And, like Kobb said, this ain't the best place to camp."

"With him dead, don't need to overnight. And sooner we're there, sooner everyone's safe," said Kobb. "But, I'll not hide that I'd enjoy something hot before we head on."

Lifting one end of the hunter each, Haelen and Kobb moved him to the edge of the tunnel and piled broken branches over him. By the time they'd finished, Anessa had cleared enough space for a fire and brewed a pot of porridge.

Warmth from his portion easing the aches in his body, Kobb rested against a stump while Anessa scoured the last of the oats. Finally, her desire to be heading on overcame her determination to find another hint of porridge in the depths.

As she started back the way they came, Kobb eased to his feet. He moved to follow but Haelen rested a hand on his elbow. "I reckon we don't tell her," whispered Haelen, "about there not being anywhere safe."

Kobb studied Haelen's face. While his brow was furrowed, his gaze was steady. Kobb had hoped he was the only one who realised what an enemy that could move through things meant. "Agreed. We'd need to set watches anyway."

The rest of the journey back to the settlement passed in silence. Cold smacked Kobb across the face as he emerged from the ragged tunnel. His collar tugged up further, he compared the broken huts to his memory; the wreckage seemed unchanged.

Anessa peered at the sky. "Daylight'll hold for a couple more hours. Press on?"

"They came through here several times." Kobb considered the tree line. "Might be nothing, but there might be a reason. Worth making sure."

Working until twilight, Kobb found only broken wood, tatters of cloth, and the occasional battered tool. Either the insects passed on the way to somewhere else, or they achieved their goal before he arrived. "Anessa, where's the best place for a cold camp?"

"Cold camp?" Anessa frowned at him.

Haelen trudged over to them. "Don't want to attract too much attention."

"Boar's easier to dodge than the weather." Anessa pointed up. "Clear sky means it might be bitter tonight. Better off with a small fire, maybe in one of the broken areas so there's shelter."

"Makes sense." Kobb lifted a section of roof. "There's plenty of dry wood, so we won't get smoked out."

Half-an-hour later, chill biting his spine despite the fire, Kobb was glad all over again that he hadn't sent Anessa straight home. "Not ideal supper conversation I know, Haelen... how easy's this trepanning?"

"Found a drill, so that'll help, but it's not something healers do any more..."

Anessa's head snapped up. "You've never done it?"

Kobb reached forward to stir the soup. A suspiciously oaty resistance met the spoon. "Safer to try on a boar first. Do it in daylight, in the clearing, no need to worry if the insect objects."

"And how are we supposed to catch one?" asked Haelen.

"Most hunters use spears." Anessa reached for the oat sack, then drew her hand back when Kobb raised an eyebrow. "But we don't have any, and these boars're even better at breaking things. Don't want it dead, neither."

"We could feed it some of this soup." Kobb loosed his grip. The spoon remained upright for a moment.

"Covered pit'd work." Anessa glared at Kobb. "Assuming they ain't changed since last time."

"I like the soup idea." Haelen kept a straight face for a moment, then winked at Anessa. "But, seriously, won't digging a pit take too long? Shouldn't we move on?"

Anessa lifted a huge scoop from the pot and splatted it into her bowl. "We can't leave people like that."

"Weren't what I meant. Don't want to get caught here if they come back quick." Haelen raised his palms. "Things got better in Alcston soon as you stopped the Korha. Might not have to save everyone."

Lifting the spoon from Anessa's hand as it passed by, Kobb took a less excessive portion. "Stopping whatever they're planning isn't the same as getting rid of them. It's worth the delay so we find out if it doesn't work before we need it."

Haelen nodded slowly. "Practice wouldn't hurt."

"We've got till tomorrow evening anyway," mumbled Anessa. "From the way the footprints froze, boars come through every five days, maybe six. Plenty of time to dig a pit and get it covered again."

"One, yes. Not enough for all those breaks." Haelen swept his arm around. "Assuming they don't break through somewhere else."

"That's why we don't put it by the tree line," replied Anessa. "We put it in the middle of the village."

"Still no guarantee the boar'll run over that bit."

"That's the second part of the plan." Anessa set her shoulders. "Soon as we hear crashing, I stand by the pit. The boar charges me, and goes in."

"And if it doesn't?"

"I run like I've got a mad boar after me." Anessa's eyes belied her humour.

Part Twenty-Seven

Kobb added a scoop of dried fruit to the pot, and stirred it through. Third of a sack of oats gone. One sack in each pack, so if they didn't have porridge for every meal they'd have plenty. He sifted another handful of oats into the pot. "I don't suppose anyone found a stock of shovels they haven't mentioned?"

"Reckon there's a bigger problem," said Haelen. "Boar bursts from the forest, sees Anessa, and charges."

Anessa eyed the lightening sky. "That's the plan."

"Won't the insect get suspicious with you sidling about?"

"Sidling?"

"He's right," Kobb said. "Won't know quite where the boar's coming from until it emerges. So, you'll need to line yourself up."

"Don't see much we—"

"You stand on the north side of the trap," said Haelen. "Soon as the boar appears, you run over the pit. Once you're over, veer till you're heading straight away from the beast. It'll think you panicked." Haelen pointed at the wreckage. "Easy enough to weaken some of these planks so they almost break under your weight."

Anessa frowned. "Suppose. We'll need a pit first, though. How deep you reckon?"

"I thought you'd...?"

"I hunt for food, Haelen; not a messy death."

Kobb divided the porridge between their bowls. "Biggest one we've seen was a touch under two yards, and a yard-and-a-half tall. Seven feet square and as deep as we can seems good."

"Thanks, Reverend." Haelen blew on his breakfast. "Suppose neither of you've ever dug a big hole either, or built a platform?"

Kobb shook his head. If Anessa answered, it was lost beneath the draughts of oats she was inhaling.

"Right. Been a while since I put up a hut, but...." Haelen peered around. "Floorboards'll probably make the best spades. Anyone sees a barrel or some sacks, would help with moving the soil away."

Five hours, and several planks each, later, the hole came past Haelen's shoulders. Throwing the broken remains of his latest improvised tool away, he patted Kobb on the shoulder. "If we want time to test the cover, that'll have to do. And I thought laying foundations near a marsh was tiring."

Arms aching, Kobb didn't argue. Clambering from the hole, he staggered toward Anessa. "We're done."

Anessa grinned. "Good. Another stint and I might let the boar hit me."

"Not over yet." Haelen dragged one of the unbroken floorboards closer. "We still need to make the cover."

Kobb rolled his shoulders and winced. "I'll be no use there. Best if I start piling clean snow on the muck."

Haelen snorted. "Would be a little obvious, otherwise. If you put the end on that pile, Anessa, I'll just..."

As Kobb picked up another improvised spade, Anessa jumped onto the plank. Nothing happened.

Cold biting into his fingers, Kobb ploughed plankfuls of snow across the mess of soil and snow. Hopefully, the insects wouldn't care about footprints. Hacking echoed across the clearing, followed by the thud of a plank being dropped.

He'd covered a small—but encouraging—patch, when a creak joined the hacking and thudding. A short while later, a jagged crack rang out.

"Bit less than that, then," said Haelen. "You want to gather or cut, Anessa?"

Kobb knuckled the small of his back. "Or, one of you could shift snow. Wouldn't want anyone to feel I hogged the easy bits."

Anessa studied the expanse of dirty ground for a moment before her shoulders slumped. "Suppose I do need a rest after all that standing on planks."

Racing the sun, they managed to get the trap covered and the worst of the mud hidden. The last of the light slipped away as they staggered into their crude shelter.

"What if it comes in the dark?" Haelen collapsed back against his pack.

Kobb fumbled his flint out. "Plan's the same. We try to keep it in the pit overnight. Kill it if we can't."

"Pit was the hardest part," said Anessa. "So, worst, we put another cover on it."

"True enough." Ignoring the dull ache it sparked, Kobb bent forward to puff the kindling to life. "And all that digging kept us warm."

"I'll give Anessa the pit," Haelen let his head fall back. "But don't see a Blessing in the digging."

Keeping his eyes open long enough to bank the fire, Kobb let himself doze. A distant crashing woke him. From the light creeping over the treetops, he'd slept the night through.

"Reckon that's it." Anessa grabbed a handful of dried fruit. Gaze resting on at the sack of oats for a long moment, she jogged toward the pit.

Kobb eased his Courser free. The joys of being young. He remembered fighting all day, sleeping on the ground, then doing it again the next day. Now, he'd be lucky if he had the energy for more than one shot. Of course, if it worked, he wouldn't need even one. Shuffling sideways, he settled down with a good view of Anessa. A subtle shift in the air indicated Haelen had joined him.

The moments weighed on his eyelids, but the boar finally burst into sight. Steam rising from its flanks, the beast angled toward Anessa without hesitation.

Legs pumping, she staggered away. A vague thudding marked her passage across the pit.

Drumming echoed as the monster pounded onto the cover. The monster lurched as cracks rang out, but it surged on.

Anessa's hands clawed at the air in a vain attempt to pull herself forward faster.

With a final snap, the trap gave way. The boar's haunches sank as the ground fell away beneath its back legs. Hooves scrabbling, it slid backwards.

But didn't fall. Eyes fixed on Anessa, it hung on the edge of the pit.

Kobb took aim; but before he could act, Anessa ran across his line of sight. Dropping her right shoulder, she slammed into the beast's snout and stumbled back.

The boar's scrabble became a flail as it slid over the lip.

"What were you thinking!" Haelen sprinted toward Anessa. "You could have been killed!"

Anessa blinked and gestured vaguely at the trap.

"If you ever do something like—"

"Breathe, Haelen." Kobb forced his legs to jog after the healer. "Risk was worth taking."

Haelen spun round. "What would you know? You've never... She was brave, wasn't she?" Shoulders shaking, he gathered Anessa into a hug.

A ragged gasp came from the pit, followed by the thud of something smacking dirt. Kobb peered in.

The boar shuffled back and then jerked forward. The thump was loud, but with only a few inches of clear space, it barely scratched the packed earth. "Your patient seems energetic. Might as well have breakfast. Let it wear itself out on the earth."

As Kobb took his first mouthful of oats, the thudding stopped. Moments later, a sharper impact sounded, followed by tearing.

Colour drained from Anessa's face as she let a spoon of porridge trickle back into the bowl. "Just remembered, a boar got to Harlan Roblin's field one winter when I were little. He said it rooting around broke the ground better than days with a pick."

Part Twenty-Eight

"How fast can they–? Never mind." Kobb rested his bowl on the ground and ran for the hole, followed by the others.

Anessa loaded her crossbow as she raced past him. "It might still tire itself out. If I hit it in the leg–"

"You'll have to kill it," said Haelen. "That insect's not going to stop until the boar's dead."

"It was worth trying, but we failed." Kobb drew his Courser. "Don't think we can afford more time on it.""Wait." Anessa grabbed his arm. "What if we drop things into the pit?"

Kobb frowned. "Knocking that hunter out almost killed him."

"No. Around it. If it can't move–"

"–it can't hit the sides as hard." Kobb holstered his weapon and grabbed a piece of broken wood.

Unsettled by the lack of squealing, he peered into the trap. Chunks of soil scattered the bottom, and the front edge already looked shallower. He quickly threw his burden in.

The boar broke it with a single blow, but it was still one less tuskful of earth smashed from the pit.

The first few journeys took an age, barely slowing the beast's attempts to break free. Slogging through the drifts Kobb had so carefully built, the three of them hurled in whatever they could find.

But each time pressed the snow down a little, making the next trip easier. Soon they fell into a pattern: if the boar moved to the front, Anessa filled more of the space behind it; if it shuffled back, Kobb added to the tangle of wood protecting the front; and Haelen filled the space to either side.

The beast twisted and smashed, but soon lost too much leverage to break the thicker wreckage. Hemmed in on all sides, it glared up at them in utter silence.

Kobb knuckled the small of his back. "Not something I'd want to do again. But, a person'll be easier to restraint. Best get it done, Haelen."

Jogging over to his pack, Haelen returned with a drill and knife. He held them out to Anessa. "I'll want both hands to get in place. Stand on the left. Hand me the knife first. Soon as I toss it to the right, give me the drill."

After walking along the edge of the trap for a moment, eyeing the back of the boar, Haelen grabbed the jutting end of a beam. Swinging his legs clear of the spurs, he dropped down.

The boar spasmed and bucked, but couldn't shake him before his left hand clasped a bone spur. Kneeling, Haelen snatched the knife from Anessa's outstretched grip and hacked at a patch of bristles on the beast's head.

The creature wrestled harder. Knuckles white against the spur, Haelen fought to stay upright. His face as pale as his knuckles, he pressed the knife to the shaved patch and sliced at the flesh below.

The boar's hindquarters dropped, then surged up. Balance gone, Haelen fell forward as the creature snapped its head up. The knife arced from Haelen's hand, falling just outside the trap.

Lips drawn over clamped teeth, Haelen pushed against the bucking monster with his free hand. With a tearing sound, he straightened. Red blossomed across the side of his tunic, matching the glistening coating of a bone spur.

Kobb snatched his Courser out.

"No." Haelen took a firm grip with his right hand on another spur and held out his left. "Almost done."

As soon as Anessa thrust the drill into his grip, he pressed it to the cut. Drawing a deep breath, he shifted his right hand from the spur to the drill and twisted in one motion. Without his hands bracing him, the boar's writhing sent him sliding sideways.

But the drill stayed in place. A dull crunch sounded as Haelen smacked into a spur. For a moment, Kobb thought it had broken Haelen's ribs. Then Haelen yanked the drill up, grin fighting against the pain.

Kobb lunged forward and grabbed Haelen's arm. Ignoring the icy stabbing that ran up his spine, he jerked Haelen toward him. Haelen smashed into him, knocking him to the ground and adding hollow lungs to the backache.

"It worked." Anessa helped Haelen up. "There's smoke."

Kobb struggled to his feet. The boar rocked, froth coating its snout and wisps of something rising from its head. Moments later, the area above it flickered.

Tendrils flailing, an insect rose above the pit. Unlike the rapid lunges of the others, this one listed, chitin cracking as Kobb watched. Ichor dripping, it drifted toward him before jerking sideways. After spiralling twice, it dropped into the snow.

Unsure whether the drift would provide some protection, Kobb unleashed his Courser. When the light faded, wing fragments and odd organs lay in the mud. "Haelen, how bad are you?"

Squealing drowned out Haelen's answer.

Kobb looked into the pit, careful to stay well away from the remains of the insect. The boar, eyes rolling and sides heaving, thrashed uncontrollably. With a sickening crunch, one of the bone spurs cracked against a joist. Kobb raised his Courser.

"Stop!" Haelen lurched over. "You're not killing it now."

"But—"

"We need to see if it lives." Haelen reached for the end of a plank. "We let it out."

Anessa grabbed Haelen's shoulder. "It's not that important."

Holstering his Courser, Kobb eased Haelen's hand free. "You need to see to your wound. I'll do it."

Moving to the left, Kobb tugged out a baulk and cast it aside. Anessa started on the other side. The first few were easy enough; but, as the boar's freedom to move increased, it hurled itself around more violently.

Anessa reached for one of the beams near the front but jerked her hand away as the beast reared up. "I don't think we—"

"Take from the back."

Working together, they cleared the highest of the obstacles.

Instinct proved more destructive than the insect's cunning. Twisting, the boar faced them. Gashes in its flanks smeared gore across the wood, but still it fought.

"It's too dangerous. Either it struggles free or it doesn't." Kobb pulled Anessa away.

Anessa jogged beside him, stealing glances over her shoulder.

The squealing intensified followed by the sound of breaking wood. Anessa began to run. With nothing to lose if the boar wasn't clambering free, Kobb sped after her. Reaching the flimsy shelter of the camp, he looked back.

Swaying, the creature wandered around the edge of the hole.

The cold seeped through the knees of Kobb's trousers as he waited.

After several long moments, the beast settled on north and meandered into the forest.

"So, only a scratch," said Haelen.

"A scratch?" Anessa crouched next to him. "You're covered in blood."

"I meant the boar. But, people have taken worse and not even stopped. Eh, Reverend?"

Kobb nodded. He'd been wounded worse himself. "Most of them got a strip torn off by a healer for doing it, though."

"Fair point." Haelen held himself straighter. "Auxiliary Lok, do that again and I might not heal you. Apologies, Medicus Lok. Carry on, auxiliary." He chuckled before spitting into the fire.

"You mean you're all right, then?" said Anessa.

"I wouldn't say no to the rest of breakfast," Haelen settled back. "But after that, we head on. People to save."

Kobb looked away. People had taken worst wounds and carried on. But the ones who recovered usually spent days in the healer's tent. For a moment, he considered arguing. It wasn't his choice though. Haelen had decided it was worth the risk. Wouldn't be right to override him.

PART TWENTY-NINE

Kobb closed the straps on his pack. "Best plan is travel parallel to the broken trees. Not guaranteed, but possessed creatures wouldn't use a harder route without reason, so less chance of trouble. If we don't find their lair by early afternoon, we stop until morning."

Haelen sat up, weight resting on his left arm. "No need to—"

"Nothing to do with your injury, Haelen. Biggest weapon we've got is the sun. Don't want to stumble on them as we lose the light." Although, giving him more time to rest was an added Blessing.

Anessa dropped the scoured pot into her pack. "Problem is, once we're in the trees, we can't dodge so well, so if we do meet anything... I say we go slower to so we're quiet. Best not talk unless we need to, neither."

Kobb and Haelen nodded, probably for the same two reasons.

Tense against the expected threat, Kobb oscillated between pulling his hat down hard and letting the chill bite at his ears. But midday passed with nothing other than shattered pines to indicate they weren't travelling into untouched lands.

Although the bloodstain on Haelen's tunic formed a constant reminder of the risk, he kept pace without complaint. A worryingly short distance later, Anessa signalled a possible camp site under a tree. Bowed beneath the weight of snow, its branches touched the ground. And inside, the litter remained dry, close-packed needles holding back the snow.

Sheltered from the wind, they were spared the worst of the cold. Unwilling to risk the light of a fire, they still passed the night huddled together.

Next morning, after forcing down a paste of snow and oats, they headed on. The exposed areas of Haelen's face looked as pale as the drifts. But an argument about him turning back risked making things worse—whether or not Kobb won.

Soon, a second stretch of tangled and shattered branches emerged from the gloom on the other side of their path. If the boar runs converged, they must be close. Anessa slowed further, clearly having the same thought.

Short of midday, the ground sloped up. After creeping to the top of the rise, Anessa held up her hand and slipped back. Gesturing for them to hold their heads together, she leaned in so close Kobb felt her lips brush his ear. "Something tall through the trees."

Kobb pointed around the group, then held his hand at waist level. Moving it slowly up and out he flattened it as it reached shoulder height. The others nodded and followed him to the base of the slope.

Moving from a crouch to a crawl as he approached the crest, Kobb slid forward until he peered between two trees. The forest thinned ahead, opening out into another clearing a few hundred metres on. Beyond the tree line, something tall and conical glinted in the sun.

As they sneaked closer, the air carried the scents of wood smoke and hot metal. Regular whooshes coincided with brief bursts of dull orange light. Standing out against the smoothness of the cone, a crude scaffold ran up one side to a circular opening.

Closer still, Kobb realised people staggered around the clearing, pushing small carts. A few wore leathers, but most only tattered rags. From their relative speeds, the workers took the contents to what he assumed was a smelter, then returned north to gather another load.

After watching until one of the people completed a full circuit, he signalled a retreat. Once they were crouched behind a massive trunk, Kobb leaned in. "Looks like the creatures attacked the village to get workers. The reason for the work's in that tower. So, that's where we need to go."

"We have to rescue the villagers, too," Anessa breathed.

"And we will," said Kobb. "After we work out what's going on."

Haelen frowned. "Stopping the insect's plan's more important. But, don't reckon we can sneak through all those people. Looked like weren't that many pushing carts. If we snatch them from the clearing one at a time, trepanning wouldn't need long."

Kobb brushed his pendant. If the cone was full of insects, they couldn't risk being noticed. Which made leaving all the villagers as much of a risk as being seen rescuing them. "I'll try capturing one. If I can do it without getting caught, we'll decide whether to rescue more or sneak past."

Anessa pointed at her chest and shrugged.

Kobb shook his head. "No question, you're quietest. But grabbing someone silently takes practice."

After a moment, Anessa nodded.

Stopping to reassess the cover each time, Kobb scuttled between trees until he reached the edge of the clearing. Moments later, a young woman shuffled past toward the smelter. Kobb rose up behind her. Slapping his left hand over her mouth, he wrapped his right arm around her waist and yanked backwards.

Arms flailing, his prisoner staggered with him toward the tree line.

Kobb shifted his grip. Her feet scuffed as he dragged her into the pines, but only slowed his progress. As Kobb inched away from the clearing, a man shuffled around the cone. Even if Kobb stayed motionless, his wriggling burden would stand out.

Hoping the bone weakness was confined to their heads, Kobb hurled them to the ground then rolled until he was on top. The woman bucked beneath him. Bearing down with all four limbs and his head, he held her deep enough into the snowy carpet of needles to muffle her struggles.

The man tilted his head. Shuffle turning to a swaying walk, he approached the woman's abandoned cart.

Part Thirty

The snow soaked through Kobb's trousers, making his joints ache. He didn't want to harm either of the villagers, but he wouldn't be able to rescue anyone if the alarm were raised. No one else was close, for the moment. If he kept the woman silent long enough to use his Courser, he'd only have to kill one of them... hopefully.

The second worker halted, peering at the cart.

Kobb rolled more of his bodyweight onto his right side until the strain on his left arm from the woman's struggling became almost unbearable. Torso broader than his prisoner, his shoulder bore on her arm, pressing it harder against the ground.

Twisting his head, he peered down. The gap between them should be wide enough for him to get his hand in, but he'd need to let go of her arm briefly; which meant he didn't have time for a second attempt. Phantom pain rising at the expectation of what he needed to do, he returned his focus to the man.

His limbs moving out of rhythm, the second worker gripped the handles of the cart and lifted.

Kobb forced himself not to hold his breath, as the man staggered toward the smelter with his new burden. Hoping he wouldn't glance back, Kobb rolled his weight evenly onto his prisoner's torso.

The worker continued to shuffle away.

Taking a moment to feel his captive's movements, Kobb released her left wrist and snapped his arm toward her head. She bucked, but his hand settled over her mouth before she could react.

His right arm curling in as he rocked sideways, he restored his grip on her torso.

The snow and needles cushioned her lashing enough that she only made a light scuffing noise. The possessed woman wrestled against him, but the insect's willingness to harm its host couldn't overcome both unfamiliarity with her body and Kobb's experience. Rolling her over him, Kobb lifted his right knee and braced his foot on the ground. As she fought his throw, he reversed it.

Caught by surprise, she rolled against his thigh.

Bracing his left leg the same way, Kobb pinned her between hislegs. With the need to clutch her torso reduced, it was the work of moments to lever them to a sitting position and then achieve a better hold.

Nevertheless, Anessa's arrival was most welcome. Prisoner struggling in their arms, they crept to Haelen. Between them, they wrestled her to the ground, her head in a shaft of sunlight.

Leaving Anessa to hold in place, Kobb drew his Courser.

Not bothering to shave away her hair, Haelen made a confident incision on the crown of their prisoner's head and pressed the drill straight in. Casting the knife away, he gripped the bit and twisted hard. With a wet crunch, it sank into her skull.

Haelen lifted the drill smoothly, and then hurled himself backwards. Anessa rolled away a breath later.

An insect, wings twitching, rose into the sunlight. Then the sound of fluttering ceased as Kobb's Courser ended another life.

Kobb glanced toward the clearing. "Something's very odd. Another worker noticed her cart, but just pushed it away."

"Maybe the insects don't think about things the same way we do?" Haelen eased himself up, face creased. "No sign they need the broken trees, yet the boars crashed straight through them."

Anessa brushed damp needles off Kobb's sleeve. "So, you think we could—"

Limbs flailing, the woman's body curled inward. Her head rose, then smashed to the ground.

Kobb leapt forward, attempting to brace her head, while Anessa threw herself across the woman's legs. Eventually the writhing stopped, leaving the woman pale-skinned and flaccid.

After staring into her tawny eyes for a moment, Haelen ran his fingers over her torso and limbs. "Between whatever the monster did and those spasms, her body's taken too much. She could survive, if she gets enough rest. But left alone in these conditions..."

"You'd better stay, Haelen." Kobb forced his gaze to not even brush the bloodstains on Haelen's tunic. "Anessa and I'll have to sneak in without you."

Anessa frowned. "We're not going to rescue any more?"

"I was lucky this time. But I nearly wasn't. Even both of us together, might not do it silently. And if Haelen's wrong about how the insects think, they'll notice a second worker going missing."

Anessa loaded her crossbow. "Suppose. Soon as we deal with whatever's in that building, we're getting the villagers, though."

"Definitely." Kobb unsheathed his weapons. Assuming those people could be rescued: if the tower was the only thing keeping the insects here...

Anessa in the lead, the two of them sneaked toward the tree line. Workers, movements seeming wrong when seen from the corner of Kobb's eyes, continued to cart something to the smelter. The centre of the clearing remained in sun, but the shadows of the trees stretched nearer to the middle than before. He leant closer to Anessa. "We have to cross soon."

"They're too close together. If we wait for one to leave, the next will see us. We need more shadow to hide us."

"Trying to escape without the sun to protect us would be worse. If we left straight after a villager passes and keep moving, there's time to get to the gantry. They don't change pace or look back." There wouldn't be time hide a body before the next worker came rounded a corner, though. So, if they were noticed, the only option would be to kill everyone who saw them to keep the details secret.

A boy, tattered remnants of britches dragging behind his left ankle, shuffled into sight.

The moment he pulled level, Kobb rose. Having overcome the desire to ease each foot forward, he struggled against the contrary urge to move faster; an urge made stronger by Anessa's swift yet silent advance.

His gait further disrupted by the cloth bunched around one foot, the child limped on, seeming unaware of their presence. Nevertheless, Kobb kept an eye on him, ready to use his Courser if needed. Attention divided, he failed to see the branch until it was too late.

Dry despite lying in a snowdrift, it collapsed beneath his foot with a sharp crack.

The boy slowed, head tilting back and forth.

Raising his Courser, Kobb brushed his free hand against his pendant. If the child didn't stop, the sound of the snow under the wheels might cover Kobb's footsteps.

Still creaking slowly on, the villager looked at one side of the cart then the other. Apparently satisfied, he returned to a faster stagger. Kobb walked to the gantry, eyes on the ground ahead of him. His neck itched, but if the child hadn't glanced back then, he wouldn't do it now.

Crouched behind the rickety frame of rope and branches, the two of them waited for the next worker to pass going the other way and clambered up. The gantry creaked and swayed, but they reached the top safely. A circular hole in the tower, small enough Kobb would have to hunch, spilled an insipid green light onto the platform.

Kobb rested a hand on Anessa's elbow and pointed at himself.

Crouching lower, she pressed herself against the metal to one side of the hole.

The corridor beyond looked as narrow as the entrance. Waddling forward, knees bent so his gaze wasn't forced down, Kobb stepped past the lip.

His stomach roiled, and a cold sweat washed over him. Bile filling his mouth, he tumbled to the ground, sight blurring.

Part Thirty-One

Anessa crouched next to the door, gaze sweeping the clearing for signs of villagers acting odd. Her shoulders curled inward as warmth oozed through the back of her jacket.

A low grunt came from behind her, followed by brief clattering. Then something heavy thudded. Peering around the edge of the entrance, she saw the sole of Kobb's right boot. After flicking her gaze across the clearing, she slid sideways, crossbow ready.

Kobb lay face down on the curved floor, Courser and rapier further along the corridor. As Anessa stepped forward, her gut twisted. A faint odour seeped over her, raising memories of Dereck threatening to throw her in a slurry pit when she was six. She swallowed hard and crouched, wobbling from the slanted footing. "Kobb? Reverend?"

He didn't respond; but he was still breathing. She rolled him half over, then stopped as her elbow thudded on the wall. After a long moment straining her ears, she decided no one had noticed the noise and tried to turn Kobb over again.

On the third try, she managed it. His eyes were shut and sweat coated his brow. The green light made him seem on the verge of death—at least she hoped it was the light. He twitched when she shook his shoulder, but his eyes stayed closed. If only Haelen were here.

Shuffling past Kobb, she lifted his shoulders. Another wave of sickness rose in her gut as she pushed. She let him settle back onto her folded knees. If she took her time, she could get him onto the gantry; she couldn't carry him across the clearing fast enough, though.

She pictured the gantry. As long as the workers stayed with the carts, they wouldn't notice anything; but there was nowhere to hide Kobb from someone going in or out of the tower.

Above her, several dark holes led up, each less than a foot across. No use for humans; a good size for one of those creatures, though. Their living quarters. Kobb'd be found if she didn't do something soon. The corridor curved away down and to the right, with no doors on either side. Her only chance was to find somewhere deeper in the tower.

She shook Kobb's shoulder again. He shifted again, his pendant sliding against her hand. She straightened it, then paused. There was one other thing she could try.

Hands shaking, she wrapped her fingers around the pendant. Her mind went blank. There'd be special words. She didn't even have Maker's Share....

She pulled a bolt from her belt. Letting go of the pendant for a moment, she gripped the shaft by each end and brought it down over her knee. Pain jolted through her leg, but the bolt didn't break. A foul taste coating her mouth, she tossed the bolt onto the gantry. It'd have to do.

She squeezed the pendant again. "I'm Anessa. Anessa Tanton. Everyone always says you ain't to be bothered. But Kobb's a good man, and he's doing what needs doing. And I want to help him, and I don't know how. And he deserves to have people admit he was right, and have a feast for him, and go back to his family..." Did Kobb have a family? He had to, or how would he stand to do this without breaking. "...and to not to die here. So make him better; and if someone's got to pay, then he's done enough so take it out on me."

Her fingers aching, she held the pendant tighter. Kobb didn't wake. Letting the pendant fall, she gathered up his weapons. Whatever happened, he should have them with him. The Courser settled easily, but his scabbard was tangled under his torso. She'd almost freed it when a low juddering sound filled the corridor. Bone ache joined the urge to throw up. Rapier snapping up, she waited for something to turn the corner.

The green light ahead flickered, then faded away as the noise stopped. After swapping the rapier for her crossbow, she crept forward along the wall. The corridor continued downward, the gloom making it hard to make out details. The ceiling was free of holes though, so less chance of insects. The smell of manure'd faded too. Maybe she could find somewhere to hide Kobb in the darkness.

She sneaked a little further, gaze flicking around. Still no side rooms or signs of what the tower was for. Moving Kobb out of sight of the door'd be a good start though. Gut feeling more settled, she turned and slipped around the curve. Bile flooded her mouth.

Caught by surprise, she stumbled back a few steps. The sourness faded, along with the shake in her limbs. The green light: it didn't make Kobb look sick, it made him sick. Taking a deep breath, she headed over to him, stride faltering into a shuffle as she went. Crossbow slung, she dragged him deeper. Each step seemed harder than the last.

Until she rounded the corner. The urge to vomit gone, she lowered Kobb and crept forward. Ahead, the corridor opened into a room wreathed in shadows. Didn't seem natural, being able to see when there weren't windows or lights, but there wasn't the green glow. She moved into the doorway.

Apart from another doorway in the far wall, the room was empty. A gloomy corner was better than the middle of the corridor, though. She headed back to Kobb. As she dragged him into the room, a buzzing noise approached from the deeper in the tower.

She brought her crossbow up as two insects glided into the room. The lead insect fell to the floor, her bolt jutting between its eyes.

Anessa drew her turf hook as the second creature lunged toward her.

Part Thirty-Two

Anessa pointed the tip of the blade at the remaining insect. Even with her arm straight out, what had been a comforting weight on her hip seemed to add little to her reach.

The creature hovered for a moment above its fallen companion, then shot into the corner of the room.

Eyes straining against the gloom, Anessa turned to keep her blade between her and the creature. Why didn't it attack? If it was an animal, she'd think it was nervous; why would an insect-thing be scared? She'd get one swing and then— She squeezed her left hand hard enough to hurt. No use dwelling on what happened if she missed.

The creature drifted deeper into the shadows and settled on the wall. Without light glinting off its body, it was almost invisible.

Anessa tensed in anticipation of a lunge. It still didn't attack. Keeping the turf hook up, she crouched and reached for her crossbow.

Before she could load it, the creature flew at her, wings whirring.

She leapt to her feet, and swung her blade.

The insect flicked sideways, avoiding her weapon, then returned to the shadows.

It only attacked if she posed an immediate threat. Flying creatures didn't need a ladder, so their prisoners must come in. No wonder it was waiting: why risk being hurt when help would arrive soon.

Knuckles white on the turf hook, she lunged for the creature.

Flicking its wings, it jerked away, leaving her cutting empty air.

As she twisted to face it again, purple flared across the room. The insect tumbled from the air, tendrils and legs twitching.

"Needed surprise." Kobb's Courser clicked against the floor as he slumped back.

Anessa slung her weapon. "You're all right!" Gathering up her crossbow, she reloaded before crouching at his side.

"Been better."

"The green light makes us sick. I had to drag you deeper. I couldn't—"

"Good thinking." Kobb holstered his Courser. "Help me up. We need to find whatever the tower protects."

Kobb's weight bearing down on one shoulder, Anessa shuffled across the room. As they approached the exit, she slowed. "It's too narrow to go side-by-side. Stay here. I'll—"

"Whatever's there needs both of us."

"At least wait while I see what's ahead."

Kobb nodded.

Anessa steered him over to the wall. Once he was propped, she crept along the corridor. As she followed it down, a faint tinge stained the walls ahead. After a half turn, they opened out into a room filled with pale green light. Odd metal objects lay scattered across the floor. On the far side, another green-lit tunnel lead deeper still. Braving the glow for a moment, she sneaked forward enough to check the near corners. No ambush, but no shadows either. Deeper meant slogging through the light. She trudged back.

Kobb's skin was pale and clammy, but he no longer leaned against the wall. "Is it safe to go on?"

"No insects. It's full of green light, though. The corridor goes deeper. I'll go on. You make sure they don't sneak up from outside."

"No. Most of the pain's in my head. Must have knocked myself out when I fell. Caught me by surprise. Now I'm expecting it, I'll cope."

Anessa stared at him. He wouldn't lie to her. But wasn't his entire life about thinking things were better than they seemed? That and— "Shoot the light. We don't need it to see, so destroy it."

Kobb studied the wall. "A Courser doesn't do much to inanimate objects, so it won't damage the tower. It might unmake whatever magic makes us ill, though."

Creeping forward until her stomach lurched, Anessa knelt. The sound of their breathing vanished as purple flashed past her shoulder.

When it faded the green glow returned. Another bolt washed across the far wall, again with no effect.

"It's no good," Kobb said. "Without some idea of what the magic is, I've nothing to aim at."

"What if you shoot everything?"

"Might work. But each time weakens me. Another two, perhaps three, times and I'll lose consciousness when the light touches me. If we go through now, we might make it to something important."

Hoping Kobb was right, Anessa moved on. Her attention shifted, one ear cocked for signs of Kobb faltering and the other for approaching insects. Aim wobbling with every step, she crept deeper. After more than a complete circle, the corridor opened out into a room the width of the tower and over ten feet high. Several thin metal frames jutted from the floor. Beyond them, cloaked in shadows, a massive circular carving covered the far wall.

Anessa straightened. "The magic doesn't reach the—"

Grabbing her shoulder, Kobb stopped her lunge forward. "Don't move any closer. Don't look at it."

She spun away. As she did, the carving shifted in the corner of her eye.

The light dimmed. Her urge to throw up faded. But she found no comfort as a scent of rotting hair gusted past.

Anessa's neck ached from the effort of not looking.

Purple flickered and flashed, then cut out as Kobb collapsed to one knee.

She turned. The carving flowed and twisted. Dark tentacles like old fungus, each of different length and shape, stretched from the depths.

Anessa loosed a bolt. Soaring toward the centre of the carving, it disappeared into the distance without ever reaching it.

"Run!" A fit of coughing ran through Kobb, dropping him to the floor. He raised his Courser, but his arm trembled too much to draw a bead.

The tentacles groped further along the wall, revealing they were the tips of thick, oddly jointed limbs.

Anessa stepped back, then set her shoulders. She couldn't leave Kobb. Dropping her crossbow, she dived to the floor next to him and grabbed his hand. "I can't use it, but I can still aim."

Kobb's head sagged to one side, and his eyes were almost closed, Then, one corner of his mouth twitched.

She pointed the Courser at the mass of limbs. "Now."

Purple wreathed the thickest tentacle.

Twisting and flailing, it shrank toward the centre of the carving, then began to grow again.

"Again."

The second blast made the limb pull back further before it groped out once more; but had no effect on the other tentacles.

"It's not dying."

Kobb took a jagged breath. "Can't die... Pain..."

Hoping he meant enough pain made it flee, she moved his aim to the longest tentacle. "Now."

Shifting between shots, they hit it again.

This time the limb didn't reach out after it withdrew, and the creature's groping slowed.

"It's working." Anessa aimed at another fleshy mass. "Again."

Wreathed in purple, the limb folded inward, the others following it.

As the carving stilled, the green glow blinked out in the corridor.

Anessa rested Kobb's arm on his chest. "It's gone. We did it."

After a moment, Kobb's eyes opened. Inching his hand up, he settled the Courser back in place.

Something clanged in the distance. A breath later, a judder ran through the floor.

Anessa yanked Kobb to his feet. Wrapping one arm around his waist, she half carried him to the mouth of the corridor. Part of the wall crashed down behind them as she thrust Kobb forward.

Somehow, he found the strength to keep upright. Floor bucking, they stumbled through the tower. Despite making no attempt at stealth, it seemed longer than the way down; but finally a tint of daylight coloured the metal ahead, and they staggered onto the top of the gantry.

Villagers converged from every direction, limbs spasming.

Part Thirty-Three

Anessa drew her turf hook. "We dealt with the monster. Why are the people still...?"

"I don't think it brought the insects here." Kobb straightened and unsheathed his rapier. "It think they summoned it."

The gantry rocked as the closest villagers pulled themselves up it.

Anessa's weapon drooped. "We can't—"

The platform lurched beneath them. A jagged tearing sound drowned out the clatter of metal. Fragments of tower spun inward, leaving the back of the gantry unsupported. Anessa dived toward Kobb. Wrapped around him, she bounced and jolted to the ground.

Agony ran along her spine as she crashed onto the tangled mass of wood, but she kept her fingers gripped tight on the handle of her turf hook.

Kobb rolled off her, groaning.

Teeth clamped against the pain, she jerked up and flicked her gaze over the clearing.

Each villager rocked in place, eyes fixed on the pit where the tower had stood. As one, they fell forward, insects rising from their heads. Mandibles clacking and spasming, the creatures spiralled upward in a mass.

As the swarm rose above the line of the trees, the setting sun caught them. Their flight lost rhythm, but the insects surged higher, ichor and chitin raining down. Moments after, the first of them plummeted to the ground.

Anessa curled tight, arms wrapped around her head.

An age later the sound of impacts ended. She eased herself up. Chunks of odd flesh and twisted shell coated the clearing, vapour rising. A few villagers twitched. After forcing down a wave of nausea, she crouched over Kobb. "They're dead... all dead. Why did they...?"

Kobb wiped ichor from his face and rose to a sitting position. "They failed their god. Perhaps, they sought to atone."

A god? But wasn't there only one god? "That thing was a god?"

"Not a true one." Kobb brushed his fingers over his pendant. "But they worshipped it as one."

Why would anyone...? "We should fetch Haelen. Can you stand?"

"My clothes took the worst of it. I'll do." Kobb picked up his fallen rapier and clambered to his feet.

Something niggled at Anessa. Kobb was bareheaded. She peered around, but couldn't see his hat. As it didn't seem to bother him, she scooped up her turf hook and led the way through the forest. Despite their victory, she found herself creeping, afraid of attracting attention.

Haelen crouched over the injured woman, muttering. He whirled round as she approached, fear melting into relief. "You're alive! I heard that noise and thought..." He leapt up and drew her close.

"We... I don't really understand, but we stopped them." Anessa eased herself out of his arms. "The villagers collapsed. We need to..." She trailed off as Haelen's grin faded.

"I couldn't save her." Haelen's head drooped. "All the life drained away. The other captives... I don't think..."

Anessa looked past him. The woman sprawled, cheeks sunken and eyes staring.

"The creatures left by choice after we destroyed their portal." Kobb rested a hand on Haelen's shoulder. "It might make the difference."

Haelen raised his head, jaw set. After rolling his shoulders, he nodded once and picked up his bag. "You're right."

Anessa jogged after him as he strode to the clearing. A breath later, he stumbled to a halt. "I didn't realise there were this many." He bent over the nearest villager, then straightened. Shaking his head, he repeated his actions with the next captive. "Their skulls broke when they collapsed."

Moving on, he crouched and examined a boy. "He's still alive. But he'll not last the night without shelter."

"What if we used this?" Anessa pulled a handful of rock from the nearest cart. "We wrap him up. If we reach the settlement—"

"Him, maybe." Haelen ran his gaze around the clearing. "But how many others won't survive without us? We need to take them all. And there's only one way to do that."

Kobb frowned. "Transporting the three of us was hard, don't know if I can transport more."

"You said the insects had a portal here," said Haelen. "You returned from Alcston with just someone's attempt. Won't a working one make it easier? You've got to try. We can't just leave them."

"We'd better get this wreckage cleared." Kobb walked closer to the pit. "If I'm going to, I want to be as near as possible to where the portal was."

"Thank you, both." Haelen rose. "I'll check the others while you work."

Anessa moved to join Kobb. The shadows cast by the trees turned the tangled wood into a single mass, but the first two baulks came free as they pulled; and whatever happened when the demon left, took all the metal. She'd just decided the job'd be easy when Kobb shouted for her to stop.

Clambering down, he reached under a mess of planks. Metal scrapped as he tugged something free. After fumbling again he pulled out a small bundle. He thrust his rescued hat onto his head and climbed out. The brim drooped, the crown was lopsided, and even in the twilight, Anessa could see the fresh stains.

Kobb grinned. "I think yours did better than mine."

She gaped at him, as he held out her crossbow. It looked intact. She half reached out, then let her hands drop. "I don't reckon I should. I... When we were in the tower and you were sick, I asked the Maker to help you, and I didn't have nothing proper to give so I tried to offer a bolt, but I couldn't break it. But you got well anyway, and crossbow's the only thing I've got that's real valuable, so I reckon Maker took it for you, and ain't right to take it back."

Haelen gave a choked sobbing noise that turned into a chuckle. "There you go being a bad influence again, Reverend."

Kobb stared at Haelen, the hat covering his left eye spoiling the effect, before starting to chortle.

After looking back and forth between the two of them for a moment, Anessa grabbed the next baulk and yanked. It weren't right. Just because she didn't understand things was no reason to laugh at her. She jumped as Kobb touched her elbow.

"We're not making fun of you. It's the idea of someone seeing all this and still saying I go bothering the Maker when I shouldn't," said Kobb.

"Suppose, that is a bit mad."

"Exactly. The Maker wants us to do this." Kobb held out the crossbow again. "This could have been crushed; but it wasn't scratched. The Maker wants it to be used."

Anessa stared at it for a moment, before lifting it from his hands. Kobb was right: first the tower, then the gantry, and it didn't need even restringing. She peered up at him sideways. "So, what does it mean if a man's hat gets smushed?"

Kobb snorted and gripped on the baulk.

Twilight was spent by the time they reached the bottom. Kobb settled into a cross-legged position in the centre. "I can feel it. Might be a rough trip though."

The ground fell away beneath Anessa. Flashes and odours assailed her, before something slammed into her chest.

A warm, wet breeze gusted across the side of her head. She rolled over, then froze. A giant maw, filled with blocky teeth hovered inches from her face.

"Falcon." Kobb wrapped himself around the beast's snout. "Good to see you too."

While the horse was distracted, Anessa scooted backwards and leapt to her feet. Five villagers lay on the churned snow nearby. "It worked. We saved them."

Haelen eased himself upright. "We dealt with the first problem. They're a long way from safe, though. Set up beds in the second tent. I'll watch over them and study the papers, while you two head out."

"We three." Kobb swept his arm around the patchy snow. "Falcon's uncovered what grass there was. We leave him here, he'll starve."

Or eat the tents. Along with everyone in them. Giving the beast a wide berth, Anessa stumbled into the sleeping tent. What to use as bedding?

By pressing every table and empty sack into service, she managed. Exhausted, Anessa collapsed until morning.

Still tired, she wandered in the direction of hot oats. Slumping beside Kobb, she pointed at a Stone. "That one."

"Are you sure?" Kobb stared at the fire. "Perhaps you should stay and help Haelen. Falcon and I'll investigate."

"I'm fine." She lowered her head to the spoon. "Wake up once I've had some porridge."

Bowl empty, she stood. Another portion would set her up, but there were five more mouths now. After collecting her weapons, she trudged over to Kobb. "Sooner we're off, sooner we're back."

Staring at her for a moment, he nodded. Falcon's reins in one hand, he led the way to the next stone.

The day unravelled around her.

Yet, the foulness was less this time, and her breakfast stayed down. She looked at the forest. Rain oozed through the gaps between branches. She'd been here before. Boots squelching, she jogged up the rise.

The ground dropped away to the west, trees thinning. And at the bottom of the hill, Morth. The stones had brought her home.

Part Thirty-Four

Kobb peered at Falcon's eyes, then ran his hands along Falcon's body. Falcon whickered amiably. Satisfied the transition hadn't upset his steed, Kobb considered the forest again.

Rain filtering through trees could be anywhere, but few sights would make Anessa forget her skills enough to stand on the skyline rather than in cover. The slight tremor in her otherwise rigid posture confirmed his fears were true: the stone had brought them to Morth. Keeping quiet had made sense when Haelen found the map. It still did once they knew what it meant: telling her would only have been a distraction from more immediate threats. With five stones unexplored, the chance the next one came here seemed low; so he'd decided to stay silent, just until they'd defeated enough evils that she trusted it could be done, trusted herself.

Anessa stepped down from the ridge. "Are Botherers allowed to lie? Or, supposed to always tell the truth?"

Kobb stared at the rotting leaf mould beneath his boots, glad his hat brim now drooped so low. "Lies hide what is. Deny people the path to see the Blessing. I should've..." He forced his gaze up.

Anessa kicked at the ground, hands clasped tight and face noticeably redder than usual even in the murk. "I tried... and then...."

"I understand. I—"

"You don't have to. All you ever do is save people. I wasn't thinking. And..." She began to sob.

Kobb stepped closer, trying to remember something from his training that might help.

Anessa lunged forward and grabbed his hands. "Can you forgive me? I didn't mean to say Botherer. Ain't right. But it just—" Another sob racked her. "I never asked what the proper name is."

Lost, he decided on a straight answer. "I follow the Way of Maker Guiding. Doctrinally, I am named Reverend Militant of the Order of the Maker. No one's used that in longer than I can remember, though, and there isn't anyone deserves to have to; especially not you. Mostly believers call themselves Guided." He squeezed her hands. "But saying I'm a Botherer doesn't... bother me. Haelen does it all the time. There's nothing to forgive."

Anessa let go, before scrubbing at her eyes with one hand. "If we tell Dad what we're doing, he won't let me help you."

"He allowed you to go with me last time."

She swung her arms, not meeting his eyes.

Kobb coughed. Why hadn't he listened harder to the pastoral lectures? "If you lie to him, won't that mean you think he shouldn't let you go?"

"Couldn't we find the evil and go?"

"You've seen what losing a child did to Haelen. Do you want your dad to wonder if he'll ever see you again? Whatever you tell him, don't turn down a chance to see him."

Anessa's shoulders slumped, but she nodded. "Seeing him would be a Blessing."

Kobb gathered up Falcon's reins and headed over the rise.

"Route's better if we swing south a bit and go in that way," said Anessa from behind him.

Kobb looked at the tangles of undergrowth to either side, then down the slope. The ground around the east gate seemed a little boggy. Nothing Falcon couldn't handle, though. Might even be easier than cutting across the between the trees. First impressions could deceive though, and Anessa hadn't lead him astray yet. Patting Falcon's nose, he swung left.

A long trudge later, wet, and spattered with leaf mould, they reached the south gate. A different watchman stuck his head out. Kobb braced himself to respond, but the youth just waved an arm at the open gate and withdrew into the hut. As the two of them entered, startled looks flickered between villagers and muttered conversations sprang up.

Anessa tensed. Before she could speak, Kobb rested a hand on her shoulder. "Nothing to heed. By the time we've spoken to your dad and cleaned up a bit, they'll have got over the shock."

The tension slid from Anessa, before returning threefold as Dereck Aycock swaggered between two buildings. For a moment, Kobb thought they hadn't been noticed, then Dereck pulled up and gawped at them.

"Well. Look what the Botherer brought back." Dereck ran his eyes across Anessa, tongue oozing over his lips. "Got bored of your—"

Dereck's bravado collapsed as a sharp-eyed, wiry woman, greying around the temples, pinched his ear and twisted. "I slapped you the moment you came into the world, Dereck Aycock; don't you go thinking I won't do it again till it sticks. No doubt you got somewhere you should be, so best not dawdle, eh?"

"No, Goodie Weaver." As soon as her grip eased, Dereck scurried away.

"You'd best not dawdle neither, Anessa Tanton."

Anessa blanched, then set off to her father's shop at speed.

Deciding not to risk tipping his hat, Kobb followed.

Lambart Tanton looked up when they entered, smile dying half-formed. "My thanks for bringing her safe back, Reverend. You'll have most of the day left if you start now, so I'll not keep you."

"I ain't staying, Dad." Anessa held her arms out. "I'm right glad to see you, but once we're done here, I going with Kobb. There's things that ain't right, and he shouldn't have to fix it all."

Lambart stepped closer, then drew her into a hug. Anger, joy, and sadness fought across his face. "Not saying he's not a good man, Nessy. But it's best to let Botherers alone."

Anessa broke free of her father. Eyes glistening, she shoved him away. "Ain't Botherers. It's Guided. And, if Kobb can't stay cos o'that, then I can't neither. Cos I'm one too!"

Kobb eased himself away from them. For a soul to see the path was a Blessing to be celebrated, but to show it now would only fan the flames.

"You always did take after her." Lambart shook his head and shuffled into the storeroom, leaving Anessa standing red faced and shaking. A moment later, he returned with a long Hessian bundle. "Planned to give you this next Maker's Day. Better you have it now. It was your Grandam's."

Wide steel quillons caught the lamplight as Anessa lifted the sacking away. "A sword? Grandam owned a sword? But..."

"Those stories she told about dangerous beasts. Not all of 'em were exaggerations. She said this blade kept her safe. Maybe it'll do the same, if..." Lambart sagged down onto a pile of sacks.

Anessa dropped the bundle and wrapped herself around her dad. "I never meant it. I thought I'd just be gone a few days. You could come with us. Couldn't he, Kobb?"

Kobb nodded. He could. He wouldn't, but he could. "Been a while since I used anything besides a rapier. I think I remember the drills. After we clean up, I'll—"

The door slammed against the wall behind him as Goodie Weaver ran in. "You best get out of here. Tremaine Aycock's on his way with his cronies. And I don't reckon a busted belt's going to stop him this time."

PART THIRTY-FIVE

Kobb stepped into the doorway. The gossiping groups had gone, those villagers who were visible hugging the buildings. But a growing murmur still undercut the hiss of the rain. "Best belt your sword on, Anessa. Keep it sheathed, though. No cause to escalate this."

"You don't have to face them at all." Lambart tugged on Anessa's arm. "Go out the back door. Leave the village. Goodie'll bring your horse to you by the north gate."

Kobb turned to Lambart. If it did become bloody, it would be better if Anessa weren't there. But, even if she agreed to leave, she'd sneak back the first chance she got unless he went with her; and he couldn't creep away. "They don't see us, they'll tear the shop apart anyway; maybe use the same excuse to ransack other people's homes. Meet them in the street, we keep innocents out of this. Might even make them think twice."

"You can't drag my Anessa into—"

Anessa pulled free. "It's time someone stood up to the east-siders. Aycock and the others've been treating people like muck for too long."

Kobb returned to the doorway as the murmuring broke into separate voices. "Don't intend to make a fight of it. We'll leave the village if we need to. But it's too late to sneak out anyway."

"Tanton!" Tremaine Aycock stopped in the middle of the street, right hand resting on the pommel of the sword on his belt. Dereck, Osraed, and five other villagers clustered behind him. Each carried an axe or other tool, rusty yet still dangerous. "Surrender the criminals and we'll go easy on you."

Lambart moved next to Kobb and picked up the door bar. His face indicated determination; however, the tremble in his arms suggested determination wouldn't be enough.

Kobb cursed silently. The east-siders hated him. But they didn't know what he was. Draw the Courser and drop Tremaine. Shoot the girl with the mattock before he hit the ground. The man with the turf hook next. Three dead and the group split before they knew what happened. Without a leader, they'd break. But that ease was the problem: they wouldn't fear him until after, three souls too late. He stepped into the street. "It's me you've issue with. I'll give myself up if you promise to leave the Tantons alone."

"No." Anessa rushed out the door. "You ain't done anything wrong."

The corners of Tremaine's mouth rose, but his eyes remained hard. "It's too late for that anyway. Lambart shows he ain't tainted, maybe we say he was just confused. But you've been with this man. He's put his corruption in you."

Kobb spoke before Anessa could react. "Seems we've an impasse then."

Pushing to the front, Dereck pointed his axe at Kobb. "Even if Tanton don't give up the whore, there's more than enough of us to end you here."

"Still can't count." Anessa's eyes were blazing, but she hadn't—Kobb was glad to see—touched her sword. "Everyone knows east-siders ain't worth half a real person. So, it's you don't have enough."

Lambart lowered the door bar to the ground as Goodie moved up beside him. After straightening, he swept his right arm around the street. "Whatever happens today, we've got to work together tomorrow. So let's talk it through, eh?"

"I'm a reasonable man." Tremaine's grin still didn't reach his eyes. "The Botherer gives himself up, I'll give you till dawn to pack up your shop and take her somewhere she don't offend decent people."

"Reasonable?" Anessa's hand dropped to her sword hilt. "I've met Eaters more reasonable than you. Better looking too."

"You'll soon learn your place once your boyfriends dead." Dereck lunged forward, axe raised.

Kobb shifted his weight. His left hand grabbed the descending weapon and yanked. His right smashed into Dereck's face. Axe and Aycock tumbled in opposite directions, landing with a splut.

Dereck pushed up on his elbows before collapsing back in the mud. Several of the east-siders sidled backwards, improvised weapons drooping.

Tremaine muttered something brittle and angular. For a moment, his eyes seemed to gleam despite the murky light. The east-siders squared their shoulders and gripped the tools tighter. After hanging his turf hook on his belt, Osraed helped Dereck up.

Tremaine hawked a ball of filth at Anessa's feet. "Lambart's right. No cause to go killing each other. If all three of you leave by sundown and don't come back, we won't chase you. You don't, we do this the hard way." Radiating false reasonableness, he turned on his heel and led his followers away.

Kobb's shoulders slumped. "Lambart. Best if you packed what you can. If I can't sort this by dark, you'll need to leave."

"Leave?" Anessa gazed at him wide-eyed. "We beat 'em twice. If anything, they're the ones need to leave."

"Most of them are cowards. But Tremaine's different. Those words he said that stiffened the others up. Don't know enough to understand them, but I've heard that sort of thing before. Something dark's touched him. He knows he can't scare us and can't win fair, so now he'll win any way he can."

"He's right, Anessa." Goodie rubbed Anessa's back. "Tremaine Aycock don't lose. Only reason he lives that side of Morth is cos he chose to. Don't know about dark things, but there've always been rumours about the Aycocks."

"Well, Kobb's wrong on one thing," said Anessa. "He ain't going to sort this by dusk. We are."

Goodie grabbed Anessa's chin and stared into her eyes. "Don't be an idiot, girl. Help your father. Leave it to the Reverend to do—"

"I know what needs doing." Anessa's shoulders shook but her voice was steady. "It's like when Roblin's herd got the frothing sickness."

Lambart gasped. "Anessa. You can't—"

She ignored him "That weren't over till we found the Corpse Breath growing in Back Pond. Driving the Aycock's out'd feel good. But we need to find out what the darkness is."

Kobb forced himself to smile. Dealing with the hidden source would stop the corruption. But once they went onto the east-siders' territory, Aycock wouldn't have to worry about hiding his power; and fighting people you'd known your whole life was very different from facing monsters. Known all your life... "The east-siders have been like that for years? It isn't recent?"

Anessa's eyes widened.

Part Thirty-Six

Kobb let his gaze drift around the street as he waved the others into the store. "Tell me more about the east-siders."

"Soil on the east edge of the village ain't good for growing. The folks live over that side... well, some wonder why you'd choose to." Goodie pursed her lips. "There's four families: Aycocks, Corlesses, Beekses, and Whellers. Sort of keep to themselves. But there's plenty of kin by marriage both ways so ain't exactly separate. Credit where it's due, they work hard, maybe harder than others would; and they're always the first to volunteer if there's rumours of bandits or a wild beast lurking about. Trouble is Aycock knows it."

"Plenty of people are hard workers," said Anessa. "Don't mean they go round telling others what to do."

Lambart wrapped an arm around his daughter. "We ain't saying they're right. It ain't that simple, though. Maybe the village'd get by without the lumber, and others could do more shifts on the gates; not having to's easier, though. Maybe folks don't agree with everything Tremaine wants, but reckon it don't affect them much."

"But—"

"Didn't hear you offering to stand watch instead of go into the forest every day."

"Hunting's working. And I'm better than any east-sider at tracking beasts."

Lambart shared a glance with Goodie. "I ain't saying weren't worthwhile, but you had the time cos east-siders did more than their share of other things."

"Same as everywhere," Kobb said. "Most people will let the Legion protect them, yet don't want their children joining up. Right or wrong, it means most of the villagers won't actively help them but we can't expect support unless we find something definite. So, we need a plan."

"Can't you..." Anessa glanced at his Courser and back up. "...feel it out?"

"Given time. But I don't think Aycock'll let me wander around the village with my eyes closed."

Lambart frowned. "What is it you're looking for?"

"Can't say for certain. Some sort of focus for the darkness."

"Well, they all heed Aycock, and he's not one to share," Lambart said. "So, likely it's safe in his house."

Goodie shook her head. "Been a while since I goodwifed Dereck, but don't recall anything odd about the place. Wouldn't evil have stood out, Reverend?"

"Powerful enough to make that many obey? Usually." Kobb sighed. "But if east-siders've been here for years, I fear this is more subtle. We'll have to search. At least the ground's boggy, so we needn't worry about cellars and tunnels."

"If they want us to leave, why don't we?" Before Kobb could question Anessa's sudden reverse, she winked. "Least far enough they can't see us. Then we sneak in the side they ain't expecting."

Between all the ties of marriage and the us-against-outsiders mentality of villages, knocking in doors wouldn't work for long anyway; and pretending to leave might make the east-siders drop their guard. "Agreed. It'll take time though, so best hope we're right about Tremaine wanting to keep it close."

"Wait." Goodie grabbed Kobb's elbow. "Tremaine moved after Wilber, that's his dad's accident. Built a new house when the old man passed on."

"And that was when the east-siders drew in?"

"No. They were always odd. Wilber falling in the ravine just changed which of 'em does the ruling. Although, Wilber's death were the start of them not calling on me to lay out the dead."

Simple murder or the shift into something else? "Anything unusual about the place he fell?"

"Ain't ever been." Anessa blinked. "Nothing worth hunting around there."

"Could be a reason for that." Kobb picked up his saddlebags. "Lambart packs while the two of us head out the gate, swing into the forest to this ravine, then sneak back in if we don't find the source."

Lambart grabbed his daughter's shoulders and pulled her close. "You be safe, now, Nessy. First sign of—"

Anessa broke free. "Don't get weepy. I'll see you soon as we've sorted this."

"It's... since your mother... You keep her safe, Reverend. Promise me that."

Before Kobb could respond, Goodie poked Lambart in the arm. "Don't you go asking Reverend for promises. You want her safe, give those east-siders something to keep their beady eyes busy." She turned to Kobb and nodded once.

Kobb inclined his head to her before striding out and settling his saddlebags onto Falcon. Without a brim to repel it, the rain had already annexed his neck. Pretending to pay no mind to the nearby villagers, he called back into the shop. "We'll head on and set camp. Only bring what you can carry."

Face a mixture of fear and determination, Lambart leaned out the doorway. "I'll borrow Harlan's hand cart. It's you should be getting on. Get my daughter out of here."

Kobb forced himself not to smile. Lambart pitched his voice loud enough to cross the street. He might not be a mighty hero, but he could sell a story.

Grabbing up Falcon's reins, Kobb headed for the south gate. Anessa stomped at his side, shoulders up and jaw set. With luck, people would take it for anger at having to leave.

Fortunately, the rain worsened as they left the village behind. Sneaking through the forest was unpleasant, but the closing gloom helped hide them and reduce the chance anyone else was out. Soaked and tired from struggling through mud and undergrowth, they reached the ravine without incident.

After resting Falcon's reins over a nearby branch, Kobb gestured for Anessa to lead the way. The gloom of the day drew in as they crept between the mossy rock walls, giving everything a leaden cast.

"Dead end. He must have landed back aways." Anessa turned the way they came. "We missed it in the rain."

"Landed?"

"Dad said he got to close to the edge and slipped. Hillside crumblesin places. 'Nother good reason not to go in this bit of the forest."

Kobb peered up. "A reason not to—? That makes sense. Someone falls, you don't stay away from where they landed; you stay away from where they fell. We need to be up there."

Anessa studied the ravine walls for a moment. "We go round. Uses up time, but less likely to fall."

Clambering up what Anessa declared a safe slope was enough to leave him gasping on a good day; after a morning of forcing his way through the sodden undergrowth, Kobb's lungs plain refused to keep time. Black spots fighting the weather for which could obscure his vision the most, he half-collapsed on the false crest.

Anessa crouched next to him. "Something's off. No sign of felling."

"If it's... not safe..."

"Aycock must have been up here for a reason. And not just him. Over there."

Spasms passing, Kobb eased himself up. Trees. Undergrowth. "I don't —"

"Someone's trimmed those trees."

Now he knew what to look for, he saw it. The overlapping tangle of branches started at six feet up. He'd thought that was how these trees grew, but there were small stumps on the trunks; too many to have broken off naturally. The undergrowth filled it now; someone kept a path clear at some point, though. "Good eyes. If anyone's there, they'd have heard me climbing, so let's not waste time."

Courser and rapier in hands, Kobb staggered along the remains of the track. A few yards further on, the going improved as the brambles thinned, replaced with flaccid bracken. Soon after, they emerged into an overhung clearing. In the centre, a stump jutted through the gloom.

"Cut wood?" Anessa's brow furrowed. "How'd you even get the trunk out?"

Kobb looked around. The lower limbs weren't cut away on the other trees, so this must be where the path ended. The overhanging branches and close sides suggested a rude temple. Yet, no foul miasmas mixed with the stench of rotten bracken and the darkness was only that of dense woodland in bad weather. If the source of the evil was here, it rested.

"This stump's thinner than the others." Anessa gestured at the massive trunks looming around them. "There still ain't space for a tree though. They must've cut it down before this all grew. But that'd be..."

Kobb joined her in the centre. "How long have Korha been only myths? How old is the stone circle? Seems Wilber Aycock kept this place open, doesn't mean he made it." He studied the stump. The top was almost flat; but sloped on the edges, and the wood changed colour. "You know enough about felling to say what did that?"

Anessa crouched down. "Top looks fresher, and... don't reckon this were done with an axe."

Kobb huffed in resignation. The tree had been carved into an icon or statue but someone had cut it away. "Axe'd be fastest. Only reason you wouldn't, is to avoid damaging it. Tremaine wanted to keep it close badly enough he sawed it free."

"Least we know we're looking for a wooden thing." Anessa rose to her feet. "I've been think though. Wilber's house is still there, empty. What if Tremaine built a new one so he could use his dad's for whatever he's up to?"

Kobb grimaced. Hiding a temple by building a house around it made sense, but so did using an empty property. If the old one was abandoned, it would be easier to search without interruption. But, even if the weather kept all the east-siders inside so the two of them didn't have to sneak, there wasn't time to be wrong.

Part Thirty-Seven

Kobb scanned the clearing again. Nothing visible suggested where the statue had been taken, and—even if there were clues beneath the bracken—searching would use up more time than it saved. "How would you sneak it into Morth?"

"Like Dad said, the Aycock's supporters do most of the guard duty. And no one visits them unless they've good reason. So, 'less someone noticed you through the trees, easy to bring stuff in the east gate without anyone knowing."

Kobb grimaced. He'd hoped the available routes might narrow it down. "So, once it was dark, they could move the statue anywhere they wanted. Anything else happen around the time Tremaine built his house?"

"Happened before I were born." Anessa frowned. "Don't recall, Dad ever mentioning nothing either."

"If this place weren't what he needed, Wilber could have moved the statue to his house any time he wanted. So, it seems more likely Tremaine built a hidden temple in his new house."

Anessa headed for the path out. "Makes sense."

After a final glance around, Kobb followed her. Eminently reasonable. Unfortunately, worship of dark powers wasn't the act of reasonable people.

"What about Falcon? No way to sneak him in."

"He'll be fine there till night. If we're not finished by then, well, hooking the reins over a branch is only a polite request not to wander off."

Anessa pursed her lips for a moment, before heading along the top of the ravine. A few hundred yards later, they reached a thin track that Kobb thought he recognised from their journey in that morning. Blessings were strange things. If they'd swung south straight away, they might have passed close enough to the temple that they assumed the area wasn't worth investigating.

Cutting across, Anessa slipped into the tangled undergrowth. Glad only his hat had lost its vim, Kobb pushed after her. The thorns grew taller as he pressed on, catching at his arms and chest; he was glad of the resistance as the hill sloped steeper, though.

Thighs aching, he broke free onto level yet marshy ground. The rain redoubled its attempt to reach his boots the long way round. Foul water oozed up with each step as he crept across to the fence.

As he pressed against it, Anessa lent in. "Watch box faces up the path, so won't see us. Might hear something if we're not lucky... I mean Blessed, though"

Kobb nodded, knowing as well as she did that his lack of skill posed the biggest risk but glad she hadn't mentioned it all the same. Rolling the tension out of his shoulders, he squelched after her again.

The weather, defying the promise of shelter, seemed to become worse. The daylight melted into leaden slurry. If he hadn't been looking for it, he'd have missed the spill of the watchman's lantern altogether. Knowing a sudden gasp carried further and caught the ear more, he forced himself not to hold his breath as the two of them slipped through the gate.

Curtains of rain gushed over crude windows, both raising the spectre of unseen watchers and tempting Kobb to assume no one would see him. Trusting Anessa to avoid trouble, he focused on seeking tiny hints of more than mundane unpleasantness in his surroundings.

A few yards further on, Anessa ducked into a narrow alley between two houses. Glancing ahead as he followed her, Kobb say Dereck trudging along the street. An acrid whiff of decay mixed with something else rose up from beneath Kobb's feet. Reminding himself that whatever it was wasn't the worst his boots had faced, he sneaked deeper into the alley. Through the murk, he saw Anessa silhouetted against the far end.

Certain he was deep enough not to be seen from behind, he felt the tightness in his shoulders slacken. Only to return as light spilled across the street, before fading as a shadow stretched over it. Copying Anessa, he froze.

"Foul day, innum," called out a voice ahead.

Anessa took a step back, before freezing again. The pounding of rain filled Kobb's ears as the silhouette shifted. The light cut off. The inhabitant must have—

"No use skulking. I know 'es there."

As Anessa backed towards him, Kobb turned and headed the way he'd come. Behind him, he heard a fist hammering on wood followed by heavy boots splashing through muck.

Before Kobb reached the far end of the alley, the sounds of pursuit grew to include a hue-and-cry. His hand dropped to the hilt of his rapier as he emerged. Dereck stood, half-turned, between the alley and the east gate. To the west, the first doors were already opening. Kobb flicked his blade free and spun into the middle of the street.

Anessa burst from the mouth of the alley, a hulking shape hard on her heels.

Spinning his weapon in the hope it would discourage her pursuer, Kobb considered his options. With another trained warrior, he could have held them off till it was too dark to fight; but, for all her competence,

Anessa didn't have the instincts to cover half the arc. Proving his concern valid, instead of using her lead to get clear, she turned on her heel and pulled her sword free.

The thug's mouth froze in mid-bellow as he skidded to a halt, leaving himself open to attack.

Anessa struck with the flat of her blade. But, whether through inexperience or memory of the hunter's head shattering, she pulled the blow at the last minute.

Showing no similar hesitation, the hulking villager swung one fist at her face.

She twisted away, but not fast enough. Instead of her cheek, the knuckles caught her ear. Still upright, she lost her bearings for a moment.

The thug raised his fists and lunged forward.

More east-siders approached from all directions, most clutching tools or farm implements. Kobb adopted a more defensive stance. He could fend the other villagers off or protect Anessa, not both. As long as she—

Anessa's opponent slammed her blade aside with one shoulder and slammed his other fist into her stomach.

Legs folding, she tumbled backwards.

Kobb's free hand settled onto his Courser as the thug snatched up her fallen sword.

"No!" Dereck shook off his surprise. Goggling for a moment at all the people now staring at him, he swallowed hard. "I mean, Dad will want to talk to them."

The hulking east-sider twitched Anessa's blade towards her, then lowered it to his side. Sticking it through his belt, he leered down at Anessa. "Your face, girl. Young Aycock's right. Wouldn't end you here." He gave a phlegmy chortle. "Might wish I had though."

Kobb sheathed his rapier and raised both hands. They might be obnoxious, criminals even, but the only one he knew was corrupted was

Tremaine. He couldn't deal with this many without leaving at least a few dead or close to. And unless the east-siders tried to kill someone first, that would be murder.

"Tie their hands." Dereck lacked his father's air of authority, but the east-siders rushed forward anyway. "And take the Botherer's weapons."

Part Thirty-Eight

Anessa gritted her teeth as Heb Beeks yanked her arm up her back. The east-siders might have got lucky, but she was determined not to give them the satisfaction of seeing her react. The downside of her plan was not talking to Kobb either. Behind her, breath exploded from someone's body. She twisted her head round, grin forming. Only to slump at the sight of Kobb, arms bound behind his back, folded over Dereck's fist.

Dereck worked his fingers for a moment, face creased up. "Bring them."

Another jag of pain ran across Anessa's shoulder as Heb lifted her arm again. Stumbling ahead of him on tiptoes, she headed for Tremaine's house. Dereck slouched next to her, close enough his breath stroked her face each time he leered at her. She should find the Blessing in this. Inside would be drier and warmer than the street and they wanted to go there anyway. Discovering and appreciating turned out to be different though.

Dereck threw open the front door and strode in. Anessa couldn't do anything to stop herself following, but did choose not to wipe her feet.

"Guests, Dereck?" Tremaine stood at the top of the stairs, one arm resting on the bannister. "How pleasant. Do come in Mr Kobb. I'd offer you a warm drink; you need to be getting on though."

"I'm sure we can spare the time," said Kobb, voice strained yet level. "Maybe you could give us a tour of your home? I hear it has a few intriguing features."

"Didn't know you liked carpentry, Mr Kobb." Tremaine strolled down the stairs. "The day is getting on though. You both should see my father's house before you depart."

Dereck wrapped an arm around Anessa's waist. "I've got her. You grab the Botherer, Heb."

"No, Dereck." Tremaine moved closer. "I need you to check Tanton's packing."

"But, Dad—"

"Now."

Dereck stepped back, fingers oozing down before sliding free. Holding hard to her plan of not giving people satisfaction, Anessa stayed still.

"Don't fear you'll miss all the little things only an Aycock knows. I'll take you myself." Tremaine rested a hand on her elbow. Despite Kobb's insight that Tremaine was the corrupt one, part of her felt glad it was him, not Dereck.

Anessa shivered as they left. She'd been inside long enough to start warming up, but not long enough to dry out, so the rain picked up where it stopped. Each step renewed the smell of soggy muck; at least she'd trodden that over Tremaine's floor. Although, he was an east-sider, so he probably didn't care about filth.

Unable to wipe her eyes, the journey melted into murk. She waited for Kobb to make his move, but—if he did try to signal—the torrent washed it away; and all too soon they reached Wilber's house.

When she blinked straight at it, nothing differed from the houses to either side. But as she ran her gaze across the walls, tatters of gloom seemed to creep in at the edges. Despite the lack of mould, it brought Alcston to mind.

Tremaine swung the door open with is free hand. Grinning, he swept his arm out in mockery of a polite invitation. Before Anessa could decide whether to resist or not, he yanked her over the threshold.

The stench of hot fat bubbled up as she staggered in. Light flickered ahead, but not enough to make anything out. Another tug sent her stumbling to her left. Something struck her shoulder, sending her sprawling on her face.

As she rolled onto her back, a dark shape hit the floor next to her.

"My apologies for the lack of beds," said Tremaine. "But, then you'll be sacrificed at midnight, so you won't miss them."

Sacrificed? Anessa glared into the murk. Tremaine was just visible in the doorway. "You can't. People won't let you kill—"

"The two of you left this morning. If anyone give it a thought, they'll think you got lost in the forest. Reminds them what happens if you listen to outsiders." The door closed on his chuckle.

"Kobb? What now? We have to do something."

"We consider what we've learnt. Seems certain the statue's here and the source of the evil with it. Midnight's not for a while, so—" Kobb fell silent as a plank creaked nearby. The door eased open and a dark figure slipped through.

"Should've gone when you had the chance," said Dereck.

"Go kiss a wolf," screamed Anessa.

Dereck raised his hands. "Ain't no way to talk to a childhood friend. Ain't too late to fix things neither."

"Friend? You ain't never been a friend. People'll hug horse dung 'fore they spend time with you."

"You don't mean that. It's the Botherer, messed with your head." Dereck kicked Kobb in the ankle. "Promise you'll tell everyone the sick things he made you do, and I'll convince Dad to let you stay in Morth."

"Sick things? Kobb ain't the one wants to sacrifice us. It's you east-siders who are sick!"

"You're lying. My Dad ain't sick. He's protecting us from all that evil outsiders bring. Might be a bit rough, but that's the only way to keep us pure!" Swinging his boot at Kobb again and missing, Dereck stormed out, slamming the door behind him.

Kobb made a light tutting sound. "Might be worth you playing along when he comes back. Least on of us would be free. He'd let you go if you asked, Father's permission or not."

"I'm not leaving you." Anessa paused. "What do you mean, Dereck'd let me go?"

"Not saying he wouldn't come sniffing after you." Kobb chuckled. "What it is to be young. He likes you."

"He don't! He hates me. Those things he called me. And staring at me sideways, like I got something dirty stuck on me. He tried to throw me in the slurry pit when I were six."

"That clinches it. Bet he put bugs in your hair too. It's not dirt he's peering at."

Heat rushed up her neck. She was suddenly glad of the murk. "But…"

"Feeling something and knowing the right thing to do are different things. Bullying might be the only way he knows to make anyone notice him. Gossiping about your young suitor isn't getting us free though. If I roll over, can you reach the knot?"

Young suitor? Kobb acted like it wasn't creepy. He thought it was funny. Dereck had punched Kobb in the stomach, so why'd Kobb—? To distract her from the danger, keep her spirits up. Even now, he thought of others. She twisted onto her side and fumbled behind her.

She could feel the knot, but the rain had swelled the cord. Her fingers ached by the time she gave up. Without seeing it, she had no hope. But maybe they didn't need to undo it. The entire house smelt uncared-for.

There might be something to cut their bonds on: a nail or the edge of a broken plank.

She explained her idea. Bracing each other, the two of them wriggled around until they sat against the wall. Sliding her back up, she stood then stepped sideways and sank down to a crouch while Kobb did the same in the opposite direction. The combination of repetition and darkness stole her sense of movement, making the change in texture a surprise.

For a moment, her spirits lifted. But there wasn't a handle on this side. Two shuffles later, she discovered the hinges were too flat to catch the cord, let alone break it.

As she turned the second corner, a door closed nearby, followed by a creak in the corridor. Kobb's shuffling stopped. Forcing down her disgust, she tried to think of something pleasant to say to Dereck.

The door swung open and a dark figure entered.

"Suppose you always did your share." Anessa curved the corners of her mouth up in case he could see.

"How kind of you," said Tremaine. "I'm early. But I thought you'd want time to look at the knives and the altar. Really understand what's going to happen." Two bulky shadows stepped through the door behind him.

Part Thirty-Nine

Anessa twisted her head away. Being in near Heb at all had been bad enough, but the narrow corridor focused the stink, making the scent of rotten meat almost solid. As he dragged her forward, she threw herself back and forth, trying to pull free of Heb's grasp. She wasn't sure what she'd do with her hands still tied; silent compliance hadn't achieved much, though, and if nothing else—recapturing her'd waste their time.

Hawking something that was—fortunately—too dark to make out, Heb lifted her off the ground and continued towards the dim light. Ahead, Tremaine lifted a curtain, increasing both the dirty glow and the stench of the burning fat. The spill of light revealed the second thug, the one dragging Kobb, as Coraed Wheller.

Still refusing to give up, Anessa flailed her boots against Heb's legs. He grunted with each blow, strides now staggers, but followed the others through the curtain. Anessa's struggles stopped as her gaze flicked around the large room on the other side.

Soggy mud stretched across the interior, and fat-filled lamps spattered light across damp wooden walls. A pit gaped in the centre, eight feet wide. Before it, several rough-hewn posts jutted up with lengths of dirty rope tied to them. And beyond, two filthy curtains hung over who knew what.

Kobb's voice echoed. "Maker of All, make of me the vessel of your Blessings. Let your—"

One hand clutched to his head, Tremaine hammered his knee into Kobb's gut. Pulling a rag from his coat, he dabbed at his nose and ears. New dark stains joined old dirt. Kobb's words'd made him bleed. But how?

After one last wipe, Tremaine twisted the cloth into a rope. Forcing it between Kobb's lips, he knotted the ends.

Anessa struggled to recall Kobb saying the same prayer before. As Tremaine turned, she realised it might not matter. She hadn't needed special words in the insect's lair, just the right ones. "Maker. We're in a bad place, but ain't nothing you can't make good. So show me how to do it."

Tremaine spun to face her. Eyes wide, he gave a throaty gurgle.

Anessa's back straightened and her head rose. Before she could continue praying, Tremaine's gurgling grew into a jagged chuckle. Holding his arms out and tilting at the waist, he gave her a shallow bow. He locked eyes with her as he straightened, laughter ending as if it'd never been. "You have spirit. He'll enjoy the taste of that. But you aren't special like Mr Kobb. He'll be better than years of sheep."

Tremaine strolled around the pit and drew the curtain on the right. "Promised you I'd let you see, though."

Anessa peered into the alcove beyond. A shape, roughly human but slightly bigger than life size, squatted on a tall chair. The light was too poor for details; it looked rough like bark or hacked wood, though. Despite her plight, she felt a brush of disappointment; after meeting the Korha and the insects, she'd expected the statue to be more frightening.

Bowing once toward the figure, a full bow rather than the mocking ones from before, Tremaine drew the other curtain. A waist-high table filled the rear of a second alcove. Another roughly human shape, this one much cruder and only three feet tall, stood at the back of the table, flanked by two pots.

Tremaine bowed again then lifted a tray from in front of the statue. Something caught the light as he turned. "Tie them to the posts. One at each end so they've a good view."

Heb wrapped his arms around Anessa's waist and shuffled right. Despite her making no effort to kick him, his gait seemed stiff.

Meanwhile, Coraed dragged Kobb to the far post and slammed him against it. Kobb slumped as if only the post stopped him falling. Grinning, Coraed let go and reached for one of the ropes.

Rising up and twisting at the same time, Kobb drove his left shoulder forward.

Caught off guard, Coraed staggered back.

Pretence of exhaustion gone, Kobb spun, his right foot slamming down on Coraed's.

Tremaine dropped the tray onto the table and sprinted around the pit.

"Best keep a good hold on you." Keeping his left arm in place, Heb slid the other up until it rested on her chest. Hand fumbling at her jacket, he ran his tongue across her right ear.

Anessa shuddered and tried to twist away.

Breath roughening further, Heb moved round to give his hand better access.

But also opening a larger gap between their bodies. Reaching back, Anessa clawed her hands and squeezed.

Dirty trousers gave no protection. Gut kicking in, Heb jerked away, hands flying to his groin.

Fighting against his stubby fingers, Anessa pressed harder and tugged.

A ragged moan slipped from Heb. After another attempt to pry her free, he raised both arms and hammered his fists down. Unhampered by cord and much stronger, he tore her hands free.

Anessa stumbled forward, expecting an attack. But—instead of cursing or blows—only a creaky judder came from behind her. Before she could take advantage of Heb's discomfort, a rank and angular shout spewed across the room.

The air around her fractured, cold absence oozing out of the cracks and into her limbs. As the chill clawed at her bones, she found she couldn't move. Only the tight bands wrapped through her chest stopped her screaming.

Then something shifted in the right alcove.

A body halfway between flesh and wood unfolded and lurched forward. As the dirty light flowed across its face, the shadows made a new pattern. The eyes were more sunken and the mouth a jagged crack; the resemblance to Tremaine was inescapable, though.

"Your weakness angers Him." The figure's voice slid into her ears like treacle and sand. "If these escape, I will take His dues from you."

"Rest, father." Tremaine faced Wilber. "I'll deal with this. You need your strength for later."

"Foul lusts. Distraction. He demands punishment." More sounds—but nothing Anessa's ears accepted—followed. A sound like ice giving way came from behind her. Something thudded into the mud as Heb's moans cut off.

"Mercy, Elder." Coraed said, the tang of piss joining the stench of burnt fat. "We'll—"

From the corner of her eye, Anessa made out Kobb twisting free of the distracted east-siders, and heading for the door. Only to stumble into view again a breath later.

Dereck strode into view, her crossbow braced at his shoulder.

Part Forty

Kobb backed towards the altar. A bolt to the vitals would be a clean death compared to what the two elder Aycocks intended; from the way Dereck's hands shook though, he could as easily be left crippled yet alive.

"Well done," gurgled Wilber. "I told you Dereck deserved initiation. Maybe my grandson can make up for your mistakes."

"Grandson?" Dereck's aim swung right to point at Wilber before twitching back to cover Kobb. "What is that? How did it—?"

Tremaine frowned at his son. "Bow to your grandfather. The God made him strong, as he will make me in my time."

"God? You mean like...?" Dereck spat towards Kobb.

"No." Wilber spread his arms and stepped into the light. "A true god. One who shares. One who gives us power and will give us more."

Dereck glared at the former man. "This is the secret? Dad said was about keeping Morth pure. Stopping outsiders stealing what's ours. Not becoming some... some monster!"

The crossbow twanged. Dereck looked down, as if unsure what he'd done.

Wilber collapsed to his knees, fingers around the bolt embedded his stomach.

Angular words lashed out of Tremaine's mouth. Dereck moaned as purple fire constricted around him.

Seeing a slim chance, Kobb grabbed the knife from the altar and sprinted towards Wilber.

Wilber's eyes cracked wide as he realised Kobb's intent. However, years of being master over hunters and foresters was no preparation for facing a trained warrior.

Left hand slamming down on Wilber's right wrist, Kobb flicked his right arm into the gap. Dark fluid, more black than red, spurted as Wilber's throat opened.

The blade spun in Kobb's hand, as his arm reversed direction.

Knife jutting between his shoulders, Wilber collapsed forward.

The sound of flesh hitting flesh came from behind Kobb and Tremaine's chanting fell silent. Kobb turned.

Dereck lay on the ground, fingers clasped across his mouth. Tremaine stood in the other side of the pit, his eyes tinged purple.

As Tremaine unleashed the curse, Anessa slammed into his back.

Caught by surprise, Tremaine staggered forward. Soil crumbled beneath his weight. Fingers grabbing at the air and magic replaced by a wordless gasp, he tumbled into the pit.

A breath later, Tremaine's shout ended with a wet crack.

Leaving Anessa to overcome the last of their captors, Kobb peered at Wilber. There were no signs of life, but how long had he sat in the alcove without moving? And how much had the power changed him? Kobb reached for the knife. Best to be sure.

The stench of burning fat boiled up as dirty orange light flared across the room. Kobb dropped and rolled.

The expected heat didn't come, though. He straightened. Flamed wreathed the altar. Next to it, Dereck, still swaying from the blow to his head, tugged at a second lamp.

On the far side of the pit, Anessa, crossbow in one hand, wrestled with the other east-sider. Kobb circled the pit, one eye out for loose soil. Before he reached them, the man broke free and sprinted for the door.

A wall of heat bubbled up as Dereck dropped the second lamp almost at his feet. Flames surged around him. He staggered past the burning altar, seeming intent on adding more lamps to the flame.

Kobb grabbed Anessa's shoulder as she lunged for Dereck. "We have to leave him."

"If we're quick, the flames won't–" Anessa broke off as Kobb yanked her towards the door.

He understood Anessa's instinct to save Dereck, even commended it. But he hadn't meant they might be burned. The power could pass through blood, and Dereck had been born after Tremaine became the public face of the cult: Dereck was tainted. However much Dereck hated what his grandfather had become, the magic answered emotions; every time his life didn't go the way he wanted brought a chance he'd let it loose. Once he did, it was only be a matter of time until he decided he could control it; that he wouldn't become the monster.

As they staggered from the building, Anessa twisted free of Kobb's grip. Her frown of accusation melted away as she saw the east-siders rushing towards them, led by their former captor. Grinning, she ran for Tremaine's house.

The east-siders, intent on the smoke oozing from the temple, ignored Kobb as he jogged after her.

Anessa stopped outside Tremaine's house. She hung her head for a moment before meeting his gaze. "Sorry. You knew Coraed'd bring help. You meant we leave them to rescue Dereck so we can get our stuff back."

Kobb stepped past and opened the door. Leaving Dereck to die was the right thing to do; that didn't make it any easier to live with, though. "You've nothing to apologise for."

Everything still rested on the side table where the east-siders had left it. Whether through fear or a desire to gloat for longer, Tremaine had returned to the temple without putting it away.

Weapons back in their proper place, the two of them headed for Lambart's store. Despite the clumps of villagers chattering and pointing at the wisps of smoke, Lambart continued to pile sacks into a wagon. Several of the groups muttered louder as Kobb crossed the street.

Anessa sprinted forward. "Dad. We're safe."

A sack of oatmeal spilled as Lambart spun and gathered Anessa up. "Nessy. I thought... Thank you, Reverend."

"Your daughter saved me as much as I saved her."

Anessa hugged her dad closer. "We beat the Aycocks. You can stay now."

"Maybe." Lambart stepped away, face serious. "But you need to go, both of you. Things might calm down and you can come back. But the Reverend's an outsider, and - whatever the Aycocks have done - most people here won't listen to some weird justification."

"But..." Anessa looked at Kobb, forehead creased.

"He's right, Anessa. We need to leave."

Eyes glistening, Anessa pulled her dad close. A moment later, she broke away and strode down the street, back rigid with the effort of not looking around.

Kobb nodded to Lambart, then headed after her.

Despite the foul weather and tangled vegetation, Kobb barely noticed the trip to Falcon. Losing his family had felt as if part of him had been hollowed out; what must it feel like to give them up?

He sighed and reached for the patterns around him. The world blurred and reformed into a circle of stones. Each time it seemed easier.

Shoulders rounded, Anessa stumbled towards the tents.

Kobb patted Falcon on the nose. Best to give her some room. As he turned to remove Falcon's saddle, Kobb realised his vision was blurry. He dabbed at his eyes, but the blurring remained and his hand came away dry.

He swept his gaze across the circle. The tents and everything else seemed crisp. When he looked back, he was certain the stone next to him had changed position.

They hadn't done enough. Something or someone had survived the fire.

Part Forty-One

Kobb stepped towards the stone. No wonder the trip had been so easy. If he went back now, he had time to do what needed to be done and return without Anessa knowing. The east-siders would still be distracted, either by the fire or by the aftermath.

But there was no guarantee they'd taken whichever of the Aycocks survived to Tremaine's house. Searching the entire village would take too long; assuming he could even do it without being spotted.

And Aycock's cult had existed for years. What if the connection hadn't been the Aycocks at all? Returning alone and without knowing more was too risky. He couldn't do much about being alone. Haelen needed time to recover. And telling Anessa she'd given up her home without ending the evil might break her. But he might be able to find out more.

Haelen had intended to study the mad man's notes. He might have found something to locate sources of evil. After giving Falcon a rub down and a nosebag of oats, Kobb headed to the improvised infirmary.

One of the patients muttered and twisted in his sleep, sweat glistening on his brow. Haelen looked up as Kobb entered, his face sombre. "Thought I heard you return. Another woman passed."

"It's not your fault. I'm sure you did everything you could."

"If it weren't for this…" Haelen shook his head. "But you don't seem happy. Where's Anessa? Did something–?"

"The stone transported us to her village. She's not wounded, but…"

"It's not easy when the threat's close to home?"

Kobb nodded. "Nothing her neighbours won't forgive once they calm down. She'll feel lost for a while, though. That's not the problem though. We thought we dealt with the evil. The stone's still shifting, though. I need to return. Finish what we–"

"You must have weakened it at least, shaken its hold. If you deal with the other stones, it might be enough to draw the power back here anyway."

"What if it isn't?" Kobb stepped further into the tent. "How can I let it fester?"

"Then you go after you've dealt with the rest." Haelen rested a hand on Kobb's shoulder. "We know the other stones lead to somewhere evil's growing. If Morth doesn't straighten out on its own, it's still the place with the least evil. Makes sense to leave it till last; even if you don't weigh Anessa's feelings."

"In the night." The sweating man's eyes snapped open. "Took her."

Kobb stepped forward, but stopped as Haelen placed a hand on his chest.

"A nightmare. Best let him rest." Haelen peered at Kobb. "What about you? Do you have enough of the potion?"

Kobb patted his jacket. "Should last me a while. Maybe you're right. Going back or not, I'll be better for a night's sleep." He crept to the other tent, careful not to wake Anessa.

When he woke, Anessa had already started breakfast. As he headed towards her, still unsure whether to tell her now or risk her noticing on her own, Haelen emerged from the infirmary.

Slumping onto a log, Haelen rubbed pinched his nose. "That man died this morning. I don't want... Sometimes I wonder if it's worth it."

"Man?" Anessa stopped stirring.

"I went to see Haelen after we returned. One of the men we rescued had a nightmare about some monster taking someone. Is that what killed him, Haelen? The insects did something to his mind?"

Haelen gazed at the floor. "I can't remove the things they've seen. Maybe it's better they don't wake up till it's all over."

"What about you?" Anessa spooned porridge into a bowl and held it out. "You need sleep too. I'll watch them for a bit."

"No. I'll be fine. Best way you can help is dealing with whatever affected the stones."

"You did get gored," said Kobb. "Lie down for a while. One of us will wake you if there's a problem."

"I'm grateful for the offer." Haelen pushed porridge around his bowl. "My wound's healed enough to cope, though. I don't want to delay you."

Kobb's eyebrows rose. It had only been two days. "You're the healer. It looked serious to me, though."

"I wouldn't be much of a Legion Healer if I couldn't get someone on their feet after they'd been stabbed." Haelen stood, his movements as smooth as if he were uninjured. "It's other things I can't fix. If it makes you feel better, I'll take it easier today; not study the notes."

If echoes of evil was what killed those people, re-balancing the stones as soon as possible did more good than waiting a day so Haelen could rest. Kobb nodded. "Deal. We'll finish breakfast and head out. We'll stay long enough we don't have to gulp it down, though."

As he'd hoped, Anessa heard his comment as permission to scrape every last oat out of the pot. While she was still spooning, he saddled Falcon and led him to the stone furthest from the one for Morth. Wouldn't be right to lie; that didn't mean he should throw the problem in her face, though. Even if cleaning more corruption didn't produce a noticeable improvement, a few days distance might salve the pain of separation enough she listened to Haelen's idea.

Recognising his reasoning for the veneer it was, he turned away as Anessa approached.

"Ready, Kobb."

His surroundings twisted away as he grabbed at the threads of power.

A murky grey sky boiled up and a bitter stench flooded his nostrils. Dark water stretched before him, the occasional rotting fish dotting the surface and the tattered remains of reeds marking the edge. In the distance, twisted trees clustered on a small island.

A scream tore the air behind him. Kobb spun, unsheathing his Courser and rapier.

A huge shape, covered in fur and bat-winged, but with a sharp, curving beak, arrowed towards the lake. Clasped beneath it, a man struggled.

Anessa's crossbow twanged. The creature was moving too fast, though.

Kobb brought his Courser up at the same time. Before he could use it, the beast was over the lake. If he killed it now, the man would fall in the water, end up sick or worse. But if he didn't the man was dead. Purple light lashed out.

Part Forty-Two

Heavy silence drowned the man's voice. Wreathed in purple light, the monster tumbled into the water, captive slipping from limp arms. Murky fluid fountained up beneath the impact.

A wave of foetid air struck Kobb's face as the muck slapped down. Eyes stinging, he made out the creature's prisoner surface several yards out, trying to reach shore. Blinking the tears away, he ran forward, Anessa at his side.

The former captive flapped one arm towards his rescuers. The effort almost sank him, but he did it again.

Kobb grabbed Anessa's elbow and pulled her to a halt. Locals would know the risks better than he would. But that didn't mean he couldn't help anyway. Releasing Anessa, he sprinted to Falcon and removed his tack.

The reins gripped in his fist, Kobb hurled the bridle to the foundering man.

The straps slapped into the swimmer's hand, but slipped free from his fingers before they'd closed.

Kobb jerked the reins back. The straps splutted onto the shore, dark fluids oozing out.

Careful to avoid the section that had been in the lake, Kobb picked the straps up as close to the bridle as he could and hurled it out again.

The straps slapped across the swimmer's left arm. After a false start, he hooked two fingers around the bit. His other limbs limp, he managed a third finger as the water surged over his face.

Kobb took up the slack and then backed away. After running her gaze along the length of the straps, Anessa grabbed another section. One step at a time, they towed the victim, flaccid save for his left arm, towards the shore. However, the extra resistance of the reeds proved too much.

Bit slipping from his fingers, the man flipped over. His body sank and only the matted vegetation stopped his head disappearing beneath the surface as well.

Crouched close enough to the edge that the water oozed across the tips of his boots, Kobb reached out. But he was too far away. The shwing of blade leaving scabbard sounded behind him. He rose and spun in a single move, weapons rising into a defensive stance.

Anessa stumbled away, jaw hanging open. Her sword hit the ground. After swallowing hard, she picked her weapon up and moved closer to the shore. "Hook... If you hold me, I can lean out. Hook his jacket with the point. Wipe it clean after."

Kobb sheathed his weapons and nodded. "Instincts got the better of me. Good idea. Metal won't soak any poison up."

Anessa approached the edge, trying to match caution and speed.

When she stopped, he moved right behind her and clasped the fingers of both hands through her belt. He braced his legs and extended his arms as she leaned forward. Her sword brushed the top of the man's head. Kobb shifted his left foot and then lent further. Right leg bending, he lowered Anessa forward. The tip of her sword now reached the collar of his jerkin. Less than an inch more and she'd hook him. Then, over her head, Kobb noticed several dark shapes rise from the island. "Anessa."

Anessa glanced up. "Don't have time to fight then save him. Have to risk one arm."

Three bat-winged forms surged closer, as Kobb slipped his left hand free. A jag of pain ran through his right fingers as they took Anessa's full weight.

As fast as the insects, but more ominous for being larger than an adult human, the beasts reached him before he could draw his Courser.

Then soared past, seemingly oblivious to the struggle below.

Puzzled, yet willing to grab any advantage, Kobb grabbed Anessa's belt with his free hand and shifted his stance. As he leaned further forward, his right boot slipped on the muddy ground. His toes sank into the water.

"Got 'im!" Anessa rolled her shoulder and inched her arm toward her body.

Dull ache growing in his lower back, Kobb straightened.

Arm trembling, Anessa turned her wrist then her elbow, keeping the end of her blade hooked inside the man's jerkin. As he drew closer, the two of them shuffled away from the lake. Inch by inch, they drew him through the reeds, until his head rested on the bank. Keeping the tension on his jerkin, Anessa moved to his side and thrust the sword further in.

After shifting her left hand half way down the blade, she turned. Under the renewed leverage, the man's body oozed up the bank. Another heave and his legs joined it. Anessa slid her weapon free and staggered away. Pulling her kerchief out, she wiped the blade.

Kobb crouched over the former captive, one eye on the dark muck pooling beneath him.

Eyes half-closed, the half-drowned figure drew a jagged breath. "Stay away. Skin kills."

Kobb pointed at the lake. "If you get the muck on your skin, it's fatal?"

The man nodded once, head listing to one side.

"What do we do?" said Anessa. "We know a healer. We could—"

"No cure. Tell family. Karek..." His chest stilled.

After a moment, Kobb drew Anessa away. "Did you get any on you?"

"Only the sword. But your boots..."

"They don't leak. Hopefully wiping it off will be good enough. We—" Kobb unsheathed his Courser as a group of armed men jogged into view from the direction the creatures had gone.

Part Forty-Three

Anessa unslung her crossbow. Now the men were closer, she realised some were her age. Seven armed people posed a real threat, though, whatever their ages. Each held a sword, which suggested they weren't possessed villagers; but none wore a uniform, so they might be brigands. And having the crossbow to hand'd make all the difference if the creatures returned anyway.

Weapons part way between carried and brandished, the new arrivals spread out into a row.

"Fair day." Kobb called out, keeping his Courser lowered but not holstering it.

The line drew to a halt several yards away. After considering them both for a moment, the man in the centre rested his blade over one shoulder. "Foul place for travellers. Where are you headed? And what business have you?"

Anessa stepped forward, crossbow lowered. Given how most of Morth had reacted to Kobb, it didn't seem sensible to share the whole story straight away. She pointed past them. "We're headed that way with a message from Karek."

"Karek, eh?" The leader swept his arm down. "For Anserth!"

The men charged forward, the same cry on their lips.

Anessa swallowed hard. Hesitation had cost too much in Morth. She wouldn't make that mistake again.

Purple-lit silence silenced the shouts as Kobb shot two down.

She fired from the hip. Her bolt caught another attacker in the throat, laying him flat.

Two of the remaining four, both youths, ran toward her, weapons raised. She dropped her crossbow and drew her sword.

Her attackers split, one sprinting in from each side.

Stepping right, she swung at the closest target.

But he twisted at the waist, letting her blade sweep past. His companion lunged at the same time.

Anessa bent her right leg and threw her weight forwards, dropping below the thrust, then rising up into a crouch.

The two assailants closed before she regained her feet.

With their swords sweeping in from both sides, she rolled the only way she could: backwards. The blades whistled past without finding her, but the shore was nothing like the barn at home, and she was no longer a girl of six. Her blade somehow caught her left ankle, throwing her off balance and leaving her sprawled on the shore.

Grinning, the two men raised their weapons.

Blade swinging right, Anessa hurled a fistful of mud and grass at the man on her left.

Instinct turned his swing to a dodge. Pain juddered down her arm as her sword blocked the other attack.

Clutching his shoulder, her right-hand attacker reeled.

For a moment, neither of them swung at her. She tucked her legs and rolled.

The left-hand youth stabbed down a breath too late.

Anessa's leg snapped straight.

Already bent, her attacker folded completely as her boot struck him in the groin.

With his collapsing body blocking his companion's advance, Anessa managed to clamber to her feet before the next attack.

Metal rang harshly as the two of them exchanged flailing blows.

Moment by moment, the aches in her arm and shoulder increased and her speed decreased. But her opponent's swings were even slower and wider. After swaying away from another sweep, she stepped forward before the youth recovered.

Only to feel something hit her ankle.

Her other opponent, face pale, had uncurled enough to act. At full extension and still half-mazed with pain, his blow lacked force. But it did distract her.

Given a moment to recover, the standing youth lunged.

She twisted, his blade passing her. But he continued forward, chest smashing into her right side.

Off balance, she tumbled over. A jolt ran through her as she hit the ground, bouncing her weapon out of her hand.

Sword gripped in both hands, her assailant braced himself over her.

His heaving breaths fell silent as purple light wrapped around him.

More out of instinct than thought, Anessa angled her arms up, shoving her dead opponent away. Rising, she snatched up the nearest weapon and flicked her gaze back and forth.

Kobb, dark spittle trailing from his lips, sagged over bodies of his opponents.

Anessa's remaining attacker rose to his feet, breathing ragged but sword rigid before him. She gritted her teeth. No hesitation. She raised her blade and advanced. "Drop it."

Wordless cry on his lips, the youth lifted his weapon above his head and ran at her.

Without thinking, she lunged. His blade tumbled away as hers sank into his gut.

He fell forward, tearing the weapon out of Anessa's hand—but not before his weight drove it deeper.

The blade in his stomach propping him up, he slumped on his side. Sweat congealed across his brow as his fingers flapped against the hilt. He drew a gurgling breath. "You'll never... win, sorcerer bitch. We'll..."

Anessa fell to her knees beside him. "Sorcerer? We're not sorcerers."

But he was beyond hearing.

Had she made a horrible mistake? But the men attacked. What if... But... Even if he was an enemy, she couldn't leave the sword in his gut. She eased him onto his back and grabbed the hilt. For a moment, the blade seemed part of him, then it slide free with a sucking sound.

Hot bile and half-digested oats flooded her mouth as she collapsed to her knees again.

"Anessa." Kobb's arm wrapped around her. His other hand held out a crumpled kerchief.

"I stabbed him. He were only young, and I killed him."

Kobb eased her to her feet. After dabbing vomit from her face, he fixed his gaze on hers. "This won't remove the pain. But they attacked us. And he could have put his blade up, offered surrender. But he didn't. If you'd turned your back, he'd have gone for you."

A cold void swallowing the mere emptiness of her stomach, she forced herself to stay upright. "How do you keep going?"

"Each morning, you remind yourself that this is why you try everything else first. And each evening, you remind yourself it means you still know right and wrong."

Anessa rested her fingers on his pendant. "Doesn't the Maker...?"

"There are answers in the Book of Blessings. But now is not the time for them."

She frowned. What kind of priest was he? Wasn't he supposed to tell what the book told her to do? What use was he if it didn't give the—

"Feeling angry, yet?" said Kobb.

"Angry! Of course I'm—"

"Pain's gone then?"

Her response caught in her throat. Shoulders rounding, she looked at the dead boy at her feet.

"Problem's not getting rid of the pain. Problem's how easy it is." He drew her close. "Sorry for doing it. But it's a lesson you have to feel."

She forced down a sob. "Still my fault they attacked. Thought they were Karek's friends. Thought it'd win 'em over."

"And it could have. Hating sorcerers doesn't mean they're not bad. Maybe there's more than two sides to this problem. Or maybe Karek wasn't his name and he tried to say 'Karek killed me'. The answers are the way they came. But first, you need to clean your weapons."

Part Forty-Four

Anessa searched her pack for a clean rag. Her fallen opponents no doubt had kerchiefs, or—failing that—singlets. It weren't right to riffle through their clothes, though—least not without knowing which side they were on. Using her spare shirt felt just as wrong though. Distracted, she didn't notice Falcon's approach until he pressed his nose against the back of her neck.

Arms tangled in her possessions, she tumbled forward. "Kobb! What about his bridle? How do we clean the lake water off that?"

"Not worth the time to try." Kobb strolled over and patted Falcon on the flank. "I can steer him with my knees. Reins are good to hold onto if he's galloping; I can do without until we find fresh tack, though."

Anessa struggled to her feet "Suppose you won't be riding anyway. Whatever those creatures are, they're taking people to the island. So stands to sense the evil's there." She peered around the lake. No sign of a boat, but the matted reeds might hide anything. The only way to tell was walking the shore.

"Might not be that easy. If the beasts were hunting, they'd have tried to grab us. But they didn't; ignored the man, too. That suggests there's something important over there."

"Won't killing them solve it?"

Kobb's gaze flicked to the dead men lying nearby. "We don't know who Karek is; either way, there's at least two sides to this. Easy enough to think the creatures are the problem because they grabbed a man. Common knowledge says Skithai are utterly evil, though."

Could the monsters be fighting the evil? They looked terrifying, but they hadn't attacked her or Kobb. Going to the island and killing the beasts'd be easy. Much easier than heading the way the men had come, and having to face their friends and families. But following the easy path rather than making sure was what lead to their attackers being dead.

Anessa squared her shoulders. "You're right. And whoever he was, that man asked us to tell his family."

Kobb's gaze hardened as he raised his Courser to point over her shoulder.

Anessa spun on her heel. Three bat-winged shapes rushed towards the lake, the one on the left carrying a writhing child. Purple light flared as she dived for her fallen crossbow.

From the corner of her eye, she saw something hit the ground. Shadows flickered across her. By the time she'd rolled over the beasts had disappeared.

Slotting a bolt into place, she looked back and forth. A furry mass sprawled several yards north.

Kobb lowered his Courser. "They move faster than even the Skithai did. Once I hit the first one, the others raced away."

"You saved the child, though?" She jogged towards it, crossbow raised. "Best check they're well. And make sure beast's dead."

Kobb advanced a few yards to her left, weapons raised.

The monster lay face down, a leathery wing almost covering the body of a young girl. Neither reacted as Anessa approached. Crossbow ready, she stepped closer.

A scent between mould and the sky after lightning wafted up as she crouched next to the wing. Black fur matted the top edge, thickening as it approached the beast's torso. Barely visible under the wing, the child's chest rose and fell.

One eye on the creature, Anessa placed her crossbow down and lifted the wing. The girl remained limp, but still breathed. However, her legs lay beneath the beast's body. "We'll need to lift it to get her out."

Kobb moved around and sheathed his weapons. After crouching, he frowned for a moment. "Not sure one of us could to hold it up alone. Easier if we shove it onto its back. Lift when I say."

The wing kept flopping over her, but Anessa got her hands under the beast's shoulder. As soon as Kobb called, she straightened. For a moment, the creature seemed to cling to the ground; then, all at once, it shifted.

Anessa leapt backwards. A jagged beak, the colour of red iron or ancient bronze, gaped from the front of a long head. Above it, four pits oozed a dark fluid across the fur. After a breath, she realised the sense of motion was the body settling. "What... what is it?"

"Don't know. But if it's stealing children, it's more likely than not a threat."

She'd been right. If they'd followed her idea of looking for a boat though, Kobb wouldn't have seen the monster in time to save the girl. Was that one of the Blessings she needed to find? Time enough to think later. Anessa dropped to her knees beside the child.

Removing the weight of the beast hadn't woken her up. After a moment, Anessa realised why: a spur of bone jutted from her left shin, rivulets of blood turning the ground beneath to muck.

Cloth tore behind her. When she spun, she saw Kobb hacking the nearest man's clothes into strips.

"We can't do anything for her here. If we stop the bleeding, we might be able to get her to wherever the men came from."

Anessa grabbed the strip out of his hand and started wrapping. As she finished, Kobb passed her another.

Blood blossomed across each turn, but less each time. After the fifth strip, the bandages were no longer sodden before she wrapped the next turn. "It'll have to do."

As Anessa lent away, Kobb swept the girl up in his arms and laid her across Falcon's saddle. "Might do her more good to carry her in my arms. This way we've both got a hand free to fight if we get ambushed, though."

Anessa jogged to her sword. Striding back, she wiped the blade clean on the creature's fur and sheathed it. Picking up her crossbow, she took the lead. There was only ragged turf between here and the ridge the men had approached over. No reason not to scout properly, though.

The grass continued, thicker but no taller, past the crest to another rise. Nothing stood out, but a shift in the breeze brought the scent of wood smoke. Something was burning beyond the far ridge; and the lack of a plume suggested it someone didn't want to give their location away.

After telling Kobb, she headed forward again, keeping about twenty yards ahead of Kobb and Falcon. The scent of burning wood increased as she crawled up to the crest.

Ruins of pale stone, like the ones they'd rescued Haelen from but covering a larger area, filled the valley beyond. They seemed abandoned. Her gut didn't agree, though. She inched forward and waited, letting her gaze flow over the ruins.

Long, slow breaths later, her patience was rewarded. A shadow on a roof shifted, for an instant moving like cloth. She eased back down the slope to join Kobb. "There's ruins ahead. At least one person watching from a roof. Feels like more. Still can't see the fire, so they're careful."

Kobb's shoulders slumped. "I hoped they'd just be camped. But that sounds as if they fortified. And no way to know who they are till after we announce ourselves."

"Don't reckon the fire's right at the edge. Wait for dark; we can sneak close enough to listen in."

Kobb glanced at the sky. "It's not even midday. Someone's going to miss those men, and there's nowhere to hide. Even if another group doesn't come, the girl won't last the day without more than we can offer."

The hidden figure was too deep in the ruins to see the outskirts; potentially, even faced the other way. There was a chance the guards all watched the skies or something further in; that no one paid attention to the slope down. "People are easier to sneak up on than deer. If I went on my own..."

Part Forty-Five

Bitterness slid up Anessa's throat from vomiting earlier. She forced herself not to swallow. If Kobb thought she was nervy, he wouldn't let her go on her own. "Better to try while it's cloudy. Less risk of metal catching the sun."

"Those beasts move too fast to shoot. If they come back, we've a better chance together."

"Like you said, they've ignored us before. Didn't fight even when we did. The two of us can maybe sneak closer. Falcon can't, though." She pushed away a spike of guilt. "If those creatures do attack, least I've got a chance. Without either of us, he'd be unprotected."

Kobb frowned for a moment, then sighed. "You're not trained to fight a group. And, whoever's in the ruins knows something about hiding too." He glanced at the young girl. "The alternative's worse though. Don't try to be heroic. First sign they're on to you, head back here."

"Don't worry. Probably want a fight less than they do." Anessa unslung her pack and readied her crossbow. After a last nod to Kobb, she crept up the rise.

The cloaked figure remained in the same place, and now she knew what to look for, she thought she spotted two more. None of them moved when she slid over the crest, but she still tensed as she rose to a crouch and sneaked forward. When the shouts and rain of bolts didn't come, she increased her pace to a jog.

The scent of smoke grew stronger. She still couldn't see the plume. Something about the smell niggled at her, though. Hoping it'd come to her, she slipped closer. At least the smell gave her a place to aim for.

As she crept past the first pile of rubble, the stiffness in her shoulders eased. She slipped into a puddle of shadow and listened. Breezes brushed through the gaps; the ruins were otherwise quiet, though. Which suggested a group of people close by; if it was only one occupant, there'd be some small-animal noises.

A tall pile of stone blocked the street best leading towards the scent. The next seemed clear, though. She drifted around a corner, then moved to a low wall. As she crept past it, a boot scuffed nearby. Lowering herself back behind the wall, she peered out, her head almost at ground level.

A man in a battered yet clean leather jerkin stepped into view. Anessa wasn't an expert but the sword at his hip looked similarly functional. After pausing for a moment to shift a sack from one shoulder to the other, he walked between the remains of two buildings.

Anessa rose and followed. Neither running nor creeping, he continued in a straight line. Wishing he moved more slowly so she didn't have to rush, she slipped from doorway to shadow. A few paces further on, he turned down a street to the right.

She reached the corner in time to see him enter an intact building that stood slightly apart from the others. Several other buildings nearby looked whole. Definitely the area you might put your camp in.

After waiting a moment in case he came straight out again, she crept along the street. Burnt juniper surged stronger as she approached. The doorway loomed too dark to see more than a foot. Whereas she'd be obvious as she stepped through. She slipped down the side, seeking a different way in.

Two windows opened in the wall. But, due to either accident or intent, rubble blocked both of them. The door at the back was, if anything, more firmly packed. Ears straining for the sound of boots, she moved on. Fallen stone sealed the windows on the next side too; unlike the other sides, though, a creeper, thick with age, stretched the height of the wall. After giving it a tug, she slung her crossbow and climbed up. Head tilted flat against her shoulder, she raised her head enough to see over the lip.

Dirty but unbroken flags covered the roof. Apart from an old nest in the far corner, it was empty. She slipped over the edge, then waited. The smell of juniper remained strong, yet she couldn't see even a trickle of smoke. And all the marks in the dirt looked like rain spatter rather than human feet. How'd they hide smoke holes this well without coming onto the roof? The fire must be in a different building.

Unless she missed something. If the smoke was thin enough, she might not notice it against the cloudy sky. She turned, peering at the rooftops before rising to her feet. The change in angle didn't reveal any smoke. However, she did spot a figure slip away below.

She dropped to a crouch. It looked like the man with the sack, now tucked empty through his belt. He moved differently, though. Previously, he'd walked down the middle of the street, boot heels tapping on stones, as if doing a boring yet safe task. This time, he'd stayed against the buildings, weight sliding between feet to test the ground ahead. And he'd headed away from the direction he came.

It was the same man though; and, if he'd been setting a trap, he'd have sprung it while she circled the building. So, it'd be safe enough to climb down and check inside.

Concern still niggling at her, she retraced her path round three sides of the building. Still no one attacked. Pausing for a moment next to the doorway, she strained her ears. When only the subtle crack of burning wood sounded, she raised her crossbow and stepped past the jamb in a single motion.

Back pressed against the wall, she waited.

A faint flicker washed the shadows further in, coming from rubble in the centre. A pile of wood rested next to the rubble; otherwise, the room was empty.

Anessa crept forwards and crouched down. The scent of burning juniper, now almost overpowering, boiled out of a crude arch in the back of the pile. Within, a slab had been removed and a small fire lit in a hole scraped into the floor. A hidden fire pit. Grandam mentioned building a fire that didn't give off smoke or light so pursuers couldn't find you in the forest. Anessa'd thought it just a tale; this wasn't though.

Why'd someone put so much effort into making one in an empty building? The smell made it obvious there was a fire. It didn't make sense. Everyone even half-competent at hunting knew the smell of burning juniper carried for—

The smell. With no smoke or light to see, people'd know there was a fire, yet not where. They'd have to search for it. If Anessa hadn't seen the man with his sack of wood, she'd have had to check all the intact buildings.

Which meant whoever was here wanted anyone looking for them to come to this area.

Part Forty-Six

Anessa crept sideways across the room, peering through the doorway as she went. Nothing moved in the street, and the buildings looked abandoned. Crossbow ready, she padded forward, skirting the spill of light.

Still no sign of anyone or anything odd. If they watched all the time, they'd have seen her on the roof or creeping about. Slipping around the jamb, she jogged to a pile of rubble and crouched down. A chill wind stirred the dust, but not the shadows. She let her eyes drift. Something might catch the corner of her eye if she didn't force it.

As she'd half-expected, nothing did. If there were people here, they wouldn't send someone from another place to tend the fire. And if someone saw her approaching the ruins and set up an ambush, they'd have sprung it by now. So, the area was abandoned. But was the fire a delaying tactic, or did they want to lure people here for a purpose?

The man's movements were odd too. If you stroll somewhere, then sneak away, you want to be followed for the first part. But the ruins had hidden him until she was almost on top of him; even the scuff of his boots hadn't given her much warning. So why—?

The creatures. The rubble blocked her view at ground level, but something flying'd see him from a distance. So whatever the inhabitants had planned could include all the streets he'd strolled along too. After closing her eyes for a moment to recall the man's departure, she set off after him.

Several long moments later, she reached the last place she'd seen him. Peering past the remains of a wall, she discovered a mostly clear street running in both directions. Lines of buildings stretched both ways without side turnings; but several had collapsed enough, they'd be no more than inconveniences. If his route to the fire had been a trick, he probably hadn't turned that way. That still left two directions he could have gone, though; as well as all the intact buildings he could have stopped in.

Anessa closed her eyes again. Apart from the gusting of the wind through tumbled stone, the area was quiet. And the juniper smoke removed any chance of smelling another camp. People cunning enough to make a hidden fire wouldn't let the one they were camped near smoke, anyway.

After drifting her gaze across the nearby buildings again to be sure, she guessed where the nearest of the cloaked watchers was and crept that way. Rubble blocked the back of the building she chose; but a window in the next opened onto another clear street, this one curving in the direction she wanted.

Several yards past the bend, more fallen stones blocked the street. Anessa slung her crossbow so both her hands were free for clambering, and peered into the surrounding buildings. No way through. At least the delay reduced the chance she'd catch up with the fire tender without warning.

She backtracked, but the previous side turning was a dead end too.

Finally, she found a ruin clear enough to pass through. As she crept down yet another pile of stone, a woman in leather armour clambered into sight ahead.

Anessa ducked into a side street. Two doorways gaped, and beyond them the collapsed front wall of the next building half-blocked the way. Not wanting to risk being trapped between the woman and a rooftop watcher, Anessa jogged to the rubble and crouched.

Several breaths later, the woman turned into the street. If she continued on, she'd almost certainly see Anessa; but if Anessa didn't stay still, she might notice the movement. Drawing a weapon posed the same risk, and Anessa wasn't sure she could kill someone in cold blood anyway. Thighs aching from the strain of keeping low, she sidled into the remains of the building.

"Who goes?" A harsh whisper came from above.

Anessa pressed herself against the side of the building.

A higher-pitched voice responded nearby. "Anserth endures."

Something scuffed on the roof behind Anessa, followed by the murmur of conversation. Sounded too calm to be planning an attack; it they must be talking about what the watcher had seen. She needed to get closer.

Cracks marred the wall, just wide enough for a fingertip. The lingering discomfort in Anessa's shoulders from the sword blows earlier blossomed into an ache as she pulled herself up.

"...flew over twice this morning," said the man.

"Orlin's unit fired the stables at day's turn. Karek must be getting desperate."

"Wish they'd burnt him. Him and all his kind."

"He'll have to come out soon."

Unable to get even the tip of her boot into a crack to ease the strain, Anessa felt her fingers slipping. Lips clamped tight, she lowered herself down. Karek was allied with the creatures. Which meant these people were trying to stop the evil. She didn't need to skulk around any more.

Although, the others attacked without even asking for surrender, so it might be better not to be found this close to one of their guards. Ears straining for the moment the voices fell silent or shifted, Anessa backed along the street and slipped into the ruins.

Retracing her steps meant going out of her way, but given how good the inhabitants were at sneaking, it seemed safer than crossing unknown ground. Eventually, she crested the rise. Falcon grazed, unconcerned by the risk of monsters, while Kobb sat beside the still figure of the girl.

Kobb rose as she approached. "Good to see you back."

"Managed to overhear a couple of them. Karek's the one with the monsters. The others are trying to stop him. Sounded like they've trapped him somewhere in the ruins. So, I reckon we're safe walking in."

"We'll have to risk it anyway." Kobb glanced at the girl. "The bleeding's slow, but she's been still too long. She should have twitched or moaned by now, and her skin feels odd."

"Might seem less threatening if I carry her and you follow. If those beasts come back, you're more likely to hit them than me anyway."

Kobb loosened his Courser, but didn't draw it. "Best not to prepare too much though. Might give the wrong idea."

Anessa lifted the girl and walked up the slope. She could feel what Kobb meant: the girl's skin felt cold and slippery as if wet, but Anessa's hand remained dry. Hoping the people in the ruins'd have answers, she crested the rise. Apart from her shallow breathing, the girl gave no sign of life.

Before she was halfway down the other side, five figures burst from the buildings. As she approached, she realised they each held a crossbow readied.

She dropped to her knees and curled over the girl as the first bolt whistled past her.

PART FORTY-SEVEN

Kobb dropped to a crouch, left hand snapping his Courser free. Somehow, all five bolts had—

A sharp yet mouldy smell filled the air around him as a leather-winged form slammed into Anessa. He drew a bead on instinct; the three figures were too muddled to fire without thought, though.

Falcon kicked out. Metal-clad hoof struck mangy fur, breaking the creature's grip on Anessa. She curled tighter around the girl.

Before Kobb could shoot, the monster shot into the air, wings still folded. Kobb turned in place as the creature dived down at Falcon, a scream piercing the air.

Acting on hope, Kobb unleashed the Courser across its path.

The beast jagged without warning, but purple light brushed its right leg. Wings thrashing, it crashed down behind Falcon.

Bone crunched as the horse kicked backwards. Leather and fur slammed into the ground, then tumbled back down the slope.

Falcon stepped to the side, tossing his mane as the remains of the beast slid past.

Kobb patted his horse on the flank. "Having fun?"

Falcon whickered once, before strolling over to nose at Anessa.

Anessa's left arm swung out as she rolled hard, her right reaching for her crossbow.

Falcon shook his head and whiffled, before stepping back.

Eyes wide, Anessa eased her hand off her weapon and rose into a crouch. "I thought..."

Kobb glanced behind him, then settled his Courser in place. The creatures' agility left him conflicted: it made them difficult targets; but, had that one been any slower, he'd have shot the crossbowmen. "Is the girl safe?"

"She still sleeps. Whether that's good or not..."

Kobb stood, hands drifting near his weapons, as the men approached. They wore the same clothing as the earlier group; however, each bore himself like a soldier. Crossbows angled towards the ground, but loaded and tensioned, they flicked their gaze between Kobb and the skies.

Kobb smiled. "Afternoon."

The three men in the middle of the line halted outside sword range. The ones at each end swung wide, moving out of Kobb's peripheral vision. After a longer consideration of both Kobb and Anessa, the oldest man tilted his head at Falcon. "Useful animal. What brings you this way?"

"We were travelling east when we rescued this girl from another of those creatures." Kobb gestured at the unconscious child. "She needed better healing than we could offer. The beast came from this direction, so it seemed the best way to try."

The man grunted, then nodded once. A moment later, one of his companions whispered something in his ear. The leader frowned in thought. "We'll escort you in. Elvar, take the girl. Anything happens, get her inside."

"I can carry her." Anessa glared at him.

"Maybe. But that's how I want it, so that's how we'll do it."

Anessa glared at him again, before moving out of Elvar's way.

Kobb patted her on the shoulder. "It's not an insult. If anything, it's a compliment."

She peered at him, head tilted.

"Your father's the right of it," said the leader. "If you are up to something, we can fill you full of bolts without risking the girl."

Anessa spun. "You think we're—"

"Patrol went missing this morning. Then the two of you come strolling over the rise with a warhorse."

Her shoulders drooped. Before she could speak, Kobb strode towards the line. "Sooner we head in; sooner we set your mind at rest."

The tension left Kobb's neck as the men's focussed back on him. After a breath, the leader nodded and turned.

Draping Falcon's reins over one wrist, Kobb strolled after the three warriors, ignoring the two who followed. Anessa stomped beside him, body rigid but keeping her feelings to herself.

"Came to the lake to fish, did you?" asked one of the men from behind.

Anessa whirled. "First we're an invading army; now we're fishers?"

"Just wondered, seeing how you stink of smoke."

Kobb stroked Falcon's flank, placing his hand closer to his Courser at the same time.

"Cold at night ain't it." Anessa rolled her eyes. "Anyone with an ounce of sense sleeps close to the fire. Surprised weren't first thing you thought."

The leader snorted. "She's the right of it, Col. We ain't all half-weasel; normal people feel the chill."

Now he looked for it, Kobb noted a certain weaseliness in Col's sharp features.

Hissing through his teeth in a way that—if anything—increased his resemblance to a weasel, Col waved Anessa on with his crossbow. They passed the edge of the rubble in silence.

Elvar leading, they wove through the maze of fallen buildings and blocked streets. Kobb sought to project amiability, while watching for the slightest hint whether the lack of blindfolds was a great sign or a terrible one. He still hadn't decided by the time the group halted beside an unremarkable—albeit intact—two-storey structure.

"Elvar, take the girl to a healer." Their guide-captor slung his crossbow. "Anserth will want to see you two straight away. Col, seeing you don't feel the cold, make sure the horse don't wander off."

Kobb winced. "No need. Falcon'll stay without trouble. Might even get fractious if a stranger tries to hold him."

"Don't worry. Col got the cunning as well as the features. He ain't going to mess with a warhorse."

Col huffed before slumping on a nearby block.

After draping the end of Falcon's reins on the windowsill, Kobb strolled into the building. The entire floor was an empty space, a flight of steps visible on the far side in the gloom. "Up?"

The leader shook his head. Striding over to an unremarkable slab, he kicked down on it three times and stepped back. Several breaths later, it rose up on a pair of burly arms, then settled to the side. As the arms withdrew, faint orange light spilled up from the hole, revealing a wooden ladder. Now certain events would end in one of two very different ways, Kobb climbed down into a dim room.

The owner of the arms, body of matching scale, lounged against the wall. A long-shafted hammer rested next to him. Beyond him, a door—the first Kobb had seen since they entered the ruins—stood in a recess, orange light flickering out of a small grill at eye level.

Their guide-captor raised his hand. "Wait here." Standing so his body blocked their view, he knocked twice and held something up to the grill. The door swung open, then closed behind him.

Anessa shifted from one foot to the other. Several long moments later, she began to whistle. Kobb was on the verge of shushing her when the door opened again and the patrol leader beckoned them in.

The scent of hot dust struck Kobb as he stepped through. Several braziers, giving off a dull orange light but no smoke stood against the walls. In the centre, four leather-clad people bent over a map table; they glanced up, before going back to their silent study.

As the door shut behind them, another opened in the far wall. A woman strode in, encased in dull plate from the neck down. A grey tabard with a black double band around the edge hung to her knees.

One eyebrow quirked in amusement above cold blue eyes, she considered Kobb before pressing her left gauntlet, palm flat, to her throat. "Blessings manifest for you, Militant."

"And for you." Kobb frowned. "It has been a long time since any greeted me that way."

"We're both far from home, and in strange company."

"Strange company? Then these troops aren't auxiliaries?"

The woman smoothed her tabard. "Not entitled to wear this any more. But I feel undressed without it. And it helps if people think I'm just a Legionary. But of course, you'd know about pretending to be less than you are. There's no juniper within a week's ride west of here, so how did your companion really end up stinking of it?"

Part Forty-Eight

Kobb tilted his head towards Anserth to acknowledge the point. He hoped honesty would strengthen the fragile trust. "Anessa scouted some of the ruins to discover your allegiances before we revealed ourselves."

The sound of swords leaving sheaths rang from the walls. Anessa raised her crossbow as she turned to face the soldiers behind them.

"A scout?" Anserth quirked an eyebrow. Her sword remained undrawn. Not that that would delay a veteran much. "That doesn't sound like the act of an honest traveller."

"Just good sense. Those beasts flew both ways." Kobb swept a hand back and forth, fingers flapping. The movement sent glitters of firelight off his Courser. "Wouldn't want to mistake enemies and friends."

For a moment, Anserth stared at him. Then a snort of laughter broke through. "Stand down, men. Suppose you wouldn't need to sneak up if you meant us harm. Might even be good fortune you turned up."

Anessa slung her crossbow. "What do you mean it might be lucky?"

"Karak's sealed himself up in a section of the ruins. He can't get out, but we can't get in. We'll break through; however, until we do he's free to send those creatures out to attack. You change matters though."

Kobb tilted his shoulders, trying to make it seem a random shift rather than releasing tension. He'd hoped Anserth wouldn't get in the way of redirecting the corrupted power; being asked to solve was even better. "We'll need to know how this started."

Anserth turned to the patrol leader. "Orlin, scrounge us up some water. Come into my boudoir, Militant.... But, where are my manners. Inductor Saevisa Anserth at your service. Whom do I have the honour to address?"

"Reverend Absolution is like the Silence of the Waterfall Kobb of the Order of the Maker. My companion is Worthy Anessa Tanton." Kobb ignored Anessa's startled look at unexpected title. Pausing to explain would make them seem vulnerable. "We are honoured to address the Hand of the Council."

Anserth slammed her fists together. "Blood and Stone of One Will." After a moment, she dropped her hands back to her sides. "That's the 'who's got the biggest muscles' out the way; let's talk."

Kobb followed her into a small stone vault. A single cot stood at the far end with a banded chest at the foot. Otherwise, the room was empty. "I shall have to pace myself. These luxuries might overwhelm me."

Anserth snorted. "I had a camp desk too; it was lost when a creature dropped masonry on my tent. Which is why we've moved underground, and why we set the jasmine fires. Karak's beasts still get us; this way, at least it's while we're awake, while we have a chance to fight back. But you said you wanted the beginning. Karak is a member of the University, an archaeologist. Several months ago, he approached the rector claiming he'd found mention of a hidden chamber in these ruins. The University agreed to fund an expedition. When Karak put the call out for someone to lead the guards, I took the job and added my unit to the roster."

Kobb frowned. "Guarding an academic seems a little outside the tasks of an Inductor."

"Karak, like many academics, is prone to chasing mist. Five years ago, he wrote a paper suggesting similarities between the markings found in ruins across the provinces and the patterns the Eaters carve on their masks. His proposal didn't mention more research on that theory, but the Council wished to make sure the expedition was protected if he decided to go looking for savages. Turned out they were right to worry he'd left some of his aims out; not the ones they thought, though.

"At first, no one realised it wasn't an ordinary expedition. We reached here without incident. We found the tower Karak sought still standing, and set up camp nearby. The next afternoon, he uncovered the chamber. He spent longer and longer down there each day, then had a cot moved in. Three days later, the watch leader reported Karak hadn't come up for supplies and the door to the tower wouldn't open. Before I'd left my tent, the first of those creatures had arrived." She paused as Orlin entered carrying a flagon of water. "More of them arrived soon after. We tried to hold them off, but the beasts pushed us back. We thought we were rescuing Karak; then he appeared in a window and ordered us to leave. Each time we advanced, his beasts snatched guards up or dropped masonry on us until we had to retreat. And when we did, they added more rubble to the piles in the streets. Soon there was a wall surrounding the tower too high to climb."

"What about attacking at night?" said Anessa.

"We tried. I sent five of my best fighters over. None of them came back. I thought he'd have to come out when his supplies ran out. The creatures must bring him food. There were a few wooden structures. We managed to land flaming arrows, but the fire wasn't enough to drive him out. Which left an attack on multiple fronts."

Kobb squeezed his chin. "Those beasts are fast. Even with my Courser, a frontal assault means casualties."

"It would. But it isn't your help I'm asking for." Anserth tilted her head at Anessa. "Worthy, you scouted the ruins without us realising. If it hadn't been for the smoke, we'd never have known. You could get in unnoticed."

"And what if she can't?" Kobb said. "Those creatures—"

"I'll do it." Anessa grabbed his elbow. "It'll save lives, so I'll do it."

Anserth nodded. "My thanks. Orlin, find the Worthy clothes that don't smell of juniper."

After passing a slow yet utterly clinical gaze up Anessa's body, Orlin pointed at the door. "I've a few ideas. Follow me."

Kobb waited until Anessa had left then stared at Anserth. "First sign Anessa's in trouble, I'm going in."

"And my unit will be right behind you if you do. Whatever happens, we'll put an end to this today. Once she's ready, I'll take you both forward myself."

Deciding he'd proved he was a threat enough for one day, Kobb sat on the cot and sipped the water. He'd almost emptied the flagon when Anessa returned. She still wore brown; but in place of a soft jacket and trousers, chain panels and boiled leather covered her body and limbs. He wasn't sure which worried him more: that she didn't carry herself like a warrior, or that she nearly did.

He watched her as they crossed the ruins, half-hoping the armour made her clumsy enough to demand Anserth abandoned her scheme. But it seemed Orlin had chosen well. Anessa moved with almost the same grace, and what stiffness he did see could easily be only wishes. Ahead, all too close, a broken-topped tower jutted into the twilight.

Anserth raised her left fist as they rounded the final corner, then pointed, unnecessarily, at the mass of stone blocking the street. "We believe there's only a single wall."

For a moment, Anessa seemed frozen. Then she pressed her fist to her throat and bowed her head to Kobb. Before he could decide what to say, she'd crept away.

He watched her until she reached the wall, but lost her in the shadows. If he couldn't see her even knowing she was there, then Karak wouldn't either. It was a Blessing.

So why didn't it feel like one?

A boot scuffed behind him. Giving up his fruitless search for Anessa, he turned. Col crouched next to Anserth, a large bundle in his arms. Kobb's forehead creased. It looked — "Are the healers nearby? Isn't it dangerous to bring the girl so close?"

"I didn't mention Karak's wife's an archaeologist too. They brought their daughter." Anserth shrugged. "We spotted the beast carry her over the lines this morning. Couldn't stop it, though. I hope your companion succeeds. If she doesn't, then I'll break the deadlock another way."

Part Forty-Nine

Anessa shifted her weight onto her right foot without a sound. The edge of the rubble'd been a mess of loose chips; now she'd past that the footing was mostly stable, though. However, as she moved her left leg forward, the rigid leather guard pressed against her thigh. Startled, she stumbled.

Her left hand grabbed a nearby rock, but the ill-balanced shift made the mail on her torso rattle. The night air crept through the spaces between panels, giving her another reason to miss her comfortable leathers. After tilting her head for a few moment without hearing shouts or the flap of wings, she decided she'd not been noticed.

She wondered if the armour'd been a good idea: most of the time it moved with her, then as she thought she'd got used to it, it caught or rattled. But, if Anserth's best fighters hadn't crept in, would being a little quieter make a difference anyway?

Caught between worrying about beasts and worrying about how to move, she struggled up the stones. The wind brushed her face, so less noise'd reach the tower. And at least while she was on this side of the barrier, Kobb'd see a creature well before it pounced. She focused on the rubble in front of her. No use thinking about the other side until she'd seen it.

Inch by inch, she gained another yard, then cursed inside as the night grew darker. Clear skies made her easier to spot. If she couldn't see the stones, she couldn't avoid the loose ones though; and sound'd carry where a glimpse of brown leather mightn't. And she plain didn't want to think about rain or snow. Limbs braced yet not rigid, she stopped clambering and glanced up. The rubble ahead was a mass of angular shadows, but a few feet further on, the stone shone pale.

The cold settled deeper as she glanced around. The stones to either side weren't in shadow. She tilted her head until her neck ached. Dark leather blocked the sky. Pressing closer to the rubble, she tried to tell herself knowing where the creature was was a Blessing. She wasn't listening to herself though. Only to the lack of utter silence.

The strain of that morning's exertions oozed deeper into her shoulders. She shifted more weight onto her legs. However, tensed for the expected bolt of purple fire, her body'd become too rigid; instead of her right knee bending, her foot slipped across the rubble.

Her fingers snapped closed as pain jagged along her arms. She swallowed her shout; yet could do nothing about the scuff of her boot or the skitter of mortar chips that followed. Why hadn't Kobb fired? He must've seen the beast. And even if she'd been too stealthy, the moonlight'd light up—

If he attacked, the night'd blaze purple. Even if Karak didn't have a way of sensing power, he'd see that; and know something had happened. Kobb was relying on her to sneak past. He'd fire if it pounced. But until then...

The creature hadn't though. Moving one limb at a time, she turned onto her side. Against the moon, the beast formed a single dark mass, even its wings still. The edge didn't have the angles of a beak; it faced away from her. Just as she hadn't seen or heard it until it was over her, it'd somehow hadn't noticed her.

And better still, it must've taken the skitter of stones for natural shifting. Aware she'd received a pile of Blessings already, she eased onto her stomach and drew herself up the rubble even slower than before.

Though the thought of claws brushed against her neck, she refused to check behind. Each movement was a chance for a boot to scuff or a hand to slip, a chance for the creature to turn. Muscles burning, yet skin chilled, she crawled over the top of the barrier and folded into the shadow of a broken arch.

Two lights flickered from a window in the fourth storey of the tower. Above them, jagged walls jutted into the sky. Between Anessa and the base, a strip of clear ground slashed across the ruins, she presumed where the top of the tower'd smashed the buildings then been cleared to make the barrier.

The scar'd be quicker than clambering between the ruins, yet more exposed. The creatures'd ignored her even when she'd was in the open by the lake, and Anserth's men used the smell of juniper to attract them. Maybe they didn't hunt by sight or sound. Unashamed of her desire to reach her destination, she decided on speed.

The pinch of imagined talons chased her down the slope and across to the foot of the tower. Pressed against the wall, she allowed herself to glance up. Only the stars looked down. Anserth'd said Karak sealed the door; he might have opened it again after the wall was built though. After straightening her shoulders, she circled the tower. Partway round, while she squeezed under a fallen arch, something softer shifted beneath her foot.

This time, she caught her stumble without any noise. One of the warriors Anserth'd sent. She crouched. Maybe he'd have something that'd help her. Unable to make out much in the shadow, she followed his arm.

Cloth, not leather or chain, met her fingers. Stranger still, his shoulder was covered by cloth too. Had he stripped his armour to be—? Anessa snatched her hand away. The body was a woman. Slender, but a woman. Judging a decent gap, she reached for the woman's stomach. And felt bile rise up as her fingers sank into something clammy.

Guilt struggling with necessity, she wiped her hand on the body's trousers. But instead found robes. She rocked in her heels. A fighter might not wear armour if they wanted to sneak; they wouldn't wear robes though. She must be one of the other scholars.

After an apology, Anessa crept on. It didn't feel right leaving her; Kobb could do a proper burial once Anessa'd done her part, though. Several yards further round, she stopped. A short wall jutted from the side of the tower, the body and arms of a robed man visible beyond it. A slash, edges dark in the moonlight, marred his back. But only one.

Anessa frowned. Didn't seem right. The beasts snatched people up or dropped rocks on them. They had claws, but claws left several wounds. She crept closer.

Something was very wrong. All but one of a creature's claws might have missed. A creature might've hit the woman hard enough to knock her into a gap too narrow for its wingspan. But the crossbow bolt jutting from the man's thigh hadn't been fired by any beast.

Part Fifty

Anessa slipped back behind the wall. Why'd Karak use a crossbow rather than the beasts? And why kill a fleeing man? Didn't he try to drive everyone away...? She sighed. The answers wouldn't help. She needed to find a way in; one that Karak wasn't watching.

If he guarded anywhere, it'd be the door. She hadn't seen windows on the ground floor. If there were some on the other side, they'd be the next most obvious entry; so too risky. The next storey might be safe though; he couldn't watch everywhere on his own. She reached above her head and felt for holds between the stones.

The blocks were mortared. However, as she'd hoped, it'd crumbled in places, leaving shallow but useable joins. She squeezed the side of her left boot into the wall and eased herself up. The ache in her shoulders blossomed as she pressed her other foot against a crack.

Foot seated—barely—she slipped her right hand free and stretched up. The pain in her left shoulder spread to her elbow. Teeth gritted, she hooked her fingertips into another seam. For a moment, she thought she'd done it; then her ears began to sing. Waves of tightness surging through her head, she dropped down before she fell.

She stared up the wall. Rested, she'd clamber up and still been able to run. But creeping over fallen rubble all day pushed her well past the point where she'd head for home after a day's hunting. The way in had to be obvious, but she didn't know anything about Universities or wars. If Kobb was here, he'd—

Hunting. Anserth said she sent her best fighters. They'd have tried sneaking around. But they'd failed; because not been noticed was only part of hunting. To get close, you also needed to work out what your quarry'd do. Karak hadn't done this to live alone in a ruin; he wanted to do something in there. So he wouldn't lurk on the ground floor; he'd spend his time doing that. He might even think the creatures protected him, and not keep watch. She stretched a few times to work out the worst of the fatigue and sneaked back to the door.

The handle resisted, the edges digging into her palm as it juddered down. A dull graunch came from the lock. She paused. The keyhole looked bigger than most; big enough for a small crossbow bolt. She stepped to the side and lifted her hand away. Another part of hunting was traps.

Chest pressed against the wall, she reached sideways and twisted the handle. It moved partway and stopped. She bore down as hard as possible. The ache completed its journey along her arm, but the handle moved.

Then stuck with a final jolt.

She peeled her fingers free and considered it. The handle wasn't quite vertical; it was close enough, though. Almost certain the stiffness was disuse rather than a trap, she shoved the door. If it shifted at all, she didn't feel it. Whether the door was bolted or just jammed by age, she didn't have the strength left to open it. Tiredness and frustration rounded her shoulders, but she continued her circuit. Maybe she'd find a vine. Or whoever built the tower liked having windows on just one side.

The last curve of wall was as sheer as the rest. And—while some of the nearby buildings had collapsed—the creatures'd taken any sections that'd fallen against the wall. She continued round. The closest she found to a way up was the arch where the dead woman lay. Climbing it'd gain her six feet, but there wasn't a window above it so that wouldn't help.

She slumped onto a fallen block. Why couldn't Karak have made his lair in the next ruin over? Even if the wall wasn't missing, getting on the roof'd be easy. Why did he need a whole tower? The roof of that one was big enough for the creatures to land, and he'd still have two whole storeys for his evil plans.

She shook her head. All the things he'd done, and she was annoyed about where he picked. He probably didn't have a choice though. The tower was the only ruin she'd seen taller than two storeys. The original people probably built it because whatever Karak found needed to be high up. And even if he'd had a choice, he wouldn't have picked her preferred ruin, as one of the tower's window overlooked—

If there was space for a beast to land, there was space for her to run. Then jump to the window. She chuckled. Climb into plain sight with monsters lurking in the sky, run across a roof, then leap three yards. It was mad enough that Karak wouldn't expect anyone to do it.

She clambered up before she changed her mind. At least the roof was free of debris, so she needn't worry she'd trip. Her armour'd be a problem; the alternative was saving the world with no clothes on, though. The space looked long enough to get some speed. Thinking'd only give her more to worry about, and she wasn't going to become less tired any time soon. She jogged to the far edge, faced the window, and ran.

The sound of her boots filled her ears.

For a moment, she floated.

Then weight yanked at her. She stretched her fingers for the tower. She wasn't—

Breath spurted from her as the sill kicked her in the stomach.

Her fingertips cut furrows in the grime as she slid backwards, then caught on the broken edge of a floor tile. With a surge, she dragged herself in before she slipped again. Her body tried to curl, but she forced her chest open. Three gulps later, the pain dulled enough she could clamber to her feet.

Apart from shadows and cobwebs, the room was empty. An archway broke the opposite wall. Unslinging her crossbow, Anessa sneaked through and up the stairs beyond. As she passed the next floor, the gloom ahead gave way to flickering light. She slowed her pace further.

"You have to leave." Anessa stilled as a man spoke. Why talk to the creatures like friends?

"Not until we know she's safe." The second voice was hoarse, but sounded like a woman not a monster.

"It's too risky to call them for that. If you go tonight, you'll see for yourself."

Anessa crept up the steps, crossbow raised. Anserth hadn't actually said Karak was alone; she hadn't mentioned anyone else, though. Neither voice bubbled with arrogance like the madman at the stones either. Another odd thing on top of the dead bodies. She needed to know more before she attacked anyone. Easing up from a crouch, she peered into the next floor.

A man stood with his back to her, his hands on the shoulders of a woman. The sag in his stance suggested the same tiredness evident in her face. Both wore grimy robes. Neither seemed like they plotted murder.

Instead, they looked like her parents the day Grandam died. Crossbow hanging in one hand, she stepped through the archway.

The couple separated as she entered and stared at her with matched frowns.

Anessa raised her left hand. "Blessings on you."

The corners of the man's mouth rose. For a moment, she thought they'd greet her back. Then the woman yanked a knife from her belt and lunged forward.

Anessa's breath stuttered. So this was what it felt like to get stabbed. Dull, like a punch. Not how she'd expected at all.

Part Fifty-One

Anessa folded forward as the woman drew the knife back again. The pain felt like the time Dereck hit her with a rock. But this had to be worse. Anessa's crossbow clattered to the floor as she wrapped both forearms around her gut. A person's body tried to pretend things weren't as bad. Her stomach didn't feel damp, but maybe she wasn't thinking right. The only way to be sure was look.

But that'd mean moving her arms. What if that was what held the blood in? She realised the woman hadn't attacked again; instead she seemed to be arguing.

"...take the risk."

"She could have killed either of us from the doorway," said Karak. "Instead, she revealed herself. She didn't draw her sword. Or try to dodge. We agreed we'd only hurt people if we had to."

"But she's one of them. Look at her armour!"

Armour. Anessa eased her left arm off her stomach. The chain panels. Despite all the clinking, she'd forgotten she wasn't wearing her leathers. The pain still filled her side; she couldn't see any blood on her sleeve, though. Must have stopped the blade. No wonder it felt like being punched.

She straightened and noticed Karak held the woman back by the arm. "Traveller, not soldier... borrowed armour... want to talk."

Karak held out his free hand to his companion. After a moment, she dropped the knife into it. Dropping it on a table, he turned to Anessa. "If you really are hear to talk, you'd best shed your sword. And explain yourself."

Anessa eased the buckle open. The belt tugged at her as it fell away, but her guts didn't follow. "We saw some of those creatures carrying people off, so we came... my friend and me, that is, this way. Anserth said you'd gone mad, and was sending monsters out to kill everyone. So I said I'd sneak in so no one got hurt attacking. But she didn't tell me anyone else was here, and other things is odd too. And my Dad said best way to avoid a problem's to talk."

"A sensible person, your father. This is my wife. I'm not surprised Anserth didn't tell you; somehow, a married couple and their young daughter doesn't seem as threatening as a lone figure. And Anserth is so very good at only mentioning things when it serves her purpose. Did she tell you who she really is? What she's here to do?"

"She called herself an... Inductor. Sent to keep the expedition safe."

"Keep it safe? More like keep her patrons' prize safe. She was the perfect guard master until I gained entry to the vaults. Then she revealed her orders were to take everything back to the Council, secretly. I watched her guards kill Bordis. The last I saw of Savrik, he'd been shot in the leg. The three of us made it inside and barricaded the door." Karak scuffed one foot on the floor. "I couldn't let anyone harm my little Frinna. Some of the scrolls I found talked about calling for aid. I didn't know what else to do."

Anessa frowned. "If all you want to do's escape, why build the walls?"

"I never wanted to hurt anyone. I told the beasts to keep Anserth's people out. That must be why they didn't stop you: you don't work for her."

Anessa's shoulders sagged. She hadn't sneaked past unseen. "I've seen them carry people. If the creatures do what you say, you could fly out. Let Anserth take whatever you found."

"I can control them, but the beasts aren't... natural. The scrolls warn that paying attention for too long changes someone. Seeing them from a distance, or while you give instructions, is safe. Clasped to their chest while they carried you miles, though, would leave a person witless. That's why I only have one circling the tower; I sent the rest to an island nearby. There is a potion that protects you; the inhabitants weren't like us, though: it puts humans to sleep for most of a day."

"So you'd be—"

"—helpless," interjected Karak's wife, glaring at her husband. "The potion takes time to work, and someone has to be awake to control the beasts. So we can't both go. And I'm not leaving him alone. Not with assassins creeping in."

Karak sighed. "Frinna needs you more than I do. She'll be safe now she's..." He looked at Anessa for a moment. "She'll be safe where she is. She'll be scared without us though, so you should go."

"We haven't translated everything yet. There might be better way. And with both of us here, Anserth won't risk sending anyone after her."

After her? The sleeping child must be their daughter! Anessa felt her cheeks warm. She needed to fix things, and fast. "There must be a way. What if I guided you out? As long as they think you're here and you've got the creatures, they'll—"

"So that's why you came!" Karak's wife raised her fists. "You want to trick us into an ambush. Tell us we need to go through a building, then grab us where the beasts can't rescue us."

"No." Anessa lifted her hands, palms up. Hopefully, people calmed like spooked animals. "I'm not a threat. I came in to stop anyone else getting hurt." She glanced down at her sword, then deliberately took a step forward.

"We can find a way out of this. Sounds like Anserth tricked us both, so I've no reason to help her. And the Reverend can protect you from her."

"Reverend?" Karak's eyes widened. "But why would there be...? Why did you come to the ruins?"

"There's something gone wrong... don't understand it, but Reverend Kobb does; and we followed the trail here. He's a good man. We get to him, and he'll sort this out. I'll lead you over the wall, then–" Something wrong. The Korha came from somewhere else. The insects'd made a gate to somewhere else. They couldn't let Anserth get the magic. "How long to destroy the scrolls?"

"Destroy the scrolls?" Karak grinned. "You mean escape and leave her nothing? You're right: she might not risk attacking a Reverend. Wouldn't work though. Setting the scrolls alight is easy enough; destroying the ritual circle would take until at least midday, though. Maybe you could slip out in daylight, but..."

Part Fifty-Two

Anessa studied the two archaeologists. Karak was right: they looked healthy, but didn't carry themselves like hunters. On a cloudy night, she might be able to give one person enough help to sneak out unseen. But both of them together, under a full moon... They'd be noticed as soon as they crossed the wall; assuming Karak's wife even heeded Anessa's words in the first place.

Unless the guards weren't watching. "Where does Anserth draw water? The creatures fouled the lake, so the guards must get it from somewhere else."

"Water? From cisterns." Karak shook his head. "I thought of crawling out through the conduits; there aren't any, though."

"She already knew that." Karak's wife glared at Anessa. "She's suggesting things which won't work, so we believe she wants to help. Probably isn't even with the Church. And if she is, they're here to steal our find too."

Fury flooded Anessa. "Kobb's a good man! He could've killed everyone in my village, but he let them capture him 'cos he didn't want people hurt. If this circle's what's causing the evil, he could just kill you and destroy it. But he won't! If you don't take my help, then that's your choice. But you don't get to say that about him. And I don't even know what a conduit is.

If I pour that potion in the water, the guards fall asleep. Then you can take those city ways and walk out of here while Kobb saves everyone again."

Karak swallowed hard. "That might work. I'll find you a map."

"Thank you." Anessa snatched her sword up and buckled it in place, grimacing as her gut complained.

After rifling through a couple of chests, Karak handed Anessa a yellowing scroll.

Anessa unrolled it. The ink'd started to brown; the shapes of the buildings were clear enough to find the tower, though. However, there didn't seem to be anything that looked like a well. "Where's the water?"

"Where it says— Sorry. Surrounded by archaeologists all day, I forgot not everyone reads Skithic. Look for— It's easier if I mark them for you, rather than spell it."

Anessa gave the map back, thankful for another Blessing. Karak'd agreed her plan, but city folk had strange thoughts; might change his mind if he realised she couldn't read.

Pen and scroll clutched in one hand, Karak flipped open and closed several small jars. Satisfied by the contents of the fourth jar, he pinned the map flat with the other three and dipped his pen in. "This might take a while. Could you bring the bottles of potion up, dear?"

Karak's wife peered at Anessa for a moment before stomping out of the room.

"Don't mind Brinthe. She's worried about Frinna." Karak made another mark on the scroll. "But where are my manners? You're risking yourself for us, and I haven't even asked your name."

"Anessa. Anessa Tanton."

"A pleasure to meet you, Anessa. If there's ever anything in my power I can do to repay this kindness, it's yours."

Anessa stared at her feet. "Just destroy all the things that brought those creatures."

"You have my word." He waved the scroll around for a moment, then handed it to her. "We only used one cistern before Anserth... I labelled it primary. I've marked them all though, just in case."

Anessa looked down. Fresh ink scrawled across some of the buildings; fortunately, one of the squiggles was different. Rolling it up, she tucked it into her jacket and walked to her sword. She was resettling her crossbow across her back when Brinthe stomped in, three stoneware bottles clutched to her chest.

Karak frowned. "Weren't there—?"

"There's no guarantee the girl'll manage it. So I kept one."

Anessa stiffened. "More I put in the water, better chance it don't just leave them dozy."

"And without any potion, we're trapped here. Which might be what you want." Brinthe thrust the bottles into Anessa's arms. "My husband wants to risk it, I'll go along. But don't mean I trust you."

"You want to keep an eye on me; you're welcome to follow me to the wall. But I ain't slowing for you."

Brinthe turned on her heel and headed up the stairs, shoulders rigid.

Biting down a bad word before it slipped out, Anessa glanced between the bottles and her armour. A few moments later, Karak emptied a sling bag onto the floor and held it out for her.

Even knowing the beast'd seen her but hadn't pounced, Anessa kept to the walls as she left the tower. She did make the journey faster, though. One hand braced against the bottles to stop rattling, she stopped at the top of the wall and studied the buildings. As she feared, not all the shadows seemed natural.

After ducking below the lip, she removed her jacket then replaced her weapons and the bag. Even a single clink of chain'd attract attention, and the armour wouldn't help if they spotted her, anyway. Arms and torso free again, she slipped over the wall and moved from shadow to shadow.

Two streets later, she risked a step into the light to check the scroll. After moving back she waited a few breaths to be sure no one'd noticed, then curved around to the right area. Between the damage since the map was drawn and her not understanding it, she expected a long search. However, a dull glow from a nearby building caught her eye. That had to be the cistern. Why weren't the guards hidden below like Anserth's rooms? She crept closer.

Like many of the others, the building lacked windows. A quick glance around the doorway revealed a single figure seated next to a shuttered lantern. The spill of light wasn't enough to make out their face. It did show they sat on a wooden hatch, though. Of course! The water was under the buildings, so there wouldn't be a basement to hide in.

She picked up a small section of rock. After sneaking around the corner, she lent forward and threw the stone as hard as possible the other way. A loud clatter echoed along the street as it bounced down a pile of rubble.

Several breaths passed without a response. Then, as she was wondering what else to try, the guard emerged with the lantern and headed away.

Creeping toward the door, she eased the corks from the bottles. Open the hatch, drop the entire bag in, and be out again before the man finished his search. It'd be easier with a light, but the route to the cistern was clear. Glad she'd shed the jacket, she slipped to the centre of the room. Her fingers met the handle where she expected. But the hatch didn't move.

She placed the bag down and gripped with both hands. After a moment, the hatch squealed up about a foot before sticking. Had the guard heard, or had the walls trapped it? Running footsteps answered her question.

Kicking the bag in, she straightened as a beam of light cut through the doorway. Blinded, she heard Col say, "What've we got here? You come to liven up the watch?"

Part Fifty-Three

"Thirsty work climbing over the wall twice." Anessa straightened and rubbed a hand across her lips. She hadn't noticed a bucket in the room; hopefully that meant the water level was close to the top.

Col swaggered forward, corners of his mouth curled up. His resemblance to a weasel stopped it being reassuring, but he kept the light out of her eyes. "Looks like you spilled half of it on your singlet. Best take it off so you don't catch chill."

She glanced down. Stale sweat stuck the cotton to her chest, the lantern beam highlighting every inch. He wasn't considerate; he just preferred to shine the light somewhere else. She'd a good mind to smack him in the groin. But brawling with a guard might raise suspicion. "Couldn't see a bucket, and weren't no one here to ask. Anserth told me to hurry back."

"Anserth... I didn't..." Col put the lantern down and sidled sideways. "Take the light. I'll be fine in the dark. Anything else I can do?"

Anessa frowned. He must have known Anserth asked her to do something, so what'd scared him? "Moonlight's enough to see. I'll travel faster with both hands empty anyway."

"Great idea. Only being helpful. You know that right?"

Shit piles, was he only helping. But she wanted to be gone as bad as he wanted her gone. She nodded once and strode out the door.

After the lantern, the ruins seemed dark. But her memory of the street proved good enough that she made it out of sight without incident. Pausing in a shadow, she screwed her eyes tight to speed her night sight. Seemed Anserth's people were as scared of her as Karak. So going to her was the last thing anyone'd do if they'd sense. For a moment, Anessa thought about finding Kobb and somewhere to hide until everyone was asleep.

If she didn't return though, Anserth'd tire of waiting and send more people over the wall. Going back was scary, but might mean the difference between all the guards wetting their throats and not. After offering the Maker a smile for the Blessing of walking openly, Anessa clambered up a pile of stone and sought a good route.

Rough direction picked, she set off. Collapsed buildings stopped her moving in a straight line, but not needing to hide made it easy to move around them. Sweaty, dusty, and wishing she'd really had that drink of water, she staggered to where she'd left Kobb and Anserth. Instead of the group of warriors she expected, a lone woman in dull leathers squatted in a doorway.

Anessa leaned on the jamb. "Where's Anserth?"

The guard jerked a thumb over her shoulder without shifting her gaze off the wall. "Took the Reverend and the girl to camp."

"Thanks." The news made Anessa feel less tired. If Kobb was with Frinna, she wouldn't need to creep about trying to find her. After a long stretch, she headed toward the basement. Unlike the last time, the doors stood open and the guards waved her past unchallenged.

The same group of people, Anserth now with them, stood clustered around the maps as Anessa entered. She couldn't see Kobb or Frinna anywhere though.

Anserth stepped away from the table and ran her gaze up Anessa. "Welcome back. Looks like a hard journey. Last report said one of those monsters still circled. Did you...?"

"Don't know what it's doing. I sorted things, though." Anessa forced herself not to look away. Nothing she'd said was a lie... exactly. "Best wait for morning before we go in."

Anserth moved closer, a smile softening the angles of her face. "You don't want to go now?"

Anessa felt warmth slip up her neck. Don't break eye contact. She just needed to keep it up until Kobb turned up. "Rubble's not an easy climb. Be easier in daylight."

"Good idea. It must've been hard work. You'll want a chance to relax." Anserth placed a hand on Anessa's shoulder. "You're shaking. I've a bottle of wine in my quarters I saved. Let's have a goblet each." Anserth turned, her hand moving to Anessa's back.

Each of Anserth's fingers felt obvious with only the thin singlet between her skin and the gauntlet. Stomach roiling, Anessa let herself be steered into Anserth's quarters. Wine might calm her down. And sipping it'd give her time to think. She stumbled to a halt as her companion's hand slipped away.

The Inductor tugged her gauntlets free. "Could you undo my breastplate? The danger's over; I don't need to clank around. So no reason we can't be comfortable."

Anessa peered at the thick metal plate. As soon as she undid one side, it'd twist sideways. "Err... I'm not sure how, Inductor."

"Just get close and undo both sides at once. You won't break anything." The Inductor removed the armour on her arms and dropped it to the floor. "And you're not under my command; my friends call me Serth."

"Anessa." Unsure if this was better or worse than having to talk about Karak, Anessa stepped closer. Pressing herself right up against Serth's torso, she could reach the both sets of straps at once. Her fingers felt like dough, but she managed to unhook the buckles. As the last set slid free, the breastplate dropped hard onto her chest.

She stumbled away. Serth caught her by the shoulders before she fell. The bottom of the armour pressed against Anessa's thighs.

"Grab the edges and guide it."

Fingers gripping tight enough to turn white, Anessa eased her feet back then let the plate slide. Serth's arms still bracing her, she shoved the breastplate sideways. The crash of metal hitting stone was louder than she expected, and - despite her companion's comment - she looked up in panic.

Serth smiled at her, less intimidating with half her armour gone. "Can you do my legs, too?"

Thick leather straps ran from the top of the leg pieces to a thick belt. They'd be easier to get at if she knelt. Close up, the buckles looked easy enough for someone to undo on their own; so, why did Serth need her to do it? After several moments of fumbling at straps that wouldn't loosen, Anessa began to think her fear had turned her fingers even more doughy.

A moment's peering later, she realised the plates interlocked with the groin plate somehow; meaning there wasn't enough give to unbuckle them. The big buckle in the centre of Anserth's belt opened smoothly. Happy for having worked it out, Anessa eased the metal trousers down while Anserth stepped out. A thick padded jacket thumped to the flags beside her leg.

Startled, Anessa sat down hard. Dressed in only a thin singlet and hose, Anserth was curvier. Which made sense: Anserth's leathers smoothed her chest. It was another thing seeing the difference, though.

Serth rolled her shoulders and then stretched her arms up. The hem of her singlet stayed decent... barely.

Throat tight, Anessa looked away.

"Definitely more comfortable. Thank you." After arching her back again, Anserth held out a hand to Anessa. But instead of the expected gentle assistance, she pulled hard.

Half-tripping, Anessa caught herself on her companion's chest with her free hand. Blood burning her face, Anessa snatched her fingers away. "Sorry... We should get Kobb. Save me telling things twice."

Anessa only realised Serth'd still been holding her hand when she let go. Strong fingers pressed against her chin, tilting her head up. Serth's face'd lost the last of its harshness, but that didn't make her gaze any less scary.

"So dedicated. I respect that. But you deserve to relax. Give your report in the morning."

Serth's fingers weren't pressing hard. Anessa could just step backwards. So, why weren't her feet moving?

Part Fifty-Four

The scent of sweat and spices filled Anessa's nose. A fluttering sensation joined the churning in her stomach. Muscles taut, she stepped away, a tingle running along her jaw as it drew across Serth's fingers. Unsteady - but ability to act returning - she took another pace. Only to fall as the edge of cot hit the back of her left leg, sending her sprawling.

Serth moved closer, her gaze heavy as it ran up Anessa's body, "Are you —?"

Anessa drew her legs in and shoved against at the palliasse with her fists.

"Steady." Serth dropped to a crouch and raised her hands, palms forward. "What's wrong?"

Wrong? Serth was a liar and a killer and a... "I wasn't... I..."

"You haven't been with a woman before, have you?"

Heat raced across Anessa's skin. Been with a woman? Privacy wasn't something most people in Morth had, and mostly everyone tended animals. So she'd known how sex worked as long as she remembered. And weren't nothing wrong with whatever two people wanted to do. She'd always thought that she'd marry and have a family, though—once she'd finished hunting and adventuring; that she didn't feel that way about the boys in Morth because they were cruel and stupid.

Serth rocked onto her heels, then eased upright. "I'll pour us that wine." Pulling a bottle out of the chest, Serth twisted the cork out and reached back for a battered metal tankard. She grinned at Anessa as she filled it. "Goblet's an exaggeration. But a tankard does the task."

Anessa pushed herself into a sitting position as Serth stepped closer. After snatching the outstretched drink, she slid away again until she hit the wall.

Serth sat on the chest and swigged from the bottle.

Droplets sloshed across her hand as Anessa gulped the wine. Bitter, fruity, fire snatched her breath yet did nothing to the fluttering or churning. Swallowing hard, she clutched the mug to her stomach. She needed to make it last. If she finished it, Serth'd pour more; and that'd mean her coming closer again. Anessa ignored the voice in her head that suggested Serth being close wouldn't be bad, and stared into the dark liquid.

"Would it help if you told me about the tower? You achieved a task no one else has managed."

Anessa hunched further over the mug. Serth lied to her, so why'd keeping Karak's secret feel like betrayal?

Except, Serth hadn't actually lied: not mentioning wasn't lying. Anessa took a sip—a small one—to fill the silence.

"Talking might help."

It wouldn't. Talking about the tower'd make everything— Or did Serth mean the other thing? Maybe telling Serth about Karak was the right thing to do. Then she'd stop being so nice.

The other end of the palliasse sagged.

Warm fingers brushed Anessa's ankle. "I didn't mean to... I assumed you wanted..."

Anessa looked up. No trace of the hard-faced, confident warrior remained in Serth's face. City folk had odd beliefs. What if liking women weren't natural there? Anessa pushed down the urge to take Serth's hand: comforting her'd be kind; but that could lead to... and maybe neither of them'd stop this time. "I... reckon you're right about a night's sleep before talking. I've not... I want to get it right."

The sadness on Serth's face melted, replaced by a shaky smile. She walked to the door. "Time to think's a good idea. No need to rush things. I'll have Orlin show you." Fingers on the latch, she turned. "Before you go. Why haven't you mentioned Karak's wife?"

Wine gushed across the cot as Anessa's hand dropped to the sword. "I..."

"A shame." Serth drew a long thin blade from the nape of her neck. "I do like you. And I'd hoped you were nervous because it's your first time. You didn't kill either of them did you? There's no harm done yet though, so no need for violence. Think about it overnight and you'll realise Karak's a bad person. We'll have that talk tomorrow; tell me everything and we can make it all right."

Anessa slumped against the wall as Serth opened the door. She could draw her sword and fight; someone who kept a knife in their slip'd expect whatever she did before she even thought of it, though.

At some point Orlin must've come in, because he was steering her up and out of the room. The people gathered round the maps didn't even glance up as he led her out of the basement.

Outside, they headed into an area she hadn't explored. Two streets in, Orlin drew her to a halt and stepped away. "I'll put you in the same room as the Reverend. It'll be less painful if you hand me your weapons, rather than make me take them."

Anessa bowed her head and reached for her belt. Purple light seared her vision.

Fingers tangled in the buckle, she staggered away as Orlin collapsed backwards. She blinked hard.

"Good to see you," said Kobb. "So you had a falling out with the Inductor, too."

"She's..." Anessa wasn't sure what Serth was. But she was certain she trusted Kobb. "Karak weren't like she said. He only wanted to save his family."

"And Anserth found out you hadn't done her killing for her."

"I tried to pretend, but..." Anessa hoped the night hid her blush. "There's something else she don't know though. Karak had more of the potion that made his daughter sleep. Before I went to Serth, I put it in the water."

Kobb drew her into a hug. "Brilliant! I wondered why my guards both dozed off. We'd best leave before someone notices."

"We can't. I promised I'd get Karak out if he destroyed the—"

The ruins shook as a deep note of metal on metal rang out. A breath later, purple light melted the shadows.

Anessa broke free of his arms. A blazing column speared into the sky from the direction of the tower.

"I don't think returning for him would do any good." Kobb rested a hand on her elbow. "You couldn't have known."

"He might've—"

The tone rang out again, undercut by dull cracks. Anessa fell to one knee as the ground bucked beneath her.

Kobb's lips moved as he pulled her up, but the noise of collapsing buildings drowned his words. Each with an arm wrapped around the other, they ran deeper into the ruins.

For a moment, Anessa thought they'd get away. Then the street ahead tipped, sending them sliding toward a gaping hole.

Her fingers scrabbled at the ground. All they found was loose grit.

Part Fifty-Five

The ground tilted further, turning Anessa's slide into a tumble. Dirty heat ran up her back as the rough stone shredded her singlet.

Pain lanced through her left shoulder, followed by a dull smack along her ribs as her body struck the side of the hole. Something clamped her wrist. Teeth gritted, she looked up.

Kobb hung above her, one hand around her wrist and the other hooked on something. The shifting ground had somehow lifted him up. Her outstretched fingers were just inches below the rim of the hole. Brow furrowed, he shouted over the din of falling stone. "Can't lift you up. Have to climb."

Anessa reached up, almost screaming as the shift in position drove another lance in. Fingers wrapped around Kobb's wrist, she pulled. But couldn't keep her grip. Her second try was equally unsuccessful.

Shoulder seeming on the verge of tearing free, she turned her foot against the side before gripping Kobb's arm. Hoping it wouldn't swing her out too far, she kicked up as she pulled.

The stabbing in her left shoulder eased. She squeezed her grip tighter, then kicked again. The force swung her body away from the side, but also gave her slack to bend her elbow.

A breath later, her weight fell onto her arms. Her right was yanked straight; but took enough of the strain that the agony in her left subsided to an ache. "You can let go now."

"I don't think... that's a good idea." Kobb flicked his eyes up, neck corded and teeth bared. His fingers sprang open.

She realised it was a grin— or as close as he could get. Too battered to even smile back, she inched her way up again and grabbed for the rim. Fire surged through her as she put weight on her left shoulder. Then her fingers slipped.

Fortunately, her right hand didn't. However, the pain blurred her sight. She braced her legs again. Without her weight, Kobb could jump to safety. With it, he'd eventually fall. She had to use her left arm. If she fell, at least he'd be safe. Toes scrabbling against the side, she grabbed the edge of the hole; and let go of Kobb.

After brief eternity of pain, her right hand joined her left. Jagged cold cutting the fuzziness with each movement, she hauled herself up.

Cracked slabs shifted, yet did not fall. Legs hanging into the pit, she slumped until the hammer in her head ceased. An uncertain time later, Kobb's hands grabbed her belt. Her left arm provided only agony; between her right and Kobb's tugging, Anessa's feet reached solid ground though.

"Shaking's stopped," said Kobb. "Safe to rest a while."

He was right about the shaking. But not resting. "Need to move. If it's safe for us, it's safe for them. My arm's useless. Can't let them catch us."

Kobb's fingers ran over her shoulder. "Only a strain."

"Hope so. Either way, can't brace a crossbow. And I doubt they'll run onto my sword."

Kobb peered around. "We barely avoided being crushed. Doubt many closer in still move about, and those that do have better things than look for us. Reckon I know where they were keeping Falcon."

Anessa's neck hurt from watching every shadow at once, but Kobb's prediction proved right. Despite tired feet sending loose rock skittering and aching lungs announcing each breath, no one unchallenged them as they wove through the rubble.

Kobb paused next to a mostly intact and chuckled. A soft whicker came round the corner, followed by Falcon's head. Kobb rubbed his horse's nose. "Not the only one who broke out I see. Lead the way, then."

After bunting Kobb's fingers, Falcon walked away, seemingly unconcerned by the random ground. A few yards later, he stopped and pawed at a slanted wall.

The light caught a buckle. Their packs! If she turned sideways— She fell forward as something wet hit her back. Another whicker came from just behind her ear. Ignoring the horse, she tugged her pack free then eased Kobb's saddle bags out. Sweat beaded on her brow, she patted Falcon once on the nose before snatching her fingers away. "You're smarter than you look."

"He's not the only one." Serth emerged from the shadows. Grime coated every inch, and one leg dragged behind her. But she still loomed. "Glad to see you weren't crushed, Anessa. I half-expected you'd let Karak live. But I never guessed you were a sorcerer. Guessed you'd come here though." More figures, each with a crossbow, stepped into the light. "You can't take us all, so best surrender."

Serth thought she was responsible for an earthquake? And why did Serth want to capture them? Had some of it been real?

"No need for killing." Kobb raised his palms and stepped forward, his right boot coming down on the pile of supplies.

Several of the warriors swung weapons up.

The ground lurched. For a moment, Anessa was puzzled by the silence. Then her knees slammed into snow-covered grass.

Bile flooded her mouth as her stomach added its voice to the pains in her limbs. Stones. Kobb had—

The Reverend sprawled beside her, the bolt through his chest stopping him lying flat.

"Haelen!" The last of her strength gone on the shout, Anessa collapsed next to Kobb. Her face landed less than an inch from his, but she couldn't feel his breath.

Part Fifty-Six

Needles of cold sank deeper into Anessa. Yet she remained motionless, desperate not to miss the slight twitch or puff of air that meant Kobb was only hurt. Vision blurring, she allowed herself to blink.

A series of noises came from nearby. Then something tugged at her arm, rolling her onto her back. She tried to resist; her limbs refused to work, though. A blurry shape blocked the stars. Pain exploded across her face.

Haelen crouched over her, right palm raised. "Anessa! Can you hear me?"

"What... Kobb..."

"You're battle fatigued." Haelen tugged at her shoulders. "Get up."

"Kobb." Anessa tried to turn sideways, but Haelen gripped harder.

"You need to rest; and to be somewhere warm."

Anessa let him ease her to her feet. As soon as her knees held her weight, she shook his hand off. "Can't. Need to save Kobb."

Haelen grabbed her jaw and twisted her head to face him. "I understand. But, you're tired and not thinking straight. That means you'll make mistakes. And I can't keep an eye on you and help the Reverend. If you don't go to bed, I'll have to put you there."

Tears leaving icy trails down her face, she stumbled into her tent and fell onto her furs. Tired people did do stupid things. It made sense. Haelen wasn't lying to her. He'd help Kobb.

Her hours of clambering, running, and tumbling weighted hard enough she barely pulled the furs over before her body refused to move. But her thoughts didn't join her limbs. After what seemed like days flickering between the same half-formed fears, she realised it was light outside. Each movement sending a new wave of throbbing through her head, she staggered to her feet.

Porridge. Kobb'd need a good breakfast. And—

Air gasped from her mouth as her chest hit the ground. Something tugged at her left foot.

Dampness spread through her singlet. Realising she'd been staring at the rope hooked around her ankle for long enough to melt the snow, she struggled upright and headed for the fire-pit.

A good helping of oats, and some vegetables. She added even more. Kobb needed his strength back; they could get supplies later. Plenty of water, too. Not having to chew'd let him eat faster.

Chunks of carrot and swede bobbed. The cold sank deeper into Anessa as she watched nothing happen. After a while, she leaned closer. Only clumps of ash and soggy fragments of charred wood filled the pit. What embers'd lasted overnight, she'd slopped water over without noticing. Eyelids heavy and limbs numb, she wandered the camp looking for kindling.

"Anessa." Haelen's arms wrapped around her. "You're freezing. What are you doing out of bed? Let's get you back in the warm."

"Making Kobb porridge."

Haelen steered her toward the tents. "It's a little soon for that. Maybe tomorrow."

"You mean—?"

"He isn't dead. But he needs to sleep. And so do you." Haelen angled them into the improvised hospital. "But I suppose you won't stay in bed until you've seen for yourself."

Kobb's head poked from a thick blanket. A blanket that rose and fell. Stained rags and tools filled a bucket beside him.

She twisted to face Haelen. Bags hung under blood-shot eyes. "I hoped, but..."

"Weren't easy. And no telling how long he'll need to sleep. He's tougher than most, though."

Despite Haelen's reassurances and seeing Kobb breathe, Anessa felt a sense of unease. A few moments later, she realised why: it was too quiet in the tent. The villagers lay still and silent, blankets covering them from head-to-toe.

Haelen pulled her back as she stepped closer. "They didn't survive. Now get yourself to bed, girl."

Leaving the fire unlit and breakfast unmade felt odd—until she lay down. For a moment, the image of Serth's mouth starting to smile rose up, then blankness swallowed her.

The tent was dark when she woke. Someone moved nearby. "Haelen?"

"How are you feeling?"

Her head felt clear. Most of her ached, but an old, dull ache. "Better, I think."

"See." Haelen sat on the edge of her bed. "Kobb's still asleep. But the stone's dark, so whatever you did worked."

Kobb almost killed. Karak, his wife, his daughter, and who knew how many other people dead. Didn't feel like victory. And... Serth. Even if Kobb woke up, she didn't know how to talk him about her. Haelen, though... "Can you like someone and still hurt them?"

Haelen drew back. "What do you mean? What did you see?"

"There was an Inductor. She acted like she liked me. But then she tried to have me locked up."

"It's possible to like someone and think something else is more important. Sagas are full of best friends on opposite sides of a war."

"What about...?" Heat burnt up her face, mercifully hidden by the darkness.

"You don't mean smiled-a-bit liked do you?" Haelen sucked air through his teeth. "Yes; for something meaningful enough. Inductors are trained to get the task done, whatever it takes. Don't stop them feeling, though. That's why those sagas are tragedies; isn't a way to get it all."

"Why'd she have to—" Tears boiled up.

"She weren't the only one felt something, was she? Don't get to choose who we like. And liking someone as does wrong, don't make you bad too. Take that Eater. Eaters've killed people long as anyone remembers, yet the Reverend wasn't wrong to help it."

"You don't have to tell Kobb do you?"

"Not unless you want. Although, he's sensible... for a Botherer, so I reckon he'd understand."

Anessa uncurled. Problem wasn't Kobb judging her; it was... well... the way Serth made her feel. Talking to Haelen was hard enough.

Haelen's weight shifted. "Get some sleep. I'll wake you if anything changes."

The next three days passed in a haze of inaction. She visited Kobb as often as she could; Haelen drove her out if she stayed too long, though.

She awoke dribbling on the fourth day. The scent of hot oats flooded through the tent flap. Pulling on her jacket, she ran out.

"Not exactly a feast of gratitude," said Kobb, looking up from the pot, "but porridge is mostly all we have."

"You're... Should you be...?"

"Best sleep I've had since I started having the dreams. I feel like I could outrun Falcon. Which is just as well; we need to get back to it."

"No. You need to rest."

"He'd lose that race." Haelen paused in the door of the infirmary to stretch. "He's fit enough to not waste the days away though. Especially if I'm along to keep an eye on him."

Anessa shrugged and filled a bowl. Seemed too quick—Haelen'd been right about Kobb so far, though. Scooping oaty goodness as fast as she could, she settled on a log. Just to make sure Kobb didn't rush, she filled a second big bowlful after the first.

Her stomach overruling her virtue and tongue combined, she admitted defeat partway down the third bowl and grabbed her pack.

The trip through? by? stone ended with barely a bump in a forest clearing. Winter sun took the edge from the frosty air. And—despite moving three people and a horse—Kobb stood straight and grinned at her. Haelen'd been—

Haelen stared past them, face pale. She turned to follow his gaze.

Eaters, spears raised and several deep, filled the treeline.

PART FIFTY-SEVEN

Kobb's weapons flowed into his hands without effort. The bandage tugged at his chest as he adopted a defensive stance. Apart from that, he felt great; in fact, he felt like a young man again. However—even if it weren't an illusion caused by the first proper sleep in months—it wouldn't be enough to overcome so many people.

The lines of spear-waving figures opened to reveal a hunched figure with two sets of complex golden antlers jutting from its mask and a long staff. If horns meant shaman, then this was a powerful or respected one.

Feet weaving in a pattern that moved as far to the sides as it did forward, the shaman advanced. An atonal chant counterpointed the slap of feet on ground.

Kobb flicked his gaze along the treeline and considered his options. If he used his Courser now, the shaman might not be able to dodge. However, he'd only get one attempt, and the remaining Skithai would overwhelm them even without the shaman's help. So, he needed the Skithai to not be enemies. He let his weapons hang lose. "All certitude is like the mist at dawn..."

The shaman spun its staff counter-clockwise above its head. The chant changed to a single phrase. "Anh-Tanak Rosh Skithai!"

The other Skithai began shouting and stamping.

Kobb scanned the treeline for the first sign of attack. Was this a greeting, or hadn't the shaman understood? He drove the point of his rapier into the ground and held out his pendant. Maybe it'd recognise the symbol.

Light glinted from the crystals embedded in the shaman's staff as it spun faster.

"Anh-Skithai!" Haelen stepped forward and pressed the fingers of his left hand to his chest. "Volg Tomor'ek. Volg Rosh'ek. Skithai Volg Anh-Sorda." Each time he said Volg he tapped his right fist against his left hand.

The Skithai fell silent. A loud thud filled the silence as the end of the shaman's staff hit the ground. Head tilted, the shaman peered at Haelen.

"Volg Rosh Haelen." Haelen tapped with his right fist again. "Skithai Volg Anh-Sorda."

The shaman held its empty hand out, palm down, then lowered it. Almost as one, the Skithai slung their spears. Twisting its staff hard, the shaman stuck it in the ground and then took two steps toward Haelen.

"What did you say, Haelen?" Kobb continued to scan the line of Skithai. "How did you...?"

"The previous occupant of the stones dealt with Skithai. Realised while you were in Morth that meant he learnt enough their language to not be killed on sight. Didn't seem as important as investigating the circle, but I wasn't getting anything new from the other notes so I learnt a bit of the language. Glad I did now."

Kobb agreed. A thought struck him as he sheathed his Courser: each time they used the stones they appeared somewhere significant, so arriving next to a large group of Skithai might be more than bad fortune. "Can you ask the Skithai what brings them here? And if they've seen anything odd nearby?"

"Men take Tan-Sorda." The shaman's voice sounded like the crack of branches. "Skithai hunt men. Kill men. Return Tan-Sorda to holy place."

"Tan-Sorda?" Haelen frowned. "God-Beast? An icon?"

"Not statue. Tan-Sorda. Dung of Tan-Sorda bring life. When Tan-Sorda return to holy place, carry voices of Skithai with it."

Kobb wrapped his fingers around the blade of his rapier. Careful to keep the tip pointed away from the Skithai, he tugged it out of the ground and wiped the dirt off, before sheathing it. "Men stole a creature sacred to you?"

The shaman snorted. "Cannot steal what cannot be owned."

"We can help," said Anessa. "They'd attack you on sight, but they'll talk to us. No need to kill anyone."

Kobb smiled at her optimism. She was right the four of them could get close without less chance of being attacked; even if they convinced the thieves to return this creature, though, he suspected the Skithai wanted the men dead. "You'll do better with our help."

An odd creaking noise filled the air, and the shaman began to shake. After a moment, Kobb realised it was laughing. Slapping its hands together, it straightened. "Kill you now. You kill some Skithai. Still not have Tan-Sorda. Not kill you. Maybe have Tan-Sorda and no Skithai die. Maybe kill you tomorrow anyway."

"We'll get the Tan-Sorda for you," said Haelen, "but you'll have to describe it, and we'll need more than a day."

"Tan-Sorda is tall as travelling-meat." The shaman pointed at Falcon. "But wider. Wide horns on brow, like shining tree. Sometimes stands on two legs. Scouts say men fifty spear throws that way. Give you until Anh-Volg-T'ek, then Skithai come. Kill all men."

The shaman turned on its heel and strode back into the trees, yanking the staff out of the ground as it passed. Without a sound, the other Skithai slipped from sight.

Kobb picked up Falcon's reins. "We'd best get started then. Don't suppose those notes say how long a spear-throw is?"

"No. Legion release at sixty yards, though. So say fifty throws is close on two miles."

Anessa leading, they set out in the direction the shaman had pointed. The ground rose, becoming rockier. Slightly past mid-morning, the trees started to thin. Anessa stopped at the crest of the rise and beckoned the others forward.

Ahead the forest ended at a cliff. Beyond it, a plain stretched out to a walled town. Anessa frowned. "That must be where they went. But it's vast. How will we find them?"

Kobb studied the town. To someone used to cities, it was tiny. She was right about it taking time to search, though. "How long is it till Anh-Volg-T'ek, Haelen?"

"It's not a when, it's a what. It means something like council of the warriors."

"So, we have until they talk themselves into a frenzy. A couple of days at best."

"But, won't they all die?" Anessa pointed at the walls. "The fence around Morth kept the Eaters out, and it only took a few people to drive them off with crossbows."

Haelen's shoulders sagged. "I don't think it will just be the Skithai we saw. I might not be translating it right, but I think a council needs at least nine shaman."

Kobb did a quick count in his head. "And how many shaman in a tribe?"

"The notes talked about needing to gain the trust of the shaman.

There might be more than one, but..."

"...but there might be nine tribes united, or more. Hundreds of warriors. Enough for a siege."

Part Fifty-Eight

Kobb ran his gaze across the plain again. He was no expert on sieges; however, the wide swathes of farmland suggested they didn't keep sufficient supplies within the walls to withstand a long siege—at least not without sacrificing a substantial number of inhabitants. And worse, the clear space stretched further than effective crossbow range, allowing attackers to camp around the town with little risk

Whereas—if a staff was as powerful as a Courser—each shaman could send blasts at anyone who sallied forth or even showed themselves above the parapet. Nine together might have enough power to breach a wall.

The only area defensible against those odds was inside massive inner wall that loomed over the far side of the town. But even that would fall to starvation if a relief force didn't arrive within a few weeks.

"We need to summon help," said Anessa.

Kobb swept his arm around the forest. "These trees grow across the land. Without knowing where we are, we don't know where the nearest garrison is. And, if we did chance on it, two days isn't long enough to muster sufficient forces to overcome so many tribes."

"Then we have to warn them." Anessa strode closer to the cliff and looked from side-to-side. "We can get down over there."

Haelen met Kobb's eyes, brow creased. "It might be better if we don't warn anyone. Even if we convince them of the threat, we'll spend all our time being questioned again about what we saw, what was said, how far we travelled. Whereas, if no one knows we're more than travellers, we find the beast, kill it, then return to the circle."

"Kill it?" Anessa spun to face them. "Once we have it, we stop the Eaters coming."

Kobb stepped forward and rested a hand on her shoulder. "Haelen means the Tan-Sorda could well be what's holding the power here. Killing it before the Skithai recapture it might be our only chance."

"We can't just let the Eaters kill them!" Anessa twisted away.

"I don't want to do it either," Haelen said. "But unless we realign the stones, we put more than one town at risk."

"The creature might not be the problem." Kobb focused on hiding how unlikely he though that was. "We only kill it as a last resort. And if we do, we try to sneak the body out; trick the Skithai into thinking the townspeople weren't involved." Which, given how angry the Skithai would be, probably wouldn't make a difference.

"Right. Best find the creature quick then." Anessa straightened her shoulders. "The town going to have a problem with Kobb?"

Kobb pressed his fingers to his pendant. "We're sometimes unpopular. The way Morth reacted was unusual, though; it's better to take the risk than force you two to sneak the beast out so I can check it."

Haelen turned to study the town. "The Reverend is the only one of us who can use power. Anessa's right about people not being comfortable with Botherers, though. Might be best to hide the Courser and your symbol."

A tendril of unease slid through Kobb's stomach at the thought of hiding his pendant. The faith wasn't the form, but it felt wrong to conceal it. They were right about the search being easier if he seemed like an ordinary traveller though. After tucking his pendant inside his shirt, he unstrapped his holster from his baldric and placed his Courser in the bottom of his saddlebag. "Anyone needs spiritual assistance, I'll have to act. But I won't volunteer anything."

Gathering up Falcon's reins, Kobb lead the way down the narrow path. The air still had the chill of winter, but the sun bouncing back off the rock made it almost warm. A warmth that fled again once they moved away from the shelter of the cliff across the plain.

Four guards, three with tabards matching the red-and-gold flag above the gate and one in pale blue, strode forward as Kobb approached. All four had a hand rested on their sword. "Hold. What business brings you to Sallis?"

"We're from the north." Kobb let Falcon's reins hang. "Looking for short work to replenish our purses."

The guards kept hands on hilts, but relaxed. "You'll find nothing till the festival's over."

Festival? None of the Holy Days fell at this time. Had he lost track of the days somehow in the trips through the Stones? Even if he had, only the most devout would celebrate more than Maker's Day; and that with prayer rather than festivity. "How long does the festival last? We have coin for a while."

The lead guard nodded at the mention of money. "Duke Torvan weds at the end of the week. The city holds a great hunt to celebrate his betrothed's arrival."

"Four days." Kobb swept his arms wide to keep the guard's attention, in case Anessa failed to hide her reaction. "Our purses will stand that. And they'll no doubt be plenty looking for willing hands once the celebration's over."

The guard snorted, then swung his free arm to point at the open gate. "Who could keep such a joyful man from a wedding celebration?"

As soon as the three of them were past the guards, Anessa leaned in close. "What's a great hunt?"

"The Duke and his retainers ride out each morning to hunt a more dangerous beast than the day before. Started as a way of showing a suitor had the strength to defend the new household against threats, but they're a ritual these days; caged animals released into an enclosure."

"You think that's why those men stole the creature?"

Haelen moved closer. "Makes sense. Something no one's hunted before would make good bragging."

"So, we explain the danger." Anessa's voice was low, but her eyes sparkled. "No one'd risk trapping their love in a war."

"Doubt he loves her." Haelen shrugged. "Might not have met her before the festival started. Political marriage is about power and glory. And, even if the Duke believes the Skithai are a threat, knowing the Tan-Sorda is important enough to declare war over will just make hunting it more glorious."

"Street's not the best place for this discussion." Kobb pointed at a huge tankard wrapped in ribbons hanging above a door. "We find a room first, then work out what to do."

With hiring suspended, most of the patrons were local; however, enough of the wealthy of nearby duchies had travelled in the hope of being taken for wedding guests that the only hostel with free stable space and a private chamber was in a murky backstreet. After carrying what little was available to eat up to their room, Kobb and Haelen reiterated the difference between ordinary and noble marriages to Anessa.

But before they could overcome her incredulity, the hostler banged on the door. "Forgot to change the beds. Come to the tap room; I'll pour an ale for you each... on the house, while the boy makes it up."

Kobb ran his gaze across the greyish blankets. They didn't look as if they'd been changed in months. "A moment." He glanced at Anessa's sword, before loosening his own in its sheath. Hand hanging near the hilt, he opened the door with the other.

The owner, yellow teeth exposed in a stiff grin, backed away toward the stairs. There was no sign of a boy or fresh bedding.

Kobb tilted his head. The only noise was from the street outside. He glanced along the corridor. He could swear he'd heard someone walking that way shortly before the knock, but the door to the other room was half-open. When he looked back, the hostler had ducked out of sight. Unsheathing his rapier, Kobb stepped out and faced along the corridor. "Best come out. I know you're there."

A bulky man, hooded cloak concealing his clothes and face but not the shape of the sword at his hip, emerged. Two masked figures followed him, each with a raised crossbow. "Suspect you've noted the quiet below, too. And what it means."

Kobb nodded once.

"Then you'll know you can't fight your way out. Three of you come along peaceably, no one gets hurt."

PART FIFTY-NINE

Kobb cursed silently. If he had his Courser, the two crossbowmen would pose little threat. Without it, his only option—other than surrender—was to dive back into his room, which from this distance would leave him flat on the floor; almost certainly both preventing Haelen and Anessa closing the door and re-opening his wound. Assuming his companions managed to hold the others off while he made it to his saddlebag, the noise would alert those downstairs. That wouldn't stop Kobb fighting free, but all it took was one attacker escaping for half the town to know someone had used a Courser. "I'll need to talk to my companions."

The bulky man waved one hand at the doorway.

Kobb sheathed his rapier. As he stepped back into the room, Anessa twitched her crossbow to the left and raised an eyebrow. Kobb shook his head and pushed the weapon down before slinging his saddlebag over his shoulder. "No cause to start a fight until we know which side we're on."

"But—"

"Kobb's right." Haelen grabbed his pack. "Building's surrounded. If they'd wanted us dead, they'd have just waited till we stepped out the door."

"Our employer only wants to talk." The hooded leader appeared in the doorway. "They've even done you the courtesy of coming here, so you'll not need bags."

"We'd prefer not to leave them unattended." Kobb inclined his head. "Backstreet tavern like this? You never know whose going to wander in while you're away."

A snort came from beneath the hood. "Point. You'll hand the weapons over though, until the meetings finished."

Kobb unbuckled his baldric and held it out. After a moment, Anessa unloaded her crossbow and yanked her belt off. After piling the proffered weapons across the arms of one of his companions, the bulky man waved an arm toward the stairs.

Glad they'd made the assumption nothing truly dangerous would fit in a saddlebag, Kobb led the way to the taproom. The absence of most patrons had done nothing to improve the smell. More hooded figures were dotted around the otherwise empty space: four stood around the edges with crossbows readied; while a fifth, smaller figure, cloak of velvet rather than wool, perched on the edge of a chair toward the centre.

"Which of you speaks for the others?" The woman's voice confirmed what her size and the style of her cloak suggested.

Without knowing what the woman wanted, it was hard to predict whether truth or artifice served better. Kobb strolled a few paces closer. "We prefer to discuss things."

"Very well. I understand you're seeking employment. I have a use for discreet people."

"I thought the Duke'd stopped jobbing until after the wedding?" said Haelen.

The woman chuckled. "The Duke makes whatever rules he wishes. Whether I choose to follow them..."

Anessa stiffened. "Ain't doing nothing for criminals."

The shing of drawn steel came from behind them.

Kobb let his saddlebag slip forward. Before he could reach for his Courser, the woman raised a gloved hand. "Stay, Borig."

"They should show respect." The leader lowered his sword, but didn't sheathe it.

"You did agree that no one would be hurt." Kobb resettled his bags. "Perhaps we'd best move on to the job."

"Duke Torvan's hunters captured a rare beast. I want it released back into the wild."

Perhaps it would've been better to dive backwards after all. That wasn't the sort of request you let someone turn down.

Haelen exhaled. "That's not criminal; that's madness. The Duke and his betrothed'll both've filled the place with guards to make sure nothing goes wrong."

"And if I could give you the patrol routes?"

Kobb shook his head. "That'd work for getting in. But this creature's huge. No way to get it out without at least one of the guards noticing something and telling a superior."

"Guards seeing it is only a problem if they give chase."

"You've already got fighters, so you wouldn't need us if you wanted the guards dead." An unnerving thought slid into Kobb's mind. "Getting the routes could be done with a little cunning. But having people ignore intruders? You'd need to control which guards were where. But then, Borig does, doesn't he—at least for your half?"

The woman swept back her hood, revealing porcelain skin and long chestnut hair held within a golden net. "I believe Borig expects you to call me Your Ladyship. Might I enquire what gave me away?"

Honestly? No criminal who'd survived more than a few weeks would share so much before making the deal. Or be so obvious as to clear the entire taproom. However, telling her that might sour the conversation.

"Most criminals use what they can, rather than commission in bulk; so six identical crossbows, six identical cloaks... That made me wonder. Then the way Borig reacted when we called you a criminal..."

"See, Borig. I told you my clothes wouldn't give the game away."

Borig dropped his hood. "Indeed, Your Ladyship."

Anessa looked back and forth. "So, you're getting married to the Duke?"

"Do you not recognise me? I am Lady Indee Calltrasta Semithros."

Haelen gave a half-bow. "Our apologies. We haven't spent much time in the capital."

Lady Semithros tilted her head and smiled.

Reminding himself to thank Haelen later for his skill at blatant flattery, Kobb bowed. "These are not fitting surroundings for one of your character, and we would not use more of your time. Perhaps you might tell us your offer, and how we might contact you after we have discussed the offer?"

Borig snorted. "I grow to like you, sell-blade; but that sense of humour'll get a person in trouble. Ten weights if you sneak the beast out. Another twenty if you manage it without anyone seeing you."

"Fifteen to get it out. Half up front," said Kobb. "And another thirty if no one notices until we're gone."

Borig sheathed his sword. "Nothing till it's done."

For half a breath, Kobb considered spitting on his palm to see how far he could push it. However, the situation was clear enough to not need the risk. He held out his hand. "Done."

"Why don't you ask the Duke to release it," said Anessa. "Surely, he's not going to kill it if you want it alive."

"Not want it killed? Don't be ridiculous, child. I want that fat idiot to work for it." Lady Semithros rose and resettled her hood, before swishing for the door. The four crossbowmen formed up around her.

Left eyebrow twitching once, Borig clasped Kobb's hand. "I'll send a man with the schedules." Releasing his grip, he marched out behind his mistress, followed by the remaining guards.

As soon as the door closed, Anessa grinned. "Never understand nobles. But getting money to do what we wanted anyway…"

"We won't be paid. Semithros wants to make the Torvan look incompetent. He'll know she was responsible, but can't say anything without proof. If we're lucky, they'll let us run rather than killing us."

Part Sixty

"She definitely won't if we don't do what she wants." Kobb strolled to the bottom of the stairs. "Let's get our weapons and take a closer look at the hunting enclosure."

"What about the guard schedules?" said Anessa. "Shouldn't we wait for the messenger?"

"They'll find us." Kobb glanced between the matted straw and the food-stained tables. "Unless you want to remain here?"

Anessa's nose wrinkled. "No, but— How'd they find us so fast?"

"The Reverend told the guards at the gate we sought work. Semithros wouldn't do this on a whim; her retinue'd be keeping an eye out for suitable people. Likely her guard paid someone to follow us while he sent a message to her."

Anessa nodded slowly, then her eyes widened. "If the ones in blue are hers, that means the patrols'll be mixed. The Duke's guards'll see us, too."

"Semithros isn't telling us everything" Although, she had shared more than she needed to. "She'll have some hold over at least a few of the Duke's people."

Haelen chuckled mirthlessly. "Or we're a distraction, and we're supposed to be seen. Either way, our chances don't get better standing here—apart from the chance of catching something."

Their weapons lay in a neat row on their blankets. After checking for adulteration, they strapped them on and headed out. A few people moved along the street outside the hostelry, each avoiding eye contact and keeping well apart from the others.

A crowd formed as soon as they turned the corner, growing to a shuffling roiling mass as they pressed forward. Hands near, but not resting on, his pouches, Kobb surveyed the area. Tight-packed crowds. Narrow streets edged by a myriad hawkers, improvised stalls, and other obstacles. And it got no better closer to the Duke's palace. Even if Lady Semithros had a way to strike all the guards blind, they wouldn't have room to lead the Tan-Sorda out for witnesses, let alone escape notice. And, if his experience of previous festivals were any guide, the streets would be filled with clumps of revellers well into the night.

Ahead, a boy, maybe six-years-old but stunted by hunger, cut a purse from a man's belt, then strolled toward an alley. Only to stumble to a halt as Anessa grabbed a handful of greasy hair. Despite the press, the crowd moved away, leaving a narrow clear space around the struggle.

"Best let go, outer." The cutpurse spat on Anessa's boot. "Less you like being dead."

Anessa yanked hard, dragging the boy further from the alley. "You'll give that back. Or I'll wallop you and take it anyway."

Kobb ran his gaze across the crowd, as Haelen did the same. The thief wasn't a threat; the rest of his crew might be, though. His head snapped round when the cutpurse gasped.

Staring hard at Anessa's waist, the boy threw his prize up in the air. "Have it then."

Anessa only glanced it for a moment, but that was enough for him to twist free and slip into the crowd, leaving a few greasy hairs behind. Forehead creased, Anessa scooped up the purse. "Didn't think a whalloping'd be that scary."

"Don't believe it was you." Haelen tapped the hilt of her sword. "The Duke's hunt means they'll have been hunters of all sorts coming through for months. I reckon he saw this and mistook you for someone who'd abandoned the comforts of home and family to protect humans from the monsters lurking in the wilds." He quirked an eyebrow.

"So that's how we get in," said Anessa. "Pretend we work for the hunt."

"Even if they are still looking, it's unlikely they'd let us near the Tan-Sorda." Haelen turned back. "Does give me an idea though."

"What about...?" Anessa waved the purse in the direction its owner had been.

"A Blessing to fund our efforts." Haelen shrugged in response to Kobb's glare. "Best get somewhere more private."

After looking around the crowd, Anessa slumped. "Don't seem right. But don't see a way to give it back."

Kobb rested a hand on her shoulder. "Nothing is beyond the Maker. We might turn a corner and be Blessed to find the owner coming the other way."

Shoving through the mass of competing smells and shouted deals in reverse, they headed for their room. As he rounded the corner, Kobb noticed several heavily muscled people in nondescript clothes taking a strong interest in cobblestones, doors, and other things that weren't the front of the hostelry. Not the owner of the purse; and, from the lack of squared shoulders and suspiciously clean areas, not Lady Semithros keeping an eye on them; but someone with an interest.

"Reckon they're here for us," muttered Haelen.

Kobb slowed his pace slightly to gain time. "Other room was empty when we left. Seems likely."

"Want to make sure everyone knows you don't mess with their gang."

"You mean... the purse?" Anessa frowned. "They rushed here for that?"

"That would be a rush," said Haelen. "They're here because we made a deal on their territory. Although, they'd have been better waiting until we'd been paid."

Kobb snorted. "If they knew that much about us, they'd have ambushed us inside the hostelry."

The sounds of commerce and revelry faded slightly behind them. Kobb rolled his shoulders. "Seems they've decided to do it this moment."

Part Sixty-One

Kobb considered the two figures swaggering from further down the street. Turning his leg out, he stepped forward. Weight shifting sideways, he hooked his right fingers around the quillons of his rapier and drew upward. The hilt smashed into the jaw of the thug lunging from a side alley before slipping into Kobb's left hand.

Body following his hand, Kobb drove his knee into the reeling attacker's groin. The foetid gust of onions and rotten teeth washed over Kobb. A crisp strike to the back of the thug's neck with his now-empty right hand laid his opponent face down on the cobbles.

Ambush falling apart before them, the two approaching assailants abandoned their saunter for a run, pulling knives as they came.

A breath later, one staggered to a halt, Anessa's bolt jutting from his left thigh.

Dropping her crossbow, Anessa grabbed her sword. Still unused to the weapon, she twisted as she drew, binding the hilt on her jacket.

Knife fisted tight, the thug lunged forward.

Only to crash to the ground as Haelen hurled himself into his legs.

Lips pulled back in a rictus, the wounded attacker advanced.

Kobb spun as a boot scuffed behind him. Two more thugs stalked along the street, these experienced enough to neither rush nor bunch up. Letting his saddlebag drop off his shoulder, Kobb flicked his gaze between attackers, seeking an opening.

Glancing past Kobb, the thug on the right broke into a run.

Unsure which of the gasps and flesh striking flesh behind him were whose, and unwilling to take the time to check, Kobb sprinted to meet him, hoping the extra distance denied the other attacker an opening for long enough to strike the first.

Too aware of the need to end this to be merciful, Kobb lead with the point.

His opponent lashed out at the oncoming rapier, knocking the blade aside.

Kobb rolled his wrist the block, snapping the blade back in line as his right leg kicked forward. Three inches of steel sank between the thug's ribs. Throat spasming in a half-cough, the man collapsed to the cobbles.

Running feet echoed. Twisting the blade free and turning in a single motion, Kobb prepared to meet his second opponent. However, instead of the expected attack, the man sprinted for an alley, Kobb's bags clutched in his arms and Haelen in pursuit. Before Kobb could follow, metal clattered and Anessa screamed.

Sword lying on the ground, she backed away from the thug she'd shot earlier. Hampered by his wound, he couldn't press his advantage; but disarmed, she could only defend.

Needing no time to choose, Kobb charged to her aid. Blade catching the attacker's out-thrust knife, Kobb turned his wrist, rotating the rapier around while pushing the blade aside. Not breaking stride, he hammered the hilt into the thug's forehead.

Eyes rolling back, the attacker collapsed to the floor.

Kobb staggered to a halt. With no opponents in sight, the little aches he never used to feel made themselves known. Blade hanging, he drew a deep breath and turned.

Purple light flared from the alley. Twinges forgotten, Kobb sprinted for the narrow alley.

Three shapes lay against the wall, the shadows of buildings robbing them of detail. Feet slipping as mud replaced cobbles, Kobb advanced.

The nearest shape shifted. "Rev... Reverend."

Closer now, Kobb realised the bundle next to Haelen was the last thug; and the third, his saddlebags, contents half-spilt. "Haelen? What happened?"

"Bag caught on the wall. He must have decided to grab what he could and leave the bag." Haelen pushed himself to his feet. "He had your Courser in his hand when I reached him. We struggled. Purple and silence. I was slammed back; banged my head. I... I thought he'd shoved me, but he must have hit himself and fallen into me."

"How'd he use it?" said Anessa.

"If someone's barely connected to the power, they might never know. Even strong emotion'd only bring it close to the surface—not all the way. Holding the Courser must have been enough." Kobb considered his possessions. Even in the gloom, he made out stains from the filth coating the floor. This wasn't the time to care about getting the muck on everything, though. Stuffing everything into the bag, he pushed the Courser back under his spare clothes.

Haelen shuffled past Anessa. "We'd best get inside. Don't want to be standing around if someone does investigate, and I've still a plan to share."

"Better be one that doesn't need us to stay here." Kobb nodded toward the thugs sprawled on the street. "If the gang took a dislike because we hadn't cut them in on the deal, they try worse once they find out we did this."

"That'll depend on how long it takes to get what we need." Haelen stepped around an unconscious body. "Once we're ready, doing it'll only need an hour."

The hostler gaped at them as they entered, before ducking through a door behind the bar. Seemed like the gang would find out sooner rather than later. Tiredness from the fight and tiredness at the venality of humans weighing on him equally, Kobb trudged up the stairs. Waving the other two into the room, he glanced into the second room before returning. "What's the plan then?"

"I had an idea when that thief mistook Anessa. They'd never let hunters in unexpected. Don't mean they won't let other strangers who seem to have a reason in, though." Haelen grinned up from his seat on the bed. "So, we pretend you're a Reverend. Here to bless the special quarry, so killing it's even more meaningful."

Pretend he was–? Kobb struggled not to laugh, failing when he saw Anessa's puzzled expression.

"But he is a Reverend! I thought we wanted to hide that. And how does it help us get it out?"

"Stones," said Haelen.

Anessa's forehead crumpled further. "Don't think acting like we've a right'll make everyone ignore a giant beast."

"No. I mean Kobb uses the Stones to move us and the Tan-Sorda to the Circle, then we go back through."

Kobb nodded. "We arrive near the Skithai, and none of the guards knows where to start looking for us. Travelling that way exhausts methough, so best to only take the Tan-Sorda. Unlikely they'd let me lead Falcon into the cages anyway, so the two of you ride out and we'll meet in the forest."

"Haelen maybe." Anessa's hand dropped to her sword. "But you'll need someone in case it goes wrong."

"You'll need something else, too." Haelen glanced up and down Kobb's clothes. "No one'll believe a Reverend Militant's come to do the ritual; especially one who looks like he's been on the road for weeks."

Kobb sighed. "Fair point. If it were real, they'd send someone senior. Which means we have to convince the nearest cloister to give us vestments I'm not entitled to—without telling anyone why we need them."

Part Sixty-Two

Kobb emptied his bags on the floor. When he'd set out in search of the source of his dreams, he hadn't expected to lead a congregation; and those rituals he did perform would be in mountains and woods. None of his clothes disgraced his calling; however, none seemed other than practical and hard-wearing. Pushing them back into the bag, he opened his credens and pulled out his stole. A waft of must rose as he let it unfold; yet, Blessedly, the iron box had protected it from stains. He might not be ready to convince Duke Torvan he was a Reverend Eminent, but he could prove he was a Reverend. "If I hurry, I can reach the temple before dusk service."

"Might be better if we arrived during." Haelen nodded his head toward the other room. "Easier to hide in a crowd if we have to."

Kobb pressed his forehead against the hem of his stole, then placed it inside his jacket. "Getting the vestments without raising suspicions will be hard enough. Calling someone away from devotions would make it worse."

"Do we need to ask? If everyone's at the service—"

"I'll not steal from my Order."

"But borrowing without explaining's fine?" Haelen quirked an eyebrow. "Are perfect records that much a virtue?"

Anessa rested a hand on each of their shoulders. "Kobb's right. But Haelen's right too; stopping evil's most important. Won't the Maker—?"

Kobb raised a finger to his lips as a plank creaked outside.

A moment later, someone tapped on the door. "Honoured guests? You've a visitor."

Sword drawn, Kobb eased the door open. The hostler jumped back, revealing one of the guards from earlier, still clad in a cloak.

"How may I help you, townsman?" Kobb lowered his sword point an inch.

The guard thrust a scroll toward Kobb. "Times and routes. Send your apprentice to the south gate if you need to contact Borig."

"Our thanks," said Kobb to the man's back. After staring at the hostler until he scurried away, Kobb closed the door.

"Send a message?" Haelen snorted. "Him turning up just after we did screams they've got us watched. So, best do nothing that don't look like Semithros' plan."

"Going to the temple's fine, isn't it?" Anessa picked up Kobb's Book of Blessings. "Weren't popular at home, but enough people in towns go to see a Reverend it ain't odd, right?"

In Kobb's experience, faith became rarer the more civilised a place was. However, that might be an advantage; it meant the watchers probably wouldn't know the intricacies of liturgy and vestment. "Enough her guards will think we want a bit of extra luck. We don't need to get an Eminent's chasuble either; I can requisition a Militant's vestments."

"Might work to disguise you so we lose the watchers," Haelen said. "But the Duke'll spot the difference straight away."

Kobb shook his head. "The Duke's not a hunter. He isn't going to visit the beast pens. And all the guards will see is what I am: a Reverend performing his duties. They won't know what my rank is, and they won't dare keep me waiting while they seek permission."

"What if Haelen heads off now?" Anessa crouched next to Kobb's bag. Pausing, she pressed her forehead to the book before tucking it away. "Might lead the watchers off."

"No. We want them to think we're staying. If Haelen remains until we've left, they've less time to realise something's wrong. Best we don't wait though. They'll expect us to do something. Haelen, head down to the taproom; make it seem you're settled in."

Haelen sauntered out, every inch a person with nowhere to be.

Anessa frowned. "What about me? They'll see you're a Reverend, but why'd the guards let me in?"

"I'll tell them—" Kobb raised his fingers to his throat. "You're right. It's past time anyway." He unclipped his pendant. "Anessa Tanton. Do you accept the Maker has placed Blessings in his Creation?"

"What...? Err, yes."

"Do you accept we should seek for these Blessings?"

"I... I do."

Kobb clipped the pendant around her neck. "Having proved yourself worthy of it, I gift you the Blessing of Unity that your faith might be seen by all persons." For an instant, the world seemed to still. He stepped back as the next breath came. "Best tuck it away for now."

Her fingers shook as she lifted the pendant. "This'll fool the guards?"

"It'll convince the Sacristan that you're entitled to lay robes."

"Oh... and then you can have it back."

Kobb patted her shoulder. "That's yours now. You've more than earned it."

"I..." Anessa peered at her boots. "Thank you." Cheeks red, she rushed out the door.

Kobb followed her from the hostelry. The streets were every bit as packed as he'd feared. Even with the townsfolk's joy-fuelled willingness to give directions, dusk loomed perilously close by the time they reached the temple.

Kobb paused in the vestibule, hand rising to his throat. "Stay two steps behind me. If anyone talks to you, bow and keep walking; they'll assume you're my apprentice and leave you alone."

Shoulders back, Kobb strode up the nave. After pausing facing the altar for three breaths, he headed along the transept to the chapter house. Second left, then first right, and they reached the Sacristy. Blessings on the strictures of architecture.

A wild-haired, yet impeccably tidy, woman in a white soutane smiled at them. "Blessing on your day. I am Sacristan Obedience Is a Candle Unlit Elviga. How might I assist, Worthy...?"

"Reverend. Reverend Militant Absolution is like the Silence of the Waterfall Kobb. This is Worthy Tanton. We have need of formal vestments."

"A Militant?" The Sacristan frowned and squeezed her chin. Peering around, she scratched her head. "I'm not sure there are any Militant chasubles in storage. Your calling are so enamoured of pomp I barely have time to clean them before they're out of my hands again." She crouched and opened the bottom drawer of a cabinet. Purple cloth bulged up. "You're in luck. It seems some remain."

"Your preparation does you credit." Kobb held his tone flat. "I will be certain to tell any of my calling that you hold more than enough to meet their needs."

Elviga straightened, arms draped in embroidered cloth. Eyes bulging for a moment, she surrendered to a chuckle. "Indeed. Although, not all would find my humour so to their taste."

"In all things reside joy." Kobb tipped his head toward a wide-eyed Anessa. "Perhaps we'd best reclaim decorum though, before my companion loses her respect for our offices."

The Sacristan laid the vestments across Kobb's arms. "Truly is it written that the serious youth perceives hidden troubles."

"Reverend?" A sharp voice came from the doorway. "I was not notified of your arrival."

Kobb turned. An Eminent in full regalia peered at him, the jut of his chin revealing him a man who'd continued to point out even the smallest of hidden troubles in later life. "I did not wish to bother anyone, Eminent. Events separated me from my vestments. I intended merely to replace them and move on."

"So, you are not called here for any special cause?" The Eminent's chin rose. "Nor racing after some evil?"

"We but pass through. Once vested, we shall depart without troubling you further."

"Nonsense. We will not send you into the night. The hospitality of the chapter-house is yours."

"Our thanks, Eminent." Kobb bowed his head. Whatever ended the conversation fastest. By the time the Eminent realised they weren't in the dormitory, they'd be back at the Stones; and if he did meet the Eminent again in the future, he'd come up with an excuse then.

"A Blessing for us both. Our Lector has an inflammation of the throat. Had you not arrived I would have had to give the readings. Now I can devote my time to more important matters. Your acolyte will assist you... after she's scrubbed the filth off."

More important matters? Kobb reminded himself that the Eminent might not mean it the way it sounded. He might merely be careless in language rather than careless of souls. There was no way to avoid the request without raising suspicion, though; and no time to warn Haelen the timing had changed.

Part Sixty-Three

Kobb bowed his head to the Eminent, then turned to Elviga. "If my companion is to assist, she will need formal vestments."

"See to it, Sacristan. Then escort them to one of the guest cells to change; the Reverend has no time to dawdle."

Kobb sighed as, chin cleaving the air, the Eminent swept from the room. It was hard to find the Blessing in this. At least today wasn't holy, so the service would be shorter. Even better, the Eminent hadn't told him the Lector's reading; and they only had a short while to robe before dusk, so there wasn't time to check. Today's verses could be ones that fitted Kobb's purposes. But which? Istrid's Gamble suited any circumstance—but needed an explanatory sermon to show its relevance. The Parable of Unrecognised Talent was among the shortest—but an itinerant Reverend giving a sermon on the worth of all to a congregation of the rich and noble might draw attention.

Maybe the answer was to avoid the standard lessons altogether. If an Eminent asked a Reverent Militant to give the lesson, then no one could complain if it were stark rather than elegiac or comforting. None could find anything other than the Maker's Truth in the Laying of Hands; and few would obstruct a warrior who'd just preached we were blessed with two hands and only one head that we might apply ourselves to issues not devote our time to contemplation or debate.

Elviga draped a simple robe across Anessa's arms. "Follow me, Reverend. We'll have you vested before you realise it."

"Deep breath, and then one foot after the other," Kobb whispered as he strode past Anessa. He set his face in a severe frown in the hope of further discouraging anyone they met.

A few moments later, they rounded the corner to the cells. As Kobb hoped, the curtain of each hung open. The chapter were either at tasks or already in temple.

The Sacristan paused a third of the way down. "These two are unoccupied. Your acolyte will be close."

Neighbouring cells was better than being corridors apart, but still risked someone addressing Anessa while they were separated; and made it harder for him to explain the duties everyone expected his acolyte to already know. "We would not impose on your hospitality. Having her sleep on stone will be good practice for the road. We shall share."

"You know her flesh best." Elviga's expression remained innocent.

Knowing it only supported her suspicion, but seeing no way to avoid it, Kobb steered Anessa past her. "No doubt our arrival has taken you from duties. I'll not delay you further. Anessa can vest me."

"As you wish." The Sacristan tugged the curtain across the doorway. Her footfalls receded.

Anessa shifted her gaze between him, the vestments, and the stone walls. "How am I...? What...?"

"Your weapons go in the chest at the foot of the cot. The alb... the long tunic goes over your clothes, then wrap the cord around your waist twice and cinch it in front of the left hip. My vestments will be the same then the chasuble and stole over the top."

"I meant..." Anessa stepped to the chest, then turned back and laid her robe on the cot. "...all of it. I've never even been to a service. How can I assist?"

"Faith is the only requirement of service." Kobb rested his pile next to hers. "Follow behind me, head bowed. When we reach the lectern, stand at my left side. The choir will sing a greeting. When that ends, I'll rest my fingers on the start the lesson so you see where it is. There'll be a small silver hand-bell beside to the Book of Blessings. When I ring it, read the rubric... the sentence of red text after the verses I've spoken. Then I read, and you read the next rubric. The choir will— What's wrong?"

Anessa stared at her feet. "Can't read." She stumbled backwards. Cheeks flushed, she pressed herself into the corner. "I should have told you, but I wanted to help you and I thought... and now I've made it worse...and..."

Kobb cursed himself. Why would a shopkeeper's daughter need to know more than simple tallies? Lambart had even complained she spent too long off in the woods, not the shop.

He'd already decided to avoid a common lesson; this merely changed which one he picked. "It's not your fault. The Enlightenment of the Province of Descar has no rubric. I'll read that."

"And I just stand next to you in silence?" Anessa looked up. "No one'll think it's strange?"

"The Enlightenment lists the mistakes of the people of Descar and the costs they bring in extensive detail. It's not my favourite section, but it is appropriate for a Militant. Walk in after me. Listen in respectful silence. Follow me out. The only issue is the Enlightenment is longer than I'd hoped. The longer the service lasts, the more risk someone recognises us."

"So I've put us—"

Kobb stepped closer and rested a hand on her shoulder. "You've done more good than most already, and done it gladly. If we are recognised, then it is because there is a Blessing in it to be found. Now, haste, we must vest ourselves."

Faced with a practical issue, Anessa moved purposefully again. After adding his rapier to the chest, Kobb took a moment to appreciate the Blessings that came from difference; he'd spent years considering formal vestments a problem to avoid, yet Anessa found in them a way to avoid her distress.

Swathes of purple cloth grabbing at his arms, Kobb flailed into the chasuble. Being recognised felt more unlikely by the breath. Any spies in the congregation would expect people of stealth and action, not tapestries on legs. A final wriggle settled the vestments in place.

After tugging his stole straight, he pushed the curtain aside and processed along the corridor, reminding himself to step rather than stride. He slowed further and moved to the side as sandals clattered ahead.

Definitely not counting a measured pace in her head, Elviga scuttled into view. "Blessings I've caught you, Reverend. The Duke has a meeting with Eminent Valk tonight. He's in the congregation. I wanted to warn you."

Questions flooded Kobb's mind; however, before he could speak them, she flapped back around the corner.

The Duke was present. Elviga's words sounded as if it were not a common occurrence. But was the Duke here to avoid seeming rude before his meeting, or to impress his subjects? A man wishing to appear powerful might leap at the chance to be publicly seen in conversation with a Militant; and the Eminent would not doubt appreciate the advantage that came from ensuring such a conversation happened.

Part Sixty-Four

Kobb straightened his shoulders. Failing to give the reading would draw attention, potentially more than standing in front of the altar. Whatever the Duke's reasons for attending, the best course was to carry on and deal with the consequences. That didn't mean not taking some precautions though. "Keep your eyes lowered until the service is over. No cause to make it easy for the watchers."

"Maybe we don't have to sneak around." Anessa leaned in close. "If we offer to bless the Tan-Sorda, we can go straight in."

"Lady Semithros isn't likely to rely on a single plan. Having the Order publicly support him gives the Duke an advantage. Even if none of the watchers recognises us, they might act if the Duke heads for the preserve with a Reverend. And if we did get there, disappearing in front of the Duke himself will cause my Order issues." Kobb gave Anessa a small smile. "It's a good thought, but politics is rarely about good thoughts; that's one reason I travel so much."

Setting his face in a mask of calm—if not serenity—Kobb continued to the temple. The heavy scent of incense flooding the corridors confirmed there was little time before the service started.

As he entered the transept, he noticed Eminent Valk seated next to a ruddy faced man in layers of velvet. Inclining his head in their direction without stopping Kobb processed smoothly yet swiftly to the lectern. Something didn't fit. The pews in the transept were for chapter, not laity; seating the Duke there was an obvious sign of favour. However, they weren't visible from the nave, so didn't display that favour publicly.

After offering a prayer that the Maker reveal the Blessing in it in due time, Kobb gazed over the heads of the congregation, trusting his peripheral vision to detect odd movement without showing his interest. However—apart from the usual skittishness of children and preening of social climbers—the pews seemed to hold the pious.

Moments later, the choir stood. Kobb's breathing slowed as the exquisite counterpoint of soprano voices and droning lutes filled the air.

After the fourth refrain, one of the lutenists fell silent for a bar before resuming her place. Kobb counted seven notes in his head, then movements matching the beat, stepped forward and threw open the Book of Blessings. Iron-bound leather slammed into the lectern as the choir hit the final note.

Thrusting his arms wide, Kobb cast his voice the length of the temple. "O, Lamentable Descar, Paragon of Iniquity, to thee..." From the corner of his eye, he noted Valk's lips twist as if he'd mistaken a lemon for an apple.

After twenty verses of black glances in Kobb's direction, Valk and the Duke rose from their pew and slipped into the chapter house.

Recalling each of his failures and imperfections, Kobb eased from castigation to sorrow as he moved through the final ten verses. The congregation might share Valk's annoyance without his option to leave, but even the most glass-eyed of audiences could contain someone in need of this seemingly harsh message.

As he lowered his arms again, the choir rose. Whether through the Maker's hand or the efficiency of the cantor, they commenced a chant of Consolation. Closing the Book of Blessings, Kobb faced the altar and pressed his fingers to his throat. If only there were a way to shed the stultifying structure of temple life while keeping the ritual and the spiritual service.

He turned to face the nave as the choir moved into the final bar. At least he could do his part to return belief to its core simplicity. After a moment of silence, he raised his arms. "Descar was burdened by flaws. But not flaws of a distant land, or of another time. The flaws we see in our neighbours. And the flaws they see in us. If the verses seem detailed, it is to teach that the difference between sorrow and Blessing hides in a single moment. If the verses seem long, it is to teach that the Maker wishes us to act on our own flaws, not sit in judgement on those of others." Forming fists, he moved his arms in, each sweeping over half the congregation before ending pointed toward the main door. "Rise with new hope, and carry it forth!"

A beat behind the ritual, the cantor lead the choir into the exeunt. For several breaths, a mass of crumpled brows and half-open mouths filled the pews. Then, the laity filed out, at first few then many, whispers growing to chatter as the doors swung wide.

Kobb lowered his arms and bent over the lectern until his forehead pressed against the Book of Blessings. The congregation would no doubt gossip about the brevity of his sermon, but in their hearts many would bless him for it. Resetting his face in a severe expression, he lifted the Book and held it out to Anessa. After a moment, she wrapped her arms around it.

Ignoring the frowns of the choir and off the chapter, Kobb spun on his heel and marched to his temporary room. After a glance into the corridor to ensure no one was in sight, he opened the chest and drew out their weapons. If they were fortunate, they'd reach the garden door before any of the chapter sought them out.

Anessa lowered the Book of Blessings to the bed. "Are services always like that?"

"The Enlightenment of the Province of Descar is not my favourite reading."

"No. It was…" She waved her hands around. "All those people together. And the singing. It was so joyful."

"Those who find joy, find the path to the Maker. However, I would be a poor Reverend if I did not heed my own sermon. Let us leave before my colleagues have the opportunity to offer their judgement of the service, at length."

After twitching his chasuble twice in an attempt to settle it over his rapier, he strode from the cell; the combination of vestment and open armament might prove more effective anyway. Hearing the clatter of sandals in the distance, he sped his feet.

Anessa, less weighted down by formality, kept pace with ease. Fortunately, their unseen pursuer did not. Marching through the empty kitchen and sweeping across the herb garden, Kobb threw open the door.

And froze, the point of a sword less than an inch from his face.

Part Sixty-Five

Anessa's shoulders slumped as the Duke's guards stepped into view. How'd the guards known Kobb would head here?

"Is there some problem?" Kobb jutted his chin at the one who held a sword on him.

"Duke's orders, Reverend." The guard lowered his blade, but didn't sheathe it "No one's to use this entrance."

Anessa frowned as Kobb stepped forward. Didn't that make him easier to attack?

"An entire congregation left through the front doors bare moments ago. Clearly, the Duke meant stop people using this gate to enter the temple." The guards moved apart as Kobb tapped the hilt of his sword. "Eminent Valk wants the wall secure. Would you like to tell him that my acolyte and I were detained from our duties?"

"We should check."

Kobb spread his hands. "We're all honest workers here, not barrack lawyers. You could send for your superior, or make me go back through the temple to the main doors then come along the wall on the outside. Or you could save me the walk, and I'll mention I found this gate well-secured."

"He's a Militant." The other one raised his palms. "My uncle was at Raveth. Don't reckon we'd stop him anyway."

The first guard swallowed and stepped aside. "Pleasant night, Reverend. How goes the watch?"

"The perimeter seems as sound as I might wish." Kobb swept through the gateway.

Book of Blessings clutched to her chest, Anessa followed him along the wall until they were out of sight. "That scared them. What happened at Raveth?"

"Dissenters overthrew the Governor and declared independence. Some had made foul pacts." Kobb slowed to a halt. "The Legion besieged Raveth, but a cultist managed to summon an abomination. Half the Legion died before Militants attached to the Legion force cast it down."

Anessa moved closer. The insects, the Korha, those flying creatures'd all been terrifying enough. A creature that killed half an army... No wonder the guards were scared of people who could defeat it.

"We should focus on the current threat, not the past." Drawing himself up to his full height, Kobb strode down a side street.

The sound of singing and shouting grew louder but no less muddled as they moved further from the temple. Small clumps of people drifted in the opposite direction, many holding each other upright. The scents of spices and vomit boiled up as they reached a main thoroughfare.

As she scuttled after Kobb, Anessa felt her robe catch on something.

"Evening, pretty." A young man wrapped in a velvet cloak and stale alcohol tugged again. Two others clad in different colours but sharing his demeanour leered at her. "How about you put that book down. I've got something better to wrap your lips round."

Anessa twisted. His grip was solid for a person drunk enough to be talking over her shoulder, though. Shifting the Book to her left arm, she snapped the heel of her right hand into his chin.

The drunkard folded backwards, eyes blank before he hit the ground.

"Blessed are those who find rest amongst the tumult." Kobb stepped in front of the man's companions, left boot landing on the drunkard's outstretched palm.

The two youths backed away.

"Faith and a strong arm? A lesser person might think himself replaced." Kobb strode through the crowd as if there were no doubt a gap would open.

Anessa stayed close, and clutched the Book closer. That thing about finding rest sounded like it was from the Book. Kobb was a Reverend, but it didn't seem right using holy words as a joke. He must be joking about her taking over too; not that it wasn't nice to image for a moment he thought she could.

The streets became less crowded and better smelling—though no less filled with singing—as they approached the Duke's residence. Somehow keeping his sense of direction in the muddle, Kobb lead them without pause to the edge of the enclosure she'd seen from the forest. After a moment's thought, Kobb followed the wall to the right.

Even this far from the hostelries and pedlars the streets weren't empty, so Anessa was almost at the narrow wooden door before she noticed it. She arranged the Book of Blessings in what she hoped was a more devout position as Kobb hammered on the centre.

After a moment, a small panel thunked back revealing a pinched face. "Who goes?"

"Reverend Absolution is like the Silence of the Waterfall Kobb. I am here to bless the Duke's prize."

Two beady eyes peered up and down Kobb's vestments before sparing a glance for Anessa. "Botherers at the gates. Don't that just make the late watch better? No offence intended."

The hatch slammed shut. After a couple of clunks, the door swung open. A wizened woman in crumpled red leaned around the edge.

"Come in then. Can't let you wander unescorted. Greff'll lead you."

A spindly boy, guard's tunic sitting lop-sided, unfolded and shuffled away.

Head bowed and shoulders thrust back, Anessa tried to match Kobb's smooth glide. As occasional torches replaced the sparse lanterns and the smell of dung grew, she gave up and walked normally—as normally as she could with a robe tangling her legs.

Two turns later, the corridor ended in two iron gates, one several yards after the other. Greff unlocked the first, then waited while they squeezed past. Once they'd both sidled in, he closed the gate behind them and shuffled along to open the second. Anessa saw how it might stop animals escaping, but why'd they make it so narrow?

"Is'm left. On the end." Unexpectedly, Greff's voice was a melodious baritone. "We kept um away so didn't fright the other beasts."

Kobb inclined his head. "Your service is welcome. Acolyte, provide Greff a ritual of Blessing before we continue. The one you offered that young man earlier would be most suitable."

Offer a ritual? She hadn't— Angling the Book of Blessings on her left arm as if about to open it, Anessa punched Greff hard between the eyes.

Kobb grabbed the youth's shoulders as he collapsed backwards like a stunned sheep and lowered him to the filthy straw. "They'll realise we're involved anyway. But this way he won't get blamed."

Turning along the stalls to the left, Anessa remained silent. In her experience, getting beat down never saved anyone a talking-to if someone was looking to blame.

A vague hint of hot metal cut the stink of old straw. Something creaked ahead, and a golden antler poked into the walkway.

Anessa stumbled to a halt. Antlers jutted. Breath steamed. She clutched the Book closer. Bark-like flanks loomed, twice the height of Falcon. When the shaman said it could stand on two legs, she'd imagined rearing up—not striding easily, double-jointed forelimbs reaching out with stubby hands.

"Not sure how close we need to be for this to work." Kobb frowned. "You open the gate and follow as soon as I step in."

In the stall...? Anessa lifted her fingers to the pendant. Kobb trusted her. She could do it. But why did the creature have to look like a more evil horse? Squeezing the Book to her chest, she slid the bolt, then pressed close to Kobb.

The scent of hot metal blossomed and everything lurched up. Legs feeling the wrong length, she staggered into Kobb.

"Sacrifices betrayed." A voice like an Eater—yet not—creaked nearby. "Walking far to not move. Mask rots below the surface. So far from home, little Tanton. And no way back."

Part Sixty-Six

Eyes sweeping the shadows, Anessa unslung her crossbow. How'd an Eater got in the circle? And where was it?

Kobb pressed down on her arm. He sucked in a rattling breath, then spat. "It was the beast."

"That thing speaks?" Her back bumped the stone.

Kobb wiped his lips with the edge of his robe, leaving a dark stain on the cloth. "The shaman did say it carried messages to their god."

"A mask worn in darkness hides a different face." Despite being in the open, the Tan-Sorda's voice echoed. With a creak, it dropped onto all fours. A hint of hot metal wafted through the air.

Crossbow angled down but not slung, Anessa stepped to the side to give herself more room. The Eaters'd attack Sallis if the beast wasn't returned; letting it kill her in the hope they didn't anyway'd be stupid, though.

"Answer me, Tan-Sorda." Kobb pointed his left arm toward it, stole draped over his wrist. "What do you serve?"

"Do servants act unknowing? I am—" The creature's head lashed from side-to-side. Black fluid splashed as skin cracked and healed. Voice shifting between words, it spoke without echoes. "We... Creator... Destroyer.... Taken.... Given..." Rising onto its hind-legs, it cackled and wept, the sounds overlapping.

Anessa braced her crossbow, eyes searching for signs of weak spots. "What is it? How's it...?"

"I think the Skithai meant carrying their voices in the literal sense; that they've somehow put their hopes and fears into a single creature. Like a living prayer."

"But it knew my name!"

Kobb frowned. "We've seen the corruption twist things before, and we know something's holding the power in place. Echoes of us travelling through the Stones must've been bound in with the prayers."

"How do we get them out?"

"Shame we left Haelen." Kobb glanced at the tents. "He'd have mentioned anything obvious he knew, though; and we don't have time to go through all those notes. The Skithai said the Tan-Sorda goes to the holy place. So, finishing the ceremony'll probably purify it."

"And if it doesn't?" The creature's chest was the best bet; a bolt through the heart dropped anything. "Doing something in the middle of an army's likely to get us killed."

The Tan-Sorda flickered and reappeared several feet further away. "How many lives buys a child's sleep?"

Anessa shivered. It moved like a shaman. And the things it said. Had it expected to be attacked? Did this make it better or worse to try now? Could she even hit it? The Eaters'd know how to keep it still, but—

"Doesn't matter." Jaw set, Kobb staggered closer to the Stone. "If we don't risk it, we doom Sallis."

"At least stay here till you've got your strength back."

Kobb frowned for a moment, then shook his head. "We made a deal with one shaman. Doesn't mean all of them'll wait. And we know they've placed scouts. The Duke will send guards out to track the people who stole his prize; if they find a Skithai..."

They'd try to capture it, or just kill it. And the deal wouldn't mean pig shit in the face of that. "At least rest on my shoulder, so you don't collapse."

"A fair exchange settles debts. And a gift to seal the contract." The Tan-Sorda spoke in a single echoing voice. Except, now she listened, it wasn't an echo; it was several voices speaking almost as one.

Kobb rested his left arm across her shoulders, and chuckled. A slight damp catch at the end robbed the laugh of the little mirth it had. "Sounds like it agrees with me."

Hot metal and sap flooded Anessa's mouth, followed by bile. Her guts lurched upward as something squeezed her entire body.

She stumbled as a large rock slammed into the sole of her boot, then to the side as Kobb's weight yanked at her. Pain spiked across her chest as she stopped him crashing into the Tan-Sorda's flank. One arm on his waist, she braced her legs and looked around.

Clouds covered the moon, hiding details and turning the forest's edge to a wall of shadows. But it seemed familiar. The Stone had returned them to the clearing. Haelen's guess was right. "It worked. We—"

Kobb coughed, dark fluid spattering her robes. His head sagged forward.

"Kobb. Reverend!"

He straightened, reducing the weight on her side. Face pale even in the darkness, he gave a weak smile.

"Are you...? How do we get the creature...?"

Before he could reply, harsh creaking syllables cut the air.

Anessa looked at the Tan-Sorda, then realised the voice'd been more natural and further away.

Staff clutched in both hands, an Eater shaman strode from the tree line.

Something about it suggested it wasn't the same one as before.

"We did it." Anessa waved her free arm at the Tan-Sorda. "We brought your beast back."

The shaman whirled his staff and uttered more jagged words.

Anessa shoved Kobb behind the Tan-Sorda as dozens of Eaters stepped from the tree line, spears raised.

Brow furrowed, Kobb drew himself up. "We fulfilled our promise. We come as friends."

Something slammed into Anessa's back, pitching her forward and sending a stab of pain along her right arm. Twisting as she fell, her crossbow tumbled from her grasp.

More Eaters lined the edge of the clearing behind them. Closer to these, she realised what the difference was. In place of the simple gaps other Eaters cut in their masks, these had carved gaping maws and jutting fangs.

Part Sixty-Seven

Anessa scrabbled for her crossbow. Her fingers slipped off. Creaking, angular voices shouted nearby. As she reached for the butt again, shadows flickered across her.

Her body curled tight as pain drove through her gut, flaring darker as her knee caught a spear shaft.

Teeth gritted, she wrapped her hands around it. Her little finger brushed binding. The spear wasn't that deep; her jacket must have slowed it. Sweat trickled down her brow as she tugged.

Black spots blossomed as the point shifted. For a moment, she thought she it'd come out; then her body tilted. Icy needles stabbed the length of her right side, as the spear in her shoulder pressed on the ground.

The chopped up voices and movements around her shattered.

A wooden face gazed down at her from the moon.

The taste of ashes and metal flooded her mouth, as the clouds fell.

Everything seemed cold. Wind thrummed nearby, and the scent of grease and dry leaves tickled her nose. The agony in her gut'd dulled to a throb. She eased her eyes open.

Tanned leather vibrated above her. Ready for the pain to return, Anessa turned her head. Light filtered between laced flaps. She lay on the floor of a small tent. The fleece of some animal covered her, leaving her feet bare.

Inching her fingers across, she felt her torso. Her jacket was gone, and something rough bulged beneath the rip in her singlet. Someone'd carried her from the clearing and bandaged her wounds.

But who? And why? She couldn't see the rest of her gear. Maybe someone rescued her, but maybe the Eaters'd decided to keep her alive to sacrifice later. She needed to know more.

She lifted her right arm. When the pain didn't flare, she pushed the fleece down. Brown stains crusted the front of her singlet, framing a large tear. However, whoever tended her'd laced it up. Would someone do that if they were going to kill her?

Beneath the thrum of the tent ropes, she heard the creak of wood. Ears straining, she waited until it came again; she still couldn't decide whether it was branches or something speaking, though. Either way, it didn't sound right outside, so she might be able to peek out without being seen.

She twisted her shoulders. The ache in her back tugged at her, but didn't grow. However, when she tried to roll onto her side, her legs seemed numb.

Her chest tightened as memories of Silas Weaver after he slipped from the roof flooded her mind. Tugging at the fleece until it slid off her, she pressed her chin down. Her trousers looked filthy yet whole, and lacked bulges. She twitched her right toes, then her left. She sagged. That meant she wasn't... that she was fine.

After a few deep breaths, she bent her left knee. Tingling burnt away the numbness as she scuffed her heels across the ground. This time, her legs turned, but wouldn't bear enough weight to get up.

She rocked her shoulders, trying to flip herself up, then stopped as the sound of boots approached. Boots was good. Eater's had been barefoot.

Something blocked the sliver of light between the flaps. A figure stepped in, hunched beneath the low roof. "Anessa?"

"Haelen? What happened? Were you captured? Where's Kobb?"

Haelen crouched by her side. "I found the Skithai just like we planned and explained the plan. The shaman told his scouts to watch the clearing and led me to this camp. We came as soon as we heard you'd arrived. Another tribe were passing nearby though. The shaman convinced them to stop. I patched you up with what I had, but I'll be happier once we return to the Stones. I'll take you to the Reverend. He'll be glad to know you're on the mend."

"I... My legs are wobbly."

"Probably from the poultices." He eased an arm under her shoulders. "Might pass once you move around. If it doesn't, I'll carry you. Compared to a Legionary in full armour, you're barely noticeable."

Anessa set her jaw and concentrated. The sensible thing was to let him carry her. But letting them get ambushed was embarrassing enough without looking like a burden too. She got her legs under her—with a certain amount of Haelen's help. Left arm wrapped across his back, she staggered out.

As she straightened, she realised the tent stood at the edge of a wide clearing, empty but for two other tents, and Falcon. "Where are they?"

"They left after the Tan-Sorda sacrificed."

"After... But weren't they waiting for the full moon?"

"They did. You slept for several days."

That explained why her legs were numb and why her wounds didn't hurt so much.

"It's a good thing in a way. The Reverend was exhausted; if you hadn't needed to stay here... Skithai gratitude isn't huge; it ran to some tents and sacks of dry vegetables, though."

The two of them swayed beside the next tent, Anessa's legs not firm enough to bear her weight without help. After almost falling, she let Haelen lower her to the ground so he could unlace the flap.

Kobb blinked as they entered, eyes threaded with red. If this was how he looked now, no wonder Haelen'd wanted him to rest.

"How much food did the Eaters leave? Can we wait a few more days?"

Haelen shook his head. "We could, as I said, I'd like to get you to the Stones, though. Even if I didn't have supplies there, we can't defend this place if trouble turns up."

"He's right." Kobb patted his pack. "Now the Gathering's over, there's no guarantee the Skithai will all leave us alone."

Anessa wiggled an eyebrow at Haelen as left the tent but he only smiled. She turned to Kobb. "But, aren't you—?"

"I don't feel young. I'll do, though. Haelen's got me up from worse than this. If he says I'm rested enough to get us there, trust him."

Kobb's lack of worry still seemed odd, but he'd know how he felt better than she did. And if he was wrong, they'd sleep as long as needed once they arrived.

Haelen ducked his head in. "I've slung our packs on Falcon for now. We've enough tents, so no reason to carry the extra burden."

"Good thought." Kobb yawned, then arched his back. "Best lie down, Anessa. We've each stumbled before."

She eased herself flat. "Wait! Where's my—?"

"I returned for it the next morning." Haelen sat beside her.

The absence of rotting wood flooded her nostrils. Damp grass slammed up into her spine. Granite jutted up around her.

After a moment to be sure her wounds hadn't reopened, Anessa pushed herself up on her elbows.

Kobb stood facing her, shoulders less square than usual but standing on his own. He stared at the stone beside her for while, then his brows drew down.

Anessa peered at it. "It looks solid. No sparkles."

"That's not... The journey felt too easy."

"Too easy?" Haelen stood. "Maybe you're getting better?"

Kobb shook his head. "It felt like it wasn't just me. As if—"

"We're most of the way done." Haelen turned and swept his arms around the circle. "The power must have rushed back. Shouldn't you be telling me it's a Blessing? That we can end this faster... once Anessa's recovered."

Anessa struggled to her feet. Five of the Stones finished—or whatever the right word was. Only two more to finally lock the evil away. And for Haelen, two more until he found where his daughter'd been taken. Hopefully...

Part Sixty-Eight

Anessa eased her head out from under her furs. Either the weather'd turned overnight, or whatever Haelen gave her'd made her feel warm too. Lying in bed sorted neither though. She stretched, wincing as pain poked her wounds. Haelen's herbs'd definitely worn off.

Moving with greater care than usual, she swung her legs out. Slight twinges, but nothing she couldn't bear. She tugged her boots on and headed toward the scent of porridge. Haelen sat beside the fire, stirring a pot. A moment later, she noticed Kobb walking from stone to stone, a bowl forgotten in one hand. "Morning.

"Anessa." Haelen spooned out a large portion as she sat. "How are you feeling?"

"Bit of pain if I stretch too fast." She inhaled a spoonful of oats. Fancy city food'd been all right, but nothing beat a good porridge. "I've been thinking. Kobb and I've gone without you, so don't have to—"

"Leaving me was different; I was healthy. We can wait till you're better."

"You'll be there and back in a day or so. I'm almost mended. I'll be fine. If you don't want to leave me that long, I'll travel with you."

Haelen looked down into his bowl, then at his tent. "Time going over those notes might save some in the end. Not much point sorting things if I can't understand them."

"But we were only just in time for Sallis... and what about your daughter?"

"Ain't worth risking you." Porridge spattered Haelen's front as he threw his spoon into his bowl. "What kind of person would I be if I sacrificed you to get her back?"

"And, I'm not going to be the reason you don't find her. You let Kobb go when he was injured."

Haelen shot to his feet, spine rigid. "The Reverend's a trained warrior. He'd be the first to tell you he's had his share of time. But you've barely lived."

"Kobb'd tell me?" Anessa stood, ignoring the twinge of pain. "Let's ask him, then!"

"If I say you're not ready, he'll..." Haelen's shoulders sagged. "If I stop you, you'll just try to prove things twice as hard next time. Suppose going might teach you to stay clear of danger."

Anessa gulped the rest of her porridge. Stay clear of danger? Sneaking around was the only thing at least one of the others wasn't better at. But, going was going...

"Morning." Kobb raised his free hand as he strode toward the fire. "Haelen said you might need more rest, so I thought I'd check the Stones; see if they felt different. Five are as solid and... stone-like as any you'd find." Kobb shared a glance with Haelen. "Reckon you're right about the power snapping back."

"You want that?" Anessa tilted her eyes at the remains of Kobb's breakfast. "Haelen was saying I'm well enough to travel, so I need to keep my strength up."

Haelen huffed, but nodded. "But, first sign you're tired, you're getting on Falcon."

The porridge shifted in her gut. She'd just have to make sure she didn't seem tired, then. Taking Kobb's outstretched bowl, she hid her discomfort.

To make matters worse, Falcon whickered as she carried her pack over to the stone Kobb'd picked, and tried to nuzzle her hair. She gripped the straps tighter. The beast hadn't hurt her yet, but those teeth and muscles... after seeing what he'd done to the Eaters, she wasn't turning her back on him. She set her feet. "Let's go."

Darkness swallowed Kobb's nod.

The ground shattered beneath her and the scent of stale blood flooded her nose. Teeth clamped hard in an effort not to lose her breakfast, she fought to throw off the effect of the journey. Then realised, the shifting and the stench were real. She was ankle deep in pieces of bone, specks of blood and other matter still clinging to them.

She stumbled to firm ground, then glanced about. The pile lay at the bottom of a narrow and rocky valley, a spattering of fragments lodged on one wall suggesting the remains'd tumbled from above. Beyond the lip, pine-clad mountains rose on every side.

"I was going to say it felt easier again." Kobb drew a shallow breath through his mouth.

Anessa unslung her crossbow and peered along the valley. "Looks like it rises that way. I'll take a look." Not waiting for a response, she crept away from the bones. Hopefully, the others'd assume her pace was caution rather than being as fast as she could go without the pain coming back.

Slowing as the floor sloped up, she flicked her gaze in wide arcs, sweeping both lips and the sky. Whatever creature threw those bones down might be able to fly. She crouched lower, not wanting to press herself to a rock wall for fear of picking the wrong one. As the path rose to barely a person's height from the surroundings, she signalled a halt and slung her crossbow. Both hands free, she clambered up until she could peer over the lip.

Several hundred yards of rough ground, covered with scrub, stretched to the edge of the forest. Not seeing any signs of attack, she turned. And gawped.

Instead of the monsters her mind'd created, a huge wooden palisade filled the centre of a bowl in the mountains. And halfway between it and the valley, a thin, bearded man in dirty robes rolled a handcart toward the point above the bones. They hadn't landed in some beast's leavings; they'd landed in a midden. Didn't mean they were safe though, not until they knew who was inside that fence.

She eased herself down, and waved her hand at the near side. There wasn't anywhere to hide Falcon. As long as the man didn't decide to glance along the valley, though, he'd empty his cart and be gone without ever knowing they were there.

The creaking of wheels grew closer, followed by a clunk of a tailboard. She pressed back as the rear end of the cart eased into view, then tilted. Bones cascaded down the valley side. After a moment, the clattering fell silent. But the cart didn't roll out of sight.

Anessa held her breath as the cart jiggled up and down, tail board flapping. A few fragments of bone tumbled onto the pile. After more shaking, the cart settled. With a muttered curse, the man into view and bent into the cart. Straightening, he hurled an armful of something over the edge. As he turned, his gaze slipped along the valley. Eyes widening, he retreated a step.

Unsure whether he was friend or foe, Anessa didn't grab for her crossbow. Then the moment passed. Howling about escapees, the man sprinted away, leaving the cart behind.

"Do we...?" Anessa waved an arm the way he'd gone.

"That many bones is odd." Haelen glanced at the other lip. "I'd suggest finding a place to hide for now. Least until we know more."

Crossbow at the ready, Anessa took the lead. The scrub wouldn't cover Falcon, but the ground was rough enough one of the ridges'd conceal them. Knowing it wasn't her height that was the problem, she still found her shoulders hunching as she sneaked between bushes. The tension left her as they slipped behind a steep rise.

Only to return a breath later, as a loud horn echoed across the bowl.

Part Sixty-Nine

Anessa eased her head over the top of the ridge, teeth gritted against the twinge in her shoulder. The breeze nipped at her face as she looked across the bowl. Moments later, a gate swung open and five riders emerged from the palisade at a walk, sun glinting on their spears and helmets. Four of them carried a large sack, while the fifth held a brass shield. She ran her eyes over the ground to either side of the ridge, before turning to the others. "Five riders. Moving slowly, so don't think anyone saw us come here."

"They will if they keep coming this way, though." Kobb glanced up the next rise. "Can we make it to the tree line?"

"Not on foot. Riding, yes—not without being seen, though."

"What about sneaking off before they arrive?"

Anessa frowned. Falcon'd be noticed as soon as he moved out. And her injuries'd limit how easily she could hide. "The scrub'll cover someone from a distance, so might be able to get away if we leave Falcon. But they'll likely spot at least one of us if they ride close, so it'd only work if they turn the other way first."

"I didn't mean all of us." Kobb gripped Falcon's stirrup. "You two sneak away while I keep watch. Once they get close or turn toward you,

I ride hard for the trees. They'll chase me, which'll give you time to slip off. That man didn't stop to do a count, so best case, they don't realise there's anyone else out here."

Haelen grabbed Kobb's elbow. "And if they do know, they'll see the ruse and split up. If we stick together, we've a better chance if they do find us.

Anessa turned back. The riders'd spread to a loose line, centred on the valley. The wide sweeps of their heads gave lie to their relaxed pace. "Running might be tricky. Looks like they're checking the valley first. No telling which way they'll go—or even if they'll stick together—till they're almost on top of us."

"Can you see any livery?" Kobb pitched his voice low enough, Anessa had difficulty making it out over the rising wind. "Anything to say who they are? Whether we're safe to hail them?"

She peered hard. "Plain leather, battered metal. Can't see flags or badges. Spears. Swords. Carrying grimy sacks. Nothing looks— Wait, they're splitting up."

The rider with the shield remained near the abandoned cart, while half of the others cantered along the lip of the valley in each direction, then reined in. Unslinging their sacks, they tipped lumps of meat onto the ground then returned. Whiffs of copper tainted the breeze. Something about the scene seemed wrong, but Anessa couldn't work out what.

A dull clanging filled the air as their leader began to beat his spear against his shield. The other four pulled brassy bundles from saddlebags and shook them out. After a moment, Anessa realised they were large metal nets. The riders swept their gazes back and forth, clearly expecting something to appear.

She turned and described everything to the others. "That man thought we were escapees. Maybe metal nets'd stop someone cutting free. But why are they waiting? And why the piles of meat?"

Kobb frowned, then looked at Haelen. Haelen shrugged.

The riders' reasons seemed destined to remain a mystery. After beating his shield for a while longer with no sign of whatever he sought, the leader called out, the words stolen by the wind. They turned as a group and galloped back to the palisade.

Once the gate'd closed, Anessa slipped down to the others. "Reckon we make for the forest, fast as we can."

"Raw meat makes me think of dangerous beasts." Haelen glanced around. "We know the power summons things, or changes them. If that's what they're hunting, won't we risk walking straight into it?"

"Sacks of meat means likely something big. Means it's better in the open. So, we're safer between trees."

"She's right." Kobb patted Falcon's nose. "Falcon's faster if there's space, but a person on foot turns quicker and fits through narrower spaces. And, if we do run into trouble, the forest might conceal the flare of my Courser. Best get moving in case they send another patrol out."

Anessa crept up the next rise and glanced back to make sure no one was in sight, before studying the ground ahead. There wasn't enough scrub to hide Falcon all the way, but the sun was low enough the forest was in shadow. Hand shaking, she pressed her fingers to the pendant around her neck. Moving slowly, they mightn't stand out from the palisade anyway.

Shoulders aching from the extended crouch, Anessa reached the tree line, the others a few yards behind. The wind blew in the wrong direction to judge sound; nothing moved in the shadows, though, so there probably wasn't a beast lurking just beyond. So, first step was getting somewhere out of sight of patrols. Bracing her crossbow to her shoulder, she picked out a route Falcon could take and slipped forward.

Despite Kobb's comment about Falcon not being good in forests, the horse made little noise moving through the undergrowth. Which brought an equal mix of relief Falcon wasn't giving them away and fear he'd as sneak up on her. She pushed the thought down, and looked for a possible clearing to stop in. But before she found one, the shadows thinned ahead. Signalling a pause, she crept on alone.

A rutted track cut across their path, the left angled toward the palisade. And from the right, on the edge of her hearing, horses clumped. She eased forward and peered through a bush.

Ten yards away, a fallen tree blocked the track. The end looked hacked rather than snapped.

Beyond it, a line of riders and people on foot approached. The riders wore the same plain armour as the ones from the palisade. Peering through the gloom she realised, the walkers were chained together. The palisade was keeping people captive then.

The lead rider raised a hand and rode forward alone. His shoulders stiffened as his gaze fell on the stump.

Before he could react, he collapsed sideways, a bolt jutting from his neck.

A panicked shout cut off as more bolts slammed into the other riders, leaving just one upright.

The surviving rider dived from his horse, only to be cut down as an armoured figure stepped out of the forest. Anessa rocked back at the sight of the attacker's jagged maw.

A breath later, she realised the bestial face was an ornate helmet, the gloom adding to the effect. A moment longer revealed something familiar about the way the warrior moved, and the tattered grey tabard they wore. It looked like—

"Rest that crossbow down slow, then slide the sword out."

Anessa turned. Elvar, clothes battered but stance firm, crouched several yards back with a readied crossbow; far enough back she couldn't knock it aside, yet close enough he'd an easy shot.

She moved her right hand away from the trigger and placed her crossbow on the ground. Anserth hadn't died in the ruins.

Part Seventy

Anessa considered her surroundings out of the corners of her eyes as she eased her sword belt off. The ground to the left seemed least cluttered. Resisting the urge to tense up, she pitched her weapon away.

And cursed inwardly when Elvar's gaze didn't even flicker from her.

"Good try, Worthy." Elvar rose to his feet. "Ease yourself up and move a couple of paces back. I'll not insult either of us by asking you to call the Reverend over."

Anessa frowned. Why would that—? He must assume they'd arranged some sort of warning. Like she would've—if she'd been any good as a scout. She had sneaked in where Anserth's soldiers couldn't, though, and then almost escaped Anserth without detection. No wonder they mistook her for someone important. Shoulders rounded she backed away.

Keeping his eyes on her, Elvar hooked her belt up, and slung it across his shoulder. When the end of one of her bolts tinked on the buckle of his baldric, Anessa sagged further; she hadn't even considered keeping the bolts. Just wanting it to be over, she watched him lift the bolt from her crossbow and tuck it through a belt loop.

"Turn around. Walk five paces along the path." Elvar twitched the end of his weapon toward the felled tree.

The dull tunk of an empty crossbow sounded behind Anessa as she shuffled away. She stiffened as she realised what Elvar'd said. Call the Reverend. Haelen hadn't gone to the ruins. They wouldn't expect him. She tried to round her shoulders again; hopefully, Elvar'd been too busy with her crossbow to notice. If they thought she was up to something, they'd take more care; maybe even question her first.

She risked a glance along the path. Several figures in brown leather, crossbows angled down but not slung, directed the still-chained line of prisoners into the treeline, while another two bent over the fallen soldiers. Anserth was nowhere to be seen.

A thrush trilled behind her. Anessa scanned the shadows. It wasn't—

A young woman, face familiar from the ruins, jogged up.

Elvar stepped around Anessa, crossbow resting across one arm. "There's a Reverend Militant west of here. Take your unit, find him, and invite him to join us. Make sure you tell him his friend's already accepted."

The woman nodded once, and ducked into the trees. She wasn't good enough that Anessa couldn't see her move; but Kobb and Haelen didn't have her skills. Haelen probably wouldn't be the advantage she'd wanted. Maybe she should shout?

But then Elvar'd shoot her. And, if Anserth's soldiers could sneak up on Kobb, they could do it while he was running. Best plan was still hoping Kobb rescued her somehow. Like he had last time.

A gentle drumming grew above. Water splashed off the top of her head. Pigshitting Anserth, and her schemes. Why'd she have to turn up again? And now it was pigshitting raining too.

Walking ahead of Elvar, she wended her way deeper into the damp gloom. Soon after, she made out the sound of muttering and a dull clink behind the hiss of the rain. Another ten yards revealed a cluster of soggy prisoners, two of them holding the chain that linked their arms across a boulder while one of Anserth's men hit it with the back of an axe. Beyond, a large tent sagged, the trees too close to put it up fully. Closer now, she realised some of the prisoners were children.

The more she knew, the better chance she had. From what she'd seen, Elvar wasn't a cruel man. Maybe, he'd tell her something. "What's going on? Why're you here?"

"That lost waif trick won't fool me again, Worthy. Not after seeing the stone-cold murderer you are."

Anessa whirled round. "I'm a murderer? Anserth's the one who tried to kill Kobb and all those people!"

"Only killing I remember is good soldiers dead cos of you. Still don't know how to tell Orlin's family." Elvar raised his crossbow. "Just get in the tent. You try this muck on the Inductor, I'll put a bolt in you."

Rain oozed down her neck as she walked through the camp. Orlin had a family? Kobb'd done the right thing, but... Thoughts swirling, she pushed the flap aside and stepped in.

Anserth looked up as she entered. Despite having removed her helmet, she seemed more threatening now. Anessa suspected she'd keep the rest of her armour on for this conversation.

Which'd be totally fine.

"Didn't expect to see you again." Anserth stared into Anessa's eyes, brow furrowed. "Suppose I shouldn't be surprised you're here, though. Answer my questions, and it'll be easier for you."

"Help you!?" Anessa stepped forward, chin jutting. "You almost killed Kobb! You were going to murder Karak and his family! Why would I help you? I wish I'd never met you! Pretending to be my–!"

"On your knees!" Elvar pressed a sword to her back. "I won't–?"

"Pretending?" Anserth raised a hand. "Step off, Elvar. I'm sure Worthy Tanton will see sense. This is the second atrocity I've found you at, girl. Do you really expect me to believe you're not involved? Is it the whole Order or just a few of them? Tell me who's behind this, what they plan. I can protect you."

"You think I'm—?"

Anserth leant closer. "Should have seen it straight away. Hero of Raveth turning up's unlikely enough. But him wandering around with some ordinary girl—?"

"Ordinary girl? Least I'm not a heartless hag with a lopsided nose!"

"Heartless hag?" Anserth's shoulders stiffened for a moment, then she stepped back. "Fury, you're good. If I didn't know what you were already, I'd mistake you for an innocent. And trying to rile an Inductor?"

"She sounds innocent because she is." Kobb moved aside to let Haelen enter. "About the only person here who is."

Anserth snorted. "And I suppose you two and your friend turning up again is just a coincidence?"

"We're hunting evil, followed it here." Kobb raised his palms. "Could be we share a goal."

Elvar spat on the floor.

"Not the most eloquent of arguments, but Elvar makes a point." Anserth quirked an eyebrow. "Why should I believe you?"

Part Seventy-One

Anessa stiffened. Kobb wasn't the one who'd lied to everyone. What right did she have to doubt him? Kobb'd sort it though; put Anserth in her place.

Inclining his head, Kobb pressed his fingers to his throat. "I promise I'm telling you the truth."

"You promise?" Anserth tapped her chin.

Anessa glanced back and forth. What was Kobb doing? Why didn't he explain about the Stones, or at least something?

"Elvar. Return their weapons."

It took Anessa a moment to make sense of Anserth's words. Elvar seemed equally puzzled. After frowning at the Inductor, he threw Anessa's kit on the floor and stomped out.

Anessa crouched. One eye on Anserth, she picked up her belt. When an attack didn't come, she buckled it around her waist. Crossbow rested across her knees, she ran her fingers over the mechanism. Everything felt true.

Everything on the crossbow anyway. She straightened and glared at Anserth. "Don't know what you're up to this time. Don't you think this'll make me trust you."

"I wouldn't expect you to. I... My apologies for the insult to your honour, Worthy Tanton." Anserth bowed sharply from the waist. "If you will excuse me, I should attend to the people we rescued." After nodding toward Kobb and Haelen, she strode out of the tent, shoulders rigid.

Anessa waited a moment, then moved closer until her head was close to Kobb's. "Reckon we make a break for it. Don't know why she gave us the weapons back. Ain't worth losing our chance, though."

"We need to stay. Find out what she knows." Kobb tugged his hat off. "Might be pleasant to dry out too."

"Stay!" Anessa looked to Haelen for support. "You can't mean to trust her. Not after last time. And just giving us the weapons for no reason... She's up to something."

Kobb rested a hand on her shoulder. "She returned them because she stopped seeing us as an enemy. The oath that lets me draw power for my Courser... there are consequences. I can't make a false promise. The Inductor knows that; as soon as I promised you were innocent, she believed us."

"Well, that just means she don't think we're involved in whatever's here. Don't see why we trust her after what she's done."

"I'm not suggesting we trust her. But we'll have an easier time if we aren't dodging her and whoever's in the palisade."

Anessa still struggled to voice her confusion when Elvar marched in. Not acknowledging their presence, he dropped an armful of Kobb and Haelen's possessions on the floor and stomped out.

The churning in Anessa's mind grew. Knowing they weren't involved and knowing they wouldn't interfere weren't the same thing. Anserth hadn't had to give the weapons back. And she'd seemed shocked when Anessa accused her of pretending to be her friend. Offering to protect her was a good way to get her to talk if she'd been involved; but what if it weren't making a deal? What if Anserth really didn't want her in trouble? Haelen'd said the sagas were full of... friends ending up on opposite sides.

Anessa sighed. This wasn't a saga.

"She didn't tell us to stay here." Haelen tilted his head toward the flap. "If you're not certain, see what she's doing."

For a moment, Anessa wondered how he'd known her thoughts. Then she realised he meant, uncertain whether it was a ploy. If Anserth didn't trust them, she'd stop Anessa poking about. Slinging her crossbow, she walked out into the rain.

The line of prisoners was gone. Bundled shapes moved in the gloom; none had Anserth's stride, though. Cold seeping down her neck, Anessa turned on the spot. Something else was missing: other tents. Even head-to-foot, the soldiers she'd seen wouldn't all fit in one tent.

No longer fixated on having been captured, she took a better look around. Some of the shadows in the undergrowth weren't the right shape. They'd built rough blinds. Probably those smokeless fires too. She crouched, then straightened and strode toward the nearest. Weren't a proper test if people couldn't see her to stop her.

To make sure she was spotted, she leaned right through the narrow doorway. A woman in thick leathers glanced up, nodded, and returned to darning a sock.

Anessa drew back and headed for another shelter. And another. No one raised an eyebrow, let alone an alarm. Either she was free to wander or she hadn't come close to the secrets yet. Torn between searching harder and returning to the dry, she realised talking came from the next blind. The rain drowned the words, but the voice was Anserth's. Now she'd find the truth of it.

Creeping closer, Anessa strained to hear. Something about riding to the rescue? And an odd slurping noise. She peered around the edge of the doorway.

Anserth sat on a log. But instead of the soldiers Anessa expected to be with her, the only other occupant was a child of six or so seated on

Anserth's lap. Holding a spoonful of stew to the child's mouth, Anserth described someone called Sire Florian leaping onto a drawbridge as it closed. This wasn't a plot; it was a story.

Anessa withdrew, more confused than ever. Returning their weapons might be a trick so they trusted her; Anserth couldn't have known Anessa'd find her, though. Didn't make sense trying to fool the child into liking her either. The only thing that was certain was crouching in the rain wouldn't do anything but make her wetter.

She crept to the tent and told the others what she'd seen.

Kobb turned his hat in his hands before placing it on the floor. "So? Prepared to stay for the moment?"

"Rescuing children ain't evil. Suppose...." She sat on a large chest, trying to make the image of Anserth caring for a child fit beside the one of her pointing weapons at them in the ruins. Several circular arguments with herself later, she was no closer to an answer.

And her discomfort increased when Anserth returned, a pot of stew and three spoons in her hands. "Apologies for the wait. And for the rain getting into the stew. Thought you'd prefer not to eat with my men."

"Doubt they'd choose to eat with us, either." Kobb lifted the meal from Anserth's grip. "After this many years, doubt swallowing a little more weather will hurt me."

Anserth paused. "Didn't just want to avoid dredging up past problems. I'd hoped one of the people we'd rescued would know why they were captured. Or the guard who survived. But, all I got is the soldiers take prisoners and horses to the palisade."

"Possibly a discussion for after we've eaten" Haelen took a spoonful of stew.

Anessa grabbed a spoon from Anserth's hand then stepped back. "If we're going to stay, no more secrets. No more lying about what we're really doing. Anserth tells us why she's here and we do the same."

Kobb and Anserth shared a glance, then the Inductor crouched. "We came across a village, mostly gutted. The tracks led in this direction. We spotted the palisade and withdrew to assess. Before we could scout it properly, we discovered the column of prisoners. Seemed a way to gain information and stop their forces growing, so we set the ambush."

"You found a village and headed off, just like that?" Anessa frowned.

"And you wouldn't? Unless ordered to perform a specific task, I have a wide remit."

"Of course I'd do something, but..."

"But you're not a heartless hag." Anserth raised a hand before Anessa could speak. "I don't hope for forgiveness, Anessa. I... Once we've dealt with this issue, we need never meet again. To speed that day, perhaps one of you might share what you know."

"They're not taking slaves." Haelen dropped his spoon back into the pot. "I didn't want to discuss it over food; I don't want risk seeming like we're hiding something, though. There's a bone pile near the palisade. Fresh human bones. I think they—"

The image of the riders emptying meat onto the floor rose up in Anessa's mind, followed by a surge of bile. Guts twisting, she curled into a ball.

Part Seventy-Two

Kobb gazed down at Anessa. They'd faced so much he sometimes forgot how inexperienced she was. All his life had been spent looking into the darkness. And Haelen had no doubt seen his share of atrocities on the battlefield. But Anessa...? A season ago, her biggest fear had been being banned from hunting. He should send her home, before he got her killed.

She wouldn't leave even if he tried, though. She'd maybe head off until she was out of sight, then sneak after him. This must be why Reverend Gannon had seemed to both keep him close and push him away. At least Anessa could go home if the horror became too much; everyone who wielded power died on the edge of nightmare, the only choice they had was which way to face.

And they lived near enough to the darkness that it spilled onto others. "Bringing a few prisoners at a time over great distances isn't efficient. Likely they're using them to feed something dark."

"They don't just kidnap people." Anserth frowned. "They gather horses, too. That'd be more meat."

Haelen sighed. "The Reverend's right. Those guards told you they captured people and horses. If this were about meat, they'd be taking livestock too. That and... like the Reverend said, we tracked an evil here."

"Don't matter." Anessa wiped the worst of the vomit off her lips. "We stop whatever it is."

Anserth nodded. "She's right. Cannibals or sorcerers, they need to die."

"Makes a difference to how we do it though," Kobb replied. "We rush in without knowing a key fact, it gets messy fast."

The inductor quirked an eyebrow. "Can't spend the time to scout properly."

"I can sneak in and out." Anessa staggered to her feet. "Caught me off guard's all. I'll be fine. This weather'll make it easier."

Anserth reached for her, then let her hand fall. "I don't doubt that. But ritual slaughter... that's different to a couple of archaeologists. And, I meant we have an opportunity if we go right now. The rain makes it harder for them to see clearly. They're expecting a convoy; let's give them one."

"You rescued those people; now you want to hand them over?" Anessa glared at her. "What—"

"No. I leave most of my people here to get the citizens to safety and back us up if needed. The rest hide short arms and pretend to be prisoners. The Reverend dresses like he's in charge." Anserth held her hands out. "Put me at the head of the coffle. Anything goes wrong, I'll be the one it hits."

Kobb poked at his hat brim. "If all else fails, I'll get a new hat. A crossbow's hard to hide; so Anessa pretends to be a guard."

"Makes— Wait... The guards ride. I've never..."

"I'll ride one of the guard's horses, and you sit on Falcon. We'll be at a walking pace and he'll follow me well enough, so you'll not need to do anything."

Anessa stared at her boots for a moment. Then nodded, jaw set.

"Put me with the prisoners," Haelen said. "If we do get away with it, there's likely people in there who need a healer. And if we don't, we'll need our best fighters ready, rather than struggling to pull a knife free."

"Anserth should be the other guard." Anessa glanced sideways at the inductor. "If we want the best fighters."

Anserth lowered her hands. "You can always tie me up after everything's over."

Kobb frowned. Inductors were trained to manipulate, but he couldn't see the advantage in reminding Anessa it might only be a temporary alliance. "We'd best get ready."

Outfitted in borrowed clothes, and in some cases clutching the ends of chains together, they rode out. Kobb hunched over his new mount. The thin brim of the pot helm kept off more rain than the remnants of his usual hat; however, the drumming of water on metal was almost worse than a wet neck.

Twitching the reins, he passed close to the pile of meat. He'd need to stop to be sure, but a glance suggested it hadn't been touched. Which, hopefully, meant whatever ate it wasn't roaming free.

Incessant drumming aside, the rest of the approach went without issue. He tilted his helm further forward as he reined in; concealment beat a wet neck. "Hallo the camp!"

A hooded head rose above the parapet. "Hallo the convoy. What's the word of the day?"

Pass phrase. Why hadn't Anserth asked— A man with a bolt in him only has a few answers in him, and she wanted the critical ones. Another bluff then. "Rain's got into everything. Password's mush by now." Kobb stared over his shoulder for a moment before looking up. "Just get the gates open. If one of those things is out, I'm not standing around."

"Don't piss your britches, old man. If it comes, you only have to outrun the captives." With a chortle, the guard disappeared. Moments later, the gate swung open.

Kobb walked his horse forward. Rough wooden cages stood either side of an expanse of churned mud, thin figures peering out of each. And beyond the cages, another palisade loomed. As the last of the fake prisoners stepped through the gate, the guard swung it shut again. "There you go. Safe as a noble's— Wait. How did you know about the experiments?"

Before Kobb could think of a reply, the guard's head tumbled free.

Wiping her blade, Anserth cantered forward. "We'll not pull the same trick twice. Elvar, take Keln and Vors, and get these citizens back to the camp. The rest of you, weapons out."

Elvar bent over the fallen guard. Pulling a bundle of keys off the body, he jogged to the cages.

Dismounting, Kobb peered around. "Don't see horses. And there isn't much space between the cages."

"So, they take them further in." Anessa scuttled closer.

"That's odd though. You don't lead horses further than you need. If they're sacrifices, why keep the horses separate; and if their not, why not keep them near the outside where the grass is? Might be another entrance, but those guards rode out of this one. A problem for after we've got past the next palisade, though."

Anessa stared at the palisade. "I might get over without being seen; couple more of us maybe. Then open it from the other side."

"Stands a better chance than hacking it apart." Anserth approached, holding Falcon and her mount. "If we wait till Elvar's done, we don't risk the civilians taking wounds."

And didn't risk them getting in the way if it came to a fight. Kobb nodded.

Blank-eyed figures milled around, as Elvar eased the gate open. A few ragged figures staggered toward freedom. Then the trickle became a flow. Legs cramped from lack of use stumbled, and a young girl fell.

A man scooped her up. For a moment, all seemed well. Then the shock of the fall caught up with her and she screamed.

Anserth's followers struggled to keep order, but the flow became a rush. Pounding feet and gasping breaths drowned out the hiss of the rain. Kobb snatched his Courser free as a hooded head figure peered over the inner parapet.

For a breath, silence and light swallowed the disorder. The guard collapsed from view.

The last of the escapees cleared the gate as a horn cleft the air.

"The gate's a bottleneck." Kobb leapt for Falcon. "We stop the first riders there, the rest lose the charge. Anessa, eyes on the parapet."

Gaze shifting between the gates and the palisade, they waited.

Shouting and running feet sounded within; but the gates didn't open and the parapet remained bare. Kobb grinned, each moment of tension another moment for people to move out of reach.

Howling shattered the air on his left, undercut by the thunder of hooves. They did have a second entrance. Wheeling Falcon, Kobb cantered to the open gate.

Halfway to the forest, figures scattered, all sense of order gone. But instead of the cavalry he expected, a mass of riderless horses boiled in pursuit. Horses that devoured the rough ground as if it were a smooth lawn, and made Falcon seem wizened.

PART SEVENTY-THREE

Kobb raised his heels, then let them drop. Even galloping, he wouldn't reach the prisoners before the horses did. Anyway, Elvar's shouted commands had already steered most of the prisoners out from the path of the stampede, and the rest sprinted toward safety. He'd do more good at the front entrance so the occupants couldn't use the distraction to sally out.

But, as he wheeled, the herd split in two, each half charging toward a group of fleeing civilians.

Elvar stood at bay. Snatching a long knife from his under his disguise, he jumped to the side as the first horse reached him, then leapt for its back. His blade arced down with his full weight behind it.

An instant before Elvar's knife met flesh, the horse twisted its head to face backward. The rain hid the detail, but not Elvar's scream as his body spun away, arm missing. A scream that cut off as another of the beasts snatched him from the air.

Snapping his Courser up, Kobb bathed a horse in silent fire.

The beast lurched, limbs losing their fluid grace. Then recovered. Panic and agony mixed with the mud as its herd-mates hit the prisoners in a wave of hooves and teeth.

Memories of the slaughter at Raveth rose up. Tears mingling with the rain, he unleashed a second bolt and then a third.

Finally—maw still snapping toward the escapees—the monster collapsed.

Kobb shifted his aim and felled another of the monsters. Ice clamped his chest as he released his sixth shot in as many breaths.

He forced down a wet cough and raised his Courser again. Before he could fire, the thunk of crossbows sounded behind him. He let his weapon drop and swung Falcon round. Killing just two beasts had left its mark. He'd lose consciousness before he felled enough to give the prisoners even the slimmest chance of survival. Whereas, his Courser might be the difference between Anserth holding and being driven from the compound.

The inner gate stood open a few feet, one of Anserth's companions sprawled next to the wedged spar that prevented it swinging further. His sacrifice had stopped the enemy cavalry, but—with Anessa the only one able to respond to the four archers on the parapet above—the remainder of Anserth's unit had been driven into cover.

As Kobb reined in, guards stepped through the gap on foot, more on their heels. The taste of iron filling his mouth, he blasted two archers from the parapet before they'd realised he was there.

The archer next to them spun away, Anessa's bolt in his throat.

His companion ducked down.

Each breath scouring his chest anew, Kobb stiffened his spine and kept his Courser raised. With luck, the foul weather would conceal the fact he lacked the strength for another shot.

Freed of the risk of bolts, Anserth's unit charged forward.

With armour, longswords, and weight of numbers, the guards grinned and advanced.

Only to stutter as Anserth's knives flew into the throats of the lead pair.

Shoulder rolling, she slammed the left guard to the floor, her hand snatching his sword from his slackened grip. Feet crossing, she lunged to the right.

Caught by surprise, another defender fell. The remainder reeled back a step as Anserth's companions took advantage of the break.

Recovering, the defenders firmed their line, their longer reach holding Anserth's men at bay. Steel rang on steel as each side sought an advantage.

Twice the defenders almost pushed forward far enough to allow more of their fellows to join them, and twice they were driven back.

The stalemate stretched, but experience began to tell. The defenders were better than bandits and thugs. But Anserth's unit had trained until they were parts of a whole, each as comfortable deflecting blows aimed at their fellows as themselves. Unable to predict when an attacker would lunge with no thought of their own defence, the guards lost rhythm, then fell.

Pressing hard, Anserth's unit cut the remnants down, before shouldering the gate closed.

Anserth wiped a dark stain from her face with one sleeve. "They'll not risk that again, Reverend."

"They might not have to. The horses aren't sacrifices. They're the reason for all this."

"How bad...?" Anserth glanced toward the gate. "Did Elvar...?"

Kobb realised the screams had stopped. He shook his head, unable to keep his shoulders from sagging.

Haelen rushed to steady him. "How did horses do that?"

"They're not..." Kobb swallowed. "I used enough power to slay three men just to cause a serious injury. They might look like horses, but they're something unnatural now. Something dark."

"Then how do we stop them?" Haelen glanced for the open gate. "If a Courser can't do it easily, what chance have the rest of us?"

Anserth shrugged. "We break, burn, or kill whatever made them. If that doesn't work, it might still give us a better idea."

"But how do we find it? Or get to it if we could?" Anessa flicked her gaze between the closed gate and the parapet. "Rest of 'em'll be waiting."

"We don't have to capture the entire fort. We go straight to the source."

"But..." Anessa frowned.

Kobb chuckled coldly. "The creatures were released from another gate. The way those riders acted at the thought of meeting one, that'll open straight on the place the beasts are kept. If we go now, we might make it while the beasts are still distracted."

Part Seventy-Four

Anessa peered through the murk at Kobb. While the creatures were distracted? Why'd they be–? Acid stung her throat as she realised what he meant. If Kobb couldn't kill them, then it'd be suicide for anyone else to try; not trying–taking advantage even–felt wrong, though. She spun as someone touched her elbow.

"Didn't mean to startle you." Haelen lowered his hand. "I'd feel safer if you'd stay with me. Let one of the Inductor's lot scout, this time?"

Anessa almost said yes, then swallowed it at the last moment. The rain'd only hide so much. Going while the creatures weren't nearby wouldn't help if the guards were on their heels. "Someone with more than a sword needs to keep an eye on the parapet. Make sure if guard see us leave message don't spread too quick. And Kobb's got the best chance to sort this out, so I'll go last."

"She's right." Anserth grinned. "Again."

Haelen twitched one eyebrow oddly. "I can–"

"Don't worry." Anserth wrapped an arm around his shoulder. "I'll keep you safe for her. Best we get the healer to the other end as fast as possible anyway. Ready, Reverend?"

Kobb swung into Falcon's saddle and nodded.

Crossbow braced, Anessa stood beside the open gate, eyes on the inner parapet. As the last of Anserth's companions jogged past, he tapped her on the back. Waiting a breath, she stepped past the gatepost. The air thinned, refusing to fill her chest.

Flanks glistened, and hooves scuffed. The horses hadn't noticed her yet, but the herd milled close to the palisade. If one of them—

One of the beasts tossed a body up, throat swelling as it swallowed its victim to the waist. The sound of rain faded. The monsters were halfway across the plain. They only looked nearby because they stood as tall as trees.

Someone shouted.

Devouring half a man at a gulp. Pounding hooves.

Something tugged at her.

A gaping maw. Shattering bone. No escape. Red mud.

Iron wrapped across her. She flailed at it, bouncing off. She was doomed. The monsters had her.

The world shifted as they dragged her off.

Figures ran before her, unable to save her from the frothing beast.

She tried to scream for help. Something covered her mouth, though.

Helpless, she slid past the palisade as the monster raced back to its lair.

Rain cascaded onto her face.

The monster'd thrown her to the ground.

Her companions clustered above her.

She tried to get them to run, to leave her, but the words wouldn't come out.

Her gaze flicked randomly. Where'd the horse gone? Why hadn't it finished her?

Haelen shouted about ague. Didn't make sense. They'd be dead before the wet mattered.

She flailed up onto her elbows. What was the beast waiting for?

A shape loomed across her view.

Before she could scrabble back, it yanked her close. The scent of sweat and rust wrapped about her. Something soft pressed over her mouth.

Warmth spread across her in tatters and jags. Air, touched with hints of barley and beets, twisted through every breath. A second tang of rotting meat undercut it.

Her body curled as tingling heat burnt away the fear.

Anessa's head tilted forward as Anserth pulled back. "What—?"

"Anessa?" The Inductor peered into her eyes, the rain stealing her expression. "Are you...?"

Questions tangled behind her lips, Anessa blurted out the first thing that came to her. "You kissed me."

"You were taken by a battle ague. Isn't time for you to sleep it off. So we needed a strong emotion to shake you up."

The fragments of memory shifted in Anessa's head. Serin Roblin pale and shaking in a tree. Like he had the ague. But he didn't; he was just mortal terrified of heights. There'd never been a horse. She'd seen them, that was all. She'd got the shakes, like Serin did. Instead of helping, she'd slowed everyone down. She turned away, unable to face the shame.

"Being kissed by someone you hate seemed the easiest way to do it." Anserth rose to her feet and stalked away.

Someone she hated? Confusion roiled up through the guilt. Did she hate Anserth? She should. Anserth'd hurt Kobb, tried to have people killed. But the kiss felt right. Like everything else didn't matter any more. Could you want to be with someone and hate them at the same time? Didn't seem possible. So had the ague messed her feelings, or...?

Either way, Anserth'd helped her. She should go after her, say thanks.

But if Anserth'd gone, whose arms supported her?

Haelen smiled as she wriggled round. "Feel able to stand?"

Why was he being so pleasant? "I got scared. I could've got people killed. You're lucky I weren't the one protecting you."

"Everyone feels fear, Anessa. Never trust someone who claims they don't. And no one knows how it'll hit till it happens. What matters is whether you try to follow the right path. Up you come."

Anessa struggled to her feet, letting him do most of the work. Even knowing the beasts weren't near, she felt the fear writhing up. "Thank you. I need to speak to Anserth... about... things."

"Later." Haelen patted her shoulder. "She's keeping an eye on the horses, so..."

Anessa nodded ruefully. So, there was every chance she'd get the shakes again if she sought Anserth out. Straightening her shoulders, she eased out of Haelen's arms and looked around. They were within another palisade. However, rather than simple stakes, this one'd been reinforced with thick bands of dark metal. A wide gate gaped, part of the forest visible beyond.

Piles of horse shit spattered the ground. But unlike the musty tang of Falcon's muck, these stank of rot and blood. She swallowed back more bile. They'd found the pen. Hoping to distract herself before the terror grabbed her again, she studied the rest of the enclosure.

Kobb approached through the murk, the fence behind him seeming different. One hand raised, he jogged over. "Either of you good with locks? There's another gate. It's likely what we want's on the other side. They've sealed it up tight, though."

"I can climb it." Anessa started back the way Kobb'd come. Even if Haelen didn't blame her, she needed to prove to the others that she wasn't dead weight.

Kobb placed a hand on her shoulder, stopping her. "Lock's built into the iron. Without the—"

Hooves hammered closer.

Boots squelched and skidded as Anserth's companions shoved at the gate. It barely seemed to move.

Part Seventy-Five

Anessa staggered back a step as Kobb and Haelen sprinted forward. Why didn't the gate close? The creatures'd get them all. There'd be nowhere to run. Why wasn't Anserth— Where was Anserth? Haelen said she went to watch the horses, so why— Unless—

The thundering in her ears drowned the sound of hooves. Anessa stared at the creeping gate. Anserth was outside. She'd be trampled.

Sweat oozing across her brow, Anessa dragged herself toward the gap. She could do this. She didn't need to get that close. Even if she couldn't kill a horse, a bolt in the leg'd— Her fingers met air.

The dregs of her courage drained away. She'd been holding her crossbow as they retreated. She must have dropped it when she panicked. She stumbled to a halt.

Kobb and Haelen added their shoulders to the effort. With a groan, the gate began to move faster.

The hooves grew ever louder, but the gap was mere feet.

Two aching breaths later, Anserth sprinted in. Spinning on her heel, she threw herself against the gate.

Anessa stumbled forward. She was safe.

The pounding stilled as a dark shape appeared. Head tilted, the horse halted and peered at the closing gap, a gap already narrower than its shoulders.

Almost as if it could think. Anessa wasn't sure if that was more or less terrifying than the creatures being stupid.

The beast no longer visible, her legs regained their strength. She jogged toward the others.

With a thud, the gate stopped, only inches from closing. Faces creased with effort and boots scrabbled as it groaned open again.

Sodden earth tearing beneath his feet, one of Anserth's companions fell. The remainder strained, but the gap widened.

A rain black snout shoved through the hole, followed by muscular body.

Snatching a knife from her belt, Anserth leapt.

The beast's head swung. Bone and muscle slammed into the Inductor, hammering her to the ground. Hooves glinting despite the gloom, the monster loomed over her.

Purple fire swallowed the shouts and ragged breathing.

Rearing up, the horse twisted away from Kobb's attack. The gate juddered as the beast shouldered through the gap and galloped into the darkness.

Back slamming against the rough wood, Anessa shoved. As the gate crashed shut, the ground beneath her feet began to shudder.

Anserth stared at the planks. "Time to pray, Reverend."

"Gate's closed. Won't that—" Anessa realised what the Inductor already knew. The gate lacked a latch or bar. Wood trembled behind her as the creatures nuzzled the other side.

They couldn't keep them out. They were going to die.

"Something's odd." Haelen looked at Kobb. "They're not howling or charging. And that one you attacked fled."

Rain faded to drizzle, heaving flanks and scuffing hooves replacing the hissing. The gate juddered again as another beast shoved at it.

"Hunger." Kobb patted his Courser. "Whatever's been done to them makes them stronger and harder to kill. Once their blood lust's sated, thought, they must return to thinking more like animals; and animals avoid pain."

"So, they're coming here because it's home?" Anserth pressed herself beside Anessa. "You prepared to bet your life they won't kill us the moment they get in? Of course you are. Same as I would."

Anessa gulped at the thin air. They weren't talking about letting the creatures in... were they?

"What choice do we have?" Kobb swept his arm around. "Without something to wedge it, they'll get in. If we risk it now, at least we'll be less tired when they do."

Anserth snorted. "You'd deny me my only chance to die in my sleep? Right. Anessa and Haelen run for the inner fence. Rest of us hold as long as we can, then follow."

A head start'd... mean her friends got killed first. Anessa shook her head. "Needs all of us to keep it closed. You'd be—"

Anserth twisted her around by the shoulder and stared into her eyes. "Do what you're told. You're too valuable to me. No one else can get that inner gate open."

Anessa's feet tangled as the Inductor shoved her away. Catching her balance, she ran, Haelen trying to keep pace. Her thoughts churned. She'd be useless if the horses broke through, but leaving felt as bad. Behind her, the sound of people straining mixed with that of flesh slamming into wood.

Moments later, the thudding ended. Boots pounded across the ground.

Gaze locked on the gate ahead, Anessa pressed her fingers to her pendant. "It's Anessa Tanton. I know finding the Blessing's my task, but if you could give me some sign..."

The sound of a sticking door mixed with hooves.

Her legs pumped harder. The creatures were inside now.

Iron wrapped across her. Her feet left the ground, Anserth's arm pulling her close.

Her stomach lurched; partially from the impact, but mostly from the realisation Anserth'd carried her before, not Haelen. Torn between remaining rigid to avoid more contact and curling deeper into the embrace, Anessa barely noticed the beasts weren't attacking.

She still hadn't worked out what everything meant when Anserth lowered her to the ground. But she didn't step away. "Thank you. And for last time."

Anserth didn't step away either. "You're important to—"

"Whoa." Kobb tugged on Falcon's reins. "Not killing us don't mean they're friends now."

Anessa looked past Anserth. The last of the horses ambled in. Definitely not friends. But not frothing horrors either. The gate slammed shut.

Anessa peered through the herd. "How'd they...?"

"A little trick of mine." A plummy voice came from above them.

Part Seventy-Six

Anessa peered up. A thin man in velvet robes smiled down at them from the parapet.

"Quite impressive." Kobb tilted his head. "If you let us in, we could discuss it in comfort."

"We could. But that spoils my chance to see whether the beasts' fury returns faster with living prey nearby."

"Maybe miss a bigger chance if you don't." Haelen tugged a crude bone pendant from his tunic.

Plummy Voice leaned forward. "A Skithai fetish? How deliciously intriguing. Were it you alone, I might be tempted. However, I suspect your Botherer friend would not consent to remain there."

"Botherer?" Kobb tugged his jacket open. "I promise you there's no pendant round my neck."

Not religious? How could Kobb break a—? Anessa snapped her jaw shut. He wasn't lying. Like the way he got the barrier around the Stones down. Unfortunately, this man didn't seem half-crazy.

"Stealing a Skithai fetish and a Courser? Persons of such ingenuity would make a delightful change from my usual dinner companions."

Plummy Voice pressed a be-ringed hand to his chest. "However, your attempt to free my prisoners raises a somewhat bitter note."

"Could say the same about your guards trying to kill us in the woods." Anserth shrugged. "Of course, doesn't matter who got our relationship off to a bad start. The Botherers are likely to turn up soon anyway."

"Don't be ridiculous. They're not going to get involved in some peasants being kidnapped by bandits, and we're too far well hidden for one of them to just wander up."

"Exactly." Haelen wiggled the pendant. "We didn't wander. Your ritual's like a beacon."

Plummy Voice stared down. "You didn't come to rescue the prisoners?"

"We followed an immense flow of power." Kobb tilted his head. "That good enough, or do you want me to promise?"

"Promise?" Plummy Voice's gawp melted into a high-pitched chuckle. Composing himself, he nodded at Kobb. "Most amusing. I think I shall allow you in after all." He strolled away.

A moment later, he reappeared. "Although, it would be remiss of me not to enquire whether the girl's gifted too. Her pallor does somewhat stand out among such hard-bitten warriors and sorcerers."

Pallor? Anessa struggled to work out what the man was up to. Was it all a game? Offer to let them in, then snatch it back. The others seemed calm, so maybe this was some sort of city thing.

"Like you said, things get tedious without dinner company." Anserth wrapped an arm around Anessa's shoulder. "She's got a hearty appetite."

Plummy Voice gave another high-pitched chuckle and disappeared. Fragments of voices, too quiet to understand, floated past the gate.

Anessa tugged free of Anserth's hug. "Why'd you tell him—?"

"Quiet." Anserth leaned closer. "Sorry. If I told him why you're with the Reverend, he'd keep a sharp eye on you. If he thinks you're my friend, might give you a chance to sneak around."

Anessa nodded automatically. Why'd telling him about her liking food make her seem trustworthy? And why'd Anserth apologised for doing it?

The inner gate creaked open, revealing a long wooden corridor. Several pikemen formed a line across it. Behind them, two scruffy men in smocks stood either side of a giant brass gong. One of the guards threw several sacks onto the ground. "Weapons in there."

Following the example of the others, Anessa placed her sword and crossbow in a sack, then stepped back. An eating knife'd be fine, wouldn't it?

After a long moment, the guard gathered the sacks up and retreated behind the line of pikes.

Anserth strolled in, hips rolling. Forcing herself to pay attention to the inhabitants, Anessa followed at her heels. Save for the cages holding horses not people, the space beyond the gate matched the other entrance.

"Do come up." Plummy Voice called from above.

Staying close to Anserth, purely to maintain the deception, Anessa headed up the stairs. Several tables of varying sizes, loaded with papers and odd objects, dotted the platform at the top. Plummy Voice stood at the far side next to a tray of wine, two pikemen in front of him. As Kobb stepped closer, the guards crossed their pikes.

"My sincere apologies." Plummy Voice inclined his head, his smile not reaching his eyes. "I trust you, but my men have demanded you prove your friendship."

Kobb nodded back, equally insincerely. "I understand completely. If you tell us a little about what you're doing, we could give you some of our insights."

"My guards are simple men; I fear you would need to provide a more... corporeal token of faith." Plummy Voice swallowed a sip of wine. "I'm sure the girl wouldn't mind showing me her appetite."

Both men snorted. The one on the left added a curled lip.

Haelen lunged forward a step, but halted as a pike swung toward him.

Blood flooded up Anessa's throat as the pieces slotted together. No way was she going to—

Anserth's fingers pressed into Anessa's jaw as she twisted her head. Noses almost touching, the Inductor growled, "Be nice to the man." Confusingly, she winked as she said it.

Still holding Anessa's face, Anserth turned back to Plummy Voice. "I trust you, but my companions are simple men. I assume you've no objection to having the meal here where we can keep an eye out?"

Hands trembling, Plummy Voice beckoned. "I'd be delighted."

Anessa stumbled as Anserth shifted her hand to her arm and stepped forward. Was this part of the plan? Why didn't Kobb or Haelen say something? She glanced sideways. More guards stood behind her companions, weapons ready.

The two men ahead parted, pikes angling toward Kobb and Haelen.

Anessa struggled to break free. Anserth's grip felt like iron, though. The meaty stench of shit filled her nose. This couldn't be the plan... they needed to trick him, but they couldn't expect her to... especially not in front of everyone.

"Very delicious." Plummy Voice licked his lips. "Is she...?"

"I guarantee you'll remember this meal for the rest of your life." Anserth's free arm flicked out. Something thudded below.

For a moment, Anessa couldn't work out why the man wasn't there any more. Then she realised what the thud was, and why someone was screaming.

The air whooshed from her lungs as a blow knocked her to the floor.

PART SEVENTY-SEVEN

As the pikeman glanced toward his master's scream, Kobb pivoted and raised his arms. From the corners of his eyes, he saw Anserth shove Anessa behind a table while her companions dived for the nearest guards. A judder ran through Kobb's left wrist as it caught the second guard's pikestaff, deflecting the lunge over his head.

For a breath, Anserth's men held the advantage. Then the enemy shook off their surprise. Thrusting through gaps in the fight, the unengaged pikemen pushed Anserth's men back.

Unarmed and with an enemy on both sides, Kobb resigned himself to the least worst option. Stepping hard left before either opponent could bring their weapon in line, he slid his arm down the pikestaff. Shoulder and elbow rolling as his weight moved, Kobb drove his fist into his enemy's crotch.

The guard's jerkin stopped the force, but not the threat. Acting on instinct, the man dodged, focus no longer on his weapon.

Kobb pivoted on his left foot, right arm driving up. Still partly folded forward to shield his crotch, the blow caught the guard on the chin and snapped his head back. Stunned, his enemy lost his grip on the pike.

Kobb threw his weight sideways, hoping to avoid his second opponent's thrust. But the falling staff slammed into his shoulder, pushing him off balance. Pain spiking through his hip, he sprawled across the floor as the pikeman lunged.

And overshot. Chest overtaking his legs, the guard stumbled then fell forward.

Anserth saluted Kobb with the poniard she'd acquired from somewhere and leapt over the guard's body.

Kobb rose to his feet as the squelch of blade meeting throat sounded behind him. Tugging a knife from a fallen opponent, he glanced around.

Those guards who'd been on the parapet lay unconscious or dead. Several pikemen ranked up the stairs, held at bay by the stolen pikes of Anserth's companions, but holding them at bay in turn. Anessa stood to one side, knife clutched in her fist and face pale beneath the dirt. Of Haelen, there was no sign.

Kobb grimaced. His heart wanted him to search for his friend, make sure he wasn't bleeding out under a pile of bodies. However, without help, the remnants of Anserth's unit would tire soon. Tucking the knife into his belt, Kobb lifted the nearest pike.

Dull throbs ran through his shoulders and down his spine as the point dragged at the shaft. No wonder pikemen always looked so grumpy. Pikestaff swaying more with each step, he staggered for the stairs.

"I've a plan, Reverend." Anserth grasped on of the fallen by the heels. "Help me move this criminal."

Pike remaining just under control, Kobb lowered it to the floor and joined the Inductor. "Where are we moving him to?"

Anserth tipped her head toward the stairs. "Rules of chivalry require the dead be returned to their own side."

Kobb flicked his gaze across the parapet. The idea was disturbing; he couldn't think of a better one, though. After heaving his end up, he matched Anserth's swing.

Unable to do anything other than stand or retreat, the unengaged ranks of pikemen stared in shock or shouted curses as the body built up speed, then arced toward them, limbs flailing. Torn between defence and respect for the dead, some attempted to swing their weapons away while some tried to fend it away. Wood and metal clattered as pikes crossed.

Disorder spreading from behind, the front rank lost ground.

After the third time, the guards broke. Taking what consolation there was in the dead feeling no pain, Kobb turned back.

Anessa knelt near one of the tables, Haelen's head resting on her leg and a hand pressed to his side. A crimson stain showed between her fingers.

"Haelen?" Kobb crouched.

"Don't worry, Reverend. Point glanced off a rib." Haelen gulped a jagged breath. "My tunic needs stitching though."

Kobb chuckled, then stopped again when Anessa glared at him. "Best get you bandaged. You don't want blood on everything."

The wound, once Anessa had been convinced to let go, was only slightly worse than Haelen pretended. Requisitioning an singlet from a fallen foe, Kobb set to work.

As he eased Haelen's clothes back into place, Anserth returned with sacks of weapons in each hand.

"You shoved him off the edge!" Anessa stared at the Inductor, eyes damp.

Anserth dropped her burden. "He deserved to—"

Anessa lunged forward and wrapped her arms around Anserth. "He wanted to hurt me but you pushed him off the edge for me, and I should have trusted you. I thought you were going to let him, but it was all a trick wasn't it."

"I saw an opportunity." Anserth broke free of the embrace and turned to the stairs. "I'd best finish securing the area. Don't want any surprises."

Anessa struggled to tug her sword out of the sack without taking her eyes of Anserth. "Wait. I can—"

"Let her go," said Haelen. "They'll be time for talking after we've searched that noble's papers."

"I can't read." Anessa fumbled with her belt. "I'd be no use here."

"Kobb and I can do the searching." Haelen patted his side. "Best I don't strain this, though. Reckon you can hold me up?"

For a moment, Anessa's shoulders sagged. Then she nodded.

Leaving the nearest tables for Haelen, Kobb strode to the far side of the parapet. After dismissing the decanter of wine, he studied the papers next to it.

The top sheet was covered in columns of numbers, each headed with a set of three letters. The sheets below proved to contain the same. Given their placement close to the pen, they were probably a list of observations on the horses rather than sorcery. He tucked them in a pouch anyway.

Several pieces of altar plate lay on the next table, mud and less pleasant substances smeared across them. Despite the seriousness of the situation, Kobb snorted. For some reason, nearly every noble who took up unnatural arts felt the need to defile the trappings of religion; as if damaging something crafted by human hand would cause the Maker to turn away leaving them to act unopposed.

"Killing him might have been premature." Haelen staggered closer, holding a bundle of papers in his free arm. "These sketches are twisted horses. The writing's not a language I recognise though."

Kobb considered the top sheet. The groups of letters didn't even seem like words.

Part Seventy-Eight

Anessa helped Haelen into a chair, then glances toward the pen. "Plummy Voice ain't screaming, and I can't hear chewing. Maybe, he ain't dead."

Kobb peered over the edge. A breath later, he shook his head. "Best not look."

The desire to look tugged at her. Kobb wouldn't have said it 'less the death was messy, though. And she didn't want to spoil Anserth's bravery with a memory like that. "Ain't Anserth good at finding answers? Maybe she knows what the words mean."

Kobb and Haelen frowned at each other.

"Why don't you trust her?" Anessa looked back-and-forth. "She saved me from Plummy Voice."

Kobb huffed. "She took the opportunity that presented itself. Whether —"

Anessa spun on her heel and marched away.

Halfway down the stairs, she admitted she hadn't trusted Anserth either till recently. Going back meant more not being able to help, though. Finding Anserth might mean finding something useful and proving she was an ally.

Dead bodies, several stripped of weapons and armour, lay in the yard. The surviving guards slumped in a cage, Anserth's companions guarding them. Beyond, a wicket gate hung open. Anessa strode through into another fenced area.

Several large huts surrounded a fire pit. She wandered closer, trying to work out which felt most like the Aycock's; crude construction aside, she couldn't see any similarities, though.

Anserth emerged from the nearest building. "Anessa?"

Anessa stared at the Inductor. Her eyes looked tired, but her shoulders were unbowed. Dirt smudged the end of her nose; the nose of a person who rushed in to fix things instead of standing around. Simplest way was to just ask her about pushing Plummy Voice over the edge; that'd set Kobb's doubts to rest.

Anessa jogged to meet Anserth. "Kobb said..." No, Kobb was only looking out for her. Wasn't right to put the blame on him. "That is, I wanted to... say sorry about calling your nose lopsided."

"But my nose is lopsided." Serth's hair shifted as she tilted her head. "And I am a heartless hag when I need to be, so don't—"

"You're not a hag. " Before she lost her nerve, Anessa rose up on tiptoes and pressed her mouth over Serth's. Lips melted together. Tingles flooded through Anessa as she wrapped herself closer.

At some point, body rigid, Serth broke the kiss. "You shouldn't..."

"You kissed me, so I owed you one." Anessa brushed her thumb across the smudge. "Don't want to be in your debt... Serth."

"If things were..." Serth stepped away, leaving a cold patch on Anessa's chest. "We need to end whatever evil's loose here." She strode toward the wicket gate.

Anessa stared at Serth's retreat. Had it all been a ploy the first time? For a moment, she'd kissed back, though. Why didn't...? Thoughts swirling, she jogged after... what was she?

Serth's gaze remained straight ahead as she marched past the cages and up the stairs. "Reverend. The immediate area's secure—potential occult risks aside. No evidence of the greater scheme."

Something sounded missing in Serth's voice. Anessa resisted the urge to wrap an arm around her.

"We haven't unravelled his secrets yet either. I'd half-hoped you'd find an obvious glowing circle or such." Kobb snorted. "Only half-hoped though."

"Can't you track the power? The same way you found this place?"

"It's not that easy." Kobb stared at the mountains. "The Maker Blessed us with a starting point, but we must—"

"He means we only get a rough idea," Haelen said.

Anessa stepped past Serth. All this hiding things from each other was wasting time. "Enough! We're trying to do the same thing, so why don't... Doing the same thing. Why did the guards have a gong?"

Serth frowned. "It's not common, but units do use them to keep time while marching."

Anessa shook her head. "When we arrived, they thought one of those beasts'd escaped. Those riders beat a brass shield to call it back. So why'd these guards have a gong ready?"

"Good question. The horses were already in the pen. So they didn't need to call them." Haelen flicked through his pile of papers. "Can't see a gong, or anything that looks like music. But, maybe there's one tune to summon them and another to hold them back."

"Gongs aren't subtle instruments." Serth frowned. "Could you play different music?"

"They put out meat, too," said Kobb. "The smell of flesh attracts the beasts. But they'd want a way to not be attacked. The sound protects against the horses somehow rather than driving them away."

"Maybe more than protects." Serth gestured at the pikes scattered across the floor. "The first group had swords and crossbows. So why were these armed with pikes? It's not a good weapon for one-on-one combat, or for stairs and corridors. But, the other advantage it has is reach. The reach you'd want against something that could cripple you with a single blow."

"But the beasts shook off my Courser. An iron point might not even break the skin.... Unless the gong suppresses the resilience as well; makes it possible to kill them."

"Easy enough to confirm, Reverend. We ask the—" Serth spun and stared into the compound. "Where are the gong-bearers? And why'd none of us think of them straight away?"

PART SEVENTY-NINE

"They probably hid when the battle started." Anessa poked Serth's arm. "You're scary sometimes. We'll find them."

Serth shook her head. "Can you describe them?"

They were...Their clothes were scruffy, and... Anessa's forehead creased. One had... They'd been toward the middle of the corridor, behind the guard with the droopy moustache. She'd seen their faces, so they must have been at least the same height as... the gong was on a frame, though, so they might have been standing on that. "I paid more attention to the guards."

"Might make sense if it were just you." Serth quirked an eyebrow at Kobb and Haelen. "But none of us remembering they were even here until we specifically thought about the gong?"

"She's right," said Kobb. "Anessa might be distracted enough they faded into the background. Haelen's a healer not a fighter, so maybe he was distracted too. I'm tired, so possibly details slipped my mind. But Inductors are trained to pick up subtle clues. There's no way Anserth wouldn't recall them at all. Unless they make people forget."

Anserth spun on one heel and glared toward the compound. "But how'd servants—?"

"I don't think they were servants." Haelen pointed at the tray of wine. "Three goblets: too many for just the noble; not enough for him and us. If he was a noble at all. The right accent and clothes and you could order anyone who did chance across it to leave."

Kobb began to pace. "Make sense. Building a compound and engaging mercenaries takes money, though. More than bandits or cultists tend to have. More likely he provided the gold in exchange for learning their secrets."

Anessa stepped into Kobb's path. "Does it matter? Shouldn't we start looking?"

"It's not that simple," said Serth. "We need to know more to find —"

Anessa shook her head. "We forgot, but we noticed them when we came in; they can't hide if we're looking at them. So we need to start hunting before they just wander away."

"I know you want to do something. I do to." Serth patted Anessa on the elbow. "But we can't rush in. They can't leave the area without meeting our rear guard anyway."

Anessa sagged. Waiting felt wrong, but then she'd never been any good at making plans for the future; she'd always just— Serth'd pushed Plummy Voice off and hoped it'd work out; why was she so cautious now? Anessa chuckled; even if she turned out to be wrong, it'd be enjoyable. Wrapping both arms around Serth's neck, Anessa kissed her hard.

Serth's hands clamped her close. Their mouths seemed to melt together.

After another few breaths—just to make sure—Anessa tilted her head back. "Kobb, Haelen! Something's messing with the way we feel. Like the Stones—"

"Stones?" Serth stared at her, cheeks flushed. "What—?"

Anessa struggled free. "Later. We need to start searching."

"She's right." Serth strode for the stairs. "We stood around while they do Raveth knows what!"

Kobb winced, then nodded. "Give me your arm, Haelen. We'll be two old fools together."

Even with Haelen's injuries, the four of them almost ran to the wicket gate.

Now she knew something odd was happening, Anessa couldn't imagine how she hadn't seen the nearest hut was a different wood. "That one."

Kobb gasped. "Anesh Oak. They built an entire building of it."

"Go." Haelen shoved Kobb. "I'll keep watch."

Anessa's stomach lurched as they opened the door. The inside of the hut looked cleaner than anything in Alcston, and her nose said the air smelt of mud and horses, but it felt like pitching into a slurry pit. Swallowing hard, she stepped in behind Kobb.

Odd patterns, again similar to the ones in Alcston, covered the walls, seeming to throb like veins. Her hand clamped around the hilt of her sword. "This is evil. We need to destroy it."

"Agreed. But we need to take time." Kobb forced a grin out. "Actually need to, this time. Break the wrong part of the pattern and the power will surge out instead of fading away. We know where it is now. Once we've found the cultists, we'll come back."

Anessa stepped toward the door. Apart from a couple of small cupboards, the room was empty. So wasn't anywhere for someone to hide. If they weren't destroying the hut, there was no reason to stay. Acid burning her throat, she staggered out.

Even the wave of horse-shit didn't spoil her gulp of air. Slumping to the ground, she tried to rub the pain from her forehead. Then froze. Fresh divots clustered around the door, like someone'd make hurrying while carrying a heavy load; and they weren't puddled with water, which meant they happened after it stopped raining.

Gaze flicking along their path, she broke into a sprint. "They've gone for the front gate."

Serth and Kobb caught up as she reached the gate. A waft of copper and shit slapped her as they shoved it open.

Three horses lay in the stables beyond, blood pooling around their torn throats. Beyond, another gate hung wide, revealing the area that had held the refugees.

And beyond that, an open gate framed two galloping horses, their riders crouched low.

Anessa lunged forward. Her crossbow was just outside. If she—

Serth tugged her back. "I had the same thought; they'd be out of range before you made the parapet, though."

Parapet? Of course, some of the guards had had crossbows. Serth was right though. "At least we know where they are."

"True. And the Inductor's people will stop them soon enough." Kobb peered at the corpses. "Brutal, no signs of ritual, though, like as not done to slow pursuit."

"Reverend!" Haelen limped over, several sheets of paper clutched in his hand. "Thought I'd be useful and search their workshop. I found more notes, but these are different." He leaned against the fence, fingers pressed to his side. "I recognise the handwriting."

Part Eighty

"You recognise the writing?" Kobb stumbled forward half a step.

"From somewhere." Haelen waved the papers vaguely. "Don't think it was about horses, though."

Kobb frowned. Didn't seem likely someone would recognise handwriting with enough certainty to get excited yet not recall any details. So Haelen wanted to keep where secret from the Inductor. "If those notes are like the others, knowing anything at all would be a benefit. Speaking of which... Anserth, best ask your companions to bring the servants back."

"Bringing them back means giving them access to their magic again." Anserth nodded toward the oaken hut. "Isn't it better if we focus on these papers Haelen's found? See if we can help him remember. People who keep so many notes tend to write everything down."

"Dark power makes people paranoid too. There's no guarantee they haven't left something out. So, I'd prefer not to rely on their records. Haelen and I will start while you fetch the prisoners."

Anserth clicked her tongue in thought. "Makes sense. Should update the others anyway. I'll ride Falcon, by your leave."

"It would save time." Kobb kept his face level. Hopefully, it wouldn't save enough that she returned before Haelen had finished sharing the rest.

As soon as the Inductor left the compound, Kobb raised an eyebrow to Haelen. "Remembered aught else?"

"You'll remember how we met?" Haelen slid down the fence until he crouched. "I was tracking the people who kidnapped Katrina. Well, it weren't a case of following footprints. All I had was a few things they left, and some words a neighbour overheard in the distance that she didn't think were 'normal'. So I sought out a historian. Maybe I should have asked more questions...."

"Take your time." Anessa crouched next to Haelen. "Kobb's not running around screaming, so I reckon the evil won't win for a while."

"Thank you. But I need to tell it all so we can fix it. He recognised enough to suggest another scholar who might have help. That didn't get me answers either; I did find out someone else'd been asking the same questions, though—only about a missing wife." Haelen tipped his head toward Kobb. "Unfortunately, not every Reverend's as forgiving of the difference between knowing and doing as Kobb, so this man had gone into hiding. But I kept searching, and finally received a letter from him. Wasn't easy, or cheap, sending letters back and forth through less than honest routes, but it seemed we were getting closer to answers. I was heading to Alcston to check a rumour when... well."

"So, you think he ended up here, not knowing what the real story was." Kobb sighed. "Compromised a little in the hope of finding the answer he needed."

"Might have done if his hand were all I recognised." Haelen fanned the papers, revealing two different types of parchment and writing. "These are in code, but dated like letters. The ones with them look like replies, in the same handwriting as the notes we found at the Stones. And they go back for years."

"You said he was hiding." Anessa patted Haelen on the shoulder. "Maybe he sent the letters from somewhere else not knowing what was happening, and it's the other man who used to be here."

Haelen shook his head. "There's a map in one of his early letters, dated before Katrina went missing. Doesn't show everything we found, but it does show the Stones. If he knew and never mentioned it..."

"Then he's neck deep." Kobb held his hand out to Haelen. Whether or not the power still affected their feelings, sitting around wasn't the answer. "I understand how this feels. But, you didn't know. In a way, him being that convincing's a good sign: if he knew enough to trick you, chances are he knows something about your daughter's kidnapping. So, I say we search the rest of the compound while we're waiting for the Inductor to bring him to us."

Haelen grinned. It didn't reach his eyes. "For a Botherer, you talk a lot of sense."

The remaining buildings provided only beds, food, and more insight into the noble's other interests than a decent person might wish. Hearing Falcon's hoof-beats approaching, Kobb abandoned his search for hidden compartments, and strode toward the gate.

Anserth, jaw jutting like a chisel and unaccompanied, leapt from Falcon's back the moment he stopped. "They shitting escaped. They rode up to Gerin bold as brass and told her we'd freed them and told them to head home for carts to carry the people who didn't make it. They seemed so shitting ragged and inoffensive that Gerin gave them a wineskin for the journey."

"And now they're out of sight, we've little chance of catching up." Kobb kicked the ground. "We'll have to do this the hard way. Between us, we carry the gong up to the parapet, and see what effect it has on the beasts. Anessa, you're the best with a crossbow."

Anessa glanced at the oaken structure, then straightened her shoulders. "Ain't it better to do something about that first? Rather than risk getting those creatures angry."

"You'll be fine." Anserth wrapped an arm around Anessa. "If you're worried you'll freeze again, you load and I'll fire."

Anessa leaned against the Inductor. "Ain't that. If the gong don't let us kill them, the beasts might break through the inner gate. And we'd have no way to stop them nor escape neither. Undoing the evil could kill them all, or get rid of whatever's making them mad."

"That gate's reinforced," said Anserth. "Those horses won't be getting in."

Haelen frowned. "Except, when we arrived, one of those fake servants thought a beast had escaped. And if he thought it could..."

"Unless you've cracked the code while I was away, what else can we try?"

"Nets! They had nets. As well as the gong-shield." Anessa pulled free of the embrace and strode into the stables. A moment later, she emerged, clutching a clinking sack. "This is yellowy metal too. Why'd they have it, if the shield was enough?"

"A good question." Kobb looked back and forth between the hut and the net. "If the nets help control the horses, maybe they limit the power itself too. We cover the building; if it feels more settled, we might not need to decode the notes."

Anserth quirked an eyebrow. "Still risky. But then, what isn't? And the guards have left us those pikes to use as supporting posts."

Foul scents seemed to boil from the walls as they pinned nets in place. And jagged shadows tugged at the corners of their eyes. But they pressed on.

As the last net settled over the roof, Kobb's chest eased and the light brightened despite the oncoming twilight. He closed his eyes, and let the sensations trickle through him. The power was still there; it tasted... squarer, though. At least, that was the closest he could come to a description. Sinking deeper into the melange of feelings, he found multiple points that sounded like chains. He opened his eyes and grinned. "Feels different: calm enough I can sense where the power's held in shape."

"I'll trust your judgement, Reverend." Anserth pressed a fist to her chest. "I suggest the rest of us move before you try unravelling it though."

"Good idea," said Kobb. He watched the others walk away; Anessa staying close to Anserth and the Inductor seeming torn between maintaining letting her and keeping a little space. Something was developing there, at least on Anessa's side. He should warn her before it went too far. If this worked, they'd leave the Anserth behind soon enough, though. And if it didn't, they'd all have bigger problems. Setting his concerns aside, he focused on the shifting patterns of power surrounding the hut.

Darkness like cold velvet crushed him as the first chain slipped free.

Part Eighty-One

Anessa latched the wicket gate. The timbers were thicker than her arm, but seemed flimsy compared to a power that shattered a city. Kobb wouldn't let that happen her though. She glanced around the yard. Kobb wouldn't; but there was no point in not being as safe as possible.

"Safest place's the parapet." Haelen glanced back. "Let's us see what happens to the horses, too."

Serth rested a hand on Anessa's shoulder. "Good thoughts. But the Reverend might need help. Take my companions. Anessa and I'll stay here, in case..."

Warmth spread across Anessa's back and through her body. Serth was going out of her way to save her having to face those creatures. She cared—or did she? The warmth faded. Half the time Serth seemed to like her and the other half she tried to avoid her. Anessa stepped to the side of the gate. "The fence'll be stronger if something goes wrong; we'll still be close enough to help, though."

Haelen looked as if he'd taken a mouthful of bad ale but nodded. Striding over to the cages, he explained the plan to Serth's companions.

"What about the prisoners?"

Serth shrugged. "I doubt they'll escape, even without guards. And we cleared the yard of weapons to link the nets together, so there's little they can do if they do get free."

"I meant, what happens if something goes wrong?"

"We don't have the forces to let enemies wander; and if the horses do break the inner gate, inside those cages might be the safest place to be." Serth snorted. "If I thought you'd go, I'd stick you in the empty one until this is over."

"You want to lock me in a cage!" Anessa stepped closer, chin jutting.

"To keep you safe. If I could find somewhere with bed or even cushions, I'd drag you there. Those cages are all I've got, though."

Anessa felt heat rush up her face, and through other places. Images of the last time they'd been in a bedroom flooded her mind. She swallowed hard to convince her throat to work. Tilting her head, she gazed into Serth's eyes. "If you promised to stay too, I might let you."

For a breath, Anessa was certain Serth would lean in, then the Inductor stepped away.

Anessa stiffened. Between Kobb trying to get rid of all that power, whatever'd been done to the horses, and a bunch of evil men plotting against Haelen, she might die here. But she wasn't pigshitting going to do it without knowing how Serth really felt. She grabbed Serth's sword belt. "No. You're not leaving it like that again. That night in the ruins, you weren't just tricking me. And earlier, when I kissed you, you kissed me back. And don't you go denying it, Goody I'm-a-hag. And you're not a hag neither; I heard you telling children's stories! So, you pigshitting admit it, or I swear I'll..." She waved her fist in the air.

"You'll hit me until I say I like you? That's—"

"Goody Weaver always said a good thrashing's the best way to deal with nonsense. Well, you're just being plain daft, so don't think I won't...!"

"I was one of the best warriors in the Legion before I became an

Inductor. I could stop you a hundred ways."

"Exactly. So, letting me grab your belt means you want me close." Anessa nodded sharply. She couldn't argue with that.

"You're not going to leave this alone, are you? Raveth! Fine. I—"

Silence swallowed Serth's words, and the rest of the world with them.

Anessa tumbled backwards as purple fire lanced into the sky beyond the fence.

By the time she'd regained her feet, Serth'd already thrown the wicket gate open. Jagged chunks of wood, the occasional yellow glint among them, surrounded a flickering column of power.

A moment later, the light collapsed, leaving a hunched figure.

Anessa dived under Serth's arm. "Kobb!"

"I'll live." Kobb clambered to his feet. "I'd not call it restful, but it's done."

Howls echoed from the direction of the pen, followed by repeated thuds and the creak of wood. They sprinted for the parapet.

Haelen met them at the head of the stairs. "Whatever you did turned the beasts worse. Soon as the light faded, they started hurling themselves up at the fences."

"With luck, they're death agonies," said Kobb. "Best stay clear of the edge until it's over."

Haelen frowned. "They're active for the dying. Not enough to leap up here; enough to stress the gate, though."

"Might be best to be sure." Kobb drew his Courser. "But the rest of you stand away, just in case."

Purple light flickered into the pen. The thundering of hooves and juddering of fences continued, but Kobb grinned. "Felled one in a single attempt. They've lost their resilience."

The juddering and creaking ended with a sharp crack and the thud of timber on timber.

Kobb spun, and discharged his Courser as fast as he could; but releasing the power's grip on the hut'd taken his strength. Frothing horses boiled into the yard behind them.

"How long till they die?" Anessa glanced down then leapt back. "Wine ain't horrible. Rather eat something proper for supper, though."

"That's not the only problem." Serth tilted her head toward the stairs. "And that's assuming someone doesn't turn up with a report and open the gates before we warn them not to. The beasts are a threat. The Reverend's shown they die now like anything else. So, it's my job to kill them."

Anessa swallowed hard, then drew her sword.

"Not you." Serth pushed her back. "I could say something pleasant. Pretend I need you to protect Kobb while he catches his breath. Truth is, we've lost the pikes, so it's going to be brutal. You'd be a liability."

Before Anessa could react, Serth'd leapt onto the stairs, her companions half a step behind.

Part Eighty-Two

The howls of the creatures below grew.

"Gongs!" Anessa spun around. "We use the gongs."

Haelen pulled her close. "They're all down there. Even if they aren't smashed to pieces already, we can't reach them."

"We need to help her. She doesn't just get to order me to stay up here! We have to do something."

"She needs you to be safe. Reckon that's all she's been doing since they found us in the forest. Might be the closest she can get to you."

That made no sense. Serth'd said she didn't think Anessa was up to stuff, so why couldn't she just hold her close and never let go. She twisted free and glared at Haelen. "What do you know? What's going on? Tell me!"

"It's only a rumour, might not even be true. Me sharing it'd probably make things worse." Haelen patted her on the shoulder. "Reckon the Inductor needs to tell you herself. Once she's ready."

"She tried." Anessa's head sagged. "She was about to, when Kobb released the power. And now she's—"

"Then, we'd best make sure she gets another chance." Kobb staggered closer to the edge.

"You're exhausted, Reverend."

Kobb straightened his shoulders. "I can still kill a few. Give them a moment to seize the initiative.... If I use everything left."

"We'd be stuck here until you'd recovered. Could be days." Haelen slumped against a table. "Do it. My Katrina wouldn't want others dying to save her."

Purple fire lanced into the yard, each flare silencing the sounds of teeth and steel meeting flesh, and the screams of pain.

Stomach churning, Anessa crept forward. Serth, one arm clutched around her side, stood back-to-back with the taller of her companions. Frothing beasts lunged in from all sides, only their urge to attack each other preventing them overwhelming the two humans.

Anessa fell to her knees. Even with Kobb's help, Serth'd die. Unless... She tugged at Kobb's jacket and pointed toward the gate. "The gong. Hit the gong."

Hand shaking, Kobb took aim.

As his Courser blazed, the writhing mass of horses surged and the power struck flesh.

The end of silence brought a chopped off scream.

Anessa's gaze snapped back to the fight.

Blade scything in wide arcs, Serth stood over her fallen companion.

Silence hammered Anessa's ears.

Followed by a teeth-juddering clang. The beasts stumbled to a halt, some collapsing where they stood.

Serth lunged forward, boots skidding on the bloody mud but aim perfect.

Kobb's Courser clattered over the edge as he slumped to the floor.

A shadow flickered past Anessa's head, and another clang echoed across the yard. Arms flailing, Haelen hurled a stream of statues, goblets, and whatever else he could reach at the gong. Most missed, but enough didn't.

The beasts milled in confusion as they were hacked down. Armour rent and coated with gore, Serth drove her blade through the side of the last horse and staggered to the stairs.

Anessa sprinted to meet her, arms outstretched. "Where are you hurt? Sit! Haelen, we need to—"

"I'll survive." Serth stepped away from Anessa's attempt to hug her. "We leave, and we burn the compound behind us. Just to make sure."

"What about the notes?" Haelen shuffled down the stairs, Kobb leaning on him.

Serth shrugged. "No one ordered me to secure this place. If they'll help you do what you need to..."

"Enough!" Anessa drew herself up. "Nobody's running around burning anything, or gathering notes, until everyone's bandaged and rested."

"Yes'm" Serth's chuckle collapsed into a wince. "Wasn't planning to do the setting fires myself. Get Col and the others to do it."

"Well... I suppose..." Anessa's chin jutted. "You're not running off fetching them either."

Kobb eased himself free of Haelen. "Falcon won't let me fall. And ride'll do me good. Nothing Haelen can do for me anyway."

Anessa frowned at his retreating back, unable to come up with a reason to stop him.

Serth limped toward the nearest gate. "Time's a wasting."

"Don't think you're wandering off!" Anessa squelched after her. "You're gonna rest, even if I have to tie you to the bed."

Serth looked back, the filth and blood smeared across her face not diluting the fire in her eyes. A breath later, she shook her head and staggered on, her initial response swallowed unuttered.

Before Anessa had decided how to respond, Haelen stepped into her path. "Go on ahead and find some water. Healing her wounds'll be easier if

I can get rid of the horse blood first. That, and she might rest if she you aren't nearby."

"But—"

"It's her secret to tell, Anessa. Water, now."

Confusion and anger churning around in her head, Anessa sprinted past Serth and out of the compound. After taking a deep breath to push her thoughts down for a moment, she turned on the spot, listening.

Without the hissing of rain or noise of horses to mask it, she located the swish of a river a few hundred yards behind the palisade. Jogging over, she chuckled. She wasn't a warrior like the others, but even she knew having your water outside the walls was daft. After peering upstream for dead animals, she filled her bottle.

When she turned, Serth lay a short distance from the gate with Haelen crouched over her. Bottle still clutched in her hand Anessa sprinted toward them.

Hearing Serth's responses to Haelen's questions, Anessa slowed.

Then staggered to a halt, face burning, when she realised Serth was naked from the waist up. Bottle stretched out behind her at arm's length, Anessa shuffled backward. Weren't the first time she'd seen a woman's chest; that'd been close friends, though. Didn't seem right to look at Serth if Serth didn't like her. "Water, Haelen. If you hand me another, I'll fill it while—"

"I'll not scream if you turn around, Anessa." Serth's voice seemed strong, but Anessa was certain it was a show.

Haelen coughed loudly, then exchanged Anessa's full bottle for an empty one.

Neck aching with the effort of not accepting Serth's offer, Anessa scurried back to the river. People got shy about being naked round people they liked. So, did that mean Serth didn't feel anything? Or that she didn't get shy?

The sound of hooves scattered her thoughts. Bottle tumbling out of her fingers, she spun.

Kobb and several other riders cantered toward Serth. Snatching the bottle from the river's grasp, Anessa shoved the stopper in and sprinted to meet them.

"Seems my friend's die when you're around." Col glared at her from the leading horse.

Anserth sat up, ignoring Haelen's attempts to keep her still. "You're a weasel-faced shitbrain, Col. Seems you're the best I've got though. You're Second now. Take the prisoners then torch the compound."

"As you command, Inductor. How soon do we depart?"

"Soon as the fire's taken hold, break camp and ride hard for the nearest city."

Haelen pushed Serth down. "You'll need longer than that before you're ready to travel."

"I know. But, we need to start the hunt for those two criminals. So, Col takes the unit as soon as it's ready to move."

Col snapped an unexpectedly crisp salute and led the riders into the compound.

Anger washed away Anessa's confusion. She stared down at Serth. "You're good at killing and stuff. But even you can't stay here on you're own. You've got to go with your people."

"Whatever you three're doing's clearly too important to wait. But Haelen's won't leave me behind, any more than you will." Serth quirked an eyebrow. "That's why I'm going wherever you are."

Kobb dismounted. "Anessa's right. Best if you travel back to the city."

"You're skilled, Reverend; but, you're not the man you were. You need another warrior."

"A warrior?" Haelen rocked back on his heels. "Or a watcher?"

"Doesn't matter does it?" said Serth. "Col will do what I order. So, you either leave me here or take me along."

"Of course we're taking you with us." Anessa glared back and forth between Kobb and Haelen. "Straight after these two apologise for treating you like a maggoty apple!"

"Anessa?" Serth pushed herself to a sitting position again. "Listen to me. They're not wrong about me. There's a saying among the Legion, 'At least Botherers have limits.' It was all a trick. I used you."

Part Eighty-Three

Kobb pinched the bridge of his nose in the hope of clearing the fog, if only for a moment. Would Anessa feel better or worse if he tried to comfort her? Running boots and sobbing told him the decision had been made for him. A breath later, Haelen sprinted after her.

Guilt mixed with relief, Kobb looked down at Anserth. Driving Anessa away meant losing the only person who'd have let her join them without a thought; and an Inductor wouldn't throw an asset like that away. Someone who didn't want Anessa to just be an asset, though... Driving her away was the most efficient course. "If you come, you'll do what Haelen tells you when it comes to health. And what I say for everything else."

Anserth grinned. "To be honest, I expected you to claim you didn't need another soldier; or claim you'd more people back at your camp."

"I considered it. Then you put Anessa's happiness above convincing us."

"Will you tell her?" For a moment, the Inductor's expression seemed utterly genuine.

"That you like her? Or that if one of those guards had turned around as you dragged her past, you'd have let him use her and waited for a more suitable opportunity? As Haelen says, it's your explanation to give or not."

"I'd thank you. But then, that wasn't actually a promise." A shutter seemed to close behind her eyes. "How soon will we be ready to travel? As poetic as it might be, brooding next to the burnt wreckage won't achieve our goals or make anyone feel better."

"I am, as you stated, not as young as I was. I'll need time to recover from overusing my Courser."

Anserth pointed at the pile of her clothes Haelen removed during treatment. "Middle pouch on the left side of my belt. Each twist of paper contains enough waking powder to keep me sharp through a night of sitting in a snowdrift. Should be enough to keep you on a horse for a few hours."

His tiredness came from more than physical exertion. Would a stimulant have any effect? At worst, he'd be wider awake to use his wits or his rapier if needed. And not trying it risked arousing suspicions while the Inductor could still order her men to detain them. He emptied a twist onto his tongue.

The taste of rotten lemons flooded his mouth. Chills raced along his limbs, followed by the feeling his skin was too tight. Everything around him blazed like staring at the sun. A breath later, everything returned to normal, leaving only a sense of well-being.

And the taste of rotten lemons. He spat to the side.

"Apologies for the flavour." Anserth tipped the contents of a second twist down her own throat, then grimaced. "Usually passes after a while."

After spitting again to no effect, Kobb turned his attention inward. The void left by the discharged power tugged at him, more roughly than previous times yet not agonisingly so. He'd likely be exhausted afterwards, but travel felt possible. Two sets of boot-steps, one almost stomping, broke his concentration.

"You're looking a little sick, Inductor." The red of Anessa's eyes spoke of tears. Her gaze was hard, though. "Just realised you forgot to kick a—?"

Kobb wrapped his thoughts around the five of them and fell upward.

Agony clawed at his temples as he sagged to his knees. Clutching his brow, he barely confirmed they were back at the Stones before another wave of pain blurred his vision. Rotten lemons flooded his mouth even stronger than before. Teeth gritted, he rose to his feet.

Anessa stared at him, anger forgotten. "Kobb, are you—"

Cramps racking her body, Anserth vomited copiously. After gazing into the distance for a moment, she collapsed onto her back.

"Haelen! What's wrong with—" Anessa paused, then stepped back. "I hope you feel terrible, you... eastsider!" Ultimate insult delivered, she turned to face Kobb. "What's that hag doing here? Why didn't you leave her—?"

Kobb half-raised one arm. "Calm down, Anessa."

"Don't you tell me to calm down! You brought—"

"Stones make us angry." Kobb hawked foul mucus onto the grass. "Don't want to you to fight like I did with Haelen."

After a moment, Anessa's back lost its rigidity. "You're right. If I kill that bitch then she'll stop feeling really, really bad." Spinning on one heel, she stomped off toward the tents.

Haelen rested a hand on Kobb's elbow. "I'll admit I'm curious too, Reverend."

"Turns out she has a strong interest in protecting Anessa. So, she'll help us until this is done."

Haelen snorted. "Or kidnap Anessa and drag her to safety."

Kobb shrugged.

"What...? Where...?" Anserth struggled up onto one elbow. "How'd we get here?"

"My turn to apologise, Inductor. I didn't know the powder would increase—"

"Stimulant!" Haelen dropped into a crouch next to Anserth. "You gave her a stimulant? Look at me, Inductor. Are your ears ringing? Hissing? Do your limbs feel light?"

"Be fine. Not first time I've—" Anserth collapsed sideways, strings of murky spittle oozing out of her mouth

Haelen eased her up again. "Bed for you. And you, Reverend!"

Kobb bowed his head and walked to sleeping tent. Still unsure which response was best, he pretended not to hear the sobs coming from beneath Anessa's furs.

Dawn brought neither the taste of rotten lemons nor the scent of oats. After glancing at the lump of bedding on the far side of the tent, Kobb decided it was as good a start as could be expected. Stretching the knots of hard age out for another day, he headed out to make breakfast.

Anserth emerged as the porridge began to bubble, a frustrated Haelen on her heels. "Morning, Reverend. Medicus Lok seems to have mistaken me for a raw recruit."

Kobb sighed. "You did agree to obey him on matters of health."

"You said that's what I should do. I never promised."

Kobb shook his head ruefully. "If she can weave words like that, I'd say she's fit to walk from a tent to the fire."

"She's not..." Haelen dropped onto a log. "Fine. But you're not allowed to complain if all your skin falls off."

The inductor paused, one hand halfway toward the pot of porridge. "Was that supposed to be a joke?"

"That was. This isn't. Reverend, I reckon might be best to stop what we're doing. Evil men wanted me to start this search, so continuing doesn't seem a good thing."

Part Eighty-Four

Kobb filled his bowl. If your enemy wanted something, preventing it was a good start for a plan. But only a start; murderers and saints often sought the same things. "No question they've betrayed you, Haelen. You've seen the evil the power's wrought, though. The conspiracy were involved in one—maybe two—of those problems. Things are going wrong even without humans interfering where they shouldn't. There's still power seeping into the world that needs stopping. We don't finish this, there's every chance things'll break down again."

"And restoring the last Stone gives those liars what they want!" Haelen glared at the fire. "Can we take the risk?"

"The Reverend's right about not leaving evil unfought." Anserth picked up another bowl. "Reckon that makes two things we agree on. As to the best way to do it? I'd need to know more than there are plotters using sorcery for unknown goals, and the Reverend can move people somehow."

Haelen glanced at her. "From what I hear, you work your way into people's trust then, once they've found a secret, you try to steal it. So, the less we tell you, the less chance you'll turn against us."

"Tell her." Anessa stomped over to the fire. "If we want to know what those pig-shitting people are up to, best person to guess is a devious hag."

Without meeting her gaze, Anserth held out some porridge. Anessa snatched it from her hand and dropped onto a log. The Inductor filled her own bowl, and strolled to the other side of the fire.

Kobb rested his spoon in his bowl. "Someone built this stone circle to shape power; the same power my Courser directs; that's how I carry us back here. Recently, the power began to seep out into the world, reawakening ancient legends and corrupting flesh and souls. We've corrected the flow through all of the stones but one. As to what happens when we realign the final Stone...? We've found notes and learnt some things ourselves; not enough to be certain, though, and it turns out some of the notes might be lies."

"This circle's ancient." Anserth scraped the last smear of porridge from her bowl. "Looks older than the ruins where we met. Which means it's been doing what it does for generations without unleashing untold horrors. Haelen's right about not handing your enemies victory. Seems containing the power makes things better, though."

Haelen shook his head. "Until those people do whatever they intend."

Anserth spooned more porridge into her bowl, then patted her knife. "Can you stab me with this, Medicus?"

Haelen frowned, then held out his hand. "What'll that prove?"

The inductor ignored him and sat down.

Kobb snorted. "Proves a blade's no use if you're not the one holding it."

"Maybe it don't matter if the circle's realigned then, if we're here to stop them taking advantage." Haelen rested his bowl on the ground. "I'll bring some notes out for the Inductor to read at over breakfast."

"Might as well study them in the tent." Anserth sucked the last flecks of oat from her spoon. "It's turned out a little chilly this morning."

Anessa peered harder into her bowl, glancing up once the Inductor had gone. "You'll want to spend time with your new friend. Suppose I'd better wash the pots."

Kobb moved to sit next to her. "It's my turn, and I'm not letting you steal it so you can sneak the rest of breakfast while no one's looking."

"How did...? Why...?" Anessa sagged against him. "I thought she... I know she's not your friend really. Go. Help them. It's daft you cleaning pots when you could be reading those papers again." She straightened.

"Are you sure? If you need to talk about—"

"They don't match." Haelen sprinted out of the tent, Anserth following him more calmly. Skidding to a halt, he waved two documents at Kobb. "The map we found in Alcston and the one from the compound. Six of the marks are close enough; but the seventh's nowhere near."

"You found a map in Alcston?" Anessa shot upright, bowl falling from her hand. "You knew the Stones lead to Morth?"

"Well." Haelen sagged. "The Reverend wanted to protect you; so you wouldn't worry until we knew more. And then there was no way of knowing which Stone went where..."

Anessa drew herself up. Jaw jutting, she spun to face Anserth. "See! That's how decent folk like Kobb act. Keeping secrets to make people's live better; not as part of some twisted plot!"

"Depending on which map you trust, the last location's either in a random area of forest or far to the south." Anserth pointed at one of the maps. "Past the Cleft."

The chords bulged in Anessa's neck, but the Inductor appeared oblivious.

"Reverend takes us through the Stone, we arrive." Haelen settled next to Kobb. "Haven't noticed the distance mattering."

"I meant, if legendary threats are returning the other side of the Cleft might not be a safe place to go. Don't the annals of your Order say the Maker formed a barrier to hold back great evil, Reverend?"

"They do. We don't have a choice, though. As Haelen says, I use a Stone and we arrive."

Haelen frowned. "Maybe we've a choice when we go. All of us need more rest. We go through all these notes in detail, see if there's anything that tells us which is right or what might happen."

After three days of studying each scrap of paper—or in Anessa's case, watching the Inductor—they'd confirmed the people involved in the plot were petty and twisted, and —if the conspiracy did know which location was correct, or what would happen afterwards—those answers were in the hands of another part of it.

Kobb dropped the Alcston map back onto the table again. "With the Korha covering everything in mould, we can't even tell which map's older. We either give up, or use the Stone."

"Seems like there's others out there who're part of this, and we've no idea who they are." Haelen sighed. "We don't finish what we started, they'll likely do it. Least if we use the Stone we might make a difference to how it comes out."

Anessa brushed her fingers across her pendant, then nodded.

Unsure what would help, they divided as much of the research as they could between their packs and bags.

"Any guidance on how to avoid vomiting?" Anserth wiggled an eyebrow. "If we do get into trouble, I'd rather not do it on a hollow gut."

Anessa loaded her crossbow. "Seems to be worse the more evil there is around. So, reckon you stand a bit away from the rest of us. Won't stop you spewing, but..."

Kobb sighed. The Inductor's choice was better in the long term, but he could do without the glares and insults it'd brought. Still, this would be over soon. Turning inward, he gathered the threads of power and shifted.

Heat and light hammered at him.

Half-blind, he looked down; but the pale stone below blazed as bright and hot.

Metal shinged behind him as Anserth drew a blade.

Squinting, Kobb peered around. Rank after rank of humans in deep purple togas, each holding a pike, ringed the edge of the stone platform.

Part Eighty-Five

Kobb shielded his eyes with his hand. The ring of warriors stood at least five ranks deep. A wall of pale stone peeped between the heads of the back rank. If it were sword-against-sword, then the four of them might cut a wide-enough path to get out; breaking that density of pikes, though, needed relentless - and costly - assaults. Sighing, he eased both arms away from his body, palms well clear of his weapons. "Easy, everyone. No reason to see enemies in every stranger."

"And he shall bear the wisdom of restraint!" A deep voice boomed across the ring of warriors. As one, the ranks split, revealing a tall man in a vastly ornate purple toga. He bowed slightly toward Kobb, then straightened and strode down the channel. "The Speaker of the Virtues greets the Killer of Innocence, the Misplaced Father, the Divided Slave, and the Pure Vessel. Your chambers stand ready."

Kobb bowed back the same amount. "We greet the Speaker of Virtues. We did not expect this welcome. Might we know how you knew we would arrive?"

"No shadow may obscure the Virtues. Come, the time of resting approaches. I shall guide you to your chambers."

"We just going to go with them?" asked Anessa.

Kobb squinted sideways at the sky. "If this is still morning, the heat'll only get worse. Best to be inside. Perhaps the Speaker could explain more on the way?"

The Speaker bowed deeply. "No mind my hold the fullness of all Virtues. And the journey to the Virtues would last into the time of resting. Those Who Are Named shall be taken to the Virtues when castigation ends."

"What?" Anessa frowned at Haelen.

"I believe he means that it will be quicker to study these Virtues ourselves rather than ask questions; but, it becomes too hot to travel soon, so we must wait until late in the day." Kobb picked up Falcon's reins and trudged toward the gap in the pikes, sweat-damp clothes tugging at his skin with each movement. After a moment, he heard the sound of the others shuffling after him.

The ranks of warriors filled a second, wider, stone ring, a channel several feet wide separating the rear rank from the wall. Shielding his eyes again, Kobb made out the beginning of a ramp leading into the gap.

Cool dimness caressed his skin as the path spiralled down past side-corridors. Moments after the point where the dropping temperature changed pleasant relief to clammy discomfort, the Speaker took a corridor on the inner wall.

Several turns later, they emerged into a round chamber with a shallow pool of water in the centre. Dim lantern-light spilled from the ceiling before dancing off the surface of the water. Several doorways led to other rooms.

"These chambers are offered to you, as is ordained." The Speaker bowed to each of them and strode out.

"Well, they got you right." Anessa glared at Anserth. "You're such a bitch, even a bunch of people on the other side of an impassable barrier know you're the Killer of Innocence."

Kobb rested his hand on Anessa's elbow. "I don't think she is."

"Well, she certainly ain't anyone's Da!"

Kobb drew a slow breath to steady himself. When the road is full of rocks, one may build either a wall or a shelter. "I'm almost certain she's the Divided Slave. I'm the Killer of Innocence. You remember those guards mentioning Raveth?"

Anessa nodded. "Your Order stopped a huge evil from escaping."

"Yes. But what I didn't tell you is I was there; Second to Preceptor Militant Gannon. I was younger then, strong enough to use my Courser as fast as I found targets." Kobb stared at the shimmering water. "Anessa, demons slip into the world like weeds, probing every crack, settling in the smallest chink to wait. If even one tainted soul remains then the creature will return. Even the briefest touch of skin on skin might pass the seed; and there is no sure way to know who is tainted. There was only one course. Gannon ordered the Legion to cordon with crossbows and led the Order in. One-by-one our companions fell or were lost to sight, until only Gannon and I remained. A... a young girl ran out of a side alley unexpectedly, hugged Gannon before he could move away. Her hair blew across his face. There was no way to tell if she was tainted or not, but we couldn't take the chance. Gannon declared himself unable to fulfil the duties of his station. As the senior Reverend, I ordered the man who raised me to provide the Maker's Grace to Raveth and retreated for the Cordon. Gannon unleashed the entirety of his power without use of Courser a few moments later. The city and everything in it was scoured away. The Annals of the Order suggest the first plant might grow in Raveth when ten centuries have passed."

Anessa collapsed against the wall, tears streaming down her face.

Part Eighty-Six

Kobb stumbled forward a step. Had telling Anessa been the wrong thing to do? He hadn't expected her to praise his actions but...

"Leave her, Reverend." Anserth stretched an arm across his path. "If she wants to be a useless ball of snot, then let her."

Anessa lifted her head again. "You... you... I'm glad you don't like me... No, I wish you did. So knowing you'll never be my friend ate into you!"

"What the Reverend's doing is too important." Anserth met Anessa's burning gaze. "Letting feelings get in the way of it isn't right."

"Feelings?" Anessa lunged forward, fists raised. "What'd you know about having feelings?"

The Inductor pivoted on one heel, letting Anessa pass by, then grabbed her from behind. "Feelings are what make you hesitate, make you let a murderer escape because she's your friend. That's why Inductors are trained to ignore them."

"Pigshit!" Anessa wriggled ineffectually. "You can't be made to not feel things. Not unless you're all evil inside already!"

"I didn't say not feel, I said ignore. Not listening properly's another thing feelings make you do. We still feel; we're trained to wall it away where it doesn't interfere with what needs doing, though. That's why they call me the Divided Soul, because I'm free to follow logic." Anserth shoved Anessa. "Can we get back to something that matters, or would you like to cry some more?"

"I hope you—" Anessa clamped her mouth shut and ran from the room.

After staring hard at Anserth for a moment, Haelen walked after her.

"I suppose you'd call it a Blessing, Reverend? Being forced to tell you all about my training."

Kobb sighed. "You weren't forced."

"Wasn't I?" Anserth pointed at him, then herself. "Which of us matters here? Finding out you killed hundreds of people would've broken her once it sunk in. But now it won't because the revulsion and confusion's directed at the ugly hag who doesn't matter. She didn't like me anyway, so it was the only sensible course of action. Just like Raveth."

"Raveth wasn't sensible, or prudent, or any of the other words that fill up reports and history books." Kobb sank onto the rim of the pool. "Raveth was horror. At the time. Then again daily for weeks after. Wondering if I could have done something differently. Someone couldn't push those sort of feelings away just by needing to. But then, what happened to you was more than training wasn't it? Who was she?"

"I suppose it is too late for half a revelation." She sat next to him. "We were in the same bunkhouse from the day we joined the Legion. Sometimes I'd top the day list, sometimes she would. The harder they drilled us, the more we excelled; and the closer we got. I'd describe her for you... but I suspect you can guess what she was like down to the way her hair moved in the breeze. The Legion doesn't encourage relationships; soldiers knowing each other well enough to fight as a perfect pair, though...? Some things are too useful to waste. We rose through the ranks, headed for greatness.

Then some half-weight flagbearer tried to be too friendly. The battle had lasted all day. We'd finally broken them at dusk. I'd gone to my tent. She wanted to stay by the fires, have one more drink to wash the dust out. This flagbearer got grabby, and she knocked him flat. Should've been the end of it; his uncle was on the Council, though, so he pushed himself up and told her to mind her place. She ignored him, so he challenged her to a duel. When she ignored that too, he said it made sense anyone who'd sleep with a mongrel would catch its morals. By the time the bystanders realised it was more than a brawl, she'd drawn through him. Worthless sack of piss wasn't even wearing his armour. Before anyone worked out what to do, she'd taken a horse and fled.

"Next morning, they posted charges. It was strongly suggested it would reflect badly on the unit if we didn't bring her in ourselves. We always did know how the other thought, so I rode out to where I knew she'd be, and there she was waiting for me. I approached on foot, begged her to come back, told her we'd find witnesses, and sort it out. She shook her head, and drew on me. Most might have thought it a bluff, but I knew her as well as I knew myself. The fight went back and forth. We always were matched, so it was inevitable we'd end up locked blade-to-blade. Then, somehow, she surprised me; just let go of her sword. My sword was deep in her side before I realised.

"I was hailed as an example of loyalty for not letting her escape. The next day, a representative of the Council offered me a way to use my skills. I'd like to say I did it to spare someone else the horror of killing a friend; really, I just wanted the pain to stop. I can't tell you how they did it. There were drugs, days without sleep, and... other methods. The process isn't pleasant, yet no one regrets the choice; because afterwards regret's only another emotion to be set aside."

"Thank you for sharing." Kobb patted her on the hand. Even if she didn't know why she had.

Boots hammering the stone, Anessa stalked into the chamber.

"Glad you returned." Kobb rose. "Might not be safe to wander too far with just Haelen for company."

"Not much chance of that." Anessa leaned against the wall. "They've sealed the exits. We checked them all."

Part Eighty-Seven

Anessa watched Serth as she delivered the news. Why hadn't she leapt up and started giving orders? She looked almost sad, as if that story'd been... No. It was just another trick. She knew her voice carried down the corridor, and now she was trying to manipulate people again.

"Sealed?" Kobb glanced past Anessa. "I don't remember seeing grates."

"Big stone slabs." Anessa mimed a large shape with her arms. "Tight enough I couldn't get a knife point in."

Haelen moved into the chamber. "Might just be their version of doors."

"Doors without handles?" Anessa frowned. He'd seemed as worried as she was when they found them. "That's not normal."

"I've been thinking. The Speaker said it gets hot during the day. Could be, they keep the heat out." Haelen strolled toward the nearest doorway. "Unless the two of you did while we were gone, we haven't even looked in the other rooms. Maybe there's a way of opening and closing the slabs; or something that helps work out what their intentions are."

Kobb stood. "You're right. No use speculating without knowing everything we can."

Keeping as much distance as she could from Serth, Anessa followed Haelen to the first room. Two thin mattresses lay in the middle, each with brightly patterned rug lying folded at one end. Two chests, large keys jutting out of the locks, stood open beyond the beds. She huffed. "Well, at least they don't want us getting a stiff back while we wait."

Apart from the patterns on the rugs, the next room was identical.

A curtain half covered the third doorway. Anessa shoved it aside. A deep pool stood along one side. Opposite it, a narrow plank jutted across a shaft at knee level. "Jakes." She spun on her heel and moved to the next, almost slamming into Serth.

Shelves lined all three walls, each containing pottery jugs, bowls, and plates; and enough food and drink to feed them for days. "Pantry. Looks like they don't plan to let us out for a while."

"Or their prophecy didn't mention what we do and don't enjoy." Haelen leaned past her and grabbed a large red fruit from the nearest bowl. "I mean, I've no idea what this is. At least they got the bedrooms right, so we don't have to share."

Anessa frowned. There were two mattresses in each bedroom, so—Haelen'd never been happy about her sharing with Kobb, so he must mean... "Don't matter either way. We're supposed to be leaving this evening anyway, so we'll be gone before we need them."

"Might be better to have a light meal then get some sleep," said Serth. "If it really is that hot during the day, these people do more at night. And we'll be fresher if anything does go wrong."

Anessa glared at her. "Anything else it's sensible to do? Maybe I'm wearing my boots oddly?"

"Light meal sounds good." Kobb stepped into Anessa's line of sight. "How about we find a few things we recognise while Haelen and Anserth shift our packs."

After a moment, Anessa sagged, then turned to the pantry. He was right: she shouldn't let Serth get in the way like that.

A search of the shelves found some bread that hadn't risen properly and a sort of runny porridge with garlic in which didn't seem too odd. No cutlery though. A plate in each hand, she followed Kobb back to the central chamber.

After taking a meal from Kobb, Serth headed into the second bedroom. "I'll eat while I unpack."

Anessa handed one of the plates to Haelen then sat on the edge of the pool. Good riddance to her. Being trapped with her was bad enough without having to see at her all the time. She scooped up a big glob of porridge; it tasted more beany than oaty, but good nevertheless.

"She doesn't have any clothes apart from what she's wearing." Haelen settled next to her. "That bag's full of maps and notes."

She swallowed her mouthful. "So?"

"So, why's she unpacking?"

"Who knows why she does things? Probably so she bitch about me not being able to read."

"Or she doesn't want to be around if it hurts you so much. Maybe you should talk to her before she goes to sleep."

Give Serth another opportunity to use her? "Suppose it has been a while since I let her insult me. Maybe you should take her advice and eat your meal."

He looked at her flatly for a moment. "I'll put that down to worry about the sealed corridors. But you heard her story, same as I did. You really think she's in there waiting to mock you?"

"How am I supposed to know? I just feel things." But she did know. Apart from insulting her about letting her heart get in the way, Serth'd been polite—helpful even. Perhaps she should calm it down a bit, so the argument didn't mess with helping Kobb. She scooped the rest of the porridge and swallowed. Didn't mean Serth was forgiven though.

Remains of the bread clutched in one fist, she rose. "Need to get her plate anyway."

Serth sprawled on the right-hand mattress, already asleep. Her plate, every trace of porridge wiped away, lay inside the door.

Anessa grabbed the plate and retreated, cheeks burning at the decidedly not furious feelings seeing Serth in only her under things raised.

By the time she'd scoured the last of the plates, Kobb and Haelen had gone through into the other bedroom. After a few strolls around the central chamber, she decided she might as well lie down.

Eyes fixed firmly on the left hand wall, she tried not to think about Serth. This was a stupid plan. She never slept in the middle of the day - unless she was really ill - so how was she supposed to do it while the garlic porridge was making her gut twitchy.

She snapped awake, Serth's face only inches from hers. She'd never noticed the Inductor had such long eyelashes before.

"Stir yourself." Serth rose to her feet. "Heard stone moving."

Anessa fumbled her belt around her waist, and staggered into the central room. Kobb emerged at the same time, Haelen on his heels.

The gentle slap of sandals grew. A moment later, the Speaker entered and bowed deeply. Straightening, he pressed his hands to his heart. "The Harrowing has passed. Are you ready to view the Virtues?"

"We are." Kobb stepped forward. "Lead on."

The Speaker bowed again. "The Speaker of Virtues means no dishonour. But weapons are not permitted in the chamber of Virtues."

Part Eighty-Eight

Anessa stared at the Speaker. "What do you mean, we can't take weapons? There were hundreds of you with them when we arrived. Why'd they get to carry them if we don't?"

"The prohibition applies only to those viewing the Virtues." The Speaker held his palms up. "Violence is prohibited within the city, so you'll be perfectly safe without them."

Serth raised an eyebrow. "If violence is illegal, why're all those warriors armed with pikes?"

"Greeting a guest armed shows that you do not believe them too weak to injure you. High Speaker Erinis commanded we welcome you with many pikes to demonstrate the extent of our respect for you. I assure you, none wish you harm"

Serth frowned. "You'll forgive us being suspicious, given you locked us in here."

The Speaker's eyes widened. "A thousand apologies. I should have explained. No one would intentionally distress you, but... well, our city has waited for Those Who Are Named since the day it was founded; some might forget politeness in their desire to look upon you.

I requested the corridors were sealed so you'd not be disturbed while you rested."

Anessa peered at the Speaker. Threatening someone as a show of politeness sounded crazy; but people back home respected those who stood up for themselves more than those who didn't, so it wasn't as mad as say, insects that lived inside your head or travelling through giant circles of rocks. And he looked horrified they'd been insulted.

Haelen stepped forward, brow furrowed. "How are we to show people the respect they deserve for the years of duty if we cannot carry weapons? Couldn't we bear them until we reach the Chamber, then leave them just outside?"

"I prostrate myself in gratitude for the honour you suggest. However, the law states no weapons may be brought, and I dare not risk that including the journey to the Virtues. Only the tools of the priesthood are exempt. Not even Those Who Are Named are safe from execution if the law is broken."

Kobb unbuckled his scabbard. "If it is the only way, then we must comply. If you wait a moment, we'll place our weapons back in our quarters."

Anessa considered for a moment, then headed back into the bedroom to stow her sword. It felt odd, but Kobb and Haelen knew more about the world than she did, so if they thought these people were friends... After silently holding the chest open for Serth, she returned to the central room. And paused.

Kobb still had his Courser holstered on his baldric. Smiling in reaction to her puzzlement, he tapped his throat.

A moment later, she realised he meant her pendant. Her frown faded: the Courser was part of his priestly equipment.

Still not quite comfortable without weapons, Anessa flicked her gaze in every direction as they followed the Speaker along a different series of tunnels and back to the surface.

Warm, dry air pressed in from every direction. Wooden stalls, some mounted on wheels, formed rough streets. People of all ages, none of them armed, stared at the four of them. In the distance, a tower of pale stone jutted above the mass.

The Speaker strode toward the tower in silence, ignoring the dense crowd. Moments before he hit the first person, the crowd parted, forming a corridor slightly wider than arms' reach.

As the people closed behind them, Serth leaned in close to Anessa's ear. "Don't worry. Between the Reverend's Courser and my training, we'll be safe enough."

Anessa glanced at the Inductor. She was still a hag, but having her there did make it easier to stay calm "Like the compound. I distract them, then you attack."

Serth swallowed and glanced down. "I meant that if they try anything, I don't need a weapon to fight. No reason to risk something unless we have to." After meeting Anessa's gaze for a breath, Serth dropped back a few steps.

Even moving at the crawl needed to pass through the crowd, the journey to the tower didn't take long; certainly not long enough you wouldn't want to do it in the afternoon heat. Did that mean the Speaker'd been lying, or did it really get that hot here?

Before she'd decided, the Speaker reach a tall arch that gaped in the side of the tower. Cold darkness clamped around her as she followed him through. Blinking hard, she managed to make out three massive stone chairs in the centre of a chamber the full size of the building. An indistinct person sat upon each.

The Speaker stopped and spread his arms wide. "As is written, Those Who Are Named arrive at the Chamber of Virtues."

"Thank you, Speaker Torva." The central figure stood.

"Welcome, travellers. I'm—"

"The rituals, First Speaker." The man on her left half-rose out of his seat.

"Calmness, High Speaker Erinis. Our guests have waited long enough without me wasting hours to get to the point." She patted Erinis on the arm, then turned. "I'm First Speaker Morheru. You must have questions."

Kobb bowed. "We do not wish to ignore your traditions."

"I'm an old woman. And I've spent that life studying the Virtues. Long enough to know they will still happen if I use two words instead of seven."

Erinis shifted, but remained silent.

Kobb inclined his head. "I too have found truth arrives without us seeking it. Perhaps you might tell us of our part in these Virtues?"

Morheru settled into her chair. "Many centuries ago, Amheru the Blessed received the Belt of Mastery from That Which Watches. Knowing that our race was not ready for its power, he built this tower to protect it while he sought understanding of its true purpose. With each year, he learnt more, and carved these truths on the walls of the tower so they would not be lost. Each new carving showed our city more of the path forward, and we prospered.

"When he realised it was time to journey on, he passed the duty of guiding the city to his three children. Over the centuries that followed, the city grew and more Speakers of Virtues were appointed to carry the Virtues to the people so the three High Speakers need not rule on every matter.

"The final Virtue, carved upon the pedestal upon which the Belt rests, tells of the day the Killer of Innocence, the Misplaced Father, the Divided Slave, and the Pure Vessel will arrive to take the Belt.

"Would you like some refreshments? Or will you take it now?"

Part Eighty-Nine

The chill of the room seeped down Anessa's back. Take this belt now, or have a meal first? Wouldn't they want to do... whatever it was you did with prophecies first? It all seemed a little too easy. "And we can just leave with it?"

"The Virtues say the Belt shall be given to you." Morheru winked. "Once you have it, what you do is your problem."

Erinis jerked upright. "I hardly think the Belt is a problem, First Speaker. Even if they are Those Who Are Named—and of course I hope they are—they'd clearly prefer we follow the rituals as much as I would."

"The path is always there, but we learn from how we walk it." Kobb nodded to Erinis. "We have no desire to rush matters of faith."

Amheru exhaled hard. "The Belt awoke from sleep a few months ago. And how blazes as bright as in the days of Amheru the Blessed. The remaining rituals are only one interpretation of the Virtues anyway. I think we have signs enough."

"Perhaps a compromise?" Erinis inclined his head reverently. "The rituals do not say that all of us must escort Those Who Are Named,

I will straight away make preparations for a feast for our guests, arrange supplies so they may leave as soon as they wish, and check upon their horse. In the time that takes, you might perform the rituals."

Anessa leaned closer to Kobb. "Something don't seem right about just taking it."

"I agree." Serth whispered. "This feels too easy."

Kobb's eyebrow quirked. "I expected to do this alone. And yet I found companions to ease the way. I will not shun another Blessing."

Anessa swallowed hard, her fingers scrabbling for the pendant. She hadn't thought of that. Was doubting a sin? Should she be doing something to make it right?

Kobb turned from the huddle. "A wise idea, High Speaker Erinis."

Erinis nodded once in acknowledgement, then strode from the room.

"I suppose we should start then." Morheru limped toward the shadows at the back of the room.

Anessa peered at the remaining seated figure. Tired eyes looked back from a wrinkled face

"Do you need help, sir?"

Morheru paused. "High Speaker Kalit doesn't speak, dear. Or leave his throne any more. The years have weighed heaviest on him."

"I'm a healer," Haelen said. "I could—"

"We will rest once our task is done." Morheru turned to face the shadows again. "You are kind to offer though."

Haelen glanced at Kobb. A look passed between them, but, the gloom prevented Anessa working out what it meant. Puzzled, she followed the First Speaker toward the rear wall. Closer now, she made out a series of pictures and symbols cut into the stone.

Arms spread wide, Morheru pressed herself against the wall. A loud click cut the air, followed a breath later by a grinding noise. Anessa's gaze flicked around as the ground began to shake.

As she watched, sections of the wall juddered out forming a broad flight of stairs that lead upward. Peering up she realised the darker patch at the head was a hole in the ceiling.

"These carvings are the Virtues?" Serth swept her arm around.

"Yes. Every teaching Amheru uncovered, recorded for the time they are needed."

Serth moved closer to the foot of the stairs. "Two figures in long robes holding curved sticks. A book with a dagger below it. Three circular objects. You'll forgive me for pointing out it will be hard for us to read them."

"I will translate any that you wish." Morheru raised a palm. "I realise you don't trust me fully either, but I hope you will come to in time." Grinning like someone's aunt, the First Speaker hobbled up the steps, leaving Serth staring at her back.

Anessa rested a hand on Serth's elbow. "Still glad you came?"

"I didn't do it because it was easy." Serth shook her head slowly. "Religion's the Reverend's area anyway. I'm only here in case it gets messy." She stepped away, and followed Haelen.

Letting her hand fall, Anessa headed up the staircase. Ahead of her, the others formed a single file, close to the wall. Morheru's pace gave plenty of time to study the carvings; however, like Serth, Anessa could make little sense of them. Struck by a sudden thought, she let her gaze settle on Serth's trousers. They were good leather, but they were tight too. How'd Serth get into them so fast when the Speaker arrived? She'd definitely not been wearing them when she lay down, so she'd heard the chamber door moving and got dressed in the length of time it took the Speaker to walk along the corridor.

Anessa felt heat sear up her neck as the thought of how fast she might be able to get them off again filled her mind. Glad the shadows would hide the colour of her face, she clamped her gaze back on the carvings. Two people not embracing. A table... not a bed a table. Wavy vertical lines.

Watching the back of Serth's head from the corner of her eye to avoid a collision, she sidled up the stairs.

"How...?" said Haelen.

Anessa's head snapped around. His lower body disappeared into the gloom as he passed through the hole in the ceiling.

Thoughts of trousers gone, she sprinted after Serth. Ignoring the drop, she pulled level with the Inductor. Together, they raced into the shadow.

The moment her head passed into the hole, a purple glow flooded her vision. A thick gold band studded with jewels the size of her fist rested on a pedestal. Blinking away the glare, she made out the other three standing against the wall. She cupped one hand around the side of her face and stumbled over to them.

"This is your belt?" Despite being beside her, Serth's voice sounded muffled.

Morheru nodded, the strange light making her face seem smoother. "The legacy of Amheru. Awoken after centuries by your journey here."

"Is that...?" Anessa waved her hands at Kobb's chest.

"It feels like the same power." Kobb squinted. "This is what we came for."

Morheru bowed deeply. "Then claim it. I shall not tell Erinis we forwent the rituals if you do not."

Kobb advanced slowly, hands moving in odd patterns. As he reached the pedestal, the light blazed brighter, enveloping him completely.

Anessa leapt forward, screaming his name. But no sound came out.

PART NINETY

Strong arms wrapped around Anessa's chest. She struggled to break free, but Haelen just lifted her feet off the ground. His breath flickered across her cheek. Whatever he said was swallowed by the silence, though. She flailed her limbs.

Despite him twitching each time a fist or boot hit him, he just continued to carry her away from the glare.

From the corner of her eye, she noticed Serth, one hand shielding her eyes, moving past them. When Haelen staggered sideways in an attempt to stop her too, Anessa intensified her thrashing.

Silent words gusting stronger, he focused his attention on Anessa.

Two steps later, Serth was a black silhouette against the purple fire. Anessa relaxed as the light bled across the edges. Kobb hadn't been much further forward. Serth had to be almost—

The glare blazed brighter, obscuring everything. Anessa clamped her eyes shut as a feeling like spikes drove into her head.

Her pain cut off. After a moment of apparent darkness, she realised the light still shone, no longer bright enough to hurt through closed lids. Half expecting a trick, she cracked one eye.

A mass of purple fire filled the centre of the room, but there was no sign of Serth. She must have passed within. Which meant it was safe.

Anessa struggled to break free.

Rather than resume his backward shuffle, Haelen turned on the spot. She went limp as Serth's body was revealed, slumped against the wall. Her face looked too pale. That had to be the glare. It had to be.

Dropping Anessa, Haelen strode toward the fallen Inductor. Knees wobbly, Anessa staggered after him. Serth couldn't be hurt. If she was, then that meant the light harmed people. And it couldn't do that, because Kobb was in it; and he was the chosen one, so he couldn't get hurt. Not like that.

Haelen crouched, and ran his fingers over Serth. Unsure whether she'd help or only be in the way, and unable to ask, Anessa halted nearby. As her gaze flicked between Serth and the purple glare, she realised Morheru was grinning.

Was it all a trap? Was there a prophecy, or did they just say there was to lure people up here so the Belt could kill them? That was why they banned weapons! Fists raised, Anessa advanced on the First Speaker, boots clumping determinedly.

The glow weakened, plunging the room into comparative darkness. "A little help, please."

Anessa spun at the sound of Kobb's voice.

Swaying but whole, he stood beside the pedestal in the centre. The Belt, jewels reduced to their initial glow, hung over one shoulder.

Forgetting her planned vengeance, she sprinted to him. Something was different. It wasn't just the glare: his hair was darker and face lined; he looked younger; still old but in the prime of maturity. She wrapped an arm around him. "Reverend! What happened...? The light..."

"Stay your curiosity a while, child," said Morheru. "He will have time to explain after he's eaten and slept."

Kobb rested his arm across Anessa's shoulders. "Might be easier if I wait a while to get it straight in my own head. What happened to the Inductor?"

Serth! Anessa forced herself not to rush as she helped Kobb away from the pedestal.

After a few steps, he removed his arm. "Reckon I've got my legs back."

Easing away, she almost leapt across the remaining floor and dropped to a crouch. Serth's eyes were open, but her gaze drifted randomly and her pupils were different sizes.

"Is she...?"

Haelen's brow furrowed.

But before he could reply, Serth's hand grabbed Anessa's neck. "Hello, pretty... Love you..." Pulling Anessa close, she kissed her hard.

Caught off guard, Anessa felt Serth's tongue slip between her lips. Hitting her head on the wall must've confused Serth. She'd mistaken her for that woman she'd killed when she was young. Didn't stop the embrace feeling real though.

Mustering every scrap of will, Anessa eased herself free and backed away. "Will she...? Is she...?"

"I've seen people knocked out for longer, shake it off in minutes." Haelen smiled, the odd light making it seem too flat. "Speaking's a good sign. She might be fine by the time we're back in our rooms. You lift her left shoulder."

Anessa crouched again. It took a couple of attempts to get Serth's arm around her shoulders—the Inductor kept trying to turn it into an embrace—but eventually the three of them ended up standing in a line. The effort of steering Serth down the stairs made Morheru's pace seem almost fast.

As they reached the door from the tower, the First Speaker bowed. "See you at the feast."

The journey across the city was similarly slow. Unable to move in single file, the gap through the crowds seemed narrower; there were moments when Anessa wasn't sure if the inhabitants had left enough space for her to pass. And the feeling of Serth's fingers fiddling with the nape of her neck didn't make it any easier. However, eventually they reached their rooms.

One ear cocked for the sound of stone closing behind them, Anessa helped Haelen settle the still-groggy Serth on a bed.

"No need for both of us to keep an eye on her." Haelen made a shooing gesture. "Talk to the Reverend for a while."

Feeling odd about leaving Serth—yet unsure why—Anessa headed into the main room and stared at Kobb. "What happened? There was that light, and silence like a Courser. I thought you'd... and then you were there. And you're..."

"Not ancient any more?" Kobb winked. "The Belt somehow accesses the same flow as the Courser. Instead of taking it gives, though. I felt the years I'd lost coming back. Not all of them; a few though."

"It makes people young again?"

He swept his arms down his body. "I think this is what I get. Tired rather than half-dead's still a Blessing, though. And I can feel the power there; I could draw on it to use my Courser instead of my own energies. Which is a problem."

"Problem. How's being able to fight without— It's connected to the Stones; keeping it means not making the Stones right."

Kobb nodded.

"That's still—"

The sound of sandalled feet echoed down the corridor. Moments later, High Speaker Erinis staggered in. "They've discovered your plan. If you give me the Belt I might be able to buy you enough time to escape."

PART NINETY-ONE

Kobb raised his hand to his Courser. "Plan? What plan? We haven't decided what to do with the Belt yet."

"There isn't time for you to pretend innocence. People know about the kidnapping." Erinis lunged toward the Belt.

Kobb stepped back, leaving the High Speaker gripping air. "We haven't abducted anyone. Check all the rooms if you wish."

"I meant the one you intend." Erinis held his arms out. "Give me the Belt. I'll stop the mob while you escape."

Something wasn't right. Lies did spring up fast, but something about this niggled at him. He needed more time to unravel what, though. "We'll talk to the populace. We're grateful for the warning. You'd best leave, though; it won't help for you to be here when the attackers arrive. I don't doubt you could stop the attack if I gave you the Belt; the Virtues commanded we should bear it, though, so that's got to be what we do."

"You don't understand. They'll..." Erinis let his head sag. "Very well. I'll leave you to prepare."

"Wait!" Anessa grabbed Erinis arm. "Who do they reckon we're going to kidnap?"

Erinis turned back, hope lighting his eyes. "First Speaker Morheru. While you can't steal the Virtues themselves, they're all in her memory."

That did make a certain sense. It wasn't true, yet it was a very plausible and rational motive for kidnapping her; too reasonable. Kobb ushered Erinis through the door. "Thank you again for trying to avoid violence."

Erinis peered at Kobb. Realising he wouldn't change his mind, the High Speaker jogged down the corridor and out of sight.

After waiting a moment to make sure he was gone, Kobb returned to the main room.

` "Will he be all right?" Anessa frowned toward the exit.

"He's a very experienced ruler. I doubt he'll let himself get in the middle of a fight."

"I meant when the mob don't find us. Now we've go the Belt, we can return to the Stones. Will they try to hurt him for warning us?"

Kobb settled on the edge of the pool. Sometimes, after all the things she'd done, he forgot how innocent Anessa was. "Erinis is the one who started the lie."

"What? No. He came to help us."

"He hoped we'd give him the Belt. I didn't realise at first either, but there are too many things that don't make sense otherwise. If he'd arranged a feast, there'd almost certainly have been fewer people on the streets not more; and signs they were setting up tables and preparing large quantities of food."

"Maybe it's all in a building?"

"Where though? I didn't see anything happening in the tunnels when we returned. And the citizens seem to set up a temporary city on the surface as soon as the sun sets, so wouldn't they hold it up there?" He stood and raised a palm. "I know that's only speculation. He got here too fast, or too slow. Erinis thought we we'd be following the rituals; Morheru skipped them all, though, so we left the tower faster than he expected. There wasn't time for him to get there then here through that crowd; yet if he came here intending to wait for us, why wasn't he surprised we were back? And many of the residents already seemed to resent us when we left the tower. But they didn't attack; which makes sense if they were waiting until after Erinis asked politely."

Anessa's eyes widened. "We didn't have Morheru with us as we crossed the city; so it don't make sense for the crowd to get angry. But... He didn't want to risk the Belt getting damaged if he could avoid it. I'll start packing." She shot into the bedroom, reiteration of Kobb's theory spilling from her mouth as she crossed the threshold. Only to emerge, a puzzled expression on her face, at Haelen's heels.

"We can't risk travelling at the moment, Reverend." Haelen frowned. "The first few times we went by the Stones, we experienced a stronger reaction. Maybe realigning them's reduced that, but maybe we've just become used to it. The Inductor's only done it twice; taking her through before she recovers from the blast might be enough to kill her."

"No!" Anessa grabbed Kobb's elbows. "We can't... We have to..."

"Don't worry. I want her safe too." Kobb pulled her into an embrace. "How long until she's fit to travel, Haelen?"

"A crack to the head? Could take days of rest to shake it off." Haelen swallowed. "Given she was hit with the same power that flows through the Stones? Might make her more vulnerable than usual."

Anessa broke free. "The power. The Belt made you better, Kobb. Why can't it do the same for Serth?"

"It may work." Kobb strode to the bedroom and wrapped the Belt around Serth as best he could.

The Inductor struggled to focus on him, then sagged back into semi-consciousness.

After a few minutes with no sign of a change, he rose to his feet. "It's not working. Maybe there's a trick to it. But without someone to explain it...

If anyone knows, it's Morheru. We'd never make it back to the tower, though, not now Erinis realises we won't surrender the Belt willingly."

Anessa dropped down beside Serth, face wet. "We have to try. Maybe healing you used up the power it'd stored. If we give it some."

It hadn't felt drained. The power might need to be—

"I couldn't use a Courser, but don't mean I can't do other things." Anessa pressed her hands to the central jewel.

Kobb suddenly realised her plan.

Before he could react, Serth knocked Anessa's hand away. "Did it to keep you safe... Not letting you..."

"What do you mean, you did it to keep me safe?" Anessa stared into Serth's eyes. "Haelen'd already pulled me back. I weren't—"

"No." Serth swallowed. "Before—"

The sound of boots clattering along the corridor covered whatever she intended to say.

Part Ninety-Two

Kobb spun on his heel and strode to the central room. Three men clutching heavy tools ran through the far doorway, followed by a woman holding a cleaver.

Seeing him, they screamed something and raced around the pool, two on each side.

He paused for a breath. The citizens had been mislead. They didn't deserve to die. If he charged one pair, he could drive them off before the others closed; but if the others ignored him, they'd have a clear run to the bedroom. Time to find out whether the Belt had given him more than a feeling of health. He drew his rapier and adopted a defensive stance.

Rather than wait and flank him properly, the four attackers charged forward as fast as they could.

As the first man reached him, Kobb whirled toward the other pair while slashing out at chest level. As intended, the tip of his blade scored along the inside of his target's forearm.

Shout becoming one of pain, his attacker clutched his wound and pulled up sharply. Blocking his companion's path.

Knees bending without even the memory of age, Kobb shifted his whirl to a low sweep toward the woman's ankles.

Her feet tangled as she attempted to reverse direction, sending her tumbling into the pool.

The third man lunged forward, bringing his improvised club whistling down over his head.

Kobb raised his arm, blade downward, as he rolled at the waist. As his opponent's weapon deflected past along the diagonal blade, Kobb punched his elbow with his free hand.

The man grunted, dropping his club.

Kobb spun, blade rising up to meet the second man's weapon as he rounded his injured companion.

His opponent winced as a judder ran along his arm.

Before he recovered, Kobb stepped sharply backwards, elbow raised at shoulder level.

Bone crunched. The attacker behind him staggered back, fingers clutching his bleeding nose.

Kobb spun his rapier and advanced in a high guard.

The still-armed man brought his club up in a hasty block.

Allowing his blade to be directed over his target's shoulder, Kobb shifted his weight across as he continued forward, then drove his knee into the man's groin.

Mouth gaping, his opponent collapsed backward.

Pivoting around three-quarters of a circle fast enough to make his coat flare out, Kobb brought his rapier to guard an inch from the nose of the dripping woman.

The cleaver splashed into the water as she raised her palms and backed away.

Arm as steady as stone, Kobb inclined his head toward the entrance.

Dripping, bleeding, and moaning, the battered former-attackers staggered from the room.

Kobb sheathed his blade.

A moment later, Anessa joined him, sword readied. "Don't seem much of a threat."

"Maybe not. But defeating them's not the problem; it's doing it without causing any mortal wounds. They don't deserve that."

"What about the guards? Why aren't they attacking?"

"Might just be ceremonial. And pole-arms don't work in narrow spaces. I think Erinis'll likely let a few groups of ordinary people charge in first, though, in the hopes we don't have the stomach for hurting civilians."

"You drove those four off easily enough. So with both of us, it'll be easy." She grinned. "Just got to hit them, right?"

He shook his head. "Once a person's blood's up, making them think they'll lose is harder than killing. There's only some opportunities you can exploit; so, it takes longer and needs thought. And, even if you're careful, accidents happen. So, we might push the civilians back, but it'll wear us down."

The scuff of feet sounded outside.

Kobb drew his rapier. "They'll be more cautious this time. I'll charge round the pool the moment they enter. You hold here in case any of them try to get past me."

Her fingers too tight and elbows too straight, Anessa raised her sword.

Kobb stepped forward and spun his blade dramatically as someone peered through the door.

The head drew back. Fragments of whispered conversation drifted from the corridor.

A few breaths later, a woman wielding a chair-leg ran in.

Kobb charged toward her, bellowing.

Eyes wide and weapon clutched vertically in both hands, she stumbled to a halt.

Kobb angled his rapier back, intending to roll around her block and hammer the hilt into her face.

However, as he engaged, two more men sprinted through the doorway and headed around the pool in the other direction.

The woman's eyes glazed as Kobb's guard struck her temple.

Continuing past her falling body, he charged the other attackers. Only to curse as two more rushed into the room behind him.

The first pair pulled up as Anessa swept her sword across sharply.

Wrist flicking in a crescent, Kobb sliced the earlobe from the one on the left.

One hand instinctively grabbing his wound, the man spun. His weapon clattered to the floor as the flat of Kobb's blade smacked his knuckles.

Kobb drove his fist into the man's gut, sending him stumbling against his companion.

Before the nearest opponent could untangle himself, Kobb cracked him on the temple with the hilt of his rapier. The man crumpled.

Sword still horizontal, Anessa whirled around.

The remaining attackers halted; then divided, one facing Kobb across the pool while the other kept Anessa between them.

Hoping his opponent was too fired up to think straight, Kobb charged through the water. As the man moved to engage, Kobb hurled his rapier.

As he'd hoped, the attacker raised his arms to deflect the missile.

Hands fisted, Kobb struck forward at stomach level, driving the air from his opponent's lungs.

A stain spreading across his crotch, the remaining opponent fled past Kobb.

Kobb reclaimed his rapier as the still conscious citizens to the chance to retreat, carrying their companions.

"Why not block the corridor?" Anessa rested the point of her sword on the ground.

"Packed in between walls, there's no room for them to run away, so they fight."

She glanced at his Courser. "I meant, block it so they can't get in. We carry Serth to the stable, and as much food as we can, and bring the ceiling down behind us."

"I don't have the— The Belt!" Kobb jogged to the bedroom.

An impression of wide spaces and great distance wrapped around him as he buckled the Belt. Courser drawn he ran into the corridor.

Seeing no new attackers nearby, he unleashed the power. Searing light washed across the wall ahead.

Chunks of stone tumbled free, and slammed silently to the floor.

Energy filling him as fast as he could use it, he brought the ceiling down.

After a final glance at the pile of rubble to confirm it blocked the corridor, he turned.

Sandals hitting the ground in perfect unison, figures in purple togas with sabres and shields rounded the far corner.

Part Ninety-Three

Kobb brought his Courser up, rapier leaping into his other hand, and cursed. They weren't limited to pikes. Of course, they weren't; a nation that lived in tunnels for centuries would've realised the issues by now. If he moved immediately, he could reach the doorway before the enemy did. The extra space would be a liability against trained fighters, though. Better to take advantage of both range and their cramped advance.

Purple light flared along the corridor as he felled soldier after soldier.

His opponents staggered to a halt, shocked by the force of his resistance.

A tactical error he was more than happy to exploit. Courser almost floating in his grip and limbs flowing as smoothly as they did in his memories of youth, he scythed down another rank. This was how it should be. Delivering justice to those who advanced under a flag of evil and lies.

More opponents moved along the corridor, and fell before his wrath. He sheathed his rapier. With the Belt to strengthen him, he no longer needed it. He'd purge the unbelievers before they even reached him. If only he'd had it at Raveth. Those demon worshippers would never have taken Gannon from him.

Palms raised, First Speaker Morheru stepped around the corner.

Now he saw the whole plan. She was part of it too. First, she sneaks in here, then the soldiers run out the main door with her among them as if they'd rescued her. But, it wouldn't work. Justice would be done.

Rubble tumbled silently to the floor as Kobb's blast seared through Morheru and into the stone beyond.

The rhythm of his boot-steps rendered staccato by bursts of silence, he advanced along the corridor.

Disarrayed, the remaining enemy fell where they stood.

Slumped against a wall, a robed figure raised a palm.

Lips drawing back, Kobb took aim. Another unbeliever to be cleansed, and he had all the power he—

Pain jolted along his arm as something smashed into his elbow. Fingers tingling yet firm, he spun.

His Courser dropped from his hand as Haelen smacked the club against his wrist.

Rage flooding through him, Kobb swung his other fist into Haelen's jaw.

The healer fell backward, but as he did, his fingers hooked the buckle on the Belt.

Kobb felt the strength leave him as the Belt slipped free. Agony flickering and jabbing from every direction, he collapsed to the floor.

When the pain faded enough to see again, he realised he lay across a soldier, little older than Anessa. Others, faces equally contorted and eyes equally blank, piled around him.

"Reverend!" Haelen, rubbing his own cheek, crouched beside him. "Are you recovered?"

Fragments of memory rose up. The soldiers had attacked, but he'd cut them all down before they'd harmed anyone... hadn't he?

They hadn't charged, though. They'd been walking calmly. And

Morheru hadn't been armed. He eased himself upright. More bodies sprawled dead along the corridor, killed as they tried to flee. He'd broken the advance and hadn't even noticed. Instead, he'd slaughtered them all.

Haelen rested a hand on his elbow. "The gems almost blinded me when you passed the door. I called out. You didn't notice me, though. I'm sorry. The club was all I—"

"You did right, my friend. I though I was using the Belt, but the taint used me instead. I killed them all."

"Not all." Haelen stepped carefully toward the robed figure. "Kalit still lives."

High Speaker Kalit pushed his hood back with a palsied hand. "Discovered Erinis plan. Wanted to warn you."

"Then we can stop this." Anessa staggered into the corridor, supporting Anserth. "You can explain Erinis lied."

Kobb sighed. "It's too late for that. If Morheru lived, maybe. But even if she were here to give her version of events, the mob might not listen. We have to leave, now."

"No, Serth could die." Anessa shook her head. "We need to wait."

Anserth swallowed hard. "Kobb's right. They won't stop. If we don't go, we'll have to kill everyone."

"No. I don't care if you're a bitch sometimes. I'll not lose you. We'll barricade the tunnels. They'll—"

"Bit tired." Anserth's head sagged. "If we're going to discuss, then... sit down for a bit."

Eyes filled with panicked love, Anessa lowered against the wall, kicking the discarded Belt aside as she did. After brushing the hair from Anserth's brow, she shot upright and rounded on Kobb. "Ain't you supposed to be good at battles? Well, you find some way to keep them all out until—"

Purple light flared behind her as Anserth drove her knife through the Belt over and over.

Part Ninety-Four

Anessa's gaze jumped around the piles of bodies as purple light drove the shadows off Kobb's face. Where'd the attack come from? Why hadn't the blast harmed–? She spun.

Serth lay on the floor, the blackened and twisted remains of a knife next to one hand. Brief flickers of energy crackled across her as the last of the jewels faded.

"Serth!" Anessa fell to her knees. "Why–? Serth! She's not–"

Kobb's arms slid over her shoulders, pulling her away. "Give Haelen some space."

Vision blurring and chest aching, she settled back into Kobb's embrace. Why'd Serth done it? She knew the Belt was dangerous.

"She's alive," Haelen said. "Her pulse is weak, but it's steady."

"We have to stay then!" Anessa jerked free of Kobb.

"Anessa could be right. Although–" Haelen tugged at Serth's clothes. "The bruising's gone. And some of her scars are too. I'd need time to be sure; the power might've healed her, though."

"I hope so." Kobb stood. "Because we can't stay here. There's another way in. We need to get her to the stables, before we're overrun."

Anessa wiped her eyes. If Serth'd been healed, then why wasn't she awake? What if Haelen was wrong? Moving her might be the worst thing to do. She dived forward, not noticing when her elbow knocked Haelen aside. "You aren't allowed to die. Not like this. You've got two things to explain now, and you're not allowed to die until you've done it! Do you hear me!"

Serth didn't react.

A moment later, Haelen coughed. "We ease her onto one of the mattresses and carry an end each while Kobb keeps an eye out for ambushes."

Anessa clambered to her feet and backed through the door. The instant the frame hid Serth, Anessa spun on her heel and raced into one of the bedrooms. Haelen caught her up as she struggled to push a mattress through the doorway.

Each slight sag or flop of Serth's body felt like being stabbed, but eventually the two of them got her onto it and lifted. Anessa stiffened as the improvised stretcher rose more easily than she expected. That had to be a good thing. Hoping she didn't have to be touching the pendant for it to work, she started praying under her breath. Serth'd tried to help Kobb. That meant she was on the Maker's side. The Maker would save her. And if she didn't explain anything, or was cruel again, it would still be a Blessing, because she'd be alive. Hands full, Anessa let the tears and snot trickle down her face.

After a wrong turn, but mercifully without meeting another person, they reached the stable. No attacks meant the Maker'd been listening. A flicker of hope sprang up; even Falcon's whicker seemed almost welcoming. The moment the mattress was settled, she crouched at the side of it and took Serth's fingers.

When the world lurched around her, she barely noticed.

"Anessa?" Haelen patted her shoulder. "She'll be more comfortable in my tent. Can you help me move her?"

She drew her hand back, a surge of joy almost knocking her over as Serth's fingers clung for a breath. Body aching with the effort of not jostling her friend, she followed Haelen into the tent and eased the mattress down again. Then returned to her place at the side of it.

A sharp yet earthy scent filled the air as Haelen mixed pinches from several jars.

Anessa leaned closer as Serth shifted slightly. Then shifted again. Pressing the fingers of her free hand to her pendant, Anessa smiled.

Kobb strode into the tent. "The Stones are dull now."

"All of them?" Haelen said.

Anessa frowned. They'd dealt with the last thing; why'd Haelen want to check? Her puzzlement slipped away again as Serth's eyes opened.

A breath later, her friend's face hardened and she glanced around. "Tent... Worked then...."

"You mean the Belt?" Anessa squeezed her fingers. "Why did you do something so idiotic?"

Kobb crouched down. "Without the Belt, there was no way to block the corridors. We'd have to leave."

Anessa looked back and forth between them, before settling on Serth. "But, you could have died. Why?"

"Even with barricade... mob might get in... need to kill them all...."

"I knew you weren't evil. It was stupid and risky, and wonderful. I knew you cared about people."

Serth shook her head. "No... Kill them all to stop getting Belt... too much risk Kobb would be overwhelmed. So, I ended the threat."

"What?" Anessa turned the words around. They didn't fit. No one thought like that. "But— What did you mean about keeping me safe? Before those people rushed in, you said you did it to keep me safe."

"Doesn't matter any more." Serth turned her head away. "I should rest."

"No. You need to keep talking. Tell her, Haelen. Tell her she has to keep talking, so she doesn't—"

The stench of burning soil flooded the tent.

PART NINETY-FIVE

Kobb shivered, then drew his weapons and sprinted out, Anessa on his heels. Everything seemed dull. He staggered to a halt, gaze sweeping the area as he sought the fire without success. The scent of scorching came from all around, but was strongest behind him.

The barrier seemed more obvious. Two feet later, he realised smoke rose where it touched the ground. He held up a hand. "Stay back. Just in case."

Power pressed down on him as he opened his mind to the connection. The edge seemed to be in the same place, yet felt heavier. He eased closer, a step at a time. Not heavier exactly: more— He halted, as crackle of light moved around the edge.

The flicker afforded him too brief a glimpse to be certain, but the ground had seemed eaten away. If the barrier had started to damage the soil, getting closer was risky. Especially if it arced out again. Safest option was to dismiss it. They'd realigned the Stones, so did they need the protection any more? He peered in every direction. No sign of anyone waiting to get in; and if someone did come, he could raise it again quickly enough. He turned his mind inward toward the threads linking him to the barrier.

Only to feel them slip from him.

Sinking to his knees, he slowed his breathing and eased his worry away. The structure floated before him. At ease, he reached out.

His mental fingers passed through, closing on nothing. He tried again, with no success. Sweat beaded on his brow as he pushed himself harder to no effect.

He inhaled sharply, as Anessa shook his shoulder. Then coughed as heat dried his throat.

"What's happening? Why's it so hot?"

He clambered to his feet. "The barrier's changed. I can't dismiss it."

"How hot's it going to get?" Anessa backed away, gaze flicking around.

"I don't know." Kobb patted her elbow. "We'll check the notes. There has to be an answer."

Anserth sat on the edge of the bed when they returned, supported by Haelen. "Whatever the Belt did to me, I feel good—a little hot, but..." The smile left her face as Kobb explained.

After easing away from his patient, Haelen moved between piles of paper, tutting under his breath. Brow creased, he held up the stained and mildewed remains of a diagram. "It's not clear how; seems the Stones need life to seal the pattern in place, though."

"We're not sacrificing anyone." Kobb snatched the page. Seven red lines linked rough rectangles to a central one. Age and misuse had destroyed most of the text. The crude figure in the middle was obvious enough, though. "There has to be another way."

Anserth sat up straighter. "I'll do it. If it's this hot now, we don't have time to research the best approach. So, we complete the mission."

"No!" Anessa wrapped her arms around the Inductor. "We're not killing you."

"Anessa's right." Kobb held up a hand before Anserth could argue. "I know all the arguments that you're the sensible choice. But using the Stones to travel's heretical enough; sacrificing someone's demon worship, plain and simple."

Anessa looked up, eyes sparkling. "What about your Courser? Could you... break the barrier or something?"

Kobb shook his head. "Courser blasts pass through each other. More power might even speed things up."

"She could be on the right path, Reverend." Haelen tapped his chin. "Not breaking through, but using the way it affects you. It doesn't just channel from somewhere else; each time you use it, you end up tired. So, the blasts contain part of your life. If you focus it on the central stone, it might be enough."

"I hope you're right." Anserth eased free of Anessa's embrace. "If you destroy the altar and it doesn't work, then we can't try anything else."

"Coursers barely damage normal rock. Might not even scratch one crafted to direct power." Kobb strode out of the tent, shoulders set. The air clutched at his lungs as he approached the altar.

His aim settled. He slowed his breathing. If his Courser did destroy the stone, it denied the Circle to anyone who might misuse it. So, one way or another, this would be a Blessing. Everything thinned as purple fire boiled out.

He dropped to his knees, focus broken, as the ground lurched beneath him. Cool air flooded his lungs. The barrier remained; the weight was gone from his mind, though. He could—

Instead of the gentle light of stars, everything had a ruddy tinge. The stars were still there, yet somehow less solid. And among them hung an immense red moon where no moon had ever been.

Courser ready, he stood. The edge of the forest loomed dark, yet thin as shadow. And visible through it, mountains jutted. Anessa gasped as she stepped into view, as shocked as he was.

A breath later, she sprinted forward, eyes locked on something just behind him. He spun into a defensive stance.

And froze. It wasn't... How...?

Leather creaked as Reverend Militant Gannon spread his arms wide. "It's good to see you, Absolution. I have so many things to tell you."

Part Ninety-Six

Kobb lowered his Courser. "Reverend Gannon?"

"No need to be formal, Absolution. How've you been? How's that cantankerous beast of yours?"

The sound of Anessa's feet had stopped. She must've decided to give them some privacy once she realised Gannon wasn't a threat. "Falcon's fine. But never mind me. How did you survive? I saw Raveth obliterated. Nothing could—"

"The Rules don't tell the whole story. Power can destroy, but no more than an axe can destroy. There are other uses. Ways to move faster, to heal. It's not the evil we were taught."

It made a kind of sense. The Skithai used power differently. The Stones allowed people to travel. But, the Belt had driven him to unspeakable fury. "I've seen reason to question the Rule, to suggest it might overstate certain risks. But I've seen horrors, too. Felt power tug me toward evil."

"Not claiming it's without risk. I've met my share of monsters. There's ways to reduce the danger, though. Same as I trained you not to let your power run wild." Reverend Gannon gestured past the edge of the circle. "Our village's only a short distance. You'll see our research for yourself."

"

If the blast at Raveth had hurled Reverend Gannon away, then it seemed reasonable he'd arrive near somewhere that used power to travel. Had help been just beyond the trees all this time? "Our...? How many of you are there? I should gather my companions."

Reverend Gannon shook his head. "Just you for now. Some of the villagers faced persecution. Several armed strangers all at once might be too much. I know this is a shock; I wasn't expecting to find you here either. But, if it were a trap, wouldn't I want to lure you all out at once?" He pressed a hand to his chest for a moment, pain squeezing his face.

———

Anessa raced forward, each step on the verge of becoming a stumble. "Ma!"

Her mother grinned back. "Nessa. My Nessa, all grown up."

Anessa stumbled to a halt. She should introduce— No. There'd be time for that later. "How'd you...? The wolves...? Everyone thought... Why didn't you...?"

"I'm sorry. The wolves did catch me. Mauled me bad. Thought I were done for, then things sort of lurched and everything went black. When I came round the others told me they'd found me half-naked near this circle. I wanted to go back to Morth, but it wasn't safe to travel alone and the others had important work to do; couldn't ask them to stop just to get me home."

Her coffin was nailed down. Da must have seen bit of Ma's bloody dress and assumed... "Don't matter. Found you now. Kobb'll keep us safe on the way."

After an instant, Ma nodded. "Meal and a good night's sleep first, though. You're looking too thin. And when did you last have a bath?"

"Ma!" Anessa tried to pretend to be annoyed, but it wouldn't stick.

Her mother collapsed forward, blood trickling over her lips.

Kobb clutched his head. A mass of slate-grey flesh lay where Reverend Gannon had stood, ichor seeping from the rents covering it. Beside it, drenched with sweat, Anserth raised her sword then drove it down through the body. After swaying for a moment, the Inductor collapsed to one knee, head bowed.

Raising his Courser, Kobb looked around. Haelen and Anessa, stood nearby, staring at the creature with the same confusion he felt.

"Katrina... I saw Katrina." Haelen sagged, tears washing away his puzzlement. "She said her kidnappers brought her here."

"My Ma wasn't..." Anessa hiccuped.

Kobb patted Anessa on the shoulder. "For me, Reverend Gannon. Somehow, that creature made us each see it as the person we missed the most. Maybe more than just made us see them. If the Inductor hadn't killed it, I'd have gone off alone with it."

"And me." Anessa swallowed hard, then frowned. "How'd you know to kill it, Serth? Why didn't it look like someone you missed?"

The Inductor glanced up, eyes like stones. "It did. I heard her calling me, so I staggered out. She'd this story about how the rest of you'd gone into the other tent to give us some privacy. I'd pushed my emotions away when we talked about needing a sacrifice, though, so whatever the beast did to inspire trust didn't work. You all leaving me with someone you'd never met didn't make sense. The blade went in just like last time, but that changed once the illusion stopped."

Anessa's eyes widened. "You didn't know it wasn't... not till after you'd stabbed her. But that's—"

"Utterly delicious."

Kobb's gaze snapped to the edge of the circle as a voice like shattering metal swallowed Anessa's words.

A man-shaped shadow emerged from behind one of the Stones, seeming to tear apart then reform rather than cross the intervening space. "Greetings, Reverend. I lost the opportunity to make your acquaintance at Raveth, but—"

Demon! Kobb raised his Courser and unleashed blast after blast. Each only passed through the gaps between shadows as the abomination flickered closer.

Part Ninety-Seven

Arm straight but not rigid, Kobb tracked the abomination as it advanced. It seemed solid enough, and yet no matter how carefully he'd picked his spot, the creature always split there the instant he unleashed his Courser.

"No need for violence, Absolution." The demon's voice sounded like Gannon's now; however, the hint of tortured metal still lurked beneath. "Join us and your friends won't be harmed."

Kobb's ears buzzed as the power struggled to be free. For an instant, the desire to attack until he was spent filled him, but he fought it down. It must know mimicking Gannon would make him less prone to negotiate, so wanted him angry. Lending further evidence to his worry it could predict his actions, the abomination—while still moving in a series of jagged flickers—slowed to the pace and predictability of a gentle stroll. He needed to try something different; something it couldn't dodge. He lacked any of the trappings; he was Blessed with lungs, though.

"Whosoever would be Blessed, before all things it is necessary—" Kobb drove the words of the Creed forth from the depths of his chest, yet they seemed muffled. "—that they hold faith in the Maker. Which faith..."

"The Rite of Abjuration?" The creature halted. Its speech shattered into myriad voices chanting the Creed as one. "...keep whole and undefiled; without such they shall face confusion and loss everlasting. And the demonstrations of faith are these—" The choir collapsed again into a single voice of torn iron. "The gate makes this as much my home as yours. Even with a chorus to sustain the harmonies you cannot send me to where I have not left."

Kobb continued to push the words out with all his will, but the abomination didn't flinch, let alone retreat. Realising he wasted his energy as surely as if he used his Courser, he fell silent.

"Gannon told me you'd see sense."

Straightening her shoulders, Anessa drew her sword. "Why are you doing this? Why try to trick us? Why can't you just leave us alone?"

A sound like breaking glass rang from the demon. "I want to share my home, my wisdom, everything. My appearance can be troubling at first, though. I thought seeing your friends, knowing you'd be among family, would be more reassuring.

Kobb frowned. Two moons. Mountains that weren't quite there. If it was set on talking, maybe it'd be arrogant enough to let something slip. "You infected hundreds at Raveth. If you wanted us to join you, you could have done the same to us. You've proved I can't stop you. Which means, you need us to choose to serve. You claimed this is as much your home as ours. That's it, isn't it? I opened the gate halfway. You need someone to complete the ritual; however, they have to do it of their own free will."

"So clever." A wisp of smoke rose from beneath the creature's feet. "The gate can only be unsealed from your side. Even the tiniest sliver of me in someone and they can't touch it. Why fight it though? If you don't open it, someone will. Already people are turning against your beliefs. I can wait. So, why not have the rewards for yourself?"

"Pigshit!" Anessa tugged her pendant out of her jacket. "There'll always be someone to fight. And you ain't got nothing we want!"

"Such passion. Even the scent is sweet." The creature juddered two feet closer to her in a blink. "I need one of you to open the way. I could embrace the rest now... or I could agree to let them leave, agree to let them live out their lives free of my love if that is what they wish."

"Go eat slurry!" Face pale but hands steady, Anessa stepped forward and swung her sword in a massive arc. Tatters of shadow floated away as the blade cleaved through the demon's torso. She struck again, slashing another wound through her opponent.

The demon tittered as the wisps twisted in the air and resealed the wounds. "Maybe losing a companion will convince one of you to see sense."

Anessa leapt back, sword raised. Boot striking a hummock, she fell backwards.

Folding forward, the creature reached for her leg.

Only to be sent sprawling as Haelen slammed into it from the side.

Seeing a chance, Kobb unleashed a blast.

Purple fire lashed out, yet the demon somehow still tore apart before it hit.

The abomination juddered for an instant and reformed standing. The shadows fractured and leapt toward Kobb.

He stepped back.

A tendril of shadow flickered out as the abomination twisted past, hooking around the end of his Courser.

Before Kobb could unleash power, inhuman strength sent his weapon spinning over the creatures shoulder.

"Perhaps you'll be more amenable without your trinket." The abomination reformed beside Anserth. "Does this one matter to—?"

Purple fire swallowed the rest of its words. The shadowy form twisted as tatters spun away, each fading rather than flowing back. Shrinking and fading, it staggered then ceased to be.

Haelen collapsed to his knees, trickles of blood marking his cheeks and chin.

"How did you—?" Anessa dropped down beside him.

He raised a palm before she could wrap her arm around him. "Explain later. Kobb needs to close gate. Paper in tent. Two wolves on the top."

For a moment, Kobb thought she'd insist on helping Haelen first; then she sprinted for the tents.

Anserth raised an eyebrow. "There's nothing with wolves on."

Haelen clambered to his feet. "It'll take her a while to find that out though. Long enough for the Reverend to get the barrier down and close the gate."

"Safe travels, Medicus." Kobb bowed his head for a moment.

Nodding back, Haelen jogged toward the edge of the circle.

Reaching within, Kobb reached for the threads. This time they unwove easily. The power screamed at him, but now the Stones seemed determined to help not hinder.

When he opened his eyes again, pale starlight shone on dense forest. And an empty space where Haelen had been.

Anessa burst from the tent, a pile of parchment clutched in each hand. "I can't find it. Are you sure it's got two... The moon's gone. What happened? Where's Haelen?"

Kobb held his arms out. "He touched the abomination. He knew he was infected."

"But, maybe he wasn't." Anessa swallowed. "Maybe it didn't..."

"He used my Courser. Only way to access power if you're not born with it's to get it from a demon. Once the infection spread, he'd have tried to convince someone to open the gate again. So, he did the only thing he could: stay on the other side."

Anessa collapsed to the ground, sobbing.

After staring at the tent for a moment, he turned to face Anserth.

"She'll need your help to get through this, Inductor. Not just the warrior; all of you."

"I don't know if I even can." Anserth's shoulders sagged. "I'm trained to put the mission first. How do I not do that?"

Kobb let his gaze drift across the dull stones. "I don't know. But because of Haelen, there's time for you to find out."

Thank you for reading the collected *Seven Stones*.

Want to make sure you don't miss my next release? Subscribe to my mailing list and you won't miss a thing.

Sign up today: www.subscribepage.com/davehigginsnewsletter

About the Author

Dave Higgins writes speculative fiction, often with a dark edge. Despite forays into the mundane worlds of law and IT, he was unable to completely escape the liminal zone between mystery and horror.

Born in the least mystically significant part of Wiltshire, England, and raised by a librarian, he started reading shortly after birth and has not stopped since. He currently lives in Bristol with his wife, Nicola, his cats, Jasper and Una, a plush altar to the Dark Lord Cthulhu, and many shelves of books.

It's rumoured he writes out of a fear that he will otherwise run out of things to read.

Discover more here: https://davehigginspublishing.co.uk